ONE NATION

MICHAEL LESLIE KARNES

TABLE OF CONTENTS

"We will no longer be a nation divided. We will not be a nation of Democrats versus Republicans or liberals versus conservatives nor North versus South. We are one nation, indivisible, with one party to guide us."

- Hank Gregor, leader of the Second American Revolution, 2019.

"This is not what our forefathers intended for us."

- Diablo05, member of the Valley Forge Network Forum, 2040.

Chapter 1

Jennifer had always hated the garish neon green and yellow colors of Stigman's Supermarket. For what was considered a Class A store, exclusive only to members of the Freedom Party and their families, Stigman's was a disappointment. She wheeled the plastic neon green cart down the produce aisle. The rubber wheels glided silently across the bright white linoleum floor. Say what you will about Stigman's it was at least clean and well lit. Everybody wanted to see everyone else and be seen. After all, having access to a Class A store was important.

Jennifer passed a woman the same age as her who laughably wore a little black dress accentuating her breasts and hips. *It was three o'clock in the afternoon for God's sake.* Even her iGlasses, the wearable tech linked to her tablet, were designer fashion that cost more than five grand. Jennifer's own iGlasses identified the woman as Tabitha Hart, a newlywed to a party official twenty years her senior. She gave the woman a curt nod as they passed one another.

The produce aisle wasn't as robust as it had been before the Florida invasion. Corn and potatoes were in abundance but tomatoes were in scarce supply, now fetching twenty-seven dollars a pound. California still produced oranges but they were now thirty dollars each. Jennifer sighed and picked up a half dozen oranges. She and Matt could afford them but she remembered the days when you could buy a dozen oranges in a bag for only a few bucks. At least lettuce was plentiful and cheap, although Jennifer wasn't sure where it came from since it was no longer imported from Mexico. The flashing targeted advertisements on the nearby OLED wall urged her to make reservations on the next shipment of oranges.

She wheeled the cart by the bakery. Bread was still baked fresh every day and, this being a Class A store, she had access to as much as she wanted. High quality too. None of the cheap grainy shit they sold in the Class C stores. Even then the amount of bread people could buy was limited because of health controls. The Freedom Party had enforced carbohydrate limits a few years earlier. Jennifer had heard rumor of a black market where carb credits were traded to one another.

Dark and covered with clear plastic the butcher section had been closed for years, falling victim to the same health controls that had outlawed most meat. Meat was declared 'dangerous' by the Party and therefore needed to be controlled in all of the citizens' diets. Steak and chicken may not be sold any longer in Class A markets but the upper echelon of the Party had access to anything they wanted.

At least a fresh selection of salmon was available. Jennifer had no idea where the salmon came from but it had been awhile since she had any. The smoked salmon filets were just south of a seventy bucks. She picked up a half dozen. Matt would probably grumble about the hit on their bank account but they got so little meat these days. He probably wouldn't care in the long run. Tofu was in abundance, and Stigman's had high quality tofu, but it wasn't the same as a good steak.

At least the Class A store had plenty of canned fruits and vegetables. They were relatively cheap and she could stock up on as much as she wanted. While she loaded her cart with canned kidney beans her iGlasses chimed in her ear. The display read, *Incoming Text - Matt Hanson*. The text read, *Wear your little black dress tonight. The one with the cleavage. And the white pearls. Love u.*

Jennifer sighed and pulled the tablet out of her purse. Other people publicly transcribed their responses aloud but Jennifer maintained her modesty and privacy. She typed back, *Yes, dear husband of mine, I will. What time are we leaving for the party?*

He texted back and told her they would leave at six o'clock for an arrival at seven. Jennifer breathed a sigh of relief. A rare early dinner and evening meant they could get home at a reasonable hour. Most of the party officials liked to host late night events grinding on until dawn. Jennifer could tolerate the parties but during the week it played hell with her own personal schedule. She had to be in her classroom at seven and it was a long day when she went straight to school from an all-night party.

Jennifer scrutinized her ugly plastic shopping cart with a sense of satisfaction. She had a good haul today. The increasingly scarce oranges were a good find as well as the salmon. She still had enough time to get home, put away groceries and get ready for the big party. It was expected to be the last big social event of the summer season.

She wheeled her cart towards the front of the store to Stigman's three open registers. Jennifer got into the shortest line behind the Tabitha Hart. The lady at the front of the line had a shaved head. Older, somewhere on the north side of forty, but well dressed. The woman was white but as far as Jennifer could tell she might have been a brunette previously. The shaved head was an unusual fashion choice as far as Jennifer was concerned. It wasn't even uniformly shaved, since it was completely uneven and gapped. The woman wasn't carrying any tech so Jennifer's iGlasses registered her as unknown.

The attendant working the register tallied up the lady's groceries. Stigman's was the only grocery store that still employed people to work cash registers. All the other grocery stores were completely automated. Stigman's liked to brag in their advertising that they gave the customer the personal touch. The attendant dutifully bagged the food as the register automatically tallied up the items.

"That will be $351.65," the attendant said.

Jennifer checked the time on her iGlasses. She hoped the lady with the shaved head wouldn't fumble around. Even though Stigman's was old fashioned, the experience should still be in and out for everybody. The lady placed her hand on the scanner so that it could read her dent. The light above the dent scanner stayed red then started flashing with an angry buzz.

"I don't understand," the lady said.

"Ma'am, please try again," the attendant said.

Jennifer caught herself rubbing her thumb against the hard bump in her right palm. Everyone had an identity chip inserted in the palms as children. Your entire life was wrapped up in the chip, from the ability to pay for things to access to buildings and anything else in life. The thought of having anything wrong with your dent gave everyone chills. The lady turned and faced the line waiting behind her. Jennifer could see she sported a black eye on the right side. The shaved head now had a whole new context. What had happened to this lady that had led her to here and now? She placed her hand on the dent scanner again. The light still showed a solid red, then blinked and repeated the angry buzz.

"Can you try it again?" the lady asked with a quiver in her voice.

"Let me check something, ma'am," the attendant said. He keyed in some commands on the register. Whatever he keyed in gave him immediate results on his own pair of iGlasses. "Ma'am, I am afraid that there are some issues with your account."

"I don't understand," she said. Jennifer checked the time on her own iGlasses again. She needed them to hurry this thing up.

"Ma'am," the attendant continued, still polite but with a hint of regret and hesitation. "It appears that your Class A privileges have been revoked. I am afraid that you are now classified as a Class C."

"That can't be," the lady said. "Let's try again." She slapped her palm angrily on the dent scanner as tears started to course down her face. "Come on, run it through."

The woman with the black dress turned around and rolled her eyes. Jennifer wanted to do the same. Whatever this lady was doing she held up the line for everyone else. She impatiently checked the time in her iGlasses again.

The attendant was patient with the lady but Jennifer could read the irritation in his demeanor. He went through the motions one more time to placate her. He keyed in his own entry in the terminal then reset it for another attempt.

"Hey, lady," Tabitha Hart called out. "You're in the wrong store." She turned to Jennifer. "I don't know why they don't check their dents before they come through the front door."

Jennifer shrugged. She didn't want to engage in conversation but she agreed.

The woman with the shaved head turned and smiled apologetically. "I'm sure it's just a mistake." Her mascara had washed down her face from her tears. The running makeup gave her the appearance of a demented clown.

A manager appeared alongside the cash register attendant. Jennifer figured the attendant had signaled him to come from the office.

"Oh, good, a manager," the lady said. "Can you help me checkout? There seems to be a problem with the dent scanner."

"There is no problem with the register, Mrs. Avendano," the manager said coolly. Jennifer tried to place the name. She didn't remember hearing of 'Avendano' in any of the Party social circles. But there were a lot of civilians who held Class A privileges without being members of the Party. "As Andy here informed you, your store privileges have been revoked. You will have to shop elsewhere. You need to leave immediately."

"But I have always shopped here," Mrs. Avendano said. "I don't go anywhere else. Please, can you make an exception? Please." Her sentence ended as a wail.

"Mrs. Avendano," the manager said with an answering plea of his own. He was uncomfortable with this situation. Finally, he sighed and waved over the security guards from covering the entrance and exit of the store. One approached left and the other from the right. A small crowd of onlookers had gathered, other customers drawn by Mrs. Avendano's plaintive wail or waiting at the checkout, completely enraptured by the drama unfolding in front of them. Were they eager for a conflict? Jennifer hoped they weren't but she felt a stab of guilt watching the scene herself. "Mrs. Avendano, these men will escort you out of the building."

"No, I have every right to shop here. You can't throw me out."

The security guards were older. Jennifer placed them somewhere in their late forties or early fifties. These were not the common overweight night watchmen who snuck off for a nap while guarding an empty warehouse. No, these men still packed on muscle. Guarding a Class A store would be a plum job for an honored vet. They might not be in the military anymore but they hadn't let themselves go. The guards appeared almost alike with their clean-shaven faces and grim demeanor. Jennifer had never paid attention to either of these men before. They were part of the store scenery, like a display of bottled water or canned vegetables, with their navy blue uniforms. The only spot of color was the blue pin with the white star, on their collar. That marked them as Party members. Jennifer had her own White Star pin on her lapel.

"Ma'am," the guard on the right said, "you'll have to come with us. You can leave peacefully or we can drag you out of here."

"No, please," Mrs. Avendano said. "Please let me just buy what I need to buy. My money is still good. I still have cash in my bank account."

It was a tight squeeze into the aisle for the register. The woman in the black dress had the lady boxed in with her own shopping cart. Her only way out was through the register exit. The guard on the left pulled away the shopping cart that Mrs. Avendano had her groceries in. The guard on the right squeezed in the aisle with her and grabbed her by the bicep.

"Let me go. You're hurting me!"

"You need to leave, ma'am," the guard repeated monotonously. He didn't care about her either way. She presented a problem in his environment and his solution was to remove her.

Mrs. Avendano screamed. Jennifer grabbed the earpiece of her iGlasses out. The microphone was set for indoors and the scream amplified in her ears. Everyone else in the room winced and did the same.

"Let me go! Let me go! Let me GOOOOOOOO!"

Whatever mercy the security guard had seemed to leave him. Now he roughly shoved her to the door. "If you make this any worse we will call the police."

"Police" seemed to be the magic word. "No," Mrs. Avendano said. "No, no police." Her eyes shot open with fear. "No police. No police. No police." Instead of screaming she let this chanted mantra trail off into a mutter. The automatic exit doors of Stigman's opened and the guards released her. They stood side by side, waiting to block her path should she try to come back in, but she left quietly while muttering.

Tabitha Hart turned back to Jennifer. "They shouldn't let those kind in here."

Jennifer agreed and felt instantly ashamed. She waited patiently for Tabitha Hart to move through the line, then took her turn. The register attendant apologized for Mrs. Avendano's behavior but Jennifer waved it off. "It's not like it was your fault. She should have known better than to come in here if her privileges had been revoked."

The attendant bagged for Jennifer as the register scanned everything through. "That will be $697.93, Mrs. Hanson."

The bill was more than Jennifer had anticipated. The salmon and oranges probably put her over budget. Still, it was better to eat healthy and pay a little more. She put her hand on the dent scanner and authorized it to complete the transaction. Another attendant bagged her groceries and walked her to her car. The exit door of Stigman's opened to a parking lot filled with black vehicles on an unseasonably hot Denver day. Jennifer wondered if the Party elite had collectively voted and chose black as their color of choice for their automobiles. Their cars of choice were almost the same. A collection of Chrysler Patriots, Chevy Suburbans, Ford Expeditions and Lincoln Towncars filled the asphalt landscape. The only spot of color was Jennifer's own car - a bright blue antique BMW roadster. Built in the last century it drew everyone's attention when she drove around the city. It wasn't just the color but the noise. All the other vehicles were quiet and electric these days, a sharp contrast to her noisy antique that could be heard coming from miles away. Gas was rationed and expensive but they could easily afford it.

Jennifer let the attendant put the groceries in the trunk then tipped him twenty dollars in cash from the amount she kept in her purse for these occasions. She climbed into the roadster, turned the ignition and sped out of the parking lot with a squeal of the tires. Her antique didn't feature any of the aid systems the newer cars had. No AI control would help her while she was behind the wheel. No, she had to manually control the car from steering, acceleration and gear shifting. When Jennifer described driving her roadster at dinner parties half the guests were aghast at the thought of doing that much work while the others stared at her with awe.

Jennifer wouldn't let the windbags in the Party know it but she loved driving her little car. There were few convertibles these days, much less foreign ones. A specialty antique shop in North Denver lovingly maintained her car. Having this car gave her the sense of freedom. She was not restricted in terms of where she could go and she could separate herself from the pack of drones that was the Party norm. Heads turned as they always did when she sped the little roadster along the Denver streets.

CHAPTER 2

Afe arriving home Jennifer unloaded everything from the car as quickly as possible. The first thing was her bag of electronics and school stuff. Not only did she have homework to grade but she had given the kids a test today so that would need to be graded as well. Jennifer hoped the party at the district leader's mansion would wrap up early. After the groceries were unloaded and put away she needed to take a quick shower. Matt would get home soon and quickly change into the tuxedo he had for these occasions.

Jennifer laid out the tux alongside her little black dress and took her shower. Only a year old, the dress still fitted her wonderfully. She remembered the first time she had worn it at a summer party the year before. Matt hadn't liked the bra she had worn with it. He had said it made her look like a cheap whore with the way the straps showed and had told her to try it without the bra. She hadn't liked the idea of going bra-less, but she had done it because he had asked her to. She had filled out the dress nicely and it had somehow still supported her without any sag. Jennifer would never admit to Matt that he was right. She also caught the eye of everyone else at parties. Jennifer commanded the attention of all the Party officials at the social gatherings. Charming these men and women helped her husband and his status in the office. So the little black dress had become her uniform to wear just as the tuxedo had become Matt's.

The house AI announced Matt was home by flashing a quick message on the OLED wall in the bedroom. The AI needn't have bothered as Matt came crashing in. "You got everything ready?"

Jennifer was putting on the pearl necklace he had asked her to wear. The necklace hung low enough to draw the eye to her cleavage. "Yeah," she said. "You just need to change."

Matt started throwing off his clothes from the day, being careful to remove the White Star pin from the collar, while Jennifer scowled. He grinned at her still showing much of the boyish charm that had helped him win many girls' hearts in college. "What?" he asked.

"You know what."

"We can worry about it later. We gotta go!"

With the tuxedo quickly donned Matt always came to the same standstill regarding the tie. Jennifer smirked at him while he struggled with it for a couple of minutes. Jennifer had learned how to tie the knot for him early in their marriage. She sighed softly as she had to tie it for him again. "What would you do without me?"

"Probably live like a pig. Never iron. Never clean. Drink lots of beer, maybe? Are we ready?"

"One thing." She twisted the White Star pin a little to the left so that the points were parallel to the bottom of his collar. "Now we're ready. Should we take the Beemer? It's such a nice night."

"There are going to be a lot of people there. You know how they feel about foreign cars."

They would be taking his Chrysler Patriot, another black SUV in a fleet of black SUVs sure to be parking along the circular drive in front of the mansion. A drone amongst the other drones. Jennifer knew they couldn't brook even the slightest criticism that they might be less than patriotic. "Okay, your car then."

Matt climbed behind the wheel of the SUV and pulled up the address in the navigation system, then told the SUV to drive. The thirty-minute drive to Belcaro gave Jennifer time to catch up on e-mails on her iGlasses. She glanced over at Matt once to see him doing the same.

The floodlights lit up the mansion behind the silhouette orange late summer dusk of the mountains to the west. The SUV dutifully pulled up behind a line of other Patriots, Suburbans and Ford Expeditions. The vehicles lined around the drive leading to the mansion with their red taillights twinkling.

"This looks bigger than the normal party we go to," Jennifer said.

"We have a guest of honor," Matt said.

A significant presence of the National Police force were patrolling the perimeter of the mansion. Jennifer had never seen so many of them at once. They police were divided into two distinct groups - the officers with their crisp uniforms and the paramilitary types with their coveralls. The only thing they had in common was the navy blue of their uniforms. "That's a lot of police. They even have their Joltvees with them." She referred to the Joint Light Tactical Vehicles that were the mainstay of the military and the police.

"Extra security. Don't let them scare you. They answer directly to the Party and then the President." Two of the paramilitary types flanked the gate leading to the mansion. Each had an assault rifle slung over their shoulder and they were holding dent scanners. Matt pulled the Patriot up between them. Jennifer pushed the power button to slide her window down.

The national policeman who approached her was as emotionless as the guards at Stigman's. If he was supposed to answer to members of the Party he seemed to be quite unimpressed with that fact. "Your dent please, ma'am."

Jennifer extended her arm out of the window and placed the palm on the scanner. Even though the policeman could read the results instantaneously he studied the digital display with scrutiny. The policeman checking Matt through was just as grim. Finally, the policeman on the driver's side said, "All clear."

A valet station at the front of the mansion was set up to receive them. With the size and scope of this party Jennifer reckoned they wanted to make sure it was a success. One of the white-coated valets opened the door and offered his hand to her while Matt gave control of the vehicle to the other valet.

District Leader Orson Baker's mansion reminded Jennifer of something from Europe. Palatial would only begin to describe it. The ten-foot tall double doors led into the black and white tiled entrance hall. On her right a staircase covered in plush red carpeting with gold accents led to the private bedrooms upstairs and was roped off from the guests. To the left was a large room the Bakers used to receive visitors. Parties here usually only had about fifteen or twenty guests, but Jennifer thought there might be twice that number tonight even without National Police. She walked into the foyer while servants coursed their way through the room with hors d'oeuvres and glasses of sparkling wine.

"You're late." The gruff voice came from Matt's right. Deputy District Leader Kyle Larson scowled at both of them.

"We are on time," Matt said with an edge in his voice. Matt frequently complained about getting unfairly reprimanded by this man. "There is more security than usual."

Larson grunted. Jennifer wasn't sure if that is a sign of acknowledgement, contempt or even direction. "Work the room. Get a feel of the guests. This is a large party and we want to make sure everything goes smoothly. The general will be seated at the head of the table. There's been a lot of criticism about the Texas Front. We need to make sure any of that criticism is silenced. Got it?"

"Yes, Mister Larson."

Larson scowled at Jennifer then grunted again before walking off. "I see he remains as charming as ever," Jennifer says.

Matt rolled his eyes. "He's my boss. You know how it goes. Excuse me, I gotta -"

"Work the room," Jennifer finished for him.

Matt grinned sheepishly before hustling off. A party with the Party was never really a party. It was always political with her husband and his colleagues. They would "work the room" making sure the right people were connected with each other and Matt always excelled at the task. Jennifer could work the room too but she found the task tolerable and only did it to help her husband. She surveyed the room of black tuxedos and black dresses to find the only flash of red.

"Work the room," Jennifer muttered. "Screw that."

In the corner of a room a petite woman in a bright red sparkly dress laughed enthusiastically as she entertained a group of American officers. Everyone else in the room was armed with a glass of sparkling wine while this woman brazenly brandished a martini glass. Her hair was short and dyed a red that matched her dress and sharply contrasted with her porcelain skin. The only other addition of color was the tattoo of a green and orange dragon crawling up her left bicep.

Jennifer knocked back her sparkling wine and deposited the empty glass on a passing tray before picking up another. She sauntered over to the woman in red and, as expected, caught the eyes of a couple of the American officers. "Now what lies are you telling these men, Maggie?" Jennifer asked.

"Jenn! You know me, I'm just entertaining the troops," the redhead said with a wink. "Men, my girlfriend has arrived. You're going to have to soldier on without me. She and I need to catch up!"

"Come on, just one more drink," one of the officers asked. He held the rank of captain.

Maggie winked at them. "I'll catch up with you all later." She grabbed Jennifer by the arm and hustled her away from the disappointed soldiers.

"Does Brad make you work the room too?" Jennifer asked. She didn't see Maggie's husband anywhere.

"For this?" She flamboyantly waved the martini glass around the room without spilling a drop. "Nah, I just do this for fun. He and Daddy are running late. Long day at the office. Let's get some air!"

The veranda attached to the reception room of the mansion was expansive and afforded them some privacy. There seemed to be an unspoken agreement among the usual party guests that this was where you could go and carry a conversation without being interrupted. Maggie led Jennifer outside and weaved her way through the small knots of people to the back rail. Jennifer shivered a bit. The sun had already set with only a subdued glow of dusk over the mountains west of them. Winter would come early this year.

"So what's the news?" Maggie asked.

"Still pending," Jennifer said flatly. "There's a backlog at the genetics lab. Several weeks they say." She and Matt had submitted their genetic application to bear children back in July. Aside from the ten thousand dollar fee, they'd had to endure a number of blood and physical tests. This was the right time for both of them to start a family, but they had to get through this hurdle first. Matt had said it shouldn't be a problem since they both came from good families.

"I don't know why you want to do this anyway. Isn't the world fucked up already without adding another kid to it?"

"Hey, maybe my kid might be the next Hank Gregor."

Maggie rolled her eyes. "Do we really need another 'hero of the Second American Revolution'? And what if your kid turns out to be a Class C idiot instead?"

"Maggie!"

"I'm sorry! You know how I feel about kids."

"I believe you called them parasites once."

Maggie winked. "Hey, is Matt working the room?"

"It's his job. How did you all end up here tonight?" Maggie didn't usually attend these types of Party functions.

"Daddy has connections. He might not be the biggest fan of the Freedom Party but he knows a lot of people. He can get things done and they appreciate it, despite his eccentricities. There are a lot of new people here for Daddy to meet."

"Is he going to piss anybody off?" David Lewis was well known in Denver society. He still believed in the outdated notion of democracy.

"Not any more than usual, I hope."

"She gets it from her old man," a voice said from behind them.

"Daddy!" Maggie said. She practically leapt into the man's arms as he laughed.

Jennifer had known Maggie's dad since childhood. David's formerly silver hair had gone completely white over the years. "Mister Lewis, good to see you again." Jennifer hugged him and kissed him on the cheek.

"Jennifer, how long has it been? Twenty years and you still call me Mister Lewis."

Jennifer blushed. "I can't help it. I don't think I could ever call you David. You're always going to be Mister Lewis."

"So who are you afraid that I might piss off tonight?"

"There are some new faces here," Maggie said. "They might not be used to you."

David waved his hand dismissively. "An old man like me? They don't even listen to our types anymore."

"Daddy, just be careful. Now why didn't you bring my husband with you?"

"He's here. He ran into Jenn's husband and they were catching up. I imagine he'll find us. I knew where you two were as soon as I got here."

Jennifer spied her husband along with Brad entering the veranda. Both men were handsome enough to have stepped out of an underwear catalog, Matt with his sandy blond hair contrasting to Brad's inky black. Jennifer and her husband were attractive enough that there shouldn't be any problem getting an approval on their gene app.

Matt's scowl gave him the worry crease on his brow right between his eyes. He was stressed as usual before a Party function. "We should get inside," he said. "They're starting to seat for dinner."

"Assigned seating?" Jennifer asked.

"Not really."

"Can Maggie, Brad and David sit with us? It's been so long and we need to catch up."

Matt arched an eyebrow and grinned. "We saw them last weekend. But, yeah, it should be okay. Come join us."

Compared to the reception room and veranda the dining room was quite narrow. Jennifer could see the dining room table had been extended with table leaves added in. She had been here before and knew the table beneath the white cloth was exquisite stained oak. Extra chairs were added around the table. They were cheaper and didn't match the dining room furniture. Matt shepherded them into the dining room. Given the number of guests seating here would be at a premium tonight. People wanted to be as close as they could to the guest of honor.

"You sit here. And you sit here," Matt directed. A couple of other office workers tried to sit closer but Matt redirected them further down to the end of the table where General Scarborough's officers sat. "You know better!"

Everyone had to be seated first before any food came out. The servers couldn't move around the room with guests still standing. Jennifer sat at Matt's right with Larson on his far side near the head of the table. Opposite of Larson sat District Leader Orson Baker. At the head of the table General Colin Scarborough stood bewildered while the guests and servants swirled around him.

General Colin Scarborough didn't need to introduce himself. He was well known as one of the original old guards of the Second American Revolution and the famed leader of the Texas Front. She had seen him in all the news vids but this was the first time she had met him in person. He never appeared to be the least bit congenial on social media and certainly didn't in person. The way the history told it he was alongside Gregor when they were fighting in the streets of Cleveland. Twenty years later he was a general in the American Army. Not necessarily a tactician general but certainly a political one.

Scarborough seated himself and scraped the chair legs along the floor as he pulled himself to the table. Startled, Jennifer and the guests turned sharply at the noise. The general smiled with amusement as he challenged the other guests with his lack of etiquette. Scarborough offered no apology as he scrutinized them quietly with his icy blue eyes. The dinner guests, uncomfortable with the stare down, turned to one another and resumed their hushed conversations.

District Leader Baker seemed unfazed by the general. Jennifer idly wondered who had more status and control here - the general or district leader? Given the general's history with Hank Gregor she thought the general held more clout but Baker might be too blind to see it. He probably had the notion that politicians always controlled the military. Baker stood with a glass of sparkling wine in his hand and tapped it with the edge of a butter knife.

"If I can get everyone's attention please. I just want to welcome everyone here tonight in honor of our guest. As you know General Scarborough commands the army on the Texas Front. He is on leave to attend to many important matters back in Washington and has graciously stopped here in Denver to join us for dinner tonight. Let's take a moment to show the general how much we appreciate his efforts. Come on everybody!" Baker set down his wineglass and started a round of applause.

Jennifer found it to be an odd gesture. She couldn't remember seeing a round of applause given to anyone at this table. The other guests glanced at each other uncomfortably while they clapped. The general blushed with embarrassment. Jennifer applauded politely while other prominent members of the party clapped enthusiastically. At the end of the table the other officers of the general's party sat as stoically as their leader.

"Let's eat," Baker said with a laugh.

This was the highlight of the evening as far as Jennifer was concerned. The thing she loved about District Leader Baker's parties was the food. It's not that Jennifer was ever in danger of going hungry, rather the food served was often not available in restaurants and markets because of the food control laws. The servers in the white coats come out again with their trays of hot appetizers. They attempted to serve the guests but the cramped dining room made it difficult to circle around them. A dish of seared scallops wrapped in bacon was placed in front of Jennifer. Scallops were still legal, but the bacon definitely wasn't. The saliva welled up in her mouth as she reached for the serving spoon. There was also smoked salmon on brioche as well as cheese stuffed mushrooms, but the scallops were the dish everyone went for. Matt reached for the serving dish first and scooped a couple for himself before passing it to Jennifer. Jennifer chose a couple of pieces then passed the plate to Maggie. Other guests reluctantly got the salmon or mushrooms as the scallops quickly ran out.

"So, General Scarborough, I was wondering if you could give us any news from the front?" Baker asked.

The general stopped devouring his own bacon wrapped scallop. Caught in mid bite when Baker asked his question the general chewed quickly and swallowed, looking disappointed that he couldn't relish the taste. "We are fighting vigilantly," Scarborough said. "Our boys on the front are doing everything they can to push the Coalition out of Texas and back to Mexico. It's only a matter of time now before our counter attack routs them."

Larson leaned forward, eager to ask a question. "General can you tell us what our biggest advantage over the Coalition is?"

With all of the scallops gone Jennifer served herself a stuffed mushroom. It had some sort of cheesy bread filling. The only guests to her right who paid attention to the conversation were Maggie, her dad and her husband. Everyone else was too consumed with the food and the length of the table excluded them from the conversation at the head.

"Our tech," Scarborough said. "That is what gives us an advantage over the Coalition. America has a professional army that has consistently been on the field of battle since World War II. Russia and China have always relied on bodies to throw into battle. We believe differently. We fight with superior tactics and weaponry. It has been our cutting edge for the last hundred years. There's hardly been a time in our history when we are not fighting. For every one of ours that they kill we kill ten of them. Maybe a hundred."

"What if we run out of soldiers," David asked. The three Party officials turned their heads and narrowed their gaze at Maggie's dad as the servers whisked away the empty appetizer plates. The other guests were too engrossed with their meals to notice the conversation.

"We no longer have our assets stretched thinly in several theaters of operations around the world. This was our biggest mistake since World War II. Bases all over Europe, Asia and the Middle East. Hundreds of thousands of troops spread around the globe. We've now backed out of policing the world."

"General," Matt interrupted. "What's China and Russia's role during the current conflict?"

The servers came out again, this time with bowls of a creamy lobster bisque. Everyone waited politely for the soup to be served. Matt's question annoyed Jennifer. Clearly he had been prepped to keep the general engaged.

He didn't care about the war one way or the other, much less anything involving China and Russia.

The general slopped some of the steamy hot soup into his mouth. The soup was scalding hot but he slurped it unfazed. "For now both China and Russia are staying out of it. China is neutral and their sphere of influence spreads across Eastern Asia. Russia leans towards the Coalition. They don't directly support them in their efforts but they are certainly sympathetic. Both Russia and China hate each other so neither one of them wants to pick sides in this fight. China is the bigger dog here so everyone is waiting for them to make a move. While they are not necessarily supportive of us, we've had long economic ties with them. They still need us as a trade partner."

Jennifer didn't care about the war or politics either way but the news didn't escape her notice. The Coalition had declared war on her country in the past couple of years and, in a surprise move, launched invasions into Florida and Texas. The Florida peninsula was occupied up to the panhandle and the Coalition had moved to the south side of Austin, Texas in recent weeks.

"General, a question if I may," David asked. "The front line has been in a stalemate for almost a year. Your advances have done nothing to push the Coalition Forces out of Texas. Can you give us a timeline when our nation will be whole again?"

Their end of the table turned silent. District Leader Oscar Baker coughed discretely and said, "David, I hardly think that is a polite question to ask our honored guest."

The general scowled at David. "No, I'll be happy to debate this with him. Are you one of those types who believe the war should be abandoned? That we should give up? Concede Texas to the Coalition? Cut and run?"

Jennifer finished her bisque and noticed the Party men at her end of the table had stopped eating. They listened to the conversation with a mix of anxiety and hostility.

David reflexively tugged at his collar. "Well I think we should examine the root causes for the current conflict, see what we can gain and what we could possibly lose and choose the best course of action."

"Haven't we lost enough? 9/11? Baghdad? Jerusalem? 11/30? Or do you think we should capitulate and give it all to them?"

"Well, no, but I think -"

"You were one of them, weren't you?"

Shock and anger flash across David Lewis' face. "A terrorist? Hardly! If I were I would be interned at Golden Gate or Fargo right now."

"No, one of those from the old school. Republicans and Democrats."

"Well, the old system might not be perfect but you have to admit that the democratic system of representation did have its benefits."

The servers cleared away the soup. They returned moments later with the main course - filets of beef and lobster tail with au gratin potatoes. The filets are definitely illegal while the lobster was only quasi-legal. With dinner served Matt and his colleagues relaxed and hesitantly picked up their forks and knives. The meal distracted the general from the dangerous turn the conversation had taken. Jennifer just wanted her steak and lobster, a rarity even in the district leader's mansion. She checked to see if the general was still scowling but even he seemed to be taken by the dinner, as he stabbed at the filet with relish. Matt, Larson and Baker cut into their steaks hesitantly, as if they expected another war of words from either Scarborough or David.

The conversation around the table was muted as the party guests enjoyed their meal. Even with these people and their elite status in Denver society, tonight's dinner fare was a rarity. Jennifer couldn't remember the last time she'd had steak. Maybe two years ago when they were skiing? And they hadn't had lobster since the previous summer.

The general savagely attacked his steak with fork and knife and ate voraciously. Even with the other diners eating quickly, the general finished his meal well before everyone else. Jennifer spied his officers at the end of the table. She had heard that the army ate their meals quickly and these men didn't disappoint. Something to do with little time between battles. It was the first time Jennifer had seen it in practice.

Scarborough tossed his linen napkin on the plate. "Mister?" With one word everyone stopped eating and waited pensively. The general regarded David with the avid interest of a predator stalking prey.

David had a bite of steak halfway to his mouth, his eyes wide and his mouth hanging open in an "O". "David Lewis," he said as he put the uneaten bite of steak back on his plate.

"Mister Lewis, I would put you at about sixty."

"Sixty-two, actually."

"So you would have been about forty during the revolution?"

"Yes, exactly. I don't understand."

The general held up one finger. "Just bear with me. Were you part of the revolution?"

David scanned the other faces around the table frantically. The crowded room along the entire table had stopped eating and waited for the next turn in conversation. "I wasn't a part of it, no. It wasn't the same here in Denver, compared to everywhere else."

"What did you do before the revolution?"

"The same thing I do now. I am an attorney."

Scarborough laughed. His officers at the other end of the table merrily joined in. A few other guests tittered nervously. "A shyster!"

David bristled. "Well I wouldn't describe myself that way."

"No, I don't imagine you would. You didn't starve before the revolution nor afterwards, did you? I doubt you suffered much during the revolution as well."

"We all suffered during that time!"

"Really? Did you lose your entire family to the flu epidemic of '19?"

"No, you know that Denver was relatively isolated during the epidemic."

"And the financial crisis afterwards? Did you lose anything?"

"I prepared for it smartly by sheltering funds in different investments here and abroad." Jennifer remembered the Lewis family had weathered the revolution. They always had money while others had to make do with less. Still, Maggie's dad had never flaunted it over anyone else. "It doesn't make me any less of an American or any less of a member of the Freedom Party."

"And what would I find if I had the National Police search your records? When was the last time you attended a Party meeting? Have you held an office in the Party? What about your activities as a lawyer? I would bet you are a defense attorney, aren't you?"

The observation was remarkably good. Jennifer remembered Mister Lewis had always been an excellent defense attorney. He had successfully defended criminals the Party had specifically targeted and his name came up in the local news quite frequently. "When did defense attorneys become outlawed, General? A defendant still deserves their right of representation or did that change since dinner started?"

Orson Baker cleared his throat. "Perhaps we should change the subject?"

"Why, Orson?" General Scarborough asked. "David and I are getting along so well. We are enjoying this lively debate, aren't we David?" His voice belied the sweetness of the sentiment.

Mister Lewis smiled sheepishly, with beads of sweat across his brow. "We are all just friends here."

"David, what was best about the old system?"

Jennifer turned sharply as she chewed on a piece of steak. This question was clearly a trap. The Party mantra dictated the old ways had failed.

"General... sir... we all know that the old ways were wrong. Which is why we had the revolution and created the Freedom Party. I am sorry that I upset you. Perhaps it is best that I leave." He picked his napkin from his lap then folded it and laid it across his unfinished meal. Did Jennifer see a hint of regret in his eye? Not in the conversation but about the unfinished steak cooling on his plate. Even with Mister Lewis' affluence he was limited to what he could purchase.

"Nonsense. Sit. Stay." The General waved his hand magnanimously as if he was making a proclamation.

Almost comically Mister Lewis tugged at his collar again. "Well, there were good things. People were well represented. Every person represented a vote and had the power to change their destiny. There was no fixed representation of government. There were no dictatorships. Sure, there were challenges with the two party system but everyone was, more or less, taken care of by the old system. People were fed. They had shelter. They had health care that wasn't rationed. Everyone was equal under a democracy."

The tinkling of silverware against the fine china plates completely ceased. Every guest remained silently still, as this conversation had gone too far. Jennifer turned right to see the four faces of the general's officers in their dress khakis glaring back with open hate in their eyes. This was considered sedition. She snapped her head back at the general. His face turned an ugly shade of red, as if his head might pop off his neck.

"Equal under Republicans and Democrats? You mean the four hundred and forty-five congressmen in the House and the hundred senators? Those leaders who made sure we were always split in half over bullshit issues while they got rich and ruined our economy in the process. You want to go back to that system? Back to lazy drug addicts living off the taxpayer? Back to greedy corporations owning people and ruining lives? Back to the killing and poisoning of the planet? You want to give up the gains we made and the hard fought battles we won?"

David slammed his palm on the table. "We're not winning now!"

Wide-eyed, Scarborough started to say something but rapidly opened and closed his mouth like a goldfish gasping for air. Finally, he resigned to say nothing more in this argument. He turned to District Leader Baker and said, "If you will excuse me, I shall take my leave." The general carefully folded his linen napkin and set it beside his plate. The dinner guests silently tracked the general warily as he exited the room with his four officers in tow. After several seconds one of the other couples murmured their apologies and excused themselves from the table. Then two more people left quickly. It was clear David Lewis had gone too far tonight.

Matt grabbed Jennifer by the hand and got up from the table. "What about dessert?" she asked.

"I don't think there will be any tonight."

A panic filled the narrow dining room as the exit was jammed with people. The dread permeated through the room, as if they were a moment away from being burned down in the lava flow of an erupting volcano. Everyone was associated with David Lewis in some way. If the general, a compatriot of President Gregor, chose to pursue the matter with the National Police then everyone in the room was at risk.

The dinner guests flooded the main hall and gasped for air. The claustrophobic room filled with the general's vitriol had raised everyone's anxiety, but even this brief respite had failed to abate the panic as the guests rushed the front door. Matt tugged Jennifer by the hand. "Matt, let go. You're hurting me." He didn't seem to hear her as he dragged her through the foyer.

Outside the mansion a brace of cold wind slammed against her exposed skin. The valets worked as quickly as they could to get everyone's car to the front, but confusion ensued because of the conformity of the Party members' choices, as the identical cars' electronic lock systems all chirped at once.

Matt abruptly stepped to the head of the line and handed his ticket to the valet. He drew a few glares from other guests, but Matt challenged them back with a glare of his own. His rank gave him privilege here.

"Matt, can you let go of my hand? You're hurting me."

He glared back at her momentarily, then caught himself as if awakened from a fugue. "Oh, sorry. I'm sorry, babe."

"It's okay." She rubbed her hand to get the blood flowing again. Matt turned away from her and glared at the other guests with clenched fists. Matt's anxiety was not a new experience for Jennifer. She rarely saw this side of him but this night was a weird experience.

After the Patriot pulled up Matt dashed to the driver's side, leaving Jennifer to the confused valet. The valet opened the passenger side door and gave her a barely perceptible shrug with sympathetic eyes. She climbed into the Patriot and she was as confused as the valet. Matt stabbed at the display with his finger and ordered the SUV to take them home on auto-drive.

The car glided silently on the asphalt, as the headlights pierced the empty night. Another set of taillights shined ahead of them while headlights illuminate them from behind. Matt fidgeted with the control panel on the center of the dash.

"Do you think anything will happen from this?" Jennifer asked.

"I hope not. It's not like David was tweaking Orson. We are familiar with David's rhetoric at dinner parties. David is old school, but we let him get away with it because we know him. The man was solid as a rock during the revolution. Not a fighter but he kept Denver organized. He should have known better with General Scarborough."

"Doesn't the general have his own issues right now?" He had only stopped in Denver on his way back to being recalled. Despite what Jennifer had heard on the news the fight in Texas was losing ground.

"He is in the hot seat for what is going on in Texas, but he is part of The Five. I can't see the president giving him too much grief about it." Matt referred to The Five Heroes of the Revolution - Colin Scarborough, Leo Jefferson, George Kingston, Jason Cromarte, and Hank Gregor who had a lifetime term as President of America. "This is bad. Bad, bad, bad. Maybe General Scarborough will have too much on his plate and forget about to-night." He tapped the display console in the center of the dash and told the SUV to pull over.

"What are you doing?"

"Let's get in the back."

Jennifer suppressed a sigh. Matt was wound up and wanted what he called a "stress fuck". This happened maybe two or three times a year. She wanted to help her husband but she hated these stress fucks. Matt didn't wait for her. He hopped out of the seat and climbed into the back. Resignedly she opened the door. Better to get this over with quickly. She climbed in the back and closed the door while Matt barked verbal commands at the SUV. It would take them all the way home without any further input from him.

He turned to face her with a panting hitch in his breath. His eyes glittered like two small diamonds in a pool of shadows. Matt didn't say anything. He propped one knee on the bench seat while the other one supported his weight against the floor. Jennifer waited while Matt unbuckled his belt and pulled off his pants. His stress fuck was all about his control. The light from cars passing them briefly illuminated his erection as it pointed at her in the dark. Only a few seconds ticked by before he launched himself at her. Matt grabbed her hips and pulled her toward him, then pushed up her cocktail dress. He pulled her panties down with a rough tug, tangling between her knees.

"Wait," she said. "Just give me a second." Her little black panties were cute and she didn't want him to rip them in half. They maneuvered their legs around each while she leaned backward on the seat. The panties had twisted around her right ankle as she opened and extended her right leg out. Once the leg was free Matt went into her with no preamble. She briefly wondered if he realized that he was going in dry. No kisses either as he grunted like a rutting wild boar.

This wasn't the first time they'd had sex in the Patriot while the SUV took them home. Matt had bought the vehicle after he had started working for the Party. The first time they had christened the vehicle it was a celebratory evening with wine and expensive dinner in the days when having a steak was legal for everyone. Jennifer remembered the night fondly as he pumped away at her now. It seemed to be going in easier. Maybe the memory helped get her wet a little?

A new problem occurred - Matt went soft on her. This happened to him sometimes as his mind wandered. He wouldn't give up though as he kept mashing his soft meat into her until he came. Jennifer didn't want this to last all night. She put her arm around his neck and pulled his ear close to her mouth. "Come on, baby, give it to me. Come on. Make me come." Her hot breath tickling his ear always worked. He was hard again and started to thrust faster.

After eight years of marriage Jennifer learned all of Matt's sexual nuances. He always went into her deeper and faster just before climaxed. Abruptly, Matt's breath caught in his chest and held there for several seconds before ending with a guttural groan. He collapsed on top of her with all of his weight. The panting resumed with Matt's breaths of relief. His erection remained inside her and he was still hard, but Matt didn't make the motions of an encore. Her husband was of those guys who took a few minutes to go soft again.

Matt finally wiggled out of her and lay silently with his back against the door. Jennifer let the silence hang between them. They were both startled when the SUV took them inside their garage. Had thirty minutes passed? Like guilty lovers they quickly reassembled themselves after the garage door closed. Wordlessly they both entered the house, with Jennifer stopping long enough to pour another glass of wine before cleaning the come that was slowly running down her thighs. Matt poured himself a bourbon and turned on the news.

The glass of wine was already half empty before she made it to the bathroom. She kicked off her shoes and peeled off the dress and underwear, then hopped into the shower. The steamy shower had never felt so good. After the shower she stood in front of the steamed mirror wrapped in a towel. Blurred, she raised a hand to wipe the mirror then hesitated. *Matt and his stress fucks. Did they help?* She felt him enter the bathroom behind her. He wrapped one arm around her waist from behind and she caught the smoky scent of bourbon.

"Hey, I just want you to know that I love you. Tonight was a little rough. I appreciate that you were there with me."

Jennifer smiled and turned to face him. She held his chin and leaned up for a kiss. "I know," she said. "At least we didn't have a late night and risk a hangover for work tomorrow."

CHAPTER 3

Three days later Jennifer got a call from Maggie.

"What is it?" Jennifer asked.

Maggie cried. "Oh my God. It's Daddy! The National Police arrested him last night."

"Arrested?"

"The charges are sedition."

"I'm sure it is a mistake." Typically, "sedition" was often a catch all charge made. "It can't be for the dinner the other night."

"I am afraid that it is. What Daddy said that night wasn't really all that terrible, was it? I mean, Daddy talks like that all the time. People just pay him no mind."

"Go to the police. See if there's any way you can bail your father out of jail."

"I'll try. Would you be able to do something for me? Could Matt talk to District Leader Baker?"

It was a lot to ask. Peddling influence to gain favors from the Party leaders was always a gamble, one that could lead to internment in one of the protective custody camps. Despite this risky proposition Jennifer didn't hesitate in saying yes.

After she got off the phone with Maggie she called Matt at the office. "Can you find out more?" she asked.

"Honey, we're risking a lot here. It might be best if we let the police handle the matter."

"It's David Lewis we are talking about here. A sixty-two year old lawyer. Hardly a suicide bomber or a mall gunner. Maggie is my best friend. Please, just see if you can find out more."

"Okay, okay. I'll poke around."

After she hung up the phone immediately rang back with a number she didn't recognize. "Hello?"

"Mrs. Hanson? This is Barbara with the Genetic Application Office."

"Oh! Yes, this is Jennifer."

"We have the results of application. An appointment is scheduled to go over this with you and your husband. Your appointment time is Friday, September 20 at ten o'clock. Your appointment will take place at the office on Freedom Avenue. Do you know where that is?"

"Yes, it's the office we have been working with."

"Thank you, Mrs. Hanson. We look forward to seeing you then." With a click she hung up. Jennifer was taken aback by the coolness, but it seemed to be a regularity with government functionaries these days. The appointment scheduling was non-negotiable. No one less than the district leader would be able to schedule a different time. After she received an appointment notification through her iGlasses she called Matt and told him the news.

"The Genetic Application office has a lot of pull these days," he said. "Okay, I can swing it at work. Can you swing it at the school?"

Jennifer chuckled. "I work with children and women who want to have children. It should be no problem."

⋏

When Jennifer got to school on Monday she ran into Principal Jeffers in the hallway. "Did you get my email about Friday?"

Principal Jeffers smiled. "Yeah, that's fine. Go! Find out about your app. Is there anyone particular you want to cover you class? We could call Theresa in."

"Theresa would be perfect. She's worked with my kids before."

They stopped their conversation while a group of kids walked by, followed by two in electric wheelchairs. Jennifer hated that the kids were stigmatized by the red armbands they wore, as a dour teacher donned all in black led them. These were the kids that were identified with developmental disabilities. She and the principal waited as the kids passed by somberly.

"This will be the last year we teach them," Principal Jeffers said.

"What will happen to them?" Jennifer asked.

"They're building a special school for them out in Castle Rock. It's scheduled to open next fall. All class IVs will go, with class IIIs being optional."

"Bussing them out there?"

"No, permanent residence. Government mandate."

"It a shame. They're just children. They can't help it."

"Well, that's why we have the genetic application office these days," he said with a smile.

⋏

Jennifer told Matt about the class IV kids during dinner. Concerned, she asked, "Honey, you don't think we will get turned down for our genetic application do you?"

"Us? No way. It would have shown up on our gene scans when we first got married. We both have clean profiles. Our babies are going to be first class all the way."

"I'm just worried, that's all. Genetic testing is still not that exact."

"Yeah? Well, I'm telling you that neither one of us have anything to worry about. Come Friday night you and I will be celebrating at Jean Paul's. Oh, I'm still trying to dig up what happened to David. I asked Mister Baker if he could find out more. He and David are old friends so it's not that big of a favor to ask. He's just as concerned for the old man as we are."

"Oh yeah? Any news?"

"The Denver Police are saying that he's not been charged but they're holding him for questioning."

Jennifer scowled. "Questioning" was a euphemism covering a variety of things. Sometimes people were held in protective custody and genuinely co-operating with the police, but more often than not it meant interrogated. It was a toss-up either way.

Matt read his wife's scowl. "It's a step better than being outright arrested. They are holding him at the garrison in Brighton. Call Maggie and give her an update. Tell her we're doing everything we can."

⟁

On Friday Jennifer and Matt went to the Gene App office. They sat in a large sterile government waiting room, devoid of any warmth with another hundred people. Party slogans adorned the flat grey walls. Jennifer could read anxious anticipation in the faces of the other couples surrounding them. Some of them darted their eyes around the room nervously, like caged animals. A handful of people seemed to be bored with the process, having spent most of their lives in one government office or another. Jennifer tried to read a novel on her tablet but she couldn't concentrate, while her husband merely read the news on his iGlasses.

"Hanson," the intercom crackled. "Hanson to the front."

With their electronic devices put away they approached the glass-encased reception booth and scanned their dent chips. A door beside the booth opened and a nurse appeared, a brunette with startling beautiful green eyes, wearing old-fashioned whites. The nurse smiled, but it felt perfunctory. Jennifer was unsure what to make of it. Was bad news coming? Or had the nurse done this job so many times that she no longer had a passion for it.

The nurse led them to the office of Doctor McCabe. The bespectacled doctor was somewhere in his forties and quite portly. Jennifer wondered idly if he was on any of the government mandated diet plans. He stood up from his desk and smiled at them congenially, then waved for them to take a seat.

"Thank you, Mister and Missus Hanson for coming in. It's always a pleasure to serve fine folks such as yourselves who want to help out America and have babies. Do either of you know how the genetic application works and why we use it?"

Matt spoke up confidently. "It's the law."

Doctor McCabe smiled. "That's true, it is the law, but there is a reason for it."

"It's so we can have a genetically positive society," Jennifer said. "The class IVs and IIIs are deemed a drain on society and it costs too much to house and feed them." She hated saying it but it was the answer he wanted to hear.

"That's right!" the doctor responded. He reminded Jennifer of a school-teacher explaining simple math to a child. She found it patronizing. "Every couple who wishes to bear children must submit a genetic application to the government for review. We take the gene scans from your marriage license and new DNA samples from you. After we take all that and run it through DNA string compiler to see what kind of child you are likely to bear."

"Well," Matt said, "we have nothing to worry about because we are both Class Is."

"True, true. In most cases Class I parents will bear a Class I child."

Jennifer didn't like the way he phrased it. She thought they were about to receive bad news. Her husband seemed to sense the same thing. "We are Class Is, right?" Matt asked.

"You are both Class Is, that much is true. The qualifications of being a Class I are to have less than twenty percent of identifiable negative recessive genes. These are the recessive genes that lead to developmental disabilities that prevent the child from keeping up with his classmates at school or bound in a wheelchair for the rest of his life."

"Doctor, do you have bad news for us?" Jennifer asked.

He frowned. "I'm afraid I do. We ran the DNA compiler. There is a seventy seven percent probability that your child will develop into a Class III. A sixty-one percent probability for a Class IV."

Hot tears welled in Jennifer's eyes. "But the kid could be normal and healthy right?"

"Of course. Genetic prediction is still an inexact science. The child could always turn out to be normal."

"You're telling us that we would likely have a class III or IV child?" Matt asked.

"I am afraid so," the doctor said.

"Whose genes are the contributing cause to the outcome?"

Jennifer turned sharply at Matt. "Is it that important?" she asked.

"Well, yeah, we deserve to know."

The doctor attempted to intervene. "Sometimes it's best if young couples like yourselves don't know."

"But you know who it is, right?" Matt asked.

"Yes," the doctor said reluctantly.

"Who is it?"

"It's your recessive traits, Mr. Hanson."

Shaken, Matt gave a quick glance at Jennifer, then turned away. "Can the test be wrong?"

Relief washed across the doctor's face at the change of subject. "It's possible."

"Can we retake it?"

"Certainly you can. You should know that the regulations here will not let us do additional testing. You would need to go to a private facility to get the test done at considerable expense. If the test results are favorable you can go through the appeal process."

It was a small relief but they had some sort of option. "We can do that."

"Your results will be reported to your physician. Missus Hanson, you will be monitored weekly by your doctor going forward."

"Of course, doctor." She could see her husband grimace at the thought of the extra doctor bills. The weekly visits were customary after a negative test result. It was not unusual for a couple with a rejected application to try and get pregnant despite the regulations. The government found the best way to prevent it was for the wife visit the family physician weekly and undergo counseling and pregnancy tests. It was a pain, but being good citizens they would go through it.

⋏

The next several days were awkward for Jennifer. Sullen and withdrawn, Matt barely spoke above more than an acknowledging grunt. His happy mid-day calls stopped and she was filled with anxiety. It felt as if he blamed her for the outcome of the gene app.

Toward the end of the week Jennifer received a call from Maggie. "Daddy is out!"

"How is he?"

"He's not saying much. Just seems to be in a daze. I got the call earlier today and I picked him up from garrison. We should celebrate! Dinner and drinks over here. I don't think Daddy is ready for a night out yet."

"Of course. I'll call Matt and let him know. I can't wait to see him."

Jennifer called her husband but his reply was terse. "Sorry, babe, I can't go out tonight. District Leader Baker wants me to attend a party rally over in Aurora. I won't get home until late."

Skeptical of the "party rally" Jennifer wanted to argue with him, but she didn't. There was always a rally somewhere but that didn't mean her husband had to attend every one of them. He didn't want to go out with her but she wasn't sure if it is because David was politically toxic or if he held a grudge over the gene app. Jennifer decided to let it go and promised to give their hosts his regrets. Jennifer jumped into the roadster and headed toward the heart of Denver. Despite the chilly evening the heater in the antique still worked well and kept her warm. Even though the streets were crowded in this part of the city she found a parking space not too far away.

Maggie and her husband lived in a spacious townhome apartment in downtown Denver, close enough that Brad could walk to the law firm. Jennifer was shocked when Maggie opened the door. A few feet behind

Maggie stood her father, stooped over and reluctant to make eye contact. He had aged a dozen years in the short time he was held at the garrison. His eyes are haunted and he eyed the open door nervously, like he could run flee at any moment.

"How are you, Mister Lewis?" Jennifer asked as she stepped inside. She reached out to caress his shoulder but he flinched.

"I am sorry," David said. "So... sorry." His stared at the polished wooden floor and lost himself in his own thoughts while muttering unintelligibly.

Brad waved her in hastily. "Come in." David wandered into the living room and stood silently with his back to them. Maggie and Brad stared at each other than at her. Jennifer thought they were like lost children who silently pleaded for help. Finally Maggie said, "Dinner is almost ready. Do you want a drink? Yes, you definitely want a drink."

"Some wine?" Jennifer asked.

Maggie grinned. "I just opened a bottle of Cab."

Jennifer smiled uncomfortably at her friend. "Are you sure this is a good time?"

"Of course," Brad said. "Your husband was instrumental in getting David out of protective custody. We're here to celebrate."

Maggie rushed past Jennifer into the living room. "Daddy?" She started to reach out to him from behind but reconsidered. Deliberately, Maggie walked around to face him from the front. "Daddy? Come to the dinner table. It's time to eat." This time she gently reached for her father to guide him to the dining room. Jennifer followed the three of them, feeling like a stranger despite coming to their house for years. She chose to sit across from David, making sure she was in his view so that she wouldn't startle him again. Several platters of food were already laid out on the dinner table. Somehow Maggie was able to scrounge up some chicken filets, along with a fresh salad and some southwest corn it made for a fine welcome home.

Maggie conspicuously served her distracted father as the food was passed around the table. David stared at Jennifer but his eyes focused past her.

Jennifer found the experience uncomfortable and concentrated on dishing out corn onto her plate.

Brad cleared his throat. "So, Jennifer, I heard about the bad news at the gene app office."

Maggie dropped the serving spoon into the corn with a loud clatter. "Brad!"

"It's okay," Jennifer said. "We can appeal and additional tests can be run. Right now Matt and I are not going to worry."

"I am an American, dammit," David blurted out. "Born and raised here. I deserve to be treated with respect!"

"Shhhh, Daddy, I know," Maggie said.

He broke down and started crying. "You don't know what it's like in there. The screaming... the place is a mad house. They kept asking me questions over and over again. I kept answering them as honest as I could but they were always the same questions. And I couldn't sleep. God, no, I wasn't allowed to sleep."

"I am sure it was all a big misunderstanding," Jennifer offered. "You're out now. They know they were wrong."

"Brad, is there anything that can be done?" Maggie asked.

"Yeah, Pop," Brad said. "We can file a grievance with the Party. Make someone pay for what they did to you."

David's eyes widened with horror. "No, leave it alone. Leave it be."

"We can't let them get away with this," Maggie said.

"Leave it alone, Maggie. Just leave it alone."

Dinner came to a standstill. Everyone eyed David warily. "I'm sorry. I want to go home," David said as he stood up.

"No, Daddy, just stay with us tonight. It's probably better here with us. I get so worried with you in that big house all alone. Especially after you just got out. Just stay with us tonight and I'll take you home tomorrow."

"I'm so tired. I just want to get some sleep."

"Sure, Daddy. I can help you get to bed." He retired to the guest bedroom with his dinner barely touched.

"Maybe I should go?" Jennifer said.

"Sure, Jennifer," Brad says. She couldn't tell if he was ashamed or apologetic. "This was probably too soon. I'll just make a plate for you to take home. Matt too?"

"Thanks, Brad. That would be great."

Maggie stayed upstairs with her father while Brad prepared two plastic dishes filled with food and covered food. Jennifer hoped to see her friend again but she never came back down. Brad returned from the kitchen with the covered food in plastic bags. He smiled apologetically. "I am sorry about this evening."

Jennifer waved it off. "No, don't worry. It was probably just too soon."

On the way home Jennifer reflected on David's behavior. He was traumatized after his experience in protective customer. Jennifer idly wondered what the experience was like and hoped she never had to experience such trauma.

A text message popped up on her iGlasses from Matt as she pulled into the driveway. *Got drinks with the guys tonight. Don't wait up.*

"Asshole," Jennifer muttered.

She uncorked a bottle of wine to go with her dinner and planned to eat Matt's dinner the next day. It was his loss for being an asshole. After her third glass she passed out watching the news. The house AI sensed she was asleep and lowered the lights in the living room.

$$\Lambda$$

Jennifer discovered her husband passed out on the couch in the morning. He must have come in during the night and fell asleep there. She sipped her coffee and ignored his snoring. Truth be told she nursed her own hangover and decided to get ready for work quietly while her husband slept.

Jennifer left for work, quietly opening and closing the door, while her sleeping and snoring husband remained on the couch. She went to school and taught throughout the day and never heard from him. She didn't care if he missed work. It was his issue and she wasn't feeling charitable since he was still behaving like an ass.

He came home after work with a bouquet of roses. No small expense given the scarcity of flowers in this economy.

"I am sorry," Matt said. "I have been an ass."

She stood in the kitchen with her arms crossed and waited for him to continue.

"I reacted badly to the doctor's news about the gene app. I was mad at you and mad at myself for such a bad result," he said.

"Do you think it's my fault?"

"No."

She reached for the bouquet. "Do you think it's your fault?"

"If it's not your fault then it has to be mine."

"Dumbass," she said softly. It wasn't an admonishment. He hadn't thought it through and she needed to do it for him. "It's a genetic application test. It's nobody's fault. If we can't have kids then we can't have kids. And the test can still be wrong. We can apply again."

"Is your heart set on it?"

"Do I want kids? Yes, I would love to have one." She wanted more than one but the law didn't allow it. "But if we can't have a child then I'm okay with it." She wouldn't be, but she didn't want to tell him. Jennifer wouldn't mind adopting a Class III but she held a lingering fear her husband might exploit the child for favor with the Party. She imagined her husband carrying the kid in his arms at a political rally to gain sympathy from people. It nauseated her.

⋏

After Jennifer left the school for the day she got a call from Maggie. "They took Daddy again!"

"What? Why?"

"I don't know! He hasn't been doing anything. He hasn't even gone to work. He's been so different. Just quiet and withdrawn. Why would they pick him up this time? Can you see what Matt can find out?"

"Yeah, yeah. I'll ask Matt to find out what's going on."

After she hung up with Maggie she transcribed a text message through the iGlasses - *David in custody again. Can you find out what's up?*

He sent a message back several minutes later. *Yeah, babe, I will look into it.*

Jennifer sent a text back to Maggie but didn't get a response. She decided to make some dinner while waiting to hear from her husband.

Matt told Jennifer as soon as he arrived home. "It was Maggie's husband," he said. "After David was taken into custody last time around he tried to muscle the Party with their law firm. He filed a complaint against the National Police. They take that shit seriously. Now the whole inquiry into David has been reopened. It's not just David this time. It's everyone that was at the dinner party when he questioned General Scarborough. District Leader Baker is pissed. This doesn't look good on anyone. Brad needs to back off from his inquiry. Can you reach her? He hasn't answered my calls."

Jennifer told her iGlasses to call Maggie but there was no answer. She left a voicemail and sent a text as well. She tried to ring up Brad but he didn't answer either.

"Do you think they're in custody?" she asked.

"Probably. It's weird that we can't find them." The only people that disappeared these days were the ones that went into protective custody.

They both watched programming on the OLED wall in the living room. Some old World War II movie that neither of them are interested in. Jennifer watched with her wine glass while Matt sipped on his bourbon. She fidgeted with her tablet and Matt was distracted by whatever he was looking at on his iGlasses.

"Oliver?" Matt says.

"Yes," the house AI responded.

"Switch this to local news."

The war movie disappeared and was replaced with a newsfeed. Jennifer set her tablet aside to watch the report.

A shapely Hispanic anchorwoman in a blue skirt and a red blouse narrated the news video rolling to the left of the screen. "Today the SWAT team of the National Police raided the law firm of Lewis, Johnson and Young. We've received reports that lawyers of the law firm have engaged in sedition."

The video showed footage from the officers' helmet cams interspersed with high-def footage from the law firm's own security cameras. The bouncing camera footage caught glimpses of office workers standing around in shock. If anything worse had happened in the law firm it wouldn't be shown here. "Everyone in the office will be detained into protective for the time being. As everyone is aware detained in protective custody is routine in matters like this. The Freedom Party would like to remind everyone that it is their patriotic duty as an American citizen to report seditious behavior."

Matt muted the audio. "So that's where they are. Thank God we're not involved."

Jennifer was ashamed to admit that she agreed with her husband.

⚔

Matt sent a text mid-morning: *NP is here. Will tell you what happens.*

She texted him back at lunch but he didn't respond. Jennifer spent the remainder of the morning fearing her husband had been taken into custody.

An hour before the school day ended a man entered her classroom. The air of the classroom chilled as he walked in and the children were visibly frightened at his presence. He wore a crisp black uniform with the White Star pin standing out on his collar. Easily over six feet tall the man towered above all of them. He removed his black dress cap with the shiny brim to reveal a shock of white blond hair that contrasted with his icy blue eyes. Handsome, he cut an athletic figure but Jennifer shivered under his stare.

The man smiled but it felt as if he'd had to practice doing it in front of a mirror every day. "I am Chief Inspector Jennings from the National Police. Would you come me with me, please?"

"What is this about?" Jennifer asked.

"Missus Hanson, we have some questions about a dinner party you attended recently."

Jennifer had never run afoul of the Party her entire life. She always believed she was on the right side of the law and the Party. The only time the Party came after you was because they thought you had done something wrong. Now she was being questioned... and this man, Chief Inspector Jennings, truly frightened her. Jennifer remained vigilant because she was confident she had done nothing wrong. Jennifer smiled and said, "I would be happy to answer your questions, Mister Jennings."

"Chief Inspector Jennings." He turned his smile up into a wide grimace.

"I am sorry. Chief Inspector. Shall we go to the teacher's lounge?"

"I am afraid this will take a while. Would you come with us?" The tone of his voice along with his icy stare belied the politeness of the question. This was an order.

"Is that really necessary?"

"I must insist."

She hesitated. "Okay. I'll get someone to take over my class."

"Please, take your time." Again, the words didn't match his eyes. Chief Inspector Jennings didn't strike her to be a patient man.

It didn't take long to get the assistant principal to come in and cover her class. Alicia Vickers skirted around Jennifer and treated her like a stranger, despite knowing each other for years. Jennifer exited her classroom to find a couple of black-uniformed officers waiting for her. They, along with the chief inspector, escorted her outside to three black Chevy Suburbans waiting for them in the parking circle at front of the school. Kids and teachers stood silently at the windows as the National Police escorted her to the waiting cars. The kids were naturally curious. The children of wealthy parents attended this school and the National Police were a novelty to them.

Jennifer didn't say anything. She entered the black vehicle calmly and sat in the back. Jennings came in right behind her and sat at her side. The doors locked automatically and there were no handles.

They traveled downtown, passing the Party headquarters along the way. A line of unmarked black Suburbans were parked out front with a flurry of activity. She thought they would stop here but the vehicle continued.

"Where are we going?" Jennifer asked.

"The police department downtown."

The Suburbans parked in front of the police station, heedless of the "no parking" signs out front. Jennings and his uniformed officers hustled out of their vehicles and escorted Jennifer inside the precinct. The entire precinct floor stopped their activity and regarded the new arrivals warily. The Denver Police uniformed officers step back and out of the way of the black clad brethren from the federal agency. Detectives and admins behind desks put down their phones and waited quietly. Even the local criminals held in custody stared. Everyone in the room watched as this tall blond blue-eyed inspector strode into the police precinct with his uniformed officers in tow, escorting a small blonde woman.

"I need a room," Jennings said with a booming voice. Everyone in the room remained frozen. Somewhere in the back a phone warbled impatiently. "Now!"

A Hispanic woman wearing a navy blue pantsuit stood up hesitantly. The nameplate on her desk read Detective Maria Hernadez. "Right this way, Chief Inspector." Detective Hernadez led them through the station via different hallways. The well-worn police precinct was a relic from the previous century with modern security cameras, but lacked the helpful OLED doors or floors to help point the way. In fact, the floors were well-scuffed ancient pea-green and white linoleum tiles with harsh fluorescent lights shining from the tiled ceiling. They reached a hallway of windowless doors painted brown. The sign above the hallway read "Interrogation Rooms".

Outside of "Interrogation Room 4" Jennings told her to scan her dent. She placed her hand through the open slot of the dent scanner next to the door. Her hand was bathed in red until it turned green indicating a successful dent scan. The display monitor read -

"Working...
"...
"Identified: Hanson, Jennifer L.

Other personal information scrolled down the screen until it ended with bold red letters; *"FLAGGED FOR REVIEW."*

She wondered what that meant but didn't dare ask. The detective opened the door and motioned for Jennifer to go through. She entered first but

Jennings stopped at the doorframe and faced the detective. "I see you are not wearing your party pin," he said.

Briefly, the detective's eyes widened momentarily with raw panic. "My pin?" she said. "It was on my other suit. I forgot to take it off when I took it to the cleaners. If the cleaners don't have my pin I can get another one."

Jennings eyed her for a moment. He could make an issue if he chose to. Jennings had the authority to cast Jennifer aside and force Detective Hernadez to submit to an interrogation. The Chief Inspector looked as if he considered this but changed his mind and entered the interrogation room with Jennifer as his sole focus for the occasion.

The windowless room was simple cinderblock walls thickly painted gray. A perfunctory government table sat in the center of the room, bolted to the floor with a hook in the center to cuff prisoners. On either side of the table were equally perfunctory government chairs. A large mirror on one side of the room covered the wall behind Jennings. Jennifer thought that this was a two-way mirror that she had seen from old movies.

Jennings motioned impatiently for her to sit down, then reached into his jacket pocket and pulled out a set of black, thick-rimmed iGlasses. He set them on the table while he took off his suit jacket and folded it over the back of his chair. Jennings pushed a button on the side of the iGlasses then put them on.

He reviewed his tablet for a few moments then spoke. "Subject: Hanson, Jennifer L. First interrogation. Today's date is October 18. Note: Need a medic team to pull blood work for a full DNA workup." Jennings tapped his pad for a few moments then continued with his focus on Jennifer. "You attended a dinner party at the residence of District Leader Orson Baker. It was three weeks ago, correct?"

"Yes, that's correct."

Jennings smiled. "Tell me about that evening."

"Well, it was a late summer evening. As you said we were at a dinner party at Orson Baker's house. He lives just outside the city on one of the mountain slopes. There were other guests, mostly members of the Freedom Party, some members of the Denver City Council and a few distinguished guests from the community. The guest of honor was General Scarborough who was on leave from the Texas front."

"Just a pleasant dinner party then?"

Jennifer wondered what he was playing at. He knew exactly what had happened at the dinner party. Several other dinner guests had already been interrogated by now. She realized that he enjoyed this. Like a cat toying with a wounded bird as it flopped on the ground.

"Chief Inspector, I imagine you have heard reports that the dinner party ended badly. An argument occurred between General Scarborough and David Lewis."

Jennings bristled at her reply. He had the expectation for people to cower from him. Even though she had done nothing wrong she still had to be careful. He was a man who could make something bad happen to her.

"Mister Lewis's behavior was described by some as seditious," Jennings said.

"By who? David is a well-respected long-standing member of this community. He's an old man from a different era. I heard the stories while I was growing up. They had a different belief system. He probably clings to some notions of that system and forgets the problems they had in those days." Everyone she grew up with learned all the problems with democracy in school.

"So you agreed with Mister Lewis's views?"

Exasperated, Jennifer rubbed her forehead. "No. I'm saying it was a heated discussion and feelings might have been hurt, but David is a far cry from a turban-clad terrorist with a bomb strapped to his chest. He didn't mean anything. He was just talking. Did anyone else at the party call David seditious?"

Jennings leaned back in his chair. "Missus Hanson, do I need to remind you that you are here to answer my questions and not the other way around?"

"I am sorry, Chief Inspector. It feels like I'm in trouble when I've done nothing wrong."

Jennings smiled again. "We will be the ones that determine that. How well do you know Mister Lewis?"

"I've known him all my life. His daughter and I are close friends. We visited her family all the time and they visited ours. We were all friends in the neighborhood. Her folks liked my folks and vice versa."

"Your opinion of Mister Lewis would be biased then?" He tapped his tablet with a stylus.

"A friend always has a favorable bias for another friend."

"If you friend asked you to shoot a police officer or blow up Party headquarters would you do that?"

"I don't know what kind of people you keep company with, Chief Inspector. My friends would never ask me to do something like that." Now Jennifer leaned back in her chair. She didn't like this man. He was a bully and used to having his way.

"Tell me about Magnolia -"

"Maggie? Nobody ever calls her Magnolia, not even her own father. She's my best friend. A bit of a free spirit and everyone loves her."

Jennings arched an eyebrow. "Everyone has enemies. Surely, she can't be that beloved."

"No enemies that I know about."

Tick-tick-tick on the tablet again. The plastic black tip of the silver stylus banged against the capacitive glass surface. "She's a member of the Jefferson Society."

"Was a member. That was in college. Kids do all kinds of stuff in college."

Tick-tick-tick. "Speaking of college, you had a spot of trouble didn't you?"

Jennifer frowned. She knew that this would come back to haunt her someday. "Like I said, kids do all kinds of stuff in college."

"It's an illegal substance."

"It was pot and it used to be legal here. It wasn't like I did coke or was nodding off on heroin. I never did it again. Are you holding me accountable for something that was resolved ten years ago?"

"Just painting a picture, Missus Hanson. We do extensive background research on everyone. If you like, we have a more secluded facility in the mountains to the west. We could carry this conversation on there?"

He was certainly a bully. There was a protective custody facility for political prisoners on Golden Gate Canyon Road. She'd heard rumors that prisoners sent there were never seen again. "That won't be necessary. I am happy to answer your questions here."

"Tell me about your husband."

"What about him? I believe he is a member in good standing with the Freedom Party."

Tick-tick-tick. "Yes." Jennings drew out the one-word answer with a tinge of disappointment. "It would appear so. We could find nothing on him. He is a regular Boy Scout. Back to the dinner party. When Mister Lewis argued with General Scarborough whose side were you on?"

"Side? I wasn't involved with the argument at all. I was more interested in my dinner than listening to their discussion."

"Let me phrase the question another way. Did you agree with Mister Lewis?"

Jennifer barely remembered the argument. She only knew that David was against the waste of the war and the general was for it, as generals always are. Jennifer didn't care one way or the other but she had learned at an early age that one never argued with the Party. "I agree with the Party. I always agree with the Party."

A soft discreet knock on the door interrupted the interrogation. Jennings scowled as he stood to answer. A white clad nurse entered with a phlebotomy kit. She was older, just short of retirement with salt and pepper hair. "I need to draw some blood, Miss. Genetic work ups and such."

Jennifer nodded. Even though they still had her blood work on file from the gene app, the Party believed in continuous genetic testing. They wanted to make sure they had the right Jennifer Hanson in the room. She resigned herself to the testing and rolled her sleeve. Jennings quietly stepped out of the room.

CHAPTER 4

The questioning went on and on. Questions regarding her parents and their party affiliation (her father was dead and her mother lived in Chicago with no interest in politics). Questions about childhood friends she had long forgotten. Questions about junior high classmates she barely remembered (such as Jonas Mitchell, who apparently had deserted his unit on the Texas front). Questions about college classmates. Questions about neighbors. Questions about colleagues. Questions about Matt's colleagues.

On and on they went. Jennings kept throwing verbal traps in front of her to trick her into an admission of guilt. She slowly and deliberately evaded the traps and stayed with her narrative, but the conversation exhausted her and a headache blossomed in the forefront of her skull.

A little after six o'clock Jennings left the room briefly. He returned several minutes later and told her she was free to go. "We may need to question you again. Do you understand?"

"Of course."

Jennings escorted her back to the main entrance of the police station. Along the way they passed the desk of Detective Hernadez. She wore the party pin on her lapel.

Jennifer got her purse back along with her tablet and iGlasses. She stuck the ear bud in and said, "Call Matt."

"Dialing," the iGlasses replied.

There was no answer. She left him a voicemail and sent a text but it was clear he was still tied up with his own interrogation. Jennifer resigned herself to getting an autocab. She debated whether she should go back to school or go home. Finally, she decided to go home and worry about it in the morning.

⚔

Jennifer arrived home and realized how famished she was after the harrowing afternoon at the police station. She grilled some tofu and placed it on a bed of greens with some pecans and feta, then drizzled it with a balsamic vinaigrette. She ate her salad mechanically while enjoying the glass of Cabernet more. After dinner she took her wineglass, along with the bottle, and drew a hot bubble bath.

"Music," she told the house AI. "Classical. Any variety." The strings of Beethoven echoed through the house.

She sipped her wine while soaking in the tub. The tension that plagued her muscles sapped away as she relaxed in the hot bath water. When the water started to cool Jennifer caught herself getting drowsy and got out of the bath. She slipped on a long T-shirt and collapsed into bed.

Matt came home before eleven o'clock. She woke up and sat on the edge of the bed despite her lethargic need for more sleep. "What happened?" she asked.

"Tomorrow," he replied.

"No, tell me now. It's okay." She yawned.

"They came this morning around nine. There were more tactical police at one time than I have ever seen in my entire life. The building was surrounded. Then the inspectors came in. Six of them. They rounded us up and put us in trucks. Everyone who was at that damned dinner party and their staffers. Most people had no idea what was going on."

"How did you do?"

"Fine, I guess. I answered their questions. I did nothing wrong and I don't have anything to hide."

"They picked me up from school."

"I know. Jennings told me."

"Chief Inspector Jennings," Jennifer corrected with a snort.

Matt grinned. "I see you got the preferential treatment from him too."

"Yeah. Did they push anyone into a confession?"

"I won't know until tomorrow. Our releases were staggered. District Leader Baker was let go first. I think I was the last. Maybe Brad can cool it with his inquiry?"

"I haven't heard from them. I think all three are still in custody."

"I hope the National Police can bust him in his chops for getting us in this mess," Matt says.

"Matthew!"

"What? If he didn't tear into this righteous crusade to vindicate his father-in-law then none of us would have had a bad day."

"I still don't want him or anyone else to get in trouble. He's my best friend's husband."

⋏

She had Matt wake up early so that he could drop her off at school. He suggested once she should take an autocab but he didn't push it with her when she answered with a scowl. At school the principal pulled her aside and asked if she was in any kind of trouble. The tone of the conversation suggested the principal worried about the school's liability. They certainly couldn't risk employing a teacher being investigated by the National Police. None of her colleagues approached her and shied away when she met them in the hallways. During the lunch period she sat alone at the teachers' table.

Jennifer received a text message from Maggie before school let out. The message read, *I am fine. Can we meet at Juno's?*

Jennifer suggested they meet after school around four o'clock. It would take her the full hour to get there and that meant she would be doing extra work when she got home. And it was closer to Maggie and more of an inconvenience for Jennifer.

Juno's Steakhouse was attached to a mall just outside of Denver. Although steak was no longer on the menu the name had never changed and Juno's had transformed into an upscale watering hole. Dark with the shades drawn, the place was decorated with overstuffed leather couches, shelves with old books and lots of wood. Only a few early patrons were present, all having drinks at the bar. Jennifer found Maggie in a back booth drinking bourbon on the rocks with her glass holding the barest trace of liquor. Maggie's eyes were red and she was uncharacteristically free of any make up.

"How are you?" Jennifer asked. "How is David? How is Brad?"

A waitress came by to take their order before Maggie could answer. She ordered a double Jack on the rocks while Jennifer opted for a glass of Shiraz.

"Brad and I were released this morning," Maggie said. "He spent the night in their infirmary. They still have Daddy. Brad is at home recuperating. He had two fingers cut off his hand."

"Oh my God!"

"They really thought he knew something. He's pretty shaken up. He's been in bed all day. I think he might have PTSD."

"How are you holding up?"

"Jennifer, nothing like this has ever happened to me before."

"Were you hurt?"

Maggie shook her head. "No, no torture or anything like that. I was just detained and questioned. But I didn't know what they were doing to Brad and I still don't know about Daddy. I mean, I was always used to Daddy tweaking the nose of the Party and I did some tweaking of my own. The Party stepped on us - hard! I always thought we were special, a different class of people. But we're not, are we?"

"It's the Party." She thought about her own trouble and the other things that went on. Her car was a gas guzzling antique that she needed a special permit for while most people couldn't even own an electric car. Even though she had privileges that allowed her to shop at the finest grocery stores, most meat was outlawed for everyone else. Why weren't they allowed to eat meat? Jennifer still wanted the occasional hamburger or hot dog with mustard that she remembered from childhood. And who was the Party to determine who can or can't have a baby? That rubbed her the most. After her experience yesterday she began to understand why everyone else in Denver sullenly glared at her as she drove around the city in her convertible. Those people had far less freedoms than she did.

Maggie knocked back her bourbon and waved for the waitress to bring another. Quickly, a fresh drink appeared in front of her. She quietly mused over her drink. "I'm not sure how this is going to turn out. As soon as Daddy is out I think the three of us should try to make it to Cuba."

Jennifer scanned the room to see if anyone listened. "Cuba?" she hissed. "Are you crazy?" This was sedition.

"It's not like it was when it was ruled by the Castros."

Jennifer wasn't sure what to believe about Cuba. She'd heard the constant stories about dissidents fleeing America for Mexico and Cuba. Some had described both locations as a paradise while others had described them as war-torn hellholes. The Coalition forces had established a foothold in the Florida peninsula from a Cuban borne invasion. "It's not that bad," Jennifer said. "This is all a big misunderstanding. Everything is going to get back to normal soon." Jennifer doubted herself even as she gave Maggie those reassurances.

Maggie took a slug of her bourbon again. "Is there any way you can ask Matt to check on Daddy?"

Jennifer shivered. Even though had autumn settled in Denver, it felt as if the steakhouse dropped several degrees. "Is that a good idea right now?"

Maggie wiped away tears from her face. "No, it's not. I know it's a lot to ask. I just don't know what else to do."

Jennifer reached out and grasped Maggie's hand. "I'll ask Matt."

⋏

Jennifer prepared a meal of grilled slices of tofu with some brown rice and asparagus spears. The tofu was as close to meat as you could get these days. Matt said he had heard that the soldiers on the front lines got a special dispensation for beef. Of course country folk were able to hunt and fish even though it was illegal. She had no idea what happened in the ghettos but had heard there was a reduced population of stray cats and dogs. Matt got home well past dark and Jennifer was a little fuzzy on the wine.

"Sorry, I'm late," he said. "Since no one was in the office yesterday we're still trying to get back to our routine."

"How are things there? How's the district leader?"

"Tense. You hear about political raids all the time but the last place you would expect it would be at local Party headquarters. Manufacturing plants and mines? Sure, dissidents get rounded up there all the time. Mister Baker seems to be shaken up. He assured the National Police that it was just a dinner party and the rhetoric got out of hand. Most of what went on had nothing to do with anyone. District Leader Baker is not pleased and hopes this does not stain his party record."

"I saw Maggie today."

"What? Honey, you need to stay away from her and her dad right now."

"She's my best friend!"

"She's a liability! The National Police are focused on her dad at the moment. The closer anyone is to her, the closer they are going to be targeted."

"Maggie wanted to know if we can find out any info on her dad."

Matt softened his tone. "I think what is happening to David is pretty shitty, but it's not a good idea to make waves with the Party and the National Police right now."

Jennifer sighed. "I know. I told her the same thing."

⋏

Tensions slowly eased over the next several days. Matt reported everything remained hectic at the Party offices. People were still trying to catch up from the questioning and they followed the strictest procedures and protocols. Jennifer's colleagues slowly warmed up to her again. The stigma of questioning had worn off. Jennifer also made an effort to reach out to Maggie every day.

Maggie reported Brad had trouble sleeping. He complained of night sweats and he awakened her nightly with nightmares. The law firm was in disarray without David's leadership and Brad's haphazard attendance. She made her own inquiries about her father but she got nowhere. Maggie only knew he was "detained".

Maggie called several days later on Saturday. "Daddy's dead."

"What?" Jennifer asked. "How do you know?"

"Chief Inspector Jennings brought Daddy's things. Said he died of 'natural causes'. As if!"

Jennifer felt a chill go up her spine. This was an open line. After being investigated by the National Police, Maggie should be more discreet. "Maybe we should go for a drink. Same place as last time?"

Maggie sounded confused. "Yeah, okay. I'll see you there."

The anxiety mounted in Jennifer throughout her drive to Juno's. Suspicion of the Party wasn't normal. All her life the Party had taken care of her and her family. With the Party to take care of her there was never anything to worry about. After recent events she regarded the Party with suspicion. Jennifer observed the cars surrounding her closely and kept checking the mirror to see if she was followed.

Since it was Saturday Juno's had a modest lunch crowd. Jennifer didn't ask Matt to accompany her. She figured he would have given her grief about it. Jennifer went inside and found Maggie sitting alone at the same table as before. Jennifer had a brief panic attack. Were they being watched? Was the table bugged? And who was really here for lunch?

She couldn't worry about it now. She was there and she would make the best of it. Her friend stood up and Jennifer hugged her when she approached the table. Regardless of her fears Maggie remained her friend and she wanted to console as best she could.

"I am sorry about your dad," Jennifer said. "It doesn't make sense. All of this. Do you have any idea what happened?"

Maggie barked a short derisive laugh. "What happened? He became an enemy of the state, that's what happened. A subject of inquiry. A person of interest. Pick one. The Party turned their eye on him and he suffered for it. All because of bad conversation at a stupid dinner party." Maggie slugged back her drink and motioned the waiter for another. "Natural causes. And the funny thing is Daddy probably did die of natural causes. He was sixty-two and had high blood pressure. All the stress from the protective custody and questioning probably killed him."

"Is there anything I can do?"

"No. I wish there was. He has already been cremated. We don't even get his body back for a funeral."

"Oh my God." It was standard procedure for people in protective custody to be cremated if they died. Why would David be treated any differently despite his long-standing reputation in the Denver community?

"The memorial service is on Tuesday. Not a full funeral. Without a body we don't need a full funeral. Would you and Matt come?"

"Of course we will."

⚔

Matt wanted nothing to do with the memorial service. Given the inquiry surrounding David and everyone else at the ill-fated dinner party Matt thought it best they not go. She and Matt argued about it. Jennifer didn't give a damn what the Party and the state thought. She would support her friend in her time of need and she went to the memorial service alone.

Apparently everyone else agreed with Matt. Sparse in attendance, the memorial service was dwarfed by the cavernous Catholic church Maggie and Brad had booked on Downing Street. Matt was right. Anyone who had any sense stayed away from this service. Jennifer assumed the National Police had the place under surveillance.

Still, she supported her friend devoutly and stubbornly clung to the belief you didn't abandon the people you were close to. Jennifer did what she could to help with the memorial service. She attended to the guests and arranged things with the priest and the clergy staff.

The priest, along with everyone else in the Denver community, regarded David highly. If he or his staff felt any notion they were at odds with the Party, they didn't show it. Jennifer also understood the Catholic faith did enjoy some leeway with the Party and the two rarely crossed paths.

Near the end of the evening Maggie and Brad approached her. "I just want to thank you for everything," Maggie said. "I don't know how I could have done this without you."

"Yeah," Brad said. He reached out and pulled her in an embrace. "What you have done for Maggie and I... well, that has really been great. No one else has been there for us. No one." Brad glanced briefly at his mangled left hand, then cast his eyes toward the floor.

Shocked, Jennifer replied, "Well, of course, you're both dear friends. Of course I'm there for you. Reach out if you ever need me."

Maggie and Brad shared a furtive conspiratorial glance around the room then at each other. "Brad, can you give us a moment?" Maggie said.

He nodded and walked to a couple of other guests.

"Is there anything wrong?" Jennifer asked.

"No. If anything, this has brought us closer together. Nothing like being under the watchful eye of the Party to back two people into the corner. Brad quit the firm. There's not a place there for him anymore. The senior partners gave him a severance package. They bought out Daddy's part of the firm. Nothing as much as what it was worth, but a fair amount of money."

"Is he going to start his own practice?"

Maggie snorted. "Do you think he would get any business? Actually, he probably could start representing some of the more common folk. Daddy's share of the firm was pretty good even if we didn't get full value of it. But Brad's not going to do that."

"What is he going to do then?"

Maggie surveyed the room to make sure no one else listened. Jennifer wasn't sure but she thought a cathedral this size would be pretty hard to bug. Maggie whispered, "We're going to make a run for Cuba."

"Are you crazy?" Jennifer hissed. "You're going to throw away your life on a fantasy."

"What life?" Maggie asked. "What do we have left? There is nothing for us in Denver. Probably not anywhere in America. We'll probably be hounded by the Party for the rest of our lives."

"You don't know that."

"You don't either."

Jennifer grudgingly had to admit to herself that Maggie had a point. If they weren't already on a watch list yet they certainly would be. Jennifer had thought she and her husband were on the periphery of this whole mess. She suppressed a sigh and acknowledged that coming there hadn't helped. Still, she didn't regret her decision to attend this memorial service. Even with this political climate of paranoia she believed that she should be loyal to her friends and family.

"Just think it through," Jennifer said.

"We have. If we stay here the money won't last long. We could go to rural Montana, but the Party will still follow us there. We're going to run."

Flabbergasted, Jennifer asked, "How? You've led the same sheltered life that I have?"

"My father was a defense attorney. I'm married to one. They know people."

"You know somebody?"

"Brad and Daddy worked a case a few years back. A hacker Brad knows. Goes by the name of Diablo05 online. He lives out in Centennial."

"What's a hacker going to do?"

"New identities and transfer of assets. A way out through New Orleans. He can get us on a boat."

"This is crazy."

"You and Matt should go with us. Things are only going to get worse."

"Things aren't that bad."

"They will be. If you ever decide to go you should look him up. Remember the name - Diablo05."

CHAPTER 5

In late November Denver buzzed with excitement as they celebrated the Thanksgiving holiday. The Broncos were out of town to play the Detroit Lions in the annual Thanksgiving game. Jennifer couldn't care less about football but Matt was an avid fan. He could have pulled some strings with the Party to get tickets to the game, but it was too soon after all the recent mess in everyone's lives. Still, his mood was lightened by the big game and everyone she met with related to the Party seemed to be more relaxed.

Neither she nor Matt had family in town. Rather than enjoying Thanksgiving alone they took up District Leader Baker on his invitation to his mansion for the day. Jennifer was reluctant given what last occurred on her visit the District Leader's house but Matt said it would be good to mend relationships and move forward.

They took his Chrysler Patriot on another bright and sunny day in Denver, despite the air being cold and crisp. The streets were empty with few commuter buses running. They arrived before noon with the big game already under way in the first quarter. Excited, Matt was fortunate to see he hadn't missed any big plays yet since the score remained 0-0.

Only three other couples attended the Thanksgiving celebration with their children and they eyed Jennifer and Matt hesitantly when they walked into the foyer. She recognized them as deputies within Orson Baker's inner circle. They seemed to be at a loss as to what they should do at Jennifer and

Matt's arrival and glanced at each other anxiously. Baker put that to an end by stepping into the foyer.

"Matt," he exclaimed. "Good of you to make it. Jennifer, it is a pleasure to see you again." He rushed forward and pumped Matt's hand with a handshake then embraced Jennifer with a kiss on the cheek. With Baker's approval the other couples relaxed. Acceptance by Baker was good enough for the rest of them.

Everyone made small talk and greeted one another in the foyer for a few minutes. Despite the annoyance of small talk they were still "working the room" as they always did. These social occasions were all about Matt's career, even if some of the other wives didn't know that about their own husbands. After several minutes District Leader Baker declared, "If you ladies will excuse us, there's a big game we need to get back to." The men had a good chuckle and made their way to Baker's den.

Rebecca Baker, the District Leader's wife, beamed at the other women. "Well, turkey is in the oven. The servants tell me it will be ready in about an hour. How about some wine in the living room?"

The wives chirped with agreement and Jennifer was disappointed in herself when she chimed in with them. This ritual of separating men from women was strange to her but she went along with it. The Party was always pushing "progressive" and "equality". This "men in the den, women in the living room" ritual seemed to still be reserved for the holidays. At least they were not in the kitchen making dinner for their men. Where District Leader Baker was the chief among his men, this seemed to make his wife the de facto chief among the wives.

Rebecca led the way to the cream colored living room, off the right of the foyer. Decorated in a sedately old fashioned manner with a bland cream colored couch, matching chairs and a cherry coffee table with end tables, Jennifer stifled a yawn as she entered the boring room. A clean fireplace along the back wall of the room appeared to have been never used. Some original piece of artwork hung above the fireplace, depicting a scene of a sunny mountain lake that was equally as bland as the furniture. The fireplace mantle was adorned with framed pictures of the Baker family. Jennifer didn't want to look at them. She was afraid they might be as boring as the rest of the room. An elderly white man dressed in a white formal tuxedo stood against the north wall with several bottles of wine chilled in buckets.

"Charlie," Rebecca said. "Help these ladies with their drinks."

"Yes, ma'am," the servant said stiffly.

"Ladies, do have a seat. Jennifer, please sit next to me on the couch."

The three other wives were aghast. In this social hierarchy Jennifer had just jumped from near outcast to second in command. It seemed the district leader and his wife were going out of their way to smooth Jennifer and her husband's path back into the social circle. Essentially, they spent most of the time rehashing Party gossip. It came back around to that ill-fated dinner party back in September.

"How has Maggie been?" Stacy Larson asked.

"We had a drink together a couple of weekends ago. She's pretty upset, considering," Jennifer said. "Her life has been turned upside down. Her father is gone. Her husband has been pushed out of the firm. She's the subject of an investigation."

"It has been pretty tough on us all," Heather Nicholson said. Everyone at the party had been questioned. Still, Jennifer didn't think suffering through a few questions from the National Police was a fair comparison to what she and her friend had gone through. She wanted to tell this idiot the same thing but she held her tongue. Jennifer sighed and suppressed her resentment for going through this. At least she wasn't as self-centered as this oblivious idiot.

"You were very brave," Stacy said.

"Me?"

"To be as close to her as you are. That was why they held you longer for questioning."

"We'll, we've been friends since children. I would like to think Maggie would do the same for me." Jennifer knew her relationship with Maggie targeted her specifically for interrogation.

"I don't know if I could," Stacy said.

Jennifer bristled and doubted any of them could. Given the way the Party had intertwined itself in their lives, if you were close to the center of the Party people wanted to be close to you. If you were ostracized to the outer reaches, then you were shunned. Had it come to this? In the past personal relationships mattered. Now they seemed to be about advancement within the Party. Was Jennifer ever that way? She couldn't remember treating people as such, but after being targeted by the Party she now regarded life with a new outlook. She truly hoped she had never been as shallow.

Dinner was scheduled to be served at two-thirty after the game was over, but the game ran long and went into overtime. When gleeful shouts echoed through the hallways from the den, the ladies in the living room smiled at one another with relief. The Broncos had upset Lions 27-24.

Jennifer followed Rebecca and the other ladies into the dining room. Where it had been heated and stuffy during Jennifer's last visit there, it was now spacious and cozy with enough room for the Bakers and their guests to eat comfortably while served by the white coated servants. The men wore their iGlasses while they ate. Jennifer expected them to eat and watch the Cowboys' game at the same time. District Leader Baker had made a performance of carving the turkey. Occasionally the men muttered a few sentences about their mundane life in the office but they, for the most part, stayed focused on the game.

The talk turned back once again to the dinner party from two months before. Was there anything else to talk about? District Leader Baker anxiously changed the subject. "It's best we move on."

"What ever happened with the General," Heather asked.

"The last I heard he was back at his command post in Dallas."

$$\text{\Lambda}$$

The following Monday Matt returned home late in the evening. Jennifer had been waiting on the couch with a glass of wine. She could tell by the way he stormed in he was in a mood. "Why so late?" she asked.

He plopped his tablet case down on the in the foyer and threw his overcoat down on the little table. "Have you heard from Maggie and Brad?"

"No, not since before Thanksgiving. Why? Is there more trouble?"

"They're gone."

The first thought in Jennifer's mind was Cuba. Did they finally take off? "I haven't heard from them. I promise."

"Well, the National Police were back in the office again today. Inspector Jennings was leading the whole crew."

"Chief Inspector," Jennifer corrected him lightly.

Matt furrowed his brow. Her light jab at sarcasm over the inspector's title didn't help his mood. "Anyway, they questioned everyone in the office but we don't know anything."

"It's how they work. They keep beating at you until they find a wedge. Sometimes they find a wedge where none exists."

"It's so frustrating. I am loyal to the Party. I have always been loyal to the Party. I've never had a traffic ticket much less run afoul of the National Police. It's not fair."

"I know. It's not meant to be fair. They're fishing for something, anything, to find on you."

He sat down on the other end of the couch. Jennifer could see the exhaustion creeping over him. "Maggie didn't tell you anything?"

Jennifer was forced to make a choice here. She did know something but should she tell him? On the one hand she had always been a loyal citizen. On the other hand, the cruelty of the Party and the national police enforcement arm still resonated with her. Also, she still loved her friend even though Maggie was now a fugitive. Would Matt keep it in confidence if she told him? The bond of marriage was supposed to be a sacred one, but she suspected that her husband remained steadfastly loyal to the Party despite all the shit it had thrown at him as of late.

"No," Jennifer said. "She never told me anything. She's been upset about her dad and all. Maybe she and Brad took some time off in the mountains?"

"Maybe. But they didn't tell anybody."

"Who's left for them to tell? Neither one of them have a friend left in the world these days."

His eyes narrowed. "They have you." He let that hang in the air, as if she were a co-conspirator in Maggie and Brad's sudden disappearance.

She finished her wine glass and got up. "I'm going to bed. There's some grilled chicken in the fridge for you."

"You'll probably be questioned again," Matt said as she left the living room.

She ignored it and went upstairs. When she checked her tablet for messages sure enough an email from Chief Inspector Jennings waited in her inbox. A car would be waiting for her at eight in the morning. Thankfully there was nothing from Maggie. She sighed and typed out an email to the principal at her school. Jennifer suspected she was probably under surveillance right now. She couldn't resist the urge to peek out the window. There were cars in the street but nothing stood out as a vehicle from the National Police. Downstairs she could hear the AI tune in news programming on the OLED wall for Matt. He'd probably made himself a drink with his accusations toward her fresh in his mind. She went to bed, worried she would toss and turn all night, but the wine lulled her to sleep almost immediately.

Near midnight her husband climbed into bed. The bourbon coming off him strong enough to force her to turn away from him.

CHAPTER 6

Jennifer couldn't help but feel resentful when Matt left early for work. It was as if she had been abandoned to the National Police. The familiar black Surburban waited by the curb when she left the house. A black-clad uniformed officer stood by the open passenger door. How long had it been waiting for her? Probably a half an hour. At least long enough for every neighbor on the street to see on their way to work. They wanted the neighborhood to know that the National Police were there and were waiting for a neighbor to turn her in for something. It was a common tactic for them to show up and wait for the citizens to volunteer evidence.

Jennifer strode up to the waiting vehicle with confidence. She didn't want to give them the satisfaction of rattling her. Jennifer climbed into the dark cavern of the back seat with the officer following in behind her.

Despite the late fall chill in the air, the back of the Surburban was uncomfortably warm. She immediately shed her jacket as the SUV pulled away from the curb. Jennifer thought they would head downtown to the police station again but the Surburban turned toward the westbound turnpike and headed for the mountains.

"Where are we going?" Jennifer asked.

"Just relax, Mrs. Hanson," the officer said.

"You can't tell me where we're going?"

"Does it matter? Would it help if we sedated you?"

She took it to mean that if she didn't stop asking questions now she would be sedated. Jennifer shook her head no and faced forward. She had to concede that where they were going didn't matter in the long run. There was nothing she could do about her predicament.

They took the turnpike through Golden, then exited off and turned toward the lowest reaches of the mountain. A series of turns took them to Golden Gate Canyon Road. Jennifer noted that none of the vehicles passing were civilian. There were too many black Suburbans and camouflaged Joltvees. She was afraid the only place noteworthy in this direction was the protective custody center.

Jennifer turned and gazed through the back window as they wound up the mountain road. Denver had faded from view and been replaced with trees and broad cliffs where the road cut into the mountain. The road made a couple of twists then opened up before them to reveal a huge grey squat building flushed into the mountainside. Jennifer wondered if it was designed intentionally to spoil the mountain scenery. The road led up to a fifteen-foot concrete wall with a solid black steel gate. "Golden Gate Canyon National Police Protective Custody Center" was in black letters on gray concrete above the gated doors.

The Suburban paused for a couple of minutes at the gates. The driver simply sat behind the wheel and waited for them to slide open. Once they did they drove into the compound and revealed an open yard with many parked Joltvees and Suburbans. Black clad guards stood at their stations or patrolled the perimeter. Many rifle-toting guards stood at enclosed stations along the wall and scrutinized the entering Suburban. The only people moving about were uniformed and certainly not civilian.

The Suburban turned toward a darkened recessed garage with the sign above that read, "Processing". Jennifer's eyes adjusted to the fluorescent light as they entered and approached a short loading dock. More armed guards stood along the perimeter of the loading dock. On the platform a man and woman were seated at a desk with yet another sign on the wall above them that read "Detainee Processing".

The SUV came to a halt and the driver stepped out. He walked around to the passenger side where the other uniformed officer sat. With the door opened he stepped out and said, "If you will follow me, Missus Hanson."

She wanted to ask a million questions but she was afraid the officer would follow through with his threat to sedate her. Jennifer followed him out the door, dragging her jacket behind her.

"This way," the officer said and turned up the steps. He walked up to the table and held his tablet out to be scanned. The uniformed woman sitting at table held her tablet next to his and let the tablets complete their digital handshake and trade information with one another. Both reviewed their tablets and seemed satisfied, which ended with their respective confirmations through digital signatures. "She's all yours," the officer said and strode back to the waiting Suburban.

Jennifer turned to face the woman as she stood. Unlike the uniformed officer this new person had a nametag stitched on her breast - Giancarlo. Tall enough to be a professional model, she was leggy and fit enough to be athletic with her black hair pulled back into a severe bun. She scanned Jennifer with expressive dark brown eyes.

"Miss Giancarlo -"Jennifer started but was interrupted with a hand to stop.

"It's Sergeant Giancarlo," she said. "You can save your questions for the chief inspector. I am tasked with getting you through processing. I have no idea what you did to be here or why. The National Police has decided that you should be here so here you are. We can make this easy or we can make this hard. Which way would you like for it to be?"

"Easy," Jennifer said resignedly.

Giancarlo smiled. "Good! Who knows? You might be out by the end of the day."

This didn't encourage Jennifer because Giancarlo said it so quickly that it sounded polished and rehearsed. She reckoned it was more to put the detainee at ease and give them hope.

"This way, please," Giancarlo said. She scanned her dent under the hand scanner and the door buzzed open with a click. She held the door open for

Jennifer to enter. A couple of the standing guards crowded behind Jennifer to encourage her through.

The inside of the hallway was a stark contrast to the gloomy garage. More fluorescent lighting hung from the ceiling and they blindingly lit up the white painted cinderblock walls. The floor was covered with white tiles and two painted lines - one in pastel blue and the other in pink. Jennifer resisted the urge to shield her eyes as they adjusted to brightness. The door snapped shut behind her with an echo.

Giancarlo strode down the hallway a few steps, then turned to see if Jennifer had followed. The sergeant didn't say anything and waited patiently. Numbly, Jennifer followed the sergeant along the painted lines. Thirty feet in the blue line veered to a hallway on the right with a sign pointed to "Men's Processing Queue". The pink line continued straight for another fifty feet, then veered right into a separate area for the women.

Another set of double doors led into a new room with armed guards and windowed booths. Jennifer noted the armed guards were all women. Two other civilian women stood there, a heavy brunette and an older black woman, each with an accompanying escort.

Giancarlo escorted Jennifer to one of the open windows where an older woman with a scowl waited behind the glass. "Okay, hand over your coat and purse. Remove your jewelry, belt and shoes. Everything will be inventoried and returned to you when you leave."

"Is this necessary?" Jennifer asked.

"We can handcuff you and take it, if you like," the woman behind the glass said. Jennifer sighed and handed over her jacket and purse. Giancarlo placed both items on a sliding tray and shoved them through the other side of the booth. The woman on the other side grabbed the jacket and searched it. Satisfied, the jacket went into a clear plastic bag with a tag number recorded. The purse was dumped open on the woman's counter and every scrap was inventoried. Jennifer slipped off her shoes and unbuckled her belt. These went through the sliding tray as well.

"Follow me," Giancarlo told her after Jennifer handed over her things. The cold concrete floor chilled her through her socks as she stepped behind

Giancarlo through a side exit to the next room. The two other detained women had already arrived ahead of her. The women were taking off their clothes with their own respective escorts watching over them. Jennifer suppressed a sigh when Giancarlo commanded her to disrobe.

Each article of clothing Jennifer removed was quickly searched and placed into a tagged bag. She expected to stop when she was down to her bra and panties. Giancarlo waited expectantly.

"All of it?" Jennifer asked.

"All of it."

Jennifer quickly scanned the room and saw the other two detainees removing their own undergarments. Reluctantly, Jennifer followed suit and removed her own underwear. It was collected along with the rest of her clothes.

The two other accompanying guards waited at the door. Having already collected the clothing from their own detainees, they waited as Giancarlo finished collecting Jennifer's clothes. "Wait here," Giancarlo said after the last piece of clothing was collected. She joined the other two guards waiting at the door and all three of them left the room together.

Jennifer stood naked with the other two prisoners. It was cold in the changing area and she did her best to resist the urge to shiver. They stood for several minutes, not daring to move.

"Do you think we will disappear?" the heavy brunette asked.

"Hush," the black detainee said. "They're watching us."

Jennifer thought this was wise advice. Without moving her head she tried to check around the room for a surveillance camera. Even though she didn't see one she had the creepy feeling she was being watched.

Several minutes later, Giancarlo returned with the other two guards. The guards separated from one another and went back to accompanying their respective prisoners. "Follow me," she commanded once again. Naked, Jennifer followed the guard through the back exit of the changing area. It led to another hallway with doors to the right. This time Giancarlo and Jennifer led the way through the hallway. They entered the last door on the right.

A stainless steel barber chair stood in the middle of the room. "Wait, what's -"Jennifer began.

"Sit."

Jennifer turned to Giancarlo. "Are you cutting my hair?"

"Yes. Now sit."

"Come on now. Is this really necessary? You don't have to cut my hair!" Jennifer was knocked back with her left cheek stinging hot red. Giancarlo had slapped her so fast she didn't see it coming.

"Sit," Giancarlo said with a voice colder than the steel barber chair. Jennifer backed towards the chair while caressing her stinging cheek. She faltered climbing into the chair and nearly spilled herself onto the floor, but she finally managed. Giancarlo approached and raised her hand again. Jennifer flinched involuntarily and closed her eyes, but Giancarlo only grabbed her by the chin and pushed her head back. "Look, lady, I don't know what you did to rile up that Chief Inspector, but you are a detainee. I don't think you grasp the position you're in. You might not leave here today. You might not be alive at the end of the day. I gather you are some sort of high society type. Your social status in life means less than nothing here. Now sit back and shut up."

Jennifer was shoved back into the chair. Giancarlo brandished a cordless razor. At this point Jennifer realized that she was completely out of control here and the Party, particularly the National Police, were completely in charge of her fate. Giancarlo began to shear off Jennifer's hair as she cried in the barber chair. The shearing itself took several minutes. Jennifer simply sat still and sobbed as quietly as could. Giancarlo turned off the razor, stepped back and inspected her work. Satisfied, she said, "Follow me."

They exited the back of the room out a separate door. Jennifer followed, still naked and racked with hitching sobs, through a series of short narrow hallways to a hot and humid room. Despite the heat Jennifer shivered, cold and naked with the newfound absence of hair. Giancarlo lead Jennifer to an enclosed conveyor belt system. "Shower and delousing," Giancarlo said. "The process takes about five minutes total and it's completely automatic. Just step on to the conveyor belt and let the machine work. You'll wear goggles." Giancarlo stepped to a box next to the conveyor and pulled out a loose set of goggles. Water dripped from them. "I recommend you wear them. Otherwise the delousing spray will blind you. You'll probably want to hold your breath at that part too. I'll be waiting for you at the other end."

Jennifer put the goggles on and stepped on the conveyor belt. The belt itself was a moving metal grate and it stung her feet as she stepped on. The belt started with a loud buzz and moved her to a station called "RINSE". She had braced herself for an ice-cold shock but the rinse was surprisingly warm.

It was a human car wash. She had taken the Chrysler to an automated car wash plenty of times. The automated system was probably more efficient than shuffling people through the showers. The next station was labeled "WASH". An additional sign advised her to remove excess detergent by hand. The systems dumped a thick cream-colored detergent on her. Her skin lightly tingled against the detergent and she scraped off the excess as the sign had recommended.

The conveyor moved her to "2ND RINSE' where she scrubbed as much of the detergent off as she could with her bare hands. At the "DELOUSING" station she held her breath and pinched her nose shut as the fine mist covered her. It didn't seem to sting like the detergent did, but she noted a pungent odor when she breathed again. The final station through the human car wash was "DRYER". She was buffeted by a hot wind at the station before the belt moved her to the swinging doors in the end.

Jennifer stepped off the conveyor belt and shivered again after leaving the human car wash behind. Giancarlo waited for her with clothes and booties. "You'll find another set of these waiting for you in your cell," she said.

The pants and top fit snug and tight. Bright orange but thin, they wouldn't afford any warmth if she managed to get outside. She felt self-conscious wearing the tight outfit. It didn't take long to dress and Jennifer was relieved after being naked. After she slipped on the last bootie Giancarlo told her, "Come on. The Chief Inspector is waiting for you."

Another door led out the back. Jennifer noted they were always moving deeper into the protective custody center. A series of double doors waited for them and led outside. After spending so much time in the warm shower room, the cold mountain air shocked Jennifer. She shivered as she followed Giancarlo down the fenced path toward a building a hundred yards away and backed into the mountainside. Giancarlo didn't seem fazed by the cold air as Jennifer followed her to the next building.

The building turned out to be the cellblock. Other prisoners, male and female, milled about a common area in similar orange jumpers. A squad of armed guards patrolled on the catwalk high above. Giancarlo led Jennifer past the common area and the cells towards a series of rooms in the back. Jennifer was admitted to room "3" with two chairs and a table bolted to the floor. "Wait here," Giancarlo said, then closed the door.

Unlike the shower room the interrogation room was almost as cool as the walk had been only minutes before. The absence of hair still felt strange to Jennifer, as she rubbed her hand over her stubbly scalp. The windowless room and walls were painted slate grey. The paint was fresh and made Jennifer woozy from the chemical smell.

Chief Inspector Jennings walked in with a briefcase and his uniform cap tucked under his arm. He smiled but it was as chilly as the room. "Missus Hanson, so good to see you again."

"Chief Inspector," she acknowledged.

He waved to the seat at the far side of the table. "Won't you please sit down?"

After she sat down she asked, "My husband told me there would be more questions but I thought we would be doing this at the police station again?"

"I am afraid this time it is more serious. Given your relationship with Magnolia Farnham, we thought it best that you come here. This round of questioning may take a few days."

Jennifer's heart sank. *Days!* It dashed any hopes of leaving anytime soon. "Has anyone informed my husband?"

"Informed your husband? We're the National Police. Why would we inform your husband? Keeping your husband apprised of your situation is not our concern." He pulled out his tablet from his briefcase. He smiled again, "I do have good news though. You can be out of here in a couple of hours as long as you tell us everything we need to know."

Jennifer frowned. She recognized the lie. They didn't truck her all the way to the mountains for a few questions. "I don't know where Maggie is.

Maybe she and Brad went out into the country to take a little time for themselves. These last few weeks have been hard on her. She lost her father."

"We're quite aware."

"I mean, she's my best friend, but that doesn't mean I know about everything she does. Plus no one's been close to Maggie lately since this whole mess started."

Jennings leaned forward like a leopard ready to pounce. "What do you mean?"

Jennifer sighed. "It's just that when you are the subject of an inquiry by the National Police, you find out who your friends really are."

"So you and Missus Farnham haven't spoken lately."

"We've drifted apart. Most everyone I know has shied away from Maggie, her father and her husband." She didn't like doing this but she hoped to convince Jennings she was not a threat to the Party.

"You haven't shied away, have you Missus Hanson? You were there at her father's funeral, right by Magnolia's side. That was, what? Only ten days ago?"

"But I am telling you -"

The Chief Inspector leaped across the table and grasped her throat with his right hand. He squeezed her neck as she tried to pull his hand off. Absently, she noted in the back of her mind she had only been assaulted twice in her life and both had occurred today. Jennings dragged her towards the side of the table, his smile now replaced with a grimace. Jennifer heard his teeth creak as he eagerly ground them together. He pulled her away from the table and pushed her against the wall.

"I am telling you," he growled through his clenched teeth. "We know she and her husband are gone. No record of their dents anywhere. The day before Thanksgiving they simply disappeared. Now where are they hiding? Are they still in Denver?"

Jennifer struggled as she tried to gasp for air. The back of her skull was mashed into the concrete of the wall. "Please let me go," she choked. Hot tears streamed down her face once again.

"Are you going to answer my questions?"

"Yes!"

He relaxed his grip on her neck and regained his composure. Magnanimously, he waved for her to take a seat again as he straightened the wrinkles on his uniform. "Now, once again, is Missus Farnham in Denver?"

"She left the country."

"Where is she headed? Canada, Mexico or Cuba?"

"She said Cuba."

"Why Cuba?"

"I don't know. Probably because it is the most affluent of the three."

"It makes sense," Jennings mused. "Canada is sympathetic to our cause. To get to Mexico you have to go through Texas and that presents its own challenges right now. But Cuba, the new paradise. Now that would be a place to go. How is she going to do it?"

"I don't know."

"Now Missus Hanson, I thought we already talked about cooperation."

Jennifer's eyes bugged out in alarm. "I really don't know. I didn't help her plan this. She told me what she was going to do and I tried to talk her out of it."

"She had to tell you something. Give me something to work with here."

"She told me she was going to Cuba. There was some way to get there through New Orleans. Probably a ship or something."

"She planned this all on her own? You society types can't even plan a party without help. You expect me to believe the woman suddenly figured out a way to slip past a national surveillance system and travel a thousand miles to New Orleans and leave the country on an outbound freighter. Someone helped her. Who?"

"She said something about a man."

"A man? What's his name?"

"She didn't tell me his name."

"How did she know this man?"

"She didn't know him. Her husband did. Something about an old case file."

"You don't know the name?"

"No, I don't." But she realized she did know the name. Maggie had told her a name. She couldn't remember it now. It was like most of the conversation that day had slipped her mind outside of the fact that Maggie intended to go through Cuba via New Orleans. "I don't know the name," she repeated.

Jennings sighed. "I am so sorry to hear that. It looks like we are going to do this the old fashioned way. Guards!"

The door opened and two big men came into the room. They flanked Jennifer on each side.

"Take her to the VIP suite," Jennings said.

"Come on," the guard to her right said. He grabbed her by the upper arm and pinched her bicep with a vice-like grip. Jennifer was lifted her from seat and shoved towards the door.

"Where are you taking me?" Jennifer pleaded.

"To Special Treatment, of course," Jennings replied.

Dragged by the guards from the room, she was led away from the cell blocks, past other interrogation rooms and even deeper in the detention complex. Always deeper in the building. "I can walk," she said.

The guard on her left looked at his companion. He nodded and they released but the one on her right nudged her forward. Again it was more narrow windowless concrete hallways. No longer brightly lit these halls were dark and twisty, leading further into the complex. The guards let her walk on her own but were close to her on each side with the clack of Jennings' boot heels echoing in the hall right behind them.

The corridor twisted to a dead end but widened to about fifteen feet. Four doors waited on each side of the corridor. Screams echoed from one of the rooms. Jennifer backed up a step but the two guards closed in on her and grabbed her arms. "Please," she said. "We don't have to do this."

"I am afraid we do," Jennings said from behind. The door labeled "4" on the right side of the hallway was chosen. Her right hand was roughly shoved under the dent scanner. The little LCD monitor identified her as Hanson, Jennifer L. with her proper Social Security number. After the door clicked open Jennifer was pushed through.

The first thing she noted was that the floor was wet, as if recently mopped. *Rinsed,* she thought. A drain sat the center of the floor. Against the wall were shelves and tables with tools and knives on them. Towards the back of the room a shiny steel table stood upright on a pivot with well-worn leather cuffs for ankles and wrists.

"Secure her," Jennings said.

Wordlessly the guards spun her around and shoved her against the table. She tried to push away from the table but the big men handled her with ease. They had her wrists strapped into the leather restraints quickly and started working on the ankles.

"I have told you everything I know. Please. I am cooperating, I promise."

"Consider this an incentive," Jennings said. Jennings waved to the guards. They tilted the table back slightly but she remained upright. He started with the same questions again. Panic-stricken, Jennifer answered them as best as she could. Hot tears flowed down her face and her nose ran. "When did she leave Denver?"

"I don't know. She never told me." Her head slammed to the side. A moment later she realized that Jennings had slapped her.

"When did she leave Denver?"

"I don't know. I never heard from her during Thanksgiving." This time Jennings punched her face. The coppery blood filled her mouth and gushed from her nose.

"When did she leave Denver?"

"I DON'T KNOW!"

The answer elicited another punch from Jennings. The questioning continued and Jennifer answered the Chief Inspector's questions as best as she could. Sometimes he seemed satisfied with her answer, while other times he scowled and gave her a slap or a punch. She took punches continuously in her face and in the stomach, with each gut punch embroiling her in instant nausea.

At some point Jennifer passed out from the questioning. She came to when a bucket of cold water doused her head. Jennifer shook her head violently to clear the cobwebs and waited for her vision to clear. Jennings stood across the room and wiped his knuckles with a clean white towel. "Take her to her cell," he said.

After the guards unbuckled the leather restraints she tried to stand but collapsed on the floor. One of the guards knelt down next to her and said, "You need to walk." The guard voiced neither anger nor compassion, only simple statement of fact. Jennifer struggled to stand, prompting the guard to hook his hand under her armpit and hoist her up. Again, neither gentle nor rough, simply an action to get her moving.

The guards escorted her from the room walking with her sandwiched between them. She walked slowly, but never harassed or rushed. Jennifer stumbled a couple of times but the same guard always helped her back up. They reversed their path back towards the housing area for the detainees.

The second guard consulted his tablet and led her up to the upper level of the detention area and eventually to her cell. They scanned her dent as if a package had been delivered to the right door. The bars of her cell slid open and she stepped in.

Jennifer stood and took inventory of her cell after the gated door slid shut behind her. A small bed with a thin green rubber mattress waited with her bed linens resting on top alongside her second orange jumpsuit. A clear plastic bag of toiletries lay in the bowl of the sink. A small desk for writing and a simple stainless steel toilet stood on the opposite side of the cell. Jennifer moved the linens and second jumpsuit aside and collapsed on the moldy mattress. She wanted to close her eyes for a few seconds.

⋏

Someone shoved Jennifer enough to wake her up. She jerked awake with a start.

"Chow," a voice told her.

She rubbed her head and winced as she put pressure on her tender bruises. "What?' Jennifer said.

"Chow time." A woman with a crew-cut, in an orange jumpsuit, loomed over her. Jennifer would have put her somewhere in her early fifties and she had the well-weathered face of too much time in the sun. "It's chow time," the woman repeated.

"Can I skip it?" She just wanted to sleep some more.

The woman smirked. "Nobody skips anything around here. Plus you could probably use the food."

Jennifer's own stomach rumbled in agreement. She'd had a bagel for breakfast but nothing since she had arrived here.

A female guard peered into the cell. "Get her moving, Miriam," the guard said.

"Miriam," Jennifer said absently. She put a name to a face.

"Yeah, Miriam," the other woman in the jumpsuit agreed. "Look, I get that you're new here and judging by the bruises you received a very warm welcome. Some of these guards like Laura are sympathetic to a point, but you still got to go to chow."

"Okay," Jennifer said reluctantly. She got up from the bunk with her aches protesting the whole way. Jennifer followed Miriam out of the cell and fell into line with the other detainees. Even as she walked her muscles loosened up. "How long was I out?"

"Shh," Miriam said.

Jennifer took it to mean that they couldn't talk. She drew some stares from the other prisoners as she followed the line to chow. All female, each wearing an orange jumpsuit and sporting a shaved head or shorter hair. Jennifer followed the line quietly as the prisoners filed into Dining Hall B.

Mimicking the other prisoners seemed to be the safest course of action. She picked up a tray behind Miriam. No menu was available but Jennifer didn't expect one in a prison. The inmate working the chow line slopped some brown stuff into her tray and added scoop of mixed greens that was labeled as "salad." Jennifer picked up a small box of whole milk at the end of the line.

They sat down on long stainless steel benches at steel tables fixed to the floor. "Can we talk now?" Jennifer asked.

"Sure," Miriam said. "As long as we don't look like we're having too much fun and we keep the party down."

Jennifer put Miriam closer to her mother's age than her own. Miriam had to be from the country. Despite the well-worn face, Miriam's beautiful blue eyes stayed focused on Jennifer. Jennifer didn't know what Miriam had done to be in this place. Before coming here she would have judged someone detained in protective custody, but given that she was a detainee herself she figured that Miriam hadn't done anything worse than she had.

"All afternoon," Miriam said.

"What?" Jennifer asked.

"You were out all afternoon. They brought you to the cell after lunch. You passed out and now it is chow time. Just after six."

"Oh, I didn't know." She felt like she'd been in Jennings's torture room for hours. She was surprised to hear only minutes had passed.

Miriam snorted. "You must have done something special to get that sort of treatment. Detainees don't usually get welcomed that way. What did you do?"

"I went to a dinner party," Jennifer answered drily.

Miriam arched an eyebrow. "That must have been some dinner party."

"You have no idea. A family friend said something that offended General Scarborough. Months later I'm here."

"One of the Five? You met him?"

"The very one."

"There's more to it than that."

"I know someone who ran. They want to know where she ran to and how she did it."

"And this was all related to the dinner party?"

"Yes. A dinner party in early September." Jennifer took a forkful of the brown stuff. It didn't taste awful but she couldn't say it tasted like anything outside of it being flavored with salt and pepper. "What is this stuff?"

"It's a mystery. It seems to be something simple like oats and beef. They can mass produce it and feed us."

"It doesn't taste like anything."

"At least it's edible."

Surprised at her appetite, Jennifer continued to shovel the brown stuff into her mouth. At least the milk had flavor. "What did you do?" she asked.

"To come here?"

Jennifer nodded.

"I didn't make quota."

"Quota?"

"I own a cattle ranch in Nebraska. Sorry, I mean I run a cattle ranch in Nebraska. It hasn't belonged to me in some time now."

"People still eat meat?"

"Lots of people still eat meat. Just not here."

After the Freedom Party had taken over Jennifer had been taught that meat was bad for you, especially beef. To hear that people still produced meat much less beef cattle surprised her.

Miriam smiled at Jennifer's confusion. "No prime rib served at that dinner party?"

"We had steak and Maine lobsters with butter. When you go to a dinner party with General Scarborough you get steak."

"Some pigs are more equal than others."

"I beg your pardon?"

"Nothing. It's a little before your time. That's what the Party tells people. Beef is bad for you, but the army gets as much beef as it wants. We export it, of course."

"Export it? I thought there was a trade embargo?" Jennifer referred to the embargo that most of the world had imposed against America.

"There is an embargo, but there are still plenty of buyers. I've been told that Russia buys our beef. Most of the countries in Central Asia. Africa will buy whatever we can send them. The embargo is from Latin America, South America and the European Union."

"And the quota?"

"The Party said my farm was short. They held me responsible for not making quota. So I spend some months here as a corrective action. It's not fair."

Jennifer had suffered enough under the Party and inclined to believe Miriam when she claimed something wasn't fair.

"They don't understand beef production," Miriam continued. "You can't ship every head of cattle off to be slaughtered. You ship everything off then there is nothing next year to make quota. Then some idiot will be complaining about quota next year when there is nothing to give."

"How long are you here for?"

"I've been here three months with another three to go."

"Are you really getting out of here?"

Doubt clouded Miriam's face. "I think so."

"Have you ever been detained before?"

"No," Miriam admitted. "But most of us here aren't bad. We're just unfortunate. Some of us run afoul of the Party whether it's right or wrong. I hope I am getting out."

"I think so." Jennifer wanted to reassure the woman. She recalled the lady with the shaved head in the supermarket back in the late summer. In hindsight that woman had been a recently released detainee. Jennifer had seen other men and women with the shaved heads other times in the past.

"How about you?"

"I don't know. This has all been, well, horribly wrong. My husband is a member of the Party. Nothing like this has ever happened before. When I left my house today the last place I thought I would be is here. I know my husband will be worried and he will start asking questions."

Miriam sighed. "You seem like a nice lady. If your husband has some pull I hope he can get you out of here. Hell, I hope he can get me out of here too," she added with a grin.

A whistle sounded across the dining hall. Wordlessly the detainees stood with their trays. Jennifer followed them, but not far enough behind step to draw the ire of the guards. They all filed into a single line and returned their trays to a kitchen window. After the meal Jennifer felt better, even though she ached from the beating she had taken at the hand of Jennings earlier in the day.

All the detainees reversed their course from Dining Hall B and worked their way back into their cells. Jennifer noted that Miriam had the cell next to her own. It was probably why the guard had tasked Miriam with taking care of her.

She entered her own cell and reluctantly made the bed with the sheets that had been provided. It was better than sleeping atop the musty mattress spotted with her own blood. As far as she knew she was the only one who had been interned outside of Maggie, her father and her husband. Matt and everyone else hadn't suffered through what she had gone through so far. Still, it puzzled her. She had never run afoul of the Party. Jennifer honestly thought she hadn't done anything to merit this treatment now. Regardless, the Party that she had known all her life felt differently. She clung to the hope that her husband might be able to call in some favors and get her out of her in the morning.

Jennifer stared at the ceiling as she lay on her bunk contemplating that her life had been completely upended. Perhaps it was time to start thinking about life in America in a new direction. She had to consider that she might never leave the protective custody center, as well as the real possibility that she could end up in that threatened mass grave somewhere on a lonely wooded mountain slope. Her heart fluttered with a momentary panic. Jennifer paused for a few moments and then forced herself to breathe slowly. Whatever happened she couldn't do anything about it tonight. She tried to muse on it some more but her eyelids grew heavy with fatigue. Typically Jennifer spent her evenings on the couch with a glass of wine and the TV for company. Without either of those her own thoughts tired her almost as much as the beating from Chief Inspector Jennings. Despite her best efforts she fell asleep.

⋏

She woke up sometime before sunrise. Back in Denver the only noisy thing at home was her snoring husband. Outside of that her house was usually free of noise aside from the occasional vehicle passing by on the street. In the detention center the noise was pervasive. Snores echoed from other cells, punctuated occasionally by the clacking footfalls as the guards regularly walked the cellblock. Jennifer found herself frequently awakened at each new noise. Now she lay awake on her bunk and stared at the cracked paint on the ceiling.

Jennifer fervently hoped that she would be released today. She had nothing to offer Jennings in his investigation. Maggie hadn't given her a lot of details about her escape plans. If only the chief inspector could see reason and let her go. She would try broaching the subject. On the outside Matt had to be screaming bloody murder to anyone that would listen.

Despite her hopes she realized that the National Police could do whatever they wanted. They seemed to snatch up all kinds of people and inter them. Like Miriam, a cattle rancher whose only crime was pissing off the wrong guy in an office somewhere. All her life Jennifer had been completely unaware of what kind of country she lived in. Now she was awake in more ways than one. Despite the darkness, activity stirred in the cellblock. Guards spoke to one another in low voices and she could hear the other detainees moving about their cells. The start of a new day in the Golden Gate Canyon Protective Custody Center awaited her.

A klaxon sounded across the cellblock followed by a recorded announcement, "Detainees exit your cells and stand for count. Hands extended to record your dent." The door of Jennifer's cell slid open and she stepped outside to stand with the others. Guards walked along the cellblock waving their electronic wands over the embedded identity chips in the prisoners' hands. Each wave gave an audible chime as the guards checked their tablets. Once the count was complete the prisoners marched off to Dining Hall B for breakfast.

Jennifer wondered what the day had in store for her. Maybe she would get out today? Again an extremely hopeful wish, especially as her fellow detainees were decent women. If they were too decent to be in this place why would Jennifer expect to be treated any differently?

After breakfast she and the other prisoners were escorted to the common area of the cellblock. In the corner games such as chess, checkers and old board games from the 20th century sat on a shelf with a light layer of dust. Some exercise equipment stood at the back of the room but there was only one working treadmill while "out of order" signs hung from the rest of them. The OLED wall played twenty-four hour news with the sound turned down. One of the OLED panels kept flickering in and out. With nothing to do and her own injuries still fresh, she decided to simply watch the news station.

It wasn't long before the two men who had escorted her yesterday returned. "Chief Inspector Jennings would like to ask you some additional questions," one of them said.

Her heart raced as she stood up and contemplated another day of beatings ahead of her. Her legs trembled as she walked between the guards. They walked close to her, ready to grab her if she either ran or hesitated.

They arrived at the hall with the interrogation rooms and went into number 4 again. Chief Inspector Jennings waited for her with a smile. Freshly rinsed, the room gave Jennifer the idea it was often used, rinsed out and used again. A new addition of five gallon buckets filled with water stood near the table.

"What is this?" Jennifer asked.

The Chief Inspector smiled. "Something a little old school." Despite tensing her muscles up the two guards easily handled her and tightly strapped her onto the table again. "I think we were stuck on one point yesterday. The name of the man who helped Missus Farnham leave the country."

"I told you everything I already know about that. She never told me a name."

"Yes, yes, you said it was someone that her husband had defended in court. We still need a name."

"I don't know!"

Jennings turned to one of the guards. "Do it."

The table tipped backwards and Jennifer's face was covered with a towel. She struggled against the restraints as icy cold water enveloped her head. Jennifer attempted to gasp and immediately choked. Were they going to drown her here unless she gave up a name? She tried to shake her head while still gagging on the water caught in her throat. Jennifer didn't know if only seconds had passed or several minutes. After the table stood upright and the soaked towel was removed, Jennifer coughed up water and hot snot shot out of her nose.

"Give me a name," Jennings repeated.

"I don't know. I don't know, I don't know." She frantically tried to remember the name Maggie told her. She desperately wanted to make this torture stop but the only thing she could focus on was this hateful man and her own fear.

Jennings nodded at the guard. Jennifer whimpered as the table tipped back again. "Please, please, please..." The wet towel wrapped around her face and she immediately gagged on the water poured on top. She did her best to endure that water torture. All she could think about was an end of this.

When the table stood upright she coughed out water again as she gasped for breath. Before a question could be asked she shouted, "Please stop this. Please!"

"A name?"

"I don't know who you are looking for. Maggie never told me. Please let me go."

Jennings consulted his tablet. "Do any of these names sound familiar? Reginald Carlson? Andrew Gann? Gunther Morgan? Anthony Picollo?"

"No. I don't know. I... She never told me a name. Just some guy. I don't know." She couldn't stop crying now.

Jennings leaned in close. "Are you sure? These are all men that Brad Farnham defended in the past three years. These are the likeliest suspects from his case files." His voice barely a whisper that tickled her cheek.

"No. I have never heard of those men. I don't know who any of them are. Please let me go."

Again the table tipped back a third time with another fresh bucket of water poured over the towel on her face. After some time she returned upright and was asked the same questions. Jennifer had no new answers for the chief inspector.

Jennings swiped a scalpel from a tray as Jennifer continued to cough up water and mucus. "You're a very pretty woman, Missus Hanson. Well, you were pretty before you took a beating from me yesterday. Most of you young society types usually are. I guess you hit the jackpot with Mister Hanson." He brought the scalpel close to her face and inched it toward her eye. "It would be a shame to cut up that face of yours. You know, I bet I could pop out that eye of yours in under ten seconds. Jimmy, what do you think?"

"I don't know, Chief Inspector," the guard said warily. "Maybe?"

"Sure, I could. So here is what I am going to do. In this exact order, I am going to cut your hand, then clean it with alcohol, then stitch it up. Because that's what a great guy I am. Then I am going to do the same thing to that not-as-pretty-as-it-used-to-be face. And then I am going to pluck that eye out with this scalpel. You can watch me crush it with my fist with your remaining good eye. Just think! You can buy one of those new cyber eyeballs that came out. No more tacky iGlasses for you."

"Please," Jennifer whispered.

"See that, fellas? She's practically begging me to do it."

"No, please -"

She barely got the last word out when the back of her left hand blossomed with fiery pain. Jennings was that quick. He had swiped the scalpel with a superficial three-inch laceration on her hand. She gaped incredulously as blood dripped freely from the wound. Jennings set the scalpel down carefully on the tray and picked up the bottle of alcohol. He poured it freely over her hand and more fiery pain blossomed up. Jennifer couldn't help but scream. Jennings picked up the needle and thread. "Most days we use suture tape for this kind of thing. But since the theme of the day is old school, I want to stick with something from the past. Now hold still. If you squirm this is going to be worse. I suggest you lay your palm flat."

Jennifer struggled to keep her hand still. Despite the cool temperature of the room and the soaking wet jumpsuit beads of sweat popped out on her face. A rational part of her mind told her that she needed to stay still for the stitches despite the pain.

"You know what? I have to confess. You are holding up better than I thought you would. Jimmy, look at this hand? Barely trembling. My suture job is going to be better than usual."

Jennifer's hand throbbed with pain. She willed for it to stay still while this psycho stitched the wound. The tugs on her skin as he worked the sutures filled her with nausea. After a couple of minutes Jennings said, "There, all done! Take a look, Missus Hanson."

Jennifer tilted her head and lifted her hand against the restraint. Black crosses of suture thread had closed the wound as he promised. "Please, no more." Fresh hot tears spilled from her eyes. She didn't think she had any more tears to give. "I don't know anything. I promise."

"But Missus Hanson we're not done yet." He picked up the scalpel and brought up to her face. Jennings inched closer to her until she could feel his body pressed against hers. His hot breath caressed her cheek and he trembled anxiously. Something hard pressed against her thigh. After several seconds she realized it was his erection. *He's getting off on this!* Another wave of nausea swept through her. With his eyes locked on hers he sliced her forehead open above her left eye. Blood gushed over her face and she tried to move her head to the left so that it wouldn't pour into her eye. "Now get ready for the hard part," he said, picking up the bottle of alcohol. "You might want to close your eyes for this." The thought of letting her eyes burn from the exposure to the alcohol disinfectant frightened her. Jennifer forced her eyes shut, then kept them closed as the alcohol touched the wound. She couldn't keep from screaming though and she gagged on some of the alcohol that got into her mouth. Jennifer tried spitting the mix of blood, saliva and alcohol but she dribbled on the chest.

An impatient buzz sounded from the door. Jennings ignored the noise and picked up his suture kit. The buzz sounded again as he threaded the needle. Jennings sighed, "Can someone get that? It better be good or someone is trading in their black uniform for something orange."

The other guard, whose nametag identified him as Mullins, opened the door. Sergeant Giancarlo's eyes widened with alarm when Jennifer made eye contact with her. The sergeant broke it off quickly and addressed the chief inspector. "The prisoner has been released," she said.

"I have the authority here," the chief inspector said.

"Sir, you may want to check your email. These orders came from Director Pearson."

Jennings scowled as he wiped his hands with a fresh towel. He picked up the tablet, logged in and brought up his email. Jennings studied the tablet for a couple of minutes. Resignedly, he said, "Missus Hanson it seems like your husband has called in a few favors with the district leader."

"I am free to-to go?" Jennifer stammered out. Frightened out of her wits, she suspected this might be a ruse.

"You're free to go, Missus Hanson. Do you know what the trouble with favors is? People run out of them. I think we will be meeting again soon." Jennings stepped back and rubbed his chin. Finally, he shook his head in frustration and said, "Get her out of here."

The guards released her from the restraints and helped her to her feet. One of them gave her a towel to wipe the blood and snot off her face. Her forehead bled freely and she held the towel against the wound. Jennings simply stared coldly. Jennifer met his eyes briefly then looked down. He wasn't happy that he hadn't received the information he wanted and she feared that he would make sure they met again.

Sergeant Giancarlo took Jennifer by the bicep and said, "Walk." Giancarlo didn't push the pace with Jennifer though. She held her by the bicep and guided her out of the interrogation room. They wound their way back out through the halls and past the common area. After a few minutes Giancarlo guided Jennifer into the infirmary.

"Sit. I'll be out here after you're finished." Giancarlo left Jennifer alone to wait. She switched arms from left to right to keep the towel pressed against her head. Away from the cellblock and interrogation rooms, the infirmary afforded some uncustomary peace and quiet. Despite the lack of commotion, the anxiety mounted in Jennifer's chest again. She just wanted out of there.

A nurse in green scrubs whooshed into the room. She knelt down and removed Jennifer's hand and the towel from her head. The nurse examined the hand closely and said, "I will clean it again and put on some suture tape. It might scar a bit, but you should be able to remove the tape in about a week."

At least the pressure of the towel stopped the blood flow gushing down her face. The nurse moved Jennifer from the waiting area to an empty exam room. Jennifer sat quietly, completely unsure of what to or say after getting such treatment from Jennings. She feared that if she said anything it would jeopardize her exit. The nurse hummed tunelessly as she cleaned the wound lightly with some gauze then applied the tape. When finished she escorted Jennifer out of the infirmary to where Giancarlo waited. "She's all yours."

There was no need to return to her cell. She didn't have any belongings there. Everything she had given up in processing was returned back to her. She was allowed to change back into her clothes before being processed out.

⚔

The sun setting behind the mountains cast long shadows over the protective custody complex. A scent of pine filled the air as the cool, crisp December dusk braced her. She rubbed the stubble and missed her newly absent hair from her chilled scalp. She saw Matt standing by the SUV fifty yards away. It was all she could do to keep from running to him.

He almost ignored her when she approached their vehicle. "Matt," she said.

Matt narrowed his eyes at her. "Jennifer?"

She gave a wan smile. "It's me."

He closed the distance to her in a half dozen steps and embraced her. "My God! What happened?"

"I was questioned." She winced and stiffened at being squeezed tight. Her bruised and aching body protested at this close contact but she said nothing.

"I need to talk to someone about this!"

Horrified, Jennifer pushed out of his embrace. The thought of the two of them confronting the administrator of the protective custody center, much less Chief Inspector Jennings, resurrected her anxiety. "No, don't do anything. We need to leave. Now! Before they decide to keep both of us."

He scowled but said nothing as he walked to the driver's side. She sighed as he climbed into the SUV and slammed the door. She quietly slipped into the passenger side. He said nothing as he started up the Chrysler and drove past the standing vehicles and through the gates. Once they started down the canyon road the bulk of her anxiety lifted away from Jennifer.

"They can't get away with this," Matt said.

"They can and they will."

"Not if I do something about it."

"You can't fight the Party."

"I am the Party. I am the deputy chief of staff for the deputy district leader. That should carry weight."

"Maybe. But isn't the National Police a part of the Party as well? Between you and the chief inspector who is more influential?"

"Well, District Leader Baker is on our side."

Jennifer snorted. "A lot of good that has done us so far." A Suburban with tinted windows rushed past them in the opposite lane. Jennifer sympathized for whatever poor unfortunate soul on their way to Golden Gate.

"We had the district leader's help getting you out," he said. There was that sullen edge to his voice again.

Jennifer sighed again. She seemed to be doing that more and more. "Matt, I am grateful to be out of there. Truly, I am. But I don't know how much longer we can count on his help. Or anyone else's."

"Maybe all this is over?"

"Maybe."

They rode in silence until they hit the outskirts of Golden. The SUV guided itself on the turnpike when Matt started asking more questions about what happened to her on the inside. At least the sullenness had been replaced with genuine concern and he sounded sympathetic. She told him about the questioning and the torture. And about Miriam.

"She's in there because of a cattle quota?" he asked.

"Yeah."

"But nobody eats meat anymore."

She explained what Miriam had told him about cattle exports.

"This inspector thinks you know how Maggie left the country? Did Maggie tell you anything?"

"No, she didn't say anything." What if they bugged the vehicle? This was the Party and they had all kinds of technological marvels at their fingertips. They could easily activate one of the vehicle's built in microphones remotely and monitor their conversation. "She said she was leaving the country. She never told me how she was going to do it."

CHAPTER 7

Jennifer faced the reality of what happened in the mirror of her own bathroom. She stood naked, looking at her cut and bruised body. She had two black eyes and cuts all over her face where the skin had split open from the punches. The prominent scalpel cut above her eye had a pinkish-red tinge. She was surprised that her nose didn't break during the questioning. Her ribs sported a series of black bruises up each side of her abdomen. And her hair! Nothing left but a badly gapped razor job. All her life she'd had long hair that fell down as far as the small of her back. With the hair gone she felt like a completely different person, as if the National Police had erased a crucial piece of her identity.

She put the stopper in the tub and started running a bath. Jennifer donned a bathrobe and went to the kitchen while the tub filled. She passed Matt in the living room on the way. He sat passively on the couch, watching the news with a glass of bourbon. Had he gone back to being sullen? She didn't know but she was too beat-tired to care. Jennifer poured a glass of wine from a fresh bottle she had opened.

She shivered as she stepped into the tub with the glass of wine in her hand. Her last experience with water had occurred only twelve hours earlier and was still fresh in her mind. Despite her anxiety, the hot water in the tub relaxed her and she wanted to scrub the stench of the detention center off her skin.

Jennifer scrubbed for several minutes with a loofah, starting with the top of her head then down. Even though it stung while she scrubbed over the bruises and cuts she felt the need to be clean. The water turned pink as some of the cuts opened and bled again. Satisfied, she put the loofah aside and let the hot water seep away the aches of her bones. A few more sips of the red wine, then she closed her eyes and relaxed.

Jennifer leaned back and rested her head against the tub basin. *That damn dinner party.* Everything had spiraled out of control because that general had been tweaked at by Maggie's dad. She mused on the last day she had seen Maggie at her father's funeral. Maggie boldly telling her about her plan to run and Jennifer trying to talk her out of it. Jennifer had been so frightened because of the constant surveillance. She remembered Maggie telling her that if she ever needed to get out she needed to find...

"Diablo-oh-five," she whispered. Jennifer splashed her hand out of the water and clamped over her own mouth. Like being surprised by a long forgotten song lyric the name suddenly came to her. Maggie had told her to find Diablo05 online. He was the one who was getting her out of the country, whoever "he" might be. She repeated the name mentally so as not to forget again. But how would she find him?

Excited at coming up with the name, she ended her bath and drained the tub. After she towel dried, she stared at herself in the mirror. The cuts and bruises would heal soon enough but the badly botched job of her shaved head dismayed her. She rummaged under the sink and found the electric razor Matt kept in a case. The razor buzzed to life and Jennifer carefully shaved her own head in order to smooth out the gaps. She did this for several minutes, turning this way and that, and using a hand mirror to reflect the back of her head. Satisfied she wiped her head with a hot and wet washrag.

Diablo05.

⋏

Jennifer was too much of a fright to even think of going to school for the next few days. She sent an email off to the principal letting him know the earliest she could return would be the following week. He replied back within the hour stating that he understood and scheduled an appointment for her to come in to discuss her recent troubles. She suspected a temporary suspension would be discussed.

Her husband barely spoke to her that morning and looked at her even less. With sunlight streaming in the windows he was confronted by the visage of his battered and bruised spouse. She couldn't read him as he got ready for work. Jennifer didn't know if he was angry or ashamed at her, or even at himself for failing to keep her from harm. She had no idea what to do about it so she just let him quietly leave for work.

Her day wasn't going to be spent idly. Free from protective custody Jennifer didn't know if the National Police would pick her up again. She wanted to start working on a way out of America behind Maggie's footsteps. How would she find Diablo05? Maggie told her he could be found online. Using her tablet or iGlasses would leave too many digital footsteps leading back to her and the National Police were bound to be paying even closer attention to her. She couldn't go to a library or a cafe either. If she went to either of those places her dent would be scanned and her activity tracked. An easy way to solve the problem wasn't readily apparent. With nothing better to do she turned the TV on to the news station and read local news on her tablet.

Reading and watching the news still served a purpose. Jennifer scanned for news stories about other people who had run afoul of the Party. She wanted to see what information was out there and how other people fared, but she didn't want whoever monitored her network access to get suspicious so she read everything on the net; national news, international news, celebrity gossip and human interest stories. By all appearances she was a bored housewife looking to fill her day with entertainment.

She had the realistic expectations that most news would be altered if not outright censored. Jennifer found nuggets of useful information that could be discovered with a little scrutiny. Saboteurs had bombed a logistics company in Birmingham. Computers seized in Detroit for "unauthorized web access". A pirate radio station shut down in Bangor, Maine. Jennifer paid closer attention to the news instead of simply swallowing the lines fed to her. The war news from Texas painted a rosy outlook of gains against the Coalition forces but the front lines had shifted north from Austin to

Waco. If the news told her that American forces had advanced, then why were they retreating on a map?

⟁

Soon all the television and reading began to wear on her. She needed to get away from the TV and do something productive. Jennifer decided a nice home-cooked meal was in order and wanted dinner ready for Matt when he got home. She prepared a fresh salad topped with grilled tofu and a balsamic vinaigrette, some fresh baked dinner rolls and a savory beans and rice dish. She decided a red wine would pair well with the meal.

Jennifer anticipated Matt would get home around six o'clock and had the table set with candles lit and told the house AI to find some jazz to play. She had the music up a little louder than normal. She was certain that the place was bugged.

Matt came home at the time she anticipated. She heard him as he opened the front door. "Mmmm, what smells good?" he asked as he walked into the kitchen.

"Probably the beans and rice. Have some wine."

"I'm starving!"

"Well, let's eat."

He smiled appreciatively as he spooned out the beans and rice and the salad to his plate. After a bite he said, around a mouthful of food, "This is really good."

"I am glad you like it."

Matt worked his way through the beans and rice over the next several minutes, then paused. He reached for his glass of wine and took a big gulp. "Honey, I wanted to say I'm sorry if I seemed weird last night and this morning. This is... well, it's just so hard to take in. Why are we being treated so unfairly in all this? I mean, we're good decent people. We're both members of the Party. This shouldn't happen to people like us, right?"

Jennifer reached for her own wineglass. She noted to herself that the Hanson household seemed to fortify themselves with alcohol when presented with a problem. She was also still pissed at her husband but he was making an effort to reach out, albeit in a clumsy way. The only unfairness he had suffered was a little trouble at work while she had been beaten at the hands of the state, but she kept all that to herself as she sipped at her wine.

Finally, she said, "A lot of decent people are getting treated unfairly. I thought the protective custody center would be full of criminals but it's not. The only people that treated me badly at the detention center were the chief inspector and the other guards. None of the other detainees did anything wrong."

"Well, why are they there then?" He had that haughty tone as he worked himself into an argument.

"Because the Party put them there. There were no murderers or thieves of any sort. The impression I got was that the guards were scarier than any of the detainees."

"The Party wouldn't do something like that, would they?"

"Do you think I belonged there? I was just lucky that a Party connection… you… could get me out. Those other people aren't so lucky."

"All that is behind us now."

"Are you sure? It seems like once the Party has its cross-hairs on you they are always going to be watching you."

"I think you are overreacting."

"We should be prepared for the worse. That's all I am saying."

⅄

She watched more programming on the OLED wall the next day, constantly scanning news channels with a few other entertainment programs. Jennifer couldn't care less about the entertainment. She didn't want the Party to find a pattern in her viewing habits. Also, the tablet remained untouched. When the local news aired a story on the net about the dangers of "unauthorized web access" she took note. The story seemed to salaciously suggest that certain computer shops in the bad part of town were somewhat unsavory. Everyone in Denver avoided that area, but what if she drove to there and found one of those shops?

Bored, she grabbed the keys to the convertible and headed to the garage. She took the tablet out of her purse and laid it on top of a workbench. Jennifer mused on the tools hanging on the wall then grabbed a hammer and smashed the head on the tablet display. Nothing happened. Dismayed, she swung again. This time a series of cracks spider-webbed in the center of the display. She grinned with satisfaction, stuffed the tablet back in her purse and hopped in her car.

No traffic impeded her since hardly anyone owned a car these days. Taxes and permits for private automobiles fetched premium prices. She didn't bother to check to see if she was being followed. Surveillance cameras dotted the streets and the National Police could check the footage against the GPS embedded in her car. Jennifer couldn't hide that she was going somewhere.

She slowly cruised north on Carson Street; a desolate collection of boarded up apartments and shops with little foot traffic and even fewer cars. A couple of abandoned vehicles lined the streets with weeds growing up around them and rust adorning their roofs and hoods. On the corner of Flint stood an open garage (We Specialize in Gas Vehicles). Across from the garage stood AAA Computer Repair. The computer repair store had a sign that declared its own specialty in "motherboard boxes". Jennifer couldn't remember the last time she had seen a box computer.

She parked directly in front of the store and stepped out of the vehicle. The store was built like a red brick fortress. Heavy steel pull down gates above the doors and windows could fortify the store in an instant. Two surveillance cameras covered the door, while a third was pointed at the street. Jennifer checked carefully up and down the street, then chastised herself for automatically looking guilty where anyone could see her. She took a deep breath and entered the store.

An electronic chime announced her entry and her iGlasses went offline with a flashing red warning. Behind the counter stood a man smiling at her. "Those won't work in here," he said. He was fat, a rarity in these times, and bearded with glasses, regular glasses, not the iGlasses that everyone wore these days, and he also sported shoulder length brown hair. Jennifer guessed him somewhere in his thirties. "Firewalls," the man said.

"I beg your pardon," she replied.

"This place is protected by firewalls. They won't let your iGlasses transmit from inside. The cameras on those are disabled as well. Sorry, I don't like outsiders peeping in."

"Outsiders?"

"Bad guys. No matter who they work for." He didn't seem inclined to explain any further. "You are my first customer of the day. Probably my only customer of the day."

"Not a lot of business?" Jennifer asked. She took her iGlasses off and placed them in her purse, then examined the store closely. The shelves were cluttered with computers, monitors and other electronic parts. It clashed with her expectation that a store should be clean, neat and aesthetically pleasing to the eye. The CFL bulbs hanging from the ceiling gave the store a soft warm glow.

He shook his head. "Nope. Not since the news ran that story about 'dangerous computer shops'. That story has been running all week." He cocked an eyebrow at her. "You don't look like you're from the neighborhood. Not in that little hot rod you drove up in."

"No, Aurora."

He cocked one eyebrow up at her. "And you couldn't find the right computer store in Aurora?"

"Not looking like this." She reached up a pulled off the white woolen knit cap covering her head.

"Ah. A recently released political prisoner. I would say Aurora is less welcoming these days. Golden Gate Canyon?"

"Yes."

"When did you get out?"

"Three days ago."

"Be careful now that you're out. You wouldn't want to go back in."

"I never want to go back in there again."

"What brings you to my store?"

"This." She reached into her purse and pulled the cracked tablet.

"Let me check it out," he said as he extended his hand. Despite his meaty fingers he twisted the tablet around in his hands gracefully. He flicked the power switch on. The LED lit green but nothing was on the display. He reached under the counter and pulled out a cable which he inserted into the tablet. The other end of the cable plugged into a small computer. She noted that the little black computer, display and keyboard were all new-gen. "I'm Owen, by the way."

"Jennifer."

"These little tablets are tougher than they look but the displays are always fragile. It seems to boot up just fine but it's unhappy with being attached to my computer. Password?" He retreated two steps away from the tethered tablet and computer and invited her behind the counter.

Jennifer stepped forward and picked up the tablet. It gleefully chimed when it recognized her through its camera and asked her for a password which she typed in through a keyboard. With that done, Jennifer stepped away and waved for Owen to continue.

He started tapping on the keyboard again. "Just doing some diagnostics. Testing the memory cache integrity and the drive." The display showed a list of yellow happy faces as the diagnostics progressed. "I can clone this. I have the same exact model in the back. It will cost you $300. Friend prices for our recently released political prisoner."

"That's very generous." Typically they were $500.

"No problem. I would say you can go grab a bite to eat somewhere but this ain't the kind of neighborhood where pretty ladies walk around unescorted. You're welcome to hang out here."

"You think I'm pretty?"

"Well, yeah. Underneath those bruises and cuts, but, yeah." Owen blushed.

"Thank you. I would be happy to wait."

He exited from behind the counter and headed for the back of the store. Jennifer, with nothing better to do, wandered around and assessed the store again. Bins filled with computer parts lined the walls. She didn't know what they did but it had been a long time since she had seen a green circuit board with gold circuitry. Shelves were filled with archaic video game consoles; The Xboxes, PlayStations and Nintendos of her youth. Other video game consoles were so ancient and obscure she had never heard of them. At the far back stood a brightly lit cabinet with the name "Ms. Pac Man" emblazoned on the side. Jennifer smiled at the memory of Ms. Pac Man.

"Found it," Owen announced as he returned from the back. He spotted her next to the game cabinet. "You want to play? There's a mug of quarters next to the machine."

"No, thank you," she replied. "It does bring back memories though."

Owen took the new tablet out of the box. "I found that in an old pizza restaurant. Brought it back here and refurbished it. A nice novelty for the rare customer that comes in." He wired the new tablet to the computer and punched in some commands. A big progress bar filled the display.

"Owen, can I ask you a question?"

"Sure." He had nothing to do now except monitor the progress of the cloning procedure.

"I need to find someone but I don't know how."

"Someone under the grid?"

She had never heard of that phrase before but played along. "Yeah."

"There are ways probably."

"Have you ever heard of someone named Diablo05?"

Owen eyes widened. "No."

She had surprised him with that name and pushed too far. "I need his help."

"You saw that news report, right? About outlaw computer shops? Well, something that happens from time to time are stings for these outlaw computer shops. The National Police send in people into them asking questions, such as yours, to entrap the owners."

"But -"

"Now I know you're not wired."

"Wired?"

"Surveillance. With all the security around this place all the alarms would have gone off as soon as you walked in. And I know this dead little puppy," he held up the cracked tablet, "didn't have anything on it that would phone home when I connected it to my machine. You have to appreciate how careful a man in my position must be. Given your recent treatment you should be careful as well."

Jennifer sighed as she bit her lip. "Of course. I understand." There was an old couch sitting next to the door that led to the back room. With nothing better to do she sat and waited. From her vantage on the couch she had a clear view of Owen behind his counter while he worked on her tablet. From time to time he would glance at her then dart his eyes away with embarrassment.

Fifteen minutes later Owen announced that he finished. "Here, check it out," he said, as he handed the tablet back to her. She stared at the tablet and the blinking green LED. It came to life when the tablet recognized her face.

"Thank you, Owen. I appreciate it. How much do I owe you?

"Just the price of the tablet. Three hundred plus tax. Comes to $336.00."

He punched a button on his computer and the tablet acknowledged the charge and waited for Jennifer's approval.

"I am sorry about making you feel uncomfortable earlier," she said.

"Oh, don't worry about it. People ask me those kinds of questions all the time."

She smiled. "Well, thank you again." Jennifer turned to leave.

"Jennifer," he stammered. "Have you ever heard of Kongo Gumi?"

"No, I am afraid I haven't."

"It's a construction company in Japan. The oldest continuous operating company in the world. Well over fourteen centuries."

"That's interesting." She wasn't sure where this was going.

"When you get a chance you should read more about them on Wiki."

"I'll do that. Thank you again, Owen."

⅄

By the time she got home she was certain that Owen tried to tell her something. Kongo Gumi? What was that? She almost asked the tablet to find the entry for her right then but she didn't want alert anyone watching her digital movements. Instead, she started preparing dinner. She still had some fresh filets of salmon that she could season nicely along with a rice pilaf and a green salad. Jennifer couldn't help but turn her mind back to Kongo Gumi even as she prepared dinner. Did a secret message exist on the Wiki page? She would check it as soon as Matt went to bed.

Matt arrived home thirty minutes late. "I'm sorry," he said as soon as he walked in. "District Leader Baker called an all hands meeting at three. As usual the meeting ran long, which put me behind and late to leave." He leaned toward her and gave her a gingerly kiss on her bruised cheek.

"Everything okay?" she asked.

"Yeah, everything is fine, just going over budgets, quotas and rations again. There's going to be tighter belts for everyone else this year."

"Because of Texas?"

"Yeah, because of Texas and Florida. We're going to be okay though. The Party takes care of its own."

Jennifer kept quiet. All the proof she needed that the Party took care of its own could be found by staring at her bruised reflection in the mirror. "Hungry?"

"Yeah, is that salmon I smell? Let's eat."

She already had the white wine chilled and breathing. She served Matt first and while he dug into the salmon she poured herself a full glass of wine. Matt made small talk about his day while she picked at her meal. The big buzz was the return of District Leader Orson Baker who had just returned from a meeting in Washington. She nodded appropriately at the right places and asked the right open ended questions. Her mind kept turning back to Kongo Gumi.

With the generous helpings of wine it wasn't long before she heard the light snores of Matt coming from the living room as she cleaned up. The news broadcast boasted more gains on the Texas front, but Jennifer wondered if, when she looked up the city names mentioned on a map, she would find that the lines had shifted once again in favor of the Coalition forces. She left Matt sleeping on the couch as the house AI switch off the OLED wall and started playing some classical. Jennifer sat at the kitchen table and stared at her tablet.

She couldn't go straight to the Kongo Gumi Wiki page. She remembered that Owen said it was the oldest operating company in the world. Did a list of old companies exist on a separate page? Yes, she found it quickly. She clicked on Kongo Gumi and was immediately disappointed. There was nothing remarkable about it at all. She had seen wiki pages before. Everyone grew up with Wikipedia, but this page was no different than any of the pages she had seen in the past. She started playing with the hyperlinks on the page to see where the embedded URLs lead to, but again this proved unfruitful. After a half hour of staring at links again and again she finally had her eureka moment. The notation symbols next to the references were not the same. The first two references had this as a symbol ^. The third one had a π. Jennifer clicked on the π.

The tablet went black. With a furrowed brow she picked up the tablet and pushed the power button again, despite the LED still showing green. The tablet came back to life with a blue screen running a white script:

ESTABLISHING HANDSHAKE PROTOCOL
HANDSHAKE ESTABLISHED
INITIATING SECURE VIRTUALIZED INSTANCE
INITIATING ENCRYPTION
RUNNING SECURITY SCRIPT
RUNNING WELCOME PACKAGE
ENTERING MAIN LOBBY
WELCOME TO THE MAIN LOBBY BALDPRETTY

"Bald Pretty?" Jennifer muttered. Before she could comment any further the script continued.

WHO VOUCHES FOR BALDPRETTY?

An instant later a chime sounded with an affirmation message in the center of the screen.

THEBEARREPUBLIC VOUCHES FOR BALD PRETTY

The screen wiped clear, then displayed a user command menu to set options for her new account. Jennifer was familiar with account set ups from her other online accounts. She found the lack of a touch interface daunting. Everything had to be typed from the soft keyboard, including the commands. She found that she had two emails waiting for her. One was the standard welcome email that covered the rules of the forum (named "Valley Forge Public House"). The other email was from TheBearRepublic. It read:

> *Hi,*
>
> *We met earlier today. I trust you are bright enough not to use real names here. Sorry about your username. Finding something original is hard to do these days. I hope you find what you're looking for. Feel free to explore. The Freedom Party can't snoop here.*

Jennifer was in but she didn't know what to do next.

CHAPTER 8

Jennifer wasn't ready to play around with this right now and she certainly didn't want her husband to catch her snooping on an illegal website. Fortunately the site had a logout button that she could use. She left the tablet sitting on the kitchen counter and joined her sleeping husband in the living room. After she gave a silent command to the AI to turn on the news her husband woke up.

"Anything wrong?" he asked.

"Nothing. Just wondering if we should go to bed."

He rubbed his eyes. "Yeah, it's late. Got a big day tomorrow."

They went through the ritual of changing into sleep clothes (a short nightgown for her and underwear and a T-shirt for him). Then the teeth-brushing ritual came next. Once in bed with the lights out it wasn't long before Jennifer could sense him sleeping deeply beside her. Wide awake, she couldn't help but think about what waited for her online at that website. Jennifer tried to lie still and let sleep succumb her but she kept opening her eyes. Finally, after confirming with the clock that she had been awake for twenty minutes, she gave up and got out of bed.

She traipsed lightly to the kitchen and picked the tablet off the counter, then proceeded to grab a blanket from the closet. The living room should be safe enough for her online excursions. She swaddled herself in the blanket when she climbed onto the couch. When she turned on the tablet on she found a new icon listed on the homepage. The simple π symbol again in green without a title. She tapped the symbol and the screen went black again before the login script started. It made sense. If everyone went to the Kongo Gumi wiki page every day the hit count would show up on the National Police network metrics.

The screen chimed and displayed a welcome back message. She tapped her way to a main menu awkwardly. Owen had told her to explore so that was what she would do. Set up in an old forum style format the website interface wasn't intuitive like she was used to. A wealth of information was right at her fingertips and available for her to explore. At the top of the page were the discussion forums. She wasn't quite sure what these were about so she shied away from them for now. The next section was for a chat group. She decided to pop in and say "hi". Ten other avatars stared at back at her with digital silence. Self-conscious, Jennifer quickly dumped out of chat.

The next forum she went into was international news. This forum contained unfiltered news articles from foreign sources. She found this forum completely fascinating. There was a helpful sticky at the top that called itself "International Timeline for Newbies". She started with a familiar point of reference - the American Economic Collapse. Twenty years prior the American economy had toppled after a global pandemic. Regardless of the cause the two major political parties at that time were blamed, leading to the formation of the Freedom Party. This part of American history was taught in school. She remembered living through those times as a little girl in her parents' house. They hadn't lost their house like some others had but there were nights, and sometimes entire days, where they didn't have a meal. Denver hadn't suffered like the West Coast and East Coast cities, where riots in those places had ended in mass graves. Everyone had been relieved when the Freedom Party had stepped up and taken control of the situation in cities throughout the America. They had displayed their "One Nation" flag and white-star-on-blue armbands. The populace had rallied behind the cause immediately and the rest of the world had breathed a sigh of relief. That was the history that had been taught to her as she grew up.

This new timeline presented a different history. Despite the severity of the economic collapse America had recovered in a few short years. Domestically, many reforms had been put in place to govern the media, the Internet as well as anything related to the health and well-being of the individual. Abroad America had found new enemies in foreign nations again. Chief among them was Iran as well as Syria and Egypt. It wasn't long before a case had been made to invade Iran. The rest of the world had reacted negatively but each country had feared fighting against this revitalized and armed America. Soon afterward similar other invasions had been conducted against the other two countries.

With a base of five countries in the Middle East America started to project its power over the region. Other nations protested, of course, chief among them the lead nations of the European Union. The situation got progressively worse from there. The Freedom Party exerted its influence over Canadian politics and created a puppet state. Furthermore, the American military occupied the upper Baja Peninsula, Sonora and Chihuahua to "quell border violence and drug trafficking." That angered Mexico and the other Central and South American nations. The United Nations moved its headquarters to The Hague.

After the occupation of the Mexican territories the Coalition began to form. It included the European Union, Mexico and other Central and South American countries. China, the world's most powerful military and economy, remained strangely silent on the issue. The Chinese seemed reluctant to take a side. Russia remained neutral while sympathetic to the Coalition. Everyone, including America, tip-toed around the Chinese. That didn't stop the Coalition from moving forward with their plan. They began to funnel small arms into the American occupied territories in the Middle East and the Mexican districts to encourage an insurgency. After several years the insurgency worked in the Middle East. Logistically it became too difficult for America to fund the occupation. Bases were gradually abandoned and the American forces withdrew. The media framed this as a victory when Jennifer was in college. Stability was achieved in those Middle Eastern territories and America was no longer needed. As she read this foreign account it became clear that America had cut and run.

Emboldened by the American withdrawal the Coalition made moves to support Mexico. British and French missile subs ringed America on the East and West Coasts. American hunter subs played cat and mouse games with them. The Russians sold their main battle tanks, the T-14s and T-25s, to the Coalition and Mexican crews were trained up in their use. Finally, the invasion launched from Cuba into Southern Florida. Coalition tanks raced up the highways on both of Florida's coasts before the American military could stop them short of Jacksonville and Tallahassee. Later a second invasion launch from Monterrey in the spring of the previous year striking at San Antonio. The Coalition had the advantage of numbers. They seemed to be able to throw an infinite number of tanks, planes and bombs at the Americans. But America, a culture honed by war, faced the massive firepower with technically superior weapons systems such as the XM1202s, the aging Abrams tanks, the Raptors and JSFs. The Americans gave ground despite their technological prowess, first in San Antonio and then in Austin. Now the front line was south of Waco.

The war in Texas from the perspective from the other side fascinated Jennifer. The Coalition truly believed they were fighting the war against American oppression. Had she read something like this during the previous summer she would have scoffed at the idea that America was in the wrong. Now, after recent experiences, she could see how her country was the aggressor.

She perused another sub-forum that covered domestic activities. There were a lot of details regarding the National Police arrests of resistance cells. Many members of Valley Forge lamented for the loss of their colleagues interned in the protective custody centers or simply executed on the spot. No mention was made of any active cells. She figured that would probably compromise the group's security.

Despite her fascination with the material she found herself nodding off after midnight. She kept trying to read but succumbed to sleep. The tablet, sensing no activity, timed her out of Valley Forge.

⋏

Distracted by her previous night's discovery Jennifer barely acknowledged her husband for breakfast and almost missed the email from the principal. Matt fled the house with a cup of coffee, a mumble and the obligatory peck on the cheek. She grabbed her own cup of coffee and her tablet, then curled back up on the couch again with a blanket. She opened the email from the principal and read the mandatory meeting request for Friday. It was only a couple of days away. She frowned as she sipped the hot coffee. A meeting request on her last day of absence was bound not to be good, but it had to be better than the treatment she had suffered at the hands of the National Police. There was nothing she could do about it right now. The meeting would happen and probably end with a suspension.

The prospect of exploring the Valley Forge forum excited Jennifer and distracted her from the upcoming meeting. She powered up the tablet and tapped the π icon. She checked for any sign of Diablo05 but she found herself distracted by the entertainment forum. It was divided up into several sub-forums of Art, Literature, Television, Music, Video Games, Movies and Adult. She tried Art first. There were photographs of many paintings, drawings and sculptures. A lot of the art had dates on them from the last one hundred and fifty years. Some of the artwork was breathtakingly beautiful while others were frighteningly garish. Other pieces were provocative with either their beauty, stark subject matter or blatant erotica. All of it was banned in America. Each piece of artwork elicited its own heated discussion on the forum.

It brought back a fleeting memory from her childhood. After the revolution had ended her parents had brought her to Civic Center Park. Loaded in the back of the Prius were two boxes filled with books, CDs and DVDs. Usually her dad tried to entertain them with jokes but this time her parents had remained quiet during the drive. When they had arrived hundreds of other people carried similar boxes filled with the same. In the center of the park a large bonfire had raged. People had formed lines and carried their boxes to the bonfire where a Party officer greeted them. After the greeting the contents of their box had been hand fed, piece-by-piece into the fire. Jennifer had been too young to understand what was happening. The park even had carnival booths and there were other kids playing. The revolution, "the bad times" as Jennifer had remembered them, were over and this was a lot of fun.

Now she remembered the odd thing her father had said with a frown before they got out of the car; "Well, everything is already digital anyway."

Now she was enjoying new content that she had never heard or experienced before as she perused the forum. Music that had existed in her youth but had been suppressed as subversive. It was a welcome change from the classical and big bands she was used to on the net. The novelty of old fashioned rock and roll. The clashing guitars and wanton carelessness of heavy metal. The casual carefree nature of pop music. The raw rhythms of hip hop. She found herself getting lost in the cacophony of sounds assaulting her ear buds.

And the television shows. The lost dramas and comedies from the late twentieth century and the early twenty-first. Jennifer wanted to watch these as well but was afraid that they would consume her. As much as it ached her to leave this section of the forum, she needed to find seek out more information.

After noon she realized that she had spent the entire day in her pajamas doing nothing but checking out the forum. She reluctantly turned off the tablet, showered and changed into something casual and then made herself a lunch of grilled cheese and tomato soup. Still, as she ate her soup and sandwich at the breakfast nook in the kitchen, she had the tablet beside her open to the forum again.

An hour later is when she found the first post by Diablo05 titled "NEW ORLEANS ROUTE HOT". His avatar appeared to be a picture of black man in sunglasses. She did a quick image search in the forum and found that this avatar was from an old movie called "The Matrix". Again, she had to keep herself focused since the movie seemed interesting in itself.

Jennifer read the post regarding New Orleans and was convinced she found the right person. The post was about a smuggler route to the port of New Orleans that had recently become hazardous because he had transported two high profile citizens out of the country. It had to be Maggie and Brad.

Jennifer tapped on Diablo05's user name to find other posts by him. She understood him to be a smuggler who conducted citizens out of the country. There were a few posts about the nature of his work but not many. She wondered how Maggie ever found him in the first place. Most of the posts by him editorialized the American government and its totalitarian regime. Of that he was not particularly a big fan, but it was fair to say that none of the members of the Valley Forge Public House were. Outside of his ranting and raving about the American government he had a humorous side to him. He would often interject a disarming one-liner in the middle of a dueling diatribe between two posters deep in their conviction. It was enough to diffuse an escalating exchange and typically both parties at odds respected him and his opinion. Jennifer found herself becoming fascinated by this man she had never met. Wanting to know more she went to the movie library and streamed "The Matrix".

Even though the old movie featured outdated special effects, she found herself enjoying it anyway. Jennifer had nothing against old movies. Many of the "approved movies" made available by the Party were old classics from the twentieth century. She never cared too much for the newer ones, as they were typically simplistic war movies with America as the heroes and the Coalition forces as the bad guys. They weren't necessarily bad movies but nothing distinguished one over the others. Still, her husband couldn't get enough of them. "The Matrix" was older than her but the story was something new. She loved it and wanted to see more. Two sequels were listed in the library but sun started to set over the mountains and she needed to start dinner soon.

Jennifer checked the refrigerator and didn't like the bare shelves. She bit her lip for a moment then decided to make a run. Jennifer put on her winter coat and a wool hat over her naked head. The hat would obviously disguise her shaved head but the cold weather meant she wouldn't be out of place in the store. Most of the bruising and swelling had subsided. She might draw an eye or two but she was no longer the walking horror show that shambled around a few days earlier.

Jennifer jumped into the BMW, twisted the key and the engine roared life. She backed out of the garage and headed toward the store.

Stigman's featured only the familiar semi-full parking lot. The exclusivity granted to its customers guaranteed that her shopping experience would be stress free. Jennifer found a free parking space near the main entrance to the store. Buttoning up her coat and wrapping her scarf around her neck a little tighter she braced herself for the frigid wind as she got out of the car. A quick dash to the entrance and she was inside where they kept the shopping carts. She grabbed one of them and went into the fluorescent glow of Stigman's.

The empty shelves reminded her of how dreadfully depressing the war affected the store's dwindling inventory. Jennifer wondered if more food was getting shipped off to China. She worked her way over to the produce aisle to find only a few vegetables - small tomatoes, limp cucumbers and scrawny carrots grown in a hydroponic farm somewhere. At least the portabella mushrooms appeared to be full and fresh. She grabbed those quickly. In the seafood section the selections were fewer. Next was the bread aisle across the way and the fresh aroma aroused a hungry rumble from her belly. Jennifer grabbed a loaf of rye and placed it in the child seat of the cart. The dairy aisle held little milk but she didn't miss it. She did miss cheese though and took the last wedge of the cheddar. And wine of course. She needed wine. Jennifer grabbed three bottles of Cab.

Jennifer wheeled the cart to the front of the store and found an open register. She placed the items on the conveyor belt and the bored register attendant started to bag her items. The belt moved automatically and the scanner visually inspected the groceries and kept tab of the total. The attendant gave a cursory glance at the monitor to make sure everything on the belt had registered as he bagged the groceries.

The attendant said, "You're total is $257.60."

Jennifer placed her hand next to the dent scanner. It went through the sequential lights to show that it was working. After several seconds the scanner gave an angry buzz instead of the usual chime.

Anxiety flooded Jennifer as the attendant regarded her suspiciously with piqued interest, "Try again," he said. "Sometimes they have problems registering the first time."

It was true. She had even experienced the angry buzz before. Usually the dent wasn't close enough to the scanner or didn't get a chance to scan thoroughly. Still, the angry buzz from the dent scanner came too soon after her time at Golden Gate Canyon. She gingerly extended her hand to the dent scanner. Once again, the sequential lights worked then concluded with the same angry buzz.

"Is there something I can help with?" A man with navy blue pants and a crisp white button down shirt had appeared at her side. He had a nametag pinned to his shirt that read, "Reggie Simpson, Store Manager."

The store became morosely quiet as all the store patrons within view quietly enjoyed this new drama unfolding before them. Her drama. Some regarded her sympathetically while others were merely entertained. They enjoyed her suffering as part of the bright spot of their mundane shopping experience. There were a few who gave her reproachful accusatory scowls. They eyed her as an interloper into their small, quiet and pristine world, with scorn in their eyes just as there had been scorn in hers several months ago when she had witnessed this very thing happen to someone else.

"There seems to be some trouble with my dent," she heard herself say in a quiet voice.

He scrutinized her intently through his iGlasses. She could see the tiny display of data scrolling in front of his eyes. Jennifer noted that he didn't ask her to try the dent again.

The manager frowned. "I am afraid that your store privileges have been revoked. You are re-leveled to Class C store permissions."

Jennifer scanned furtively around her again. The other shoppers had closed in with the nose of their carts pointed like the snouts of a wolf pack. They wanted to see the show and waited for her to scream, panic, cry, threaten and wail. Having witnessed this happen not too long ago, she knew what they expected of her. She didn't want to give them the satisfaction and felt a slight pang of guilt for being so judgmental when this had happened to the other woman a few months back.

"Thank you, Mr. Simpson," she said. "I apologize. I had not received notification that my store privileges had changed. If you will excuse me."

The manager's face sagged with relief as Jennifer walked past her cart and through the register aisle, while the other shoppers scowled. She had just robbed them of the show they expected. Jennifer smiled at them as she walked out of the store.

She got behind the wheel of the BMW in the parking lot and sent her husband a text message:

Store privileges revoked. Class C only. Can you get them back for me?

Really? Came the reply. *That's weird. I don't know what happened.*

"I know what happened," she muttered. She didn't get an immediate reply so she started up the car. On her drive back a chime sounded in her ear with a message on her iGlasses:

Sorry, babe, but I can't get them back for you.

She said, "Reply. Do you still have your store privileges?"

His reply: *Yeah, mine seem okay.*

"Good. You can pick up dinner on the way home. Don't forget to pick up wine."

⌃

Jennifer woke up on Friday morning filled with a sense of dread. She was probably going to be suspended from the elementary school today She woke up at five in the morning, an hour before the alarm was due to go off, and stared at the ceiling while the late fall temperatures chilled the bedroom. Beside her Matt snored lightly.

Wrapped up in her own head about everything that had happened, she reflected that it was like a vicious circle. *The dinner party!* It had led to David's internment then death. Then Maggie and Brad had tried to push back on the Party, but had lost everything. That had led to their escape from America which had put Jennifer and Matt under more scrutiny. Now that she and her husband were under the watchful eyes of the Party, nothing would ever to be the same again. Now if only she could convince her husband of that. He still had the expectation of normality. Jennifer wondered if he got any additional pressure from his management.

When the alarm softly chimed an hour later she got out of bed and braced herself for the chill of the house. Knowing that her husband would be groggy from the previous evening and the bourbons that came with it, she went ahead to the kitchen and started the coffee maker. At least that savory delicacy hadn't been taken away from them yet. She jumped in the shower first, since her husband had slept through the alarm.

After the shower she put on a navy blue pantsuit and sat down at the vanity. She sighed at the visage in her own mirror. The bruises had faded to a light brown. Jennifer could cover that with a judicious amount of makeup. She couldn't hide her stubbly baldhead though. She had thought about buying a wig but had refused with a fair amount of ferocity. Jennifer didn't want to hide who she was, although she did concede that it wasn't wrong to hide what remained of the bruising.

She was drinking coffee with her oatmeal when Matt came into the kitchen. He poured himself a cup, added lots of cream and sugar, then nodded appreciatively after the first sip. "It'll probably be fine," he said.

"They're going to suspend me for several weeks, if not months."

"And that's the worst that can happen?"

"They can fire me."

"That's not going to happen."

"You're probably right. I don't like it, Matt. I haven't done anything wrong!" She started to tear up.

"Hey, hey, hey, easy there. I know you haven't. This has all been a huge misunderstanding. It will eventually all be in the past."

"How can you be so sure?"

"It has to pass."

"Will you be able to continue your political career?"

He sipped his coffee then said, "Yeah, probably..."

Was he trying to convince her or himself? Regardless, he sounded unsure.

Despite the bright morning filled with sunshine, Denver was bitterly cold. Even with the cold Jennifer felt flushed with anxiety. She pulled into the parking lot behind the school then cut the engine. Jennifer pondered for a few moments while her anxiety mounted. She closed her eyes and took a deep breath. She still had to go through this meeting with the principal, no matter what. Slowly she counted, letting the anxiety fade into the back of her mind like faraway static. Jennifer waited out the anxiety, then stepped out of the car and walked toward the school with confident strides.

The school had a dent scanner that kept the door bolted and locked. Jennifer waved her hand over the scanner and waited for the chime. The bolts retracted with a bang, allowing her in. The hallways were quiet and empty, since it was the beginning of the school day and all the kids were already in class. The matronly admin assistant frowned at Jennifer as she entered the principal's office.

"Hey, Sandy," Jennifer said. "How's it going? I have an appointment with Jim."

"Please have a seat," she replied coolly. "He will be right with you."

Jennifer took a seat in the armchair in front of the admin's desk. She and Sandy had known each other for years. Now Sandy treated her like a criminal, just like everyone else did. The assistant principal walked into the principal's office with another man she had never seen before. They skirted around her as if she were a rattlesnake on a hiking trail. They entered the main office without comment to her. Another minute passed when Sandy looked up from her monitor. "You can go in now."

Jennifer stood up and opened the office door gingerly. Her first thought was that she had entered into some sort of tribunal. All three of the men sat behind the principal's expansive desk. Jim remained seated while Chad, the vice principal, flanked his right in an armchair. The third man who stood on the principal's left was someone she didn't recognize. They all wore nearly identical navy blue suits with their Party pins prominently displayed on their lapels. There were no smiles between the three of them.

"Please sit down, Jennifer," Jim said. He had his hands folded on the desk and barely moved. Jennifer couldn't even tell if any of these guys breathed.

"You haven't met Joseph Gruber," Jim continued. "He is from human resources at Denver ISD."

"Please to meet you," Jennifer said.

"Please call me Joe." He stood up and came around the desk to shake her hand. He pumped her hand professionally three times and his grin widened. *He's a salesman.* Whatever is happening here today, he is here to make it easier. Her heart dropped as she realized that the meeting wouldn't go well for her. Still, Jennifer needed to go through with this charade and try to salvage something.

"I am looking forward to coming back to work," she said.

It was the first time she saw Jim and Chad break their stoic stares. Their eyes pleaded to Joe for guidance. Joe kept smiling at Jennifer.

The silence stretched uncomfortably until Jim cleared his throat and broke the silence. "Jennifer, we've had some discussions at the ISD office. Given everything that is going on with you the board feels that you... ah... are no longer suitable as a teacher for our students."

"But I was cleared of all charges."

Jim's faced turned red as he turned beseechingly to the HR man once more, but the man sat quietly with his grin. Exasperated, Jim continued. "Well, there are still some certain questions about, ah, the nature of the relationships you maintained with certain people over the years."

"We are good Party people!"

"I am sorry. You have been suspended from the school. But, ah, Joe here... well, Joe can tell you what your options are."

The HR man cheerfully jumped into the conversation. "Thanks, Jim. I would be happy to! Jennifer, here is the plan that the ISD has in mind for you. As of right now your position is suspended. The good news is that you will keep your pay and benefits. Our plan is for you to go through this temporary suspension until the matters about these allegations are cleared up. We are looking at a timeline of fall of the next school year."

"That's nine months away!"

He raised his hand up as if he warded off a yapping puppy. "We know, we know. It's the best we can do."

"And then I can come back to work here?"

This time Jim and Chad found some place else to avert their eyes.

"That's not going to be possible," Joe said. "We'll move you to East Denver. They always need more teachers over there."

The workers' districts and ghettos. It was where the poorest of the poor lived and the schools were filled with Class C kids and lower.

"Think of all the good you will be doing with those kids."

"It's not fair," Jennifer said.

Joe gave her a wounded look that felt well practiced. "It is fair. Generous, in fact."

"Can I appeal this?"

"No, I am afraid there isn't a chance for appeal"

"If there are no more questions..." Jim waved his hand toward the door.

Jennifer had a dozen questions, most of which had to do with the fairness of the situation, but they had no interest in speaking with her any longer and anxiously waited for her to leave. Jennifer numbly stood up and walked out of the office. She didn't look at Sandy as she headed for the door.

"Traitor," Sandy muttered as Jennifer reached for the door handle.

Jennifer considered twisting the handle and leaving the office, but she turned around and faced the admin. Jennifer took a little pleasure watching Sandy flinch from her gaze. "We've been friends for five years. I was the only one there for you when you got divorced two years ago."

"It doesn't change that you are a traitor."

"It certainly means you were never my friend."

She smiled as Sandy managed to somehow take offense at the remark. Jennifer simply turned and exited the office without further. She managed to make it behind the wheel of her of car before erupting into hot tears of rage at a situation out of her control, coupled with the dissipating adrenaline from her confrontation with Sandy. She tried holding a deep breath but it didn't work this time. The rage at the unfairness of it all was still there. Frustrated, she wiped the tears away with the heel of her hand and started up the car. She took a small sense of satisfaction at disrupting the peaceful school day with a squeal of tires as she peeled out of the parking lot.

Jennifer raced home through the side streets as she replayed the meeting in her head; the cowardice of the principal and vice principal, the smugness of the HR man and the stupid ignorant vitriol of Sandy. The tears kept flowing and she blinked them away as best as she could. *It was all so unfair!*

Jennifer gunned the accelerator and sped through the small neighborhood streets. As she quickly turned the corners the rubber tires squealed on the asphalt in protest. Jennifer didn't car, she just wanted to go faster. She didn't see the red light she had run and only had a moment to register the grill of the electric delivery van crashing through her passenger side window.

CHAPTER 9

Jennifer was lost inside her own hazy and broken memories. Snatches of things that happened here and there. A fleeting memory of being pulled from the wreckage by a paramedic. Flashes of being wheeled into an emergency room on a gurney. Banks of fluorescent lights flashing above like an inverted highway. They had blinded her each time only to subside long enough to see various faces in a circle above. And the hospital room. Sometimes Matt was there... and sometimes he wasn't. Jennifer couldn't keep her eyes open longer than a minute and kept succumbing to sleep.

Finally, she simply woke up and stayed awake. Jennifer had a private room with a window facing east. The warmth of the sun on her face had awakened her. Matt remained asleep on the couch under the window. She tried to sit up in the bed, but her head protested with a stab of pain. Exasperated, she sighed and lay back down.

The rustling of the sheets woke Matt up. He gave a startled snort and shook his head while his eyes searched the room. His finally settled on her. "You're awake?"

"How long?" The words came out as a croak. She licked her lips with her sandpapery tongue.

"Three days. You were in and out of it. Mostly out of it. You hit your head pretty good."

An IV snaked into her arm with several electrodes taped all over her body. The monitor by her bedside gave a constant feed on all her vitals. A sharp stab of pain banged against the back of her head.

"Are you sleepy?"

She shook her head and stopped when the pain returned. She choked out a, "No."

"We should probably get a doctor or a nurse in here." Matt reached for the call button.

Not even a minute passed before a pretty blonde nurse in a crisp white uniform strolled into the hospital room. "I see you're awake. Are you going to stay with us this time?"

Jennifer nodded feebly and croaked out, "Yes." The nurse's nametag proclaimed her as Kaitlyn Chalfant. She wore the White Star pin on her crisp white uniform. "Can I get some water?"

"Of course." Nurse Chalfant went over to the stand next to the hospital bed and poured a glass of water from a pink plastic pitcher. The ice shifted and tinkled into the glass. Finally she picked up a straw from the stand and stuck it into the glass of water. She brought the glass over and gently lifted Jennifer by the back of her head towards the waiting straw.

The delicious ice-cold water moistened her tongue with the welcomed wet relief. The coldness gave her another stab of pain but she didn't want to stop drinking the refreshing water. Finally, Nurse Chalfant pulled the glass away. "Not too much at a time. We want to sip it."

Jennifer wanted to chug the water like a beer from back in her college days, but she relented. "What happened?"

Nurse Chalfant stayed silent, turning to Matt expectantly.

"I haven't told her anything," he said. "She just woke up."

The nurse turned back to Jennifer. "You were in a car accident on Friday. That was three days ago. You were unconscious when they brought you in. The doctor determined that it was a concussion. You woke up briefly a few times, never longer than a couple of minutes. Today is the first time I have seen you lucid."

Jennifer lifted her arms. Several stapled lacerations crisscrossed her skin. "Any other injuries?"

"Remarkably, no. Lacerations to the arms and face. You have a huge cut in your scalp from where your head hit the window. No broken bones or internal injuries. You were lucky in that regard. Only the concussion."

"Lucky," Jennifer muttered.

"Oh, and good news! The baby is fine!"

"Baby?"

Again, Nurse Chalfant waited for Matt to answer. He smiled sheepishly. "It's a surprise, honey. You're pregnant."

Jennifer's heart was simultaneously elated and struck with terror. "A baby..."

"Well, I should let the doctor tell you more. He's on shift in about an hour. I'll let him know you're awake. Some breakfast should be here shortly."

When Nurse Chalfant left the room Jennifer turned to Matt and hissed, "A baby!"

He shrugged. "I know."

She had managed to somehow get pregnant in the past month despite everything that had happened. Jennifer wondered if she was pregnant before she was interred into Golden Gate. It had to be before Golden Gate. There had been little intimacy since then. "They're going to check our genetic applications and see that we were denied. I've been taking the pills!"

"Did you take them at Golden Gate Canyon?" Again, that implied accusation that the fault lied with her.

"No, I had other concerns in protective custody. And I didn't have them with me. They didn't dispense any in the infirmary either."

Matt held up his hands defensively. "I was just asking a question!"

"Think about these questions before you ask them."

"I'm sorry."

"You know that I'm not trying to get pregnant," she said softly. "With everything going on right now do you think adding that would be a good idea?"

"No! I mean, of course I know it wouldn't. We can get it taken care of while we're here. All we need to do is tell the doctor right away." Jennifer was unsure, since a myriad of possible outcomes needed to be considered. So far the nurse hadn't said anything about their genetic applications. Even in this day of modern technology gaps still existed in records processing, with layers of agency bureaucracy. They could admit they were not qualified for parenthood and ask for an immediate abortion. But that might imply that they tried to have a baby and got caught. Or maybe they simply didn't know and they were doing their civic duty by having an abortion? Or they could simply go on with the expectant parent routine and hoped that no one noticed. Too many decisions with too many possible outcomes, both good and bad.

"Let me think on this."

"What's to think? We're already in enough trouble with the Party."

"You don't think they might figure we planned this without their consent?"

"I -" He closed his mouth shut as that possibility hit him. "I don't know."

"Let me think a bit," she said. The throbbing headache worked up a staccato tempo. "How did I end up here anyway?" It was a Class I hospital. She wasn't sure how the classification system worked but she was surprised to find herself here.

"You're listed as my spouse. Plus I pulled in a few favors. By the way, I am running out of them."

"Favors?"

"Favors and friends."

⚔

For breakfast Jennifer had some flavorless cold oatmeal along with some equally cold toast. At least she enjoyed some real butter to spread on the toast, a small luxury these days but this particular hospital was known to be favored by the Party and bound to be well supplied. She idly wondered if some VIP patient in one of the suites enjoyed some scrambled eggs with crispy bacon. She tried spreading the butter on the toast but it was too cold to spread and she nearly ripped the slice of toast into two smaller triangles with the plastic knife. Finally she gave up and put the two cold pats of butter between the slices of toast and ate it as a sandwich.

She had sent Matt home before the breakfast arrived. There was nothing he could do and it was wiser if he went back to work as soon as possible. It was better for him to keep busy there and before he left she had asked that he try to listen for any gossip about their predicament.

Jennifer sighed and took another bite of her toast and butter sandwich. Even with cold butter the saliva jetted into her mouth. She relished it while she could. Matt seemed so... lost. He had a tenuous grip on a world crumbling away from him. Why couldn't he see that? They were caught in the Party's crosshairs and couldn't shake that. Maybe he was resistant to the change?

She finished her last bite when the doctor whisked into the room. "How are you feeling?" He beamed at her. He was Indian, older, with salt and pepper hair and portly in his green scrubs. The white lab coat could not button up across his girth. Clearly he didn't follow any of the carb restrictions. Jennifer wondered if his profession gave him privileges. The name on his badge read Gupta.

"My head hurts," she said simply.

He smiled. "Yes, you suffered a concussion from your accident. You also have a laceration on the scalp which we sutured. It will itch for a while. Try not to scratch. In about week you should be able to get them removed. You can come here or go to your own physician."

"Okay. Anything else?"

He grinned. "You are one lucky young lady!"

Jennifer didn't feel lucky but she smiled. She found Doctor Gupta's good cheer to be infectious and couldn't resist. "How lucky am I?"

"No broken bones. No internal bleeding. And the baby is perfectly healthy."

The baby. What should she do here? Come clean about the baby or hold on to the secret. On impulse she made a decision. "Doctor, I need to tell you something. My husband and I... we didn't get approved on our gene app."

"Really?" He furrowed his eyebrows and consulted his tablet. "There is nothing here about a failed gene app."

"But the baby..."

Doctor Gupta smiled and shrugged. "It's noted in your chart now. You and I both know the law. Pregnancy tests are a standard part of admission process. Additionally, this will likely flag your chart for review by one of the national agencies. My personal opinion is that genetic applications are detestable. I hope you can carry your baby to term, but that is not likely."

Jennifer sighed. "Yes, I know."

⚔

She wanted to leave the hospital that day and even tried to get out of bed. The attempt to leave failed. The act of sitting up alone brought waves of pain and nausea, with sweat beading on her skin. Nurse Chalfant caught her on the third attempt.

"You can't leave!" the nurse said. "Not for at least another day. Not until the doctor says it's okay."

Jennifer gave up. Even if she managed to get out of bed she wouldn't get far. She resigned herself to watching the news on the OLED wall panel on the far side of the room. Jennifer wished she had her tablet with her but that wouldn't be prudent. But where was her tablet? She had it with her in the car accident. Was it with her personal effects? Did Matt have it? Was it confiscated by the police or still with the car in some salvage lot across town?

Jennifer asked about her items when Nurse Chalfant returned. "My purse, tablet and clothes... are they here?"

"Let me see," Nurse Chalfant said. She opened a drawer on the dresser in the room. The nurse stuck both hands in the drawer. "Your clothes are here. They are ruined. Sorry. And here is your purse with your tablet and iGlasses inside."

"May I have my tablet?"

"Bored with the news?"

Jennifer smiled. "A bit."

"Here you go. If you get a headache put the tablet down."

"Okay."

Jennifer powered up the tablet and went through the login. The tablet appeared normal with the green pi symbol in the lower corner. She wanted to log in and read the forums so badly but it wouldn't be prudent. For one thing, she didn't want any of the doctors or staff to catch anything she browsed by accidental shoulder surfing. For another, she suspected that the hospital had security protocols that monitored network traffic. She chose to play the popular puzzle game Blue Aquarium instead.

⋏

Jennifer didn't get out that day or the next. Doctor Gupta didn't feel comfortable with her progress. When Matt came by in the evening he told her the gossip from the office. Actively interested in the happenings of the Party headquarters in the past, she now found the gossip to be tiresome and mundane. Matt had naively put the troubles from the past two months behind him.

While telling a story about someone who got caught cheating on her husband, Jennifer interrupted him. "Have you given any thought about the baby?"

Caught in mid-sentence his mouth hung open in an "O". "What do you mean?"

"The baby? Have you thought about it?"

"What is there to think about? We're not approved for the gene app. That means we have to get an abortion?"

We? She would get the abortion. He wouldn't be affected at all. "What if we could have the baby?"

Matt shook his head. "No, no, no. The last thing we need is more trouble with the Party. We can't take a chance. It might be a Class-C kid."

"I am Class-C now!"

"In your citizenship status. Not based on genetics. You know that is different."

"Besides, we don't know if the baby will be a Class C! Doctor Gupta thinks the gene app process is barbaric."

Despite being the only ones in the room Matt whipped his head around conspiratorially, as if caught in the act of sabotage. "Doctor Gupta can think what he likes. He's lucky he hasn't been detained yet!"

Now it was Jennifer's turn to admonish him. "You know there's a short-age of doctors. There are not enough of them to go around."

"We should get it aborted anyway. Why risk the trouble?"

He meant trouble for him. Things at the office had been rough but not nearly as rough as her experience. He still thought of his political career. Orson Baker's star didn't shine as brightly. It wasn't clear if Matt was get-ting dragged down with Baker or if Matt was doing the dragging. Jennifer suspected it had started with Baker's dinner party, followed by Matt's trouble-some wife.

"I'll talk to the doctor," Matt said.

"No! Don't! I will talk to the doctor." A new headache slowly throbbed to life.

"It's not just your decision to make!"

"Nor is it yours," she snapped. She took a breath and said, "Let's see what our options are first before we make any hasty decisions."

∧

After visiting hours Jennifer toyed with her tablet and caught up on the news. Only the light of the OLED wall and an overhead lamp by the bed lit the darkened room. Another thwarted attack by Coalition forces had occurred on the Texas front. Again, America always defended their ground but the front lines had receded north. Regardless of what the news said, the broad-casters painted a rosy picture. She desperately wanted to log into the Valley Forge forums.

Engrossed in the tablet she registered much too late that a visitor had quietly slipped into the room. Even though the room was warm Jennifer's blood chilled and her heart sank in her chest. With his long black overcoat Chief Inspector Jennings blended with the shadows in the dark. He stepped forward into what little light the overhead lamp cast throughout the room. His blue eyes glittered brightly despite the shadow covering his face. He re-moved his dress hat somewhat ceremoniously and placed it on the dresser. He set his briefcase on the floor so that he could remove his overcoat. Carefully, he hung the overcoat on a hook fastened to the door. As he pulled a chair from the other side of the room the legs squealed on the linoleum floor until he brought it by her bedside. "Chief Inspector," she acknowledged weakly.

"Missus Hanson," Jennings said with a cold smile. He sat down on the chair, opened the briefcase and pulled out his tablet. "I hope that you are recovering nicely?"

"I am. Thank you." *Thank you?* It was the last thing she wanted to say to him, but social niceties had been ingrained in her since childhood.

"After your accident last week I thought a follow up visit was in order."

Her heart beat like a jackhammer. More questions? "Chief Inspector, have I done something wrong?"

"I am afraid so."

Did he know about the tablet? The Valley Forge group? The tablet lay beside her on the bed opposite from the Chief Inspector. "I haven't done anything."

"Missus Hanson, we know that isn't true. Confess now and we'll spare you another visit to Golden Gate Canyon."

Confess? He was baiting her into blurting out anything to save herself from further torture. How many other people had he caught with open-ended questions like this? An open admission about guilt wouldn't help anything. As far as the National Police and the world was concerned she was innocent. "Can you tell me what it is that you think I've done? I'm sure it's a misunderstanding."

He tapped a stylus on his tablet. Tick-tick-tick. "You are pregnant."

She whooshed out a sigh of relief at which Chief Inspector Jennings narrowed his eyes. "Oh, is that all?" she asked.

"Is that all? It is an unauthorized pregnancy. You were supposed to report this to your doctor immediately."

"Chief Inspector I assure you that this was as much of a surprise to my husband and me as it is to you. We have been discussing this with the doctors and staff here."

"I will have a discussion with the staff here. You will not leave this hospital until this pregnancy is terminated."

"Of course, Chief Inspector." Any plan of carrying the baby to full term died.

"Why did you miss your visit with the obstetrician?"

"I assure you it was an oversight. What with the protective custody and the suspension at the school isn't it fair to say that I have been distracted?"

"I will allow that." The scowl on his faced showed that he didn't want to allow that but some shred of rationality in the back of his mind had to allow for the possibility that she told him the truth. "And now for the other matter." He waited for her to answer him.

He was fishing for her to confess to a crime. She didn't rise to the bait. "What other matter is that, Chief Inspector?"

He stared at her unblinking with his ice blue eyes. Finally he turned the tablet off and stuck the stylus in the slot. "We'll save that matter for another day." Were his cheeks flushed pink with embarrassment? Jennifer couldn't tell.

He quickly donned his overcoat and put his hat back on. "I will instruct the staff to terminate the pregnancy as soon as possible." He didn't wait for a response and rushed quickly out the door.

⚔

After the Chief Inspector left she called Matt. "I received another visit from the Chief Inspector."

"This late at night?"

"Yes, he was concerned about the pregnancy." Jennifer hoped Matt could figure out that the communications were being monitored. She didn't want him to reveal that they had discussed other possibilities.

"Did you tell him that we didn't plan this? That we were being monitored by a state obstetrician?"

"Yes, I told him. I told him that with everything going on it slipped our minds."

"That's the truth. We didn't plan for a baby at all. What else did he say?"

"That the pregnancy would be terminated before we left here."

"Of course. We expected that would happen."

Jennifer was relieved that Matt was savvy enough to stay with the script as well as the assumption that everything they did and said was being monitored. But did he sound relieved as well? She couldn't help but hate him for it. He still held to the dream that life would get back to normal. Didn't he see that the harassment from the National Police would never end?

She sighed. "Of course. Listen, I'm pretty tired. I'm going to sleep now."

"Okay, honey. I love you."

"Love you," she said, but she didn't particularly feel it at that moment.

⋏

Jennifer received her breakfast promptly at seven-thirty. Oatmeal, again, but this time someone had drizzled honey and sliced a banana on top. Jennifer scooped the banana slices first then picked out the clumps of oatmeal that glistened with honey.

As she finished her breakfast a new nurse she hadn't met before walked into the room, a young short Hispanic woman; pretty, with big eyes and pouty lips. The name on her tag Rodriguez. "I'm Laura," she said cheerfully.

"Please to meet you," Jennifer replied.

"Let's see..." The nurse consulted her tablet. "You have a procedure scheduled later this morning. At ten o'clock. Did anyone tell you about this?"

"No, but I expected it." She suppressed a sigh.

Nurse Rodriguez sensed Jennifer's apprehension. She rubbed Jennifer's arm and shoulder with sympathy. "Are you okay?"

No, she wasn't okay. She had never done this before and, quite frankly, had never given it much thought. Abortions were something that always happened to other people. People who simply had no control over their lives and much less remorse or, more likely, those people who came from the lower classes. But not her. This shouldn't be happening to her. Here she was getting ready to join the ranks of those women who had somehow become stigmatized by doing this. She still wanted to keep the baby despite the legal risks. "I guess I'll be okay," she said resignedly.

"It's hard," Maria said softly.

"Have you...?"

"Yes, twice now. It's not that I intentionally try to get pregnant. Sometimes the drugs don't take. That's why we get pregnant." Tears welled in the young nurse's eye but she smiled anyway. "I promise you, it will be okay."

"Thank you." Laura did a poor job of convincing her. Maybe she meant by "okay" that you somehow come to terms with what happened afterwards. Coming to terms with trauma was something she was getting accustomed to lately.

CHAPTER 10

After the procedure, Jennifer was wheeled back to her room early in the afternoon. She found her lunch covered with a steel lid waiting for her. Gingerly she stepped up from the wheelchair and climbed into the bed. Nurse Rodriguez pushed the wheeled tray with the waiting lunch toward the bed and pulled the lid back with a smile and a bit of flourish. "Oh, you got one of the good ones."

The tangy tomato scent of marinara filled the room. "What is it?"

"Cheese ravioli." It was accompanied with a small side salad and creamy ranch dressing, along with a soft buttery garlic bread stick on the side of the plate. "And you get to finish it with this." Nurse Rodriguez presented a pre-packaged cup of gelato, the Hershey brand, which was rare these days. The VIP hospital did have its perks.

"This is almost a feast." People were discouraged from deserts and pastas these days.

"You're in a Party hospital so that means you get Party privileges. But eat the ravioli. I promise it's good."

The cheery nurse left Jennifer to her lunch. Jennifer didn't feel like she had much of an appetite and forked one of the raviolis warily. She popped it in the mouth and chewed. It was surprisingly delicious and her belly rumbled appreciatively in anticipation of more. Despite her perceived lack of appetite she found herself voracious and enjoyed her meal. Most of what she had eaten here had been bland but this lunch would rival some of Denver's best Italian restaurants. Even the pre-packaged gelato.

She savored the last spooned scoop of gelato in her mouth when her eyelids grew heavy. Maybe the abortion procedure had made her tired or it could have been the emotional weight of the procedure itself. Jennifer couldn't shake the feeling that she just lost a vital part of herself and it filled her with melancholy. Regardless, she was tired felt the urge to sleep so she succumbed to it.

Sometime late in the afternoon she woke up to find Matt sitting on the couch under the window. "Shouldn't you be at work?"

"I got a call from the doctor."

"About what?"

"Maybe you should hear it from him." He grinned as he grabbed the call button. A minute later Nurse Rodriguez popped her head inside the door. "She's awake," Matt told her. The nurse popped back out.

"Am I getting out?" Jennifer asked.

"He'll tell you." But his smile gave away the surprise.

Doctor Gupta came into the room soon after. "There she is. How are you feeling?"

"A little tired but my head doesn't hurt."

"I think you are fine. In fact, I think you are well enough to go home. You might be tired for the next day or two, but I think that has more to do with today's procedure than your accident. Go home, take as many naps as you need and we can take those stitches out in a few days. Or, like I said, you can have your doctor do that. You are free to go." He grinned at her.

"Really?"

"Yes, really. Go home already." His good cheer brightened her mood a bit.

Fortunately, Matt had brought a change of clothes in one of her gym bags. Jennifer dressed quickly into a pair of jeans and a sweater. The tan wool knit cap included covered her scarred and injured head. She quickly checked her purse to see if anything was missing. The National Police worried her.

They could have gone through her purse anytime. Seeing that everything appeared to be in order, she stuffed the tablet and purse in the gym bag.

She was ready to toss the bag over her shoulder when Matt snatched it from her. "I will take that," he said with a smile. She smiled in return. Jennifer had always appreciated those small moments of kindness from her husband.

When they reached the hospital lobby he told her to wait while he fetched the SUV. Ten minutes later he pulled up to the front door. She only recognized it as their vehicle because Matt sat behind the wheel. Two other black Chrysler Patriots waited in the circular drive in front of the lobby entrance.

On the drive back home she asked, "My car?"

"Totaled. I'm sorry. We're going to have to get you a new car."

"I loved that car." It was expensive to drive and maintain. There were no more BMW imports so replacement parts had to be fabricated on a printer or scavenged from salvage yards. Gasoline was scarce; in a society where only electric cars existed and very few of them at that, she had always appreciated the uniqueness of the little blue roadster.

Relieved to be back home again Jennifer reflected on her homecoming as she drew a hot bath. As the tub filled she poured herself a glass of wine. The doctor was right about the stitches. They itched maddeningly and she found herself tempted to scratch. She took a sip of wine and checked her reflection in the mirror. The bruises from the interrogation at Golden Gate Canyon had faded to a light brown but now she had this four-inch stitched gash on the left side of her shaved skull. The laceration was above the raw scar from where the chief inspector had cut her forehead. Jennifer frowned at her reflection. She was a walking horror show again.

She took off her white terry cloth robe and stepped into the tub. Almost immediately the hot water leached away the aches in her muscles and bones. Jennifer was truly alone at bath time and could take time to pause, reflect and analyze the things going on in her life. Now she needed to see through that more than ever.

The suspension of her job had been almost the last vestige of her former life taken away from her. Over the last several weeks the Party had taken away her identity and turned her into something else. First the questions and then the beatings. After the beatings came the downgrade of her citizenship and the loss of her job. Matt was merely inconvenienced by things at work and everything that happened to her.

So what happens next? Sure, she spent nearly a week in a Party hospital. She was surprised that they had admitted her at all. It had seemed that the loss of her privileges to shop at Stigman's would naturally extend to the hospital. But she also knew the bureaucracies moved glacially slow as they crushed everything in their path. Maybe stripping away her privileges hadn't entirely worked its way through the system yet. Matt seemed to think that their way of life could go back to normal, but Jennifer had her doubts. She thought that whatever digital file the National Police had on her was far too large for her to continue unnoticed. The best she could hope for was frequent follow up visits by chief inspector Jennings and constant surveillance. She had to make Matt realize that they would be ground up into pebbles the way the omnipresent glacier chewed through boulders. There was still more they could lose. They could lose the house. They could lose the bank accounts. They could lose their stocks. They could even be thrown into Golden Gate Canyon together or someplace worse like Fargo.

Maggie had recognized what could happen before she made her escape. Now Jennifer experienced the same thing. If only she could convince her husband. *I can go without him!* She pushed the thought away as soon as it presented itself. Despite all that had happened she still felt like she loved her husband. Things would be so much worse for him if she left without him. The National Police would beat him to death. He had to be convinced to go.

She made a resolve to dig deeper in Valley Forge and find Diablo05.

⅄

How do you broach the subject of escape with someone who suspects you might be an agent for the National Police? Jennifer found herself in a quandary. She wanted to log into the Valley Forge sub forums and announce her intention to escape. Who could she trust? Did the members of Valley Forge even trust each other? It seemed like they did. Even their arguments about comic books, movies and old TV shows seem to have a thread of camaraderie throughout.

She had toyed with the idea of broaching the subject with Matt, but she was afraid of him either rejecting it outright or somehow managing to tell the wrong person at his office. Even though he was her husband she had her doubts about his trustworthiness. He seemed so eager to cling to a life that pulled further away from their reach. Besides, since Jennifer no longer worked she had a lot of free time now. She needed to give herself something to do.

Even though she wanted to go for a run the doctor had told her no exercise for fear of ripping the stitches out. After a shower she plopped herself on the white leather couch in front of the fireplace. She wanted to pour herself a glass of wine but it was well before noon and she suppressed the temptation. Once the tablet powered up she touched the green pi icon in the black square.

The tablet booted into the Valley Forge forum shell. She did a member search for his user name. The search yielded up one hit - Diablo05.

"Here goes nothing," she said. She clicked on his name, which gave her the option to send a private message.

> Hi!
>
> You don't know me but you helped out some friends of mine recently. She told me to find you if I should need your help. I am sure you remember her. She had a colorful tattoo on her arm. Please let me know what I need to do for you to help me on this.
>
> BaldPretty

She reviewed those four sentences once, then a second time and finally a third. It was a plea for help meant to be ambiguous in case the message fell into the wrong hands. With a sigh she hit "send".

With nothing else to do she decided to check out the movie forum. There she found a raunchy comedy about three men searching for the fourth missing man after a drunken night of debauchery. Just before the movie ended the forum inbox popped up a message notification.

She paused the movie and opened the message immediately.

BaldPretty,
Give me your name and social.
Diablo05

It was blunt. He wanted her personal information to research her further. On a forum that cherished the privacy of its individual members this was a brazen request. Jennifer reminded herself that this was the same man that had helped Maggie out of the country. Without further hesitation she typed in her name and social security number and sent the reply. With that done she watched the rest of the movie then started watching the sequel.

Jennifer thought that he would reply almost immediately but he didn't. Even by the time Matt got home the inbox remained empty. Matt surprised her with a couple of salmon filets. "The deputy director gave them to me," he explained. She put the tablet away and started on dinner. She was excited to have something with meat for a change, even if it was fish. They also had some chardonnay they could enjoy along with the salmon.

After dinner Jennifer curled up on the couch with her husband (and her third glass of wine). They watched a little bit of news. Matt took the news in without comment but Jennifer found herself debating the facts in her head. Was the news genuine or not? Everything deserved to be questioned these days. After that Matt streamed a new action vid about a spy for the National Police. She indulged him and watched the movie as well. It was disconcerting that, given all their recent history with the National Police, he was engrossed with this movie and the premise of the American spy as the hero. Still, the movie took both their minds off the recent events. The last of the bruises had faded away but she still had that stitched laceration on her scalp under the close cropped fuzz of blonde hair. A part of her considered that recent laceration as an unofficial addition to what she suffered under the National Police.

Jennifer watched the movie with her husband and with no comment about the subject matter. She had considered finishing off the wine, but wanted to keep her head clear in the morning. The over indulgence of wine of late concerned her.

After the movie concluded they went to bed. Jennifer was tempted to peek at her tablet but she didn't want to arouse any suspicion with her husband. She changed into her shorts and a T-shirt and he was in just his underwear.

Jennifer turned off the light on her side of the bed and he turned off his. A minute passed in the dark and his hand found her hip and then slid up her T-shirt. She hesitated as her breath hitched in her chest. He was making an effort and she turned toward him. His breath was hot on her neck and he lifted the T-shirt up, then finally over her head. Matt casually tossed it over her side of the bed then mashed himself on her. His right hand snaked down her abdomen and then into her underwear.

"Wait," she said.

Matt's muscles tensed up as his erection softened against her thigh. "Wait?"

"It's too soon. After the procedure, I mean."

Jennifer didn't know how Matt would react. Their love life typically centered on him and what he wanted. After a minute of silence his warm hand caressed her cheek. "You're right, honey. It is too soon. I love you, babe, and I don't want to see you get hurt." He kissed her gently on the lips. A peck, then longer with more passion. His erection came back to life. Jennifer kissed him back earnestly while the same aching, longing for physical love, rippled through her. Matt drew away, trembling, leaving her with a peck on the lips again. "I love you so much. I know you need your rest." He offered another playful peck on the lips and then he turned away to sleep.

Jennifer lay awake in the dark for almost an hour, the longing for physical love burning within her, before she finally fell asleep.

The next morning Jennifer took the time to cut up some melon and pine-apple. She mixed in some berries then finally stirred in some yogurt. By the standards of the Hanson household this was a lavish breakfast. She thought this little token of appreciation would serve as her gratitude for his efforts during the previous evening. The fresh coffee added the perfect punctuation to her gratitude.

He strode in the kitchen with his suit jacket in hand. That, in turn, was tossed casually over the back on of an empty chair. "Mmmm," he said as he sat down. "This is too much."

Jennifer smiled. "Enjoy."

He took a sip of the coffee and made an appreciative hum again. It was suited to his taste, lots of cream and lots of sugar. "We still have plenty of this?"

"For now, but you will have to come with me to do the shopping from now on."

"Don't worry, honey. We'll get that fixed soon enough."

Jennifer smiled and nodded. She didn't think her status would be fixed, but she suspected he needed to think he could make the change.

"What are you going to do today?" he asked.

"Maybe I can come up with some kind of project. I have a lot of time on my hands now." She couldn't wait for him to leave so that she could check her tablet.

"That's good! Keep yourself busy and take your mind off things." Matt grinned and put on his overcoat.

As he backed out of the driveway in the Patriot she rushed to get her tablet. Jennifer picked it up and logged into Valley Forge forum. She had to wait a couple of minutes while the Valley Forge site refreshed. The first thing she received was the new message notification. She tapped the glass to open the message.

It was from him. It said -

There is a bar on Havana Street. It's called Sharkey's, a quarter of a mile north of the exit off 70. Meet me there at 1:00 today.

How would she get there? She had no transportation and couldn't summon a cab. As soon as the dent recorded the transaction her destination would be registered to any prying eyes. The bus? Denver had a fine transit system but she had never taken the bus in her life. It was the only plan she could think of. She flipped the tablet out of the Valley Forge then back to its normal mode and found the bus schedule immediately. Surprisingly it had a route mapping feature that could tell you exactly how to get to your destination. She clicked on some routes, told the tablet where she needed to go and what time she needed to arrive. The app even helpfully suggested what time she should leave the house to walk to the bus stop. She needed to be out the door by 11:05.

The Denver skyline was overcast and the weather app on iGlasses told her the temperature was a brisk 24 degrees. Jennifer didn't look forward to any lengthy walks outside in the cold. She studied the itinerary the metro bus site suggested to make sure she knew what routes and transfers to take. Jennifer bundled herself with a thick beige overcoat, hiking boots, a set of thick wool gloves and a knitted black cap. It was about as much preparation she could make. She tossed the tablet in her purse and set off for the bus stop outside her subdivision. Upon opening the door a gust slammed through the entrance and the chill cut through her. The freezing wind discouraged her, almost enough to make her give up and go back inside. Even though the stinging tears welled in her eyes she moved forward anyway.

The wind lightened up a bit making the walk to the bus stop a bit easier. The walk took her a half a mile to get out of the neighborhood and another hundred yards down the boulevard to get to the stop. At the stop she didn't wait long. The steel grey, blue and red bus trundled down the street. The electronic placard showed that it was the 117 she needed.

Jennifer climbed aboard the bus and scanned her dent above the fair box. It gave an agreeable chime and she made her way through the coach. The bus pumped out some pleasant heat through the vents. Despite some signs of wear that comes with age, the bus appeared to be clean and even fairly full for this time of day, with a mix of people who were white, black and brown. It was more colorful than any of the usual dinner parties she attended. Jennifer took a seat midway down the aisle.

Little conversation occurred on the bus. She caught a few people stealing glances at her. Wearing her expensive clothing she stood apart from the rest of the passengers with their work clothes and uniforms. But no one said anything to her or each another. They simply looked ahead or out the window for their next stop.

The 117 took her to the depot downtown where she needed to wait twenty minutes for the 356 to depart. Jennifer got lost briefly at the depot but finally got her bearings and found the bus waiting on the other side of the station. She was on time to board the 356. From there the ride was only twenty minutes to Cason Street.

As the 356 approached the bus stop Jennifer reached up and pulled the signal cord as she had seen other passengers do. She stood, made sure her coat was buttoned and put on her mittens. The electric engine of the bus gave a whine as it slowed down, coupled with the soft squeal of brakes that would need to be replaced soon. The door opened with a pneumatic hiss and she stepped off in the bitter freezing cold again.

This was the tricky part of her plan. Jennifer deliberately got off the bus two stops early, in case the National Police had monitored her movements. She had to scan her dent to get on the bus but it never recorded when she got off. For all they knew she could still be riding for another hour. She still had another half-mile walk to find Sharkey's Bar.

Jennifer immediately regretted her decision to come here. If a city could have cancer this would be it. She thought Owen's computer shop was in a bad neighborhood, but this new area proved to be worse. Jennifer was surrounded by a bleak collection of old red brick buildings and a landscape of cracked parking lots. The buckles and ripples of the asphalt gave it the appearance of a frozen black undulating sea. The windows and doors of the buildings were covered with weathered plywood that had long turned grey. Even the graffiti appeared to be the aged hieroglyphics of a long dead civilization. Jennifer checked the iGlasses for directions and headed south.

There were scant signs of life as well. At first she heard a dog barking from far away but its yips had trailed off as she got closer to Sharkey's. She thought she would get to the bar unmolested until she saw the two black kids on the corner. They had the collars of their bright blue jackets zipped in tight around their mouths and wore baseball hats. Her path would take her past them. Jennifer put her head down and kept walking straight.

After she passed them one of them shouted out, "Hey lady! You got a dollar?"

She had to stifle a startled laugh. *No one carries money any more. It's all tied to our dents.* Despite having a little cash in her purse she knew they were looking for a reason to stop her. "I've got nothing. I gotta go. In a hurry." She never lost pace.

"Lady, this is our street. If you want to walk you gotta pay!"

She turned and stole a glance at them. They were twenty feet behind her. They had stopped and faced her with hungry stares in their eyes. Jennifer broke out into a run. She needed to find the bar quickly. It wouldn't be long before the kids overtook her. As Jennifer ran with her purse jiggling beside her, she frantically scanned the addresses on the doors she passed. It wasn't far but with the adrenaline and excitement she couldn't focus. Finally, she reached a door on her right hand side; it was painted bright blue and featured a cartoon shark chomping on a lit cigar. The number on the door matched the address. She slammed against it, then grasped the knob quickly to let herself in.

At first she thought she had stumbled into a cave. She waited as her eyes adjusted to the dark windowless room. An oppressive wave of heat blasted at her from overhead. It was like no bar she had ever seen before. Neon beer signs and mirrors hung on the walls. On the left side stood the bar itself, wooden, scraped and scarred from years of abuse. Lined up in front were metal bar stools with cracked black vinyl seats mended with silvery duct tape. On the right side of the bar, booths were lined against the wall. In the back sat an aged pool table covered in stained velvet. A jukebox in the back behind the pool table played music with a low volume.

The sea of faces that turned toward her was mostly black with a couple of brown. Most were indifferent, some curious while other faces vacillated between suspicion and hostility. She wanted to turn around and bolt away but she remembered what waited her outside. The bartender, an elderly black man with a shock of white hair, gaped at her while holding his bar towel. "You can't wear those here," he said.

"What?"

"Those glasses. We don't wear those here. If you want to stay, you need to take them off."

She quickly took them off her head and folded them into her purse. The door exploded open behind her, bathing the interior with bright sunlight and causing the patrons to wince again. Jennifer twirled around and faced the two kids that had just chased her. She didn't know if they wanted to drag her out into the street but they seemed more anxious about being inside than she did.

"This lady owes us money," the kid on the right exclaimed.

Jennifer turned around and faced the bar. She felt the need to defend herself. "No, I don't!"

"This lady don't owe you a damn thing," the bartender said. "You assholes know better than to be in here. Now get out before you get your asses whipped."

Jennifer turned around to face her pursuers. They looked at each other questioningly then slowly retreated. The way they scowled indicated they would be waiting for her to leave. She hitched a sigh a relief and the door closed, but the anxiety crept back in as she faced the bar. The patrons' faces told her she was about as welcome here as they would be at District Leader Baker's house for a Party function. It wasn't so much hostility as suspicion. Still, this was where Diablo05 asked for her to meet and this was where she was. She did what anyone would - she took a seat at the bar.

"What it'll be, Miss?" the bartender asked.

"Do you have any wines?"

He gave a wry grin. "No Cabs or Chardonnays. Our selection isn't that sophisticated. We have a decent selection of beers, and a collection of bourbon, gins, rums and vodkas. None of that fancy flavored stuff, but good anyway."

"I'll have a Coors Light."

He nodded and pulled a frozen pint glass from the cooler, then drew a beer from the tap. The frosty beer was placed on a cardboard Coors Light coaster in front of her. The excitement from the brief chase had parched her throat and the ice cold beer was refreshingly crisp and pleasant.

"How much will it be?" she asked.

"Seven dollars, miss."

"Do you take cash?" She didn't want her dent attached to this transaction but she realized that wearing her iGlasses may have already given away her movements.

"Yes, ma'am. We like cash here."

She laid out a ten dollar bill on the bar.

"What brings you to this part of town, Miss?" the bartender asked.

"I am supposed to meet somebody."

"Probably that son of a bitch over there." The bartender nodded toward the back booth by the pool table.

Jennifer took a careful glance in that direction. A muscular black man sat in the booth, wearing black jeans and a black thermal long sleeve. A single thin strand of gold circled his neck. He wasn't bulky like a bodybuilder rather lithe like a professional athlete. He had a black goatee and closely shaved head. His eyes were piercing and for a moment Jennifer wondered if she had made a mistake.

"James," the man in the booth called out. "Are you telling stories about me again?"

"What stories?" the bartender replied. "You're here on a Tuesday afternoon. She's here. I know this is part of your business."

Jennifer examined the room to see if the other half dozen patrons took notice of the conversation. Sure enough all eyes remained on her. She wondered if an informant was in their midst.

The man in booth waved to Jennifer. "Bring your beer over here and join me."

Jennifer picked up her icy beer and did as he commanded. As she sat down she noted that she had her back to the rest of the room while he faced the front door. He stared at her and said nothing.

"You're black," she said.

"Have been all my life," he said wryly. "Not used to seeing black faces?"

Jennifer blushed. "I'm sorry. I didn't mean to be rude." She took a nervous sip of her beer and stammered out, "Are you Diablo05?"

"You can call me Anthony." He extended his right hand over the table. "I presume you're Jennifer Hanson."

Despite her nervousness she shook his hand. It was warm. The social niceties still stayed with her as she told him, "Pleased to meet you."

"Likewise."

Jennifer paused for a moment then asked. "What do you need to know?"

"I'll talk first. After I'm done, you help me fill in the blanks. You probably got my screen name from Maggie. I saw her little over a month ago. You and her have been friends since childhood and are in the same spot of trouble with the Party. Once the Party locks in on you it rarely lets go. Given the haircut and faded bruises you stayed with them recently at Golden Gate Canyon. Since then you seem to have run afoul of them, one way or another. Most recently your file was flagged for an unauthorized pregnancy. Your husband's shining star with the Party is now tarnished and the District Leader is going to unhitch that star from his wagon for fear of being dragged down with the Hanson couple. You decided to get out whether that be to Mexico City or Havana or maybe Europe. Am I right so far?"

"You learned all this from my name and social security number?"

"Yeah."

"How? Personal information is supposed to be restricted."

"It is. All you need to a skeleton key."

"A skeleton key?"

"It's a hack that lets me go anywhere in the network. I cross referenced everything with your name and social, then built my own report overnight. None of the pics reflect your current haircut."

She rubbed her bristly head. "So can you get us out?"

"For a price. My fee is fifty thousand for the two of you. You will transfer all of your assets to an escrow account that I will set up. I will keep the fifty and then set up the rest in an offshore account that you can access once you are outside of America."

Jennifer thought it over. They had at least seventy thousand in the savings account. All told once their assets were liquefied they would have about half million altogether. Minus the fifty thousand, of course. "Okay, we have a deal. When do we get started?"

"I can contact you through the message board. There is a complication though. My route to New Orleans might be compromised."

"Because of my interrogation at Golden Gate?"

Anthony nodded. "I saw the interrogation video. How did you manage to not give them my screen name?"

"I'm so sorry!" Jennifer blurted out.

Anthony waved his hand and dismissed the apology. "No need to apologize. Even the most battle hardened war vets will talk under torture. I'm just amazed that you held out long enough to convince that son of a bitch that you didn't know anything."

Jennifer blushed. "I really forgot your screen name. I couldn't remember it. After I was released I just pictured myself with Maggie at the funeral and your name came back to me."

"Well, I'll check my underground railroad and make sure it isn't compromised. Everything should be set up in a couple of weeks, give or take a day or two. Now a question for you. Is Mister Hanson in agreement with this plan?"

"I haven't told him yet. I can tell him tonight."

"Wait till tomorrow. He's going to have a little more incentive to leave the country."

Jennifer's heart pounded with excitement. "You learned something with your skeleton key?"

"I wasn't kidding about the Deputy District Leader giving your husband the boot. The memo came down from the national level yesterday. The appointment's scheduled at ten o'clock. Your husband should be home by lunch and more receptive to your plan. Even then he might not be fully on board with this. Some people can see the danger in front of them. Others? Well, they still want to hold onto their old lives. If he says no do you plan to go without him?"

"He won't say no."

"Okay." His voiced lacked conviction. He didn't think Matt would follow through but he wasn't going to argue with her.

"Is there anything else?" she asked.

"Oh, there's a whole lot more but we don't need to worry about that right now. All that will come later."

"Can I ask a favor?"

He grinned. "Favors already? And we just met."

"I was chased in here by two kids. Could you walk me back to the bus stop?"

"In this weather? I'll do you one better. I'll drive you home."

Jennifer's eyes widened with surprise.

"What?" Anthony asked. "You didn't think a black man could afford a car?"

"I didn't mean -"

"It's all right. Everybody has expectations of people, some good and some bad. You just gotta set your prejudices aside."

Jennifer blushed again. "I really didn't mean to offend you."

"Who's offended? Come on. We'll go out the back." He slid out of the booth. "James, I'm going to take this young lady home. I'll holla at you later."

"Go on then," the bartender said. "We'll see you again, I'm sure."

She followed as Anthony went toward the back of the bar through the door that had a sign tacked on that read "Restrooms". He held the door open and waited expectantly for her. She followed into a dark hallway lit only by red neon beer signs. A musty scent of spilled beer mixed with the harsh disinfectant from bathrooms flooded her nostrils. Anthony kept on toward the end of the hallway to a door with a frosted glass window at the end. The sign on the door said "Emergency Exit - Alarm Will Sound". But he pushed the bar on the door and exited the building with no alarm following them. The harsh Denver cold hit Jennifer in the face as she walked into a narrow alley with a blue dumpster. On the other side of the dumpster a black car waited with its nose pointed away from the alley. She recognized an antique as old as her crashed BMW convertible. "What is it?" she asked.

Anthony grinned. "That's my Bettie. A Ford Mustang GT from the late aughties." With the glossy black paint and black wheels it appeared in mint condition. The windows were tinted to almost black.

"That doesn't look inconspicuous."

"When people see it they think some old white guy is driving. Only rich people can afford to drive these. I can drive around your neighborhood and nobody is going to think any different."

Jennifer grinned. "Well, take me home."

As she climbed into the passenger side and she noted the inside of the car was as pretty as the outside with red leather interior and brushed aluminum paneling. "This is a beautiful car," she said.

"You hear that Bettie? The pretty lady likes you." Jennifer blushed at the compliment.

Anthony started up the car and the engine responded with a throaty growl. He turned the wheel and took them from one alley to another until he hit the street. Then he opened up the throttle.

The acceleration took Jennifer by surprise. Most cars were electric or had H cells. The Chrysler Patriot puttered along with the rest of them. Her sporty BMW would have outpaced them all, but her old car was a snail compared to Anthony's. "It's really fast," she said. "Do you worry about the police?"

"No, not as many police on the roads these days. When only rich people can afford cars there aren't many cars on the road. No cars, no police."

"Not even the electronic surveillance?" She referred to the automated police systems that surveyed the roads. They had been installed decades earlier to monitor traffic violations.

"They're still out there but I have an electronics package in the truck that scrambles my signal. This car is an empty spot in the data feeds. Most electronic eyes can't see me. When they do, they think I'm some old rich white guy."

He was right about the streets and roads. Built in a time when they needed to handle the traffic capacity of thousands, they were now only sparsely populated with buses and delivery trucks. The only other vehicles were the customary Chrysler Patriots that everyone in the Party seemed to adore.

Anthony took the Mustang on the expressway and the old muscle car soared. She couldn't help but find the speed exhilarating. "How fast are we going?"

"About eighty-five."

It wasn't long before he had her back home. As he pulled into her driveway he said, "Remember, wait till tomorrow to talk about this with your husband. Keep an eye on Valley Forge for updates and instructions. There's something else you should know. Your house is almost entirely covered in eyes and ears."

"Eyes and ears?"

"Your house is planted with bugs. Your car, too. Mobile micro cameras with audio mostly. That chief inspector hasn't let go yet. He's waiting to catch you on something. I've seen the feeds."

"How long have they been there?"

"They were installed while you were at Golden Gate Canyon."

"So no talking in the car or house?"

"The bathroom is the best place. Get the shower all steamy. The steam messes up the micro cameras. The bad guys on the other side directing them usually stay clear of the bathroom. Those things are tiny but they're about ten grand a pop."

"Okay. Do I need to worry about using my tablet?"

"Use headphones. The eyes in them are not that great. From their vantage point they just see you on your tablet. But the ears on them are pretty good, so if you're watching a movie put your headphones on. If you hear a fly buzzing around you it's one of them.

"Thank you for helping us, Anthony." With a low grumble the Mustang prowled away from the Hanson house back to Denver.

CHAPTER 11

Jennifer couldn't keep her eye away from the digital clock on the tablet. Matt had left work that day thinking that everything was normal. In a few minutes he would be terminated from his position. He would still be a member of the Freedom Party but not with the same rank and privilege that he was accustomed to. It was 9:47.

She tried to distract herself with games and forum topics on Valley Forge but her eyes were always drawn to that clock in the corner of the display. When the clock read ten o'clock she thought, *well, it's happening now.* She expected him to be home sometime after that, probably around lunchtime.

Jennifer thought it would be a nice gesture to prepare lunch along with some chilled wine. She decided on a spicy bean soup in a crock-pot. It could be ready by lunchtime and would keep if Matt ran a little late. Before noon the house filled with the rich savory scent of beans and spices.

After the time passed one o'clock, she sent him a text message - *Where are you?* He didn't respond. She thought he would come home straight-away after being fired.

She reasoned that maybe he wasn't let go today. He could be busy at work right now. Anthony might be wrong about the whole thing. Jennifer relaxed a little and got caught up on the news through the Valley Forge site. It was the only news she trusted these days.

Late that afternoon she was startled when the tablet started warbling. The caller ID said it was the Denver Police Department. She hesitated, wondering if she would be summoned for more questioning. It kept warbling impatiently. The tablet would keep ringing until she dismissed the call or she answered. The tablet could see her through the optical sensor and knew she was there. Even if she set it down the Party at the other end of the line would know she dismissed the call. She debated answering this call for nearly a full minute before tapping on the answer icon.

A face appeared on the glass, a young cop with a chiseled jaw and close-cropped blond hair. "Mrs. Jennifer Hanson?" He had to already know who she was. The question was merely a courtesy.

"Yes," she replied.

"I am afraid your husband has been arrested."

"What?" Was he now being detained and questioned by Chief Inspector Jennings? Her heart raced in her chest. "What for?"

"Drunk and disorderly. We'll keep him overnight and you can post bail in the morning. We'll send a follow up email with further instructions." Then his image simply disappeared from the screen.

Jennifer realized what Matt had done. After he got let go from his position he decided to soak himself in bourbon somewhere. *Did he get into a bar fight?* The officer didn't say anything about assault charges. *He most likely made an ass of himself.*

Her tablet gave her the "new mail" chime. She tapped the icon and opened it, an email with more information regarding her husband's arrest. There was a precinct listed as well as instructions for bail. Apparently he wasn't required to go before a judge but she couldn't bail him out until morning.

Jennifer sighed. There was nothing more she could do at the moment. She poured herself a glass of red wine and ladled out some of the bean soup in a bowl. Jennifer ate the soup without any enthusiasm while reading more forum posts on Valley Forge. She still had no email from Anthony either, but she didn't expect to hear from him so soon.

Jennifer drank only a couple of glasses of wine before falling asleep while watching an old movie on her tablet. This one was about a teenage girl in some barbaric survival contest.

Jennifer woke up refreshed early in the morning. She called an auto-cab to pick her up at 7:30. The auto-cab got her to the police precinct with plenty of time to spare. A chill ran up her spine as she stood in front of the squat grey building on a cold crisp Denver morning. It wasn't quite like the police headquarters building where she had been detained the previous month but it was close enough to make her uneasy. The Denver police wore black uniforms similar to that of their National Police brethren. Other policemen stood at guard posts flanking the entrance to the station. With much hesitation Jennifer steeled her nerve and took that first step towards the door.

The door opened automatically for her and announced her name as she entered. It had the familiarity of worn linoleum tiles and flickering fluorescent lights. A desk sergeant looked up from behind his booth encased in wire and safety glass. "Over here, Mrs. Hanson," he said over the lobby intercom.

She stepped up to the desk sergeant's glass cage. "I'm here for my husband."

"Yes, ma'am." Even though the dent scanner announced her as she walked in the precinct she wondered if the desk sergeant had her dossier to review but he didn't appear to care. "Your husband's in holding filling out forms. Bail is set at five thousand dollars. I just need to scan your dent to confirm the payment?" He nodded to the dent scanner to the right of the window. She scanned her dent and it gave an agreeable chime.

After that she waited a few extra minutes. The door buzzed open, letting through various cops from the back. Finally her husband was buzzed through. She stood to greet him then stopped. He had dried vomit covering the white button down shirt he had left the house with the day before.

"I'm so glad to see you," Matt said. He smelled sour.

"I'm so happy to be here too." She made no effort to hide her sarcasm. "You won't mind if I forego the hug?"

He looked down at his disheveled blue suit. "No," he mumbled. "I understand."

"So where's the car?"

It turned out he'd spent the afternoon getting sloshed at a trendy bar near the Party headquarters called Hoppers. Jennifer had been there a couple of times. High end drinks commanding top dollar prices in a dispassionate atmosphere of neon and steel. As they climbed into the auto cab she checked her tablet to see how much money Matt had spent the night before. It was over five hundred dollars. She decided to let it go.

They spent the cab ride in silence. In this day where people were discouraged from speaking with one another it was just prudent to keep quiet. The ride to Hoppers was short anyway.

She spotted their Patriot immediately and told the auto-cab to pull over. After climbing into the SUV Matt set the auto drive and leaned the driver's seat back. Jennifer sat in the passenger seat and stared at the bustling city as people headed for their workdays.

When the SUV parked itself Matt sat up and rubbed his temples. "This headache is killing me," he said. "You haven't asked me anything. You don't even seem mad."

"I'm not mad. A little disappointed, but not mad."

"I lost my job."

"I know."

"You know? I guess Deputy District Leader Carson called you?"

"Nope."

"How then?"

She gave a sly grin. "I'll tell you later. First you need to clean up and get some sleep."

After taking a long shower Matt ate some crusty bread with some olive oil. It was a large loaf of bread but Jennifer had never seen such a voracious appetite in him before. Twenty minutes of chewing punctuated with gulps of water. At one point his chewing slowed as he turned green and sweaty. He dashed to the bathroom, retched everything up, rinsed his mouth and came back to the table in the breakfast nook. Even with a hangover working him over like something fierce, he seemed compelled to fill his belly with bread. He finished the entire loaf of bread, then a third of a fresh loaf. Matt's pallor was much better and the sweating stopped when he finished his meal. During this exercise of exorcising his hangover demons Jennifer watched passively while sipping on a glass of cranberry juice.

"You should sleep now," she said.

He rubbed the back of his neck. "Yeah, the drunk tank is not what I would call comfortable."

"Sleep. We can talk more when you wake up."

"You're still quiet. That worries me."

She couldn't help but giggle. "It's fine, really. You lost your job yesterday and have probably fallen out of favor of the Party. I can understand you being a little upset and making bad decisions. Now go to sleep."

He pushed himself away from the table warily, as if backing away from a predator, then headed upstairs to the bedroom. She cleaned up the table and went back to her tablet. There was still no email from Anthony. Jennifer settled in with some old TV programming from the 90s.

Early afternoon she got a message chime from Valley Forge site. It was a file from Anthony with the message, "Show him this." Jennifer scanned the file quickly and smiled.

Matt slept through the rest of the morning and well into the afternoon. The sun was setting when she heard him stirring around upstairs. Jennifer heard the shower start so she set the tablet aside and worked on dinner.

The spicy bean soup would be a little thicker but okay after being re-heated. Jennifer started some rice on the stove top. She had the ingredients to make Spanish rice. With a salad and some thick sliced tofu for the grill it should make a fine dinner. Jennifer opened up a fresh bottle of Cab while she cooked. After pouring a glass of wine she turned on some music. *Vivaldi would be nice,* she decided. She turned up the volume so that it filled the house.

He came downstairs wearing jeans and a Broncos T-shirt. "A little loud, don't you think?"

Jennifer smiled. "We need it loud."

"Why?" He started to reach for her tablet to change the volume.

Jennifer grabbed the tablet before he could reach it. "They could be listening."

"They?" he snorted. "You've watched too many spy movies."

She drew him close and spoke directly in his ear softly but not in a whisper. "They are listening. Just humor me on this."

"Okay." She could feel the warmth of his breath in her ear. "Tell me what's on your mind."

She pulled away from him. "Dinner first! Then we'll talk."

"You're driving me crazy with all this cloak and dagger stuff."

She was filled with the excitement of her new plan. Matt eyed her warily as Jennifer wolfed down her dinner. She washed away the last remnants of grilled tofu with her wine. "Come on, hurry up."

"Slow down. Let me finish."

She poured herself another glass of wine and grinned at him.

"I haven't seen you this excited in a while or in this good of a mood." It took him another five minutes to finish off his plate.

He started to take his plate to the kitchen but Jennifer stopped him. "Never mind that. Just come with me." She grabbed her tablet and led him by the hand upstairs.

"Is it going to be that kind of a night?" She could hear the excitement in his voice.

"It might be after we talk." Jennifer had to tug him away from the bedroom and towards the bathroom. She glanced behind her and saw confusion on his face. Jennifer said nothing and simply took him into the bathroom and closed the door. She started the shower on hot and was satisfied after steaming up the room. Jennifer closed the lid to the toilet then gestured for him to sit down.

"More cloak and dagger?" Matt asked.

"It should be safe to talk now."

"Okay, you want to tell me what's on your mind?"

"What if I told there is a way out of this mess?"

"A way out? How?"

"We leave the country like Maggie and Brad did?"

"How do you know they got out?"

"They did." She logged into her tablet then into her user account at Valley Forge. It took her several seconds to get where she wanted. She tapped the attachment to her last message from Anthony. "See for yourself."

She handed him the tablet. A picture of Maggie and Brad on a beach. In the background was the unmistakable spire of the Sapphire Tower in Havana. "It's a fake," Matt said.

Jennifer snatched the tablet out of his hand. "It's not a fake."

"It has to be a fake. There is no way they could make it to Cuba."

"They did and they sent a picture."

"How did they send it to you without the National Police seeing it?"

"I'll get to that. Now do you want to get out of this mess?"

"Not like that! Everyone we know is here."

"Where are they, Matt? Where are all those friends of ours?"

"You know how it is with the Party and our friends. Everyone has to keep their distance from us at the moment. Once this blows over we'll be back in."

"Blows over? This is never going to blow over. We've both lost our jobs. I was in a detention center. We are under constant surveillance."

"We won't be outcasts forever."

"Outcasts? You're worried about being an outcast? I'm worried about being alive next month. They're watching us, Matt!"

"How do you know?"

She went back to her tablet and tapped the second attachment on Anthony's message. After the attachment opened she handed her tablet back to husband. It was the surveillance feed from the previous weekend. Matt was in the living room watching the Broncos game while Jennifer cooked dinner. There were four video windows in all but the bedroom and dining room feeds were empty. At the top a title listed as "Summary Feed 12/15". She waited as he reviewed the feeds passively. "That is the National Police watching us."

Matt smiled. "Honey, this is great!"

"The government is spying on us. What's so great about that?"

"This is our ticket back in! This is good news!"

"What are you talking about? Ticket back in? These are the same people that beat and tortured your wife and you want to kiss their ass?"

"It's not like that. If we can do the Party a favor we can -"

"Tablet lock - Polar Volcano."

The tablet recognized Jennifer's voice and lock command. It gave a harsh buzz and flashed red.

"Give the tablet back to me," Jennifer said.

Matt held the tablet dumbly with his jaw agape. "I don't understand."

"Give me back the tablet. You can't unlock it anyway. You could take it to the National Police and they can unlock it if you want."

Matt still held the tablet in his hand, looking at it then back at her. He weighed the decision of which way to go.

"I hope you are not seriously considering turning in your own wife to the National Police?"

Abruptly, he blinked and handed the tablet to her. "No, of course not. I want us to do this together. I mean, we should take this to the National Police together."

"Matt, all they would do is question us and put us both in Golden Gate Canyon. After they were through with us we would probably be executed. Everyone else we know would be harassed as well."

"Everyone else?"

"The people who helped me plan this. Everyone I met on the way. There is a way out of this. We can get a fresh start outside of the country."

"And lose everything built together?"

"We're going to lose it anyway if we stay. At least if we start fresh somewhere else there's a way we can take some of our stuff with us."

"How long have you worked on this?"

"I guess I got started as soon as I got out of the protective custody center."

"You haven't been doing this alone?"

She shook her head. "No. I found some help."

"Who's been helping you?"

"Why do you want to know? You want to turn these people in?" Jennifer was pissed off. She had found a way out and Matt wanted to throw all that away on the hopes of gaining favor with the Party.

"If I'm going to be a part of this you're going to have to share everything."

"If you want to be a part of this then I need to trust you. I need to know that you're not going to run to the National Police with this as some lost hope for leverage."

He regarded her stonily for a minute. "Okay," he said finally. "Tell me what your plan is."

She went on to explain the plan for several minutes. How she found the computer shop where Owen gave her a hint about the underground site and then she connected with Diablo05. Jennifer didn't let on that she knew Anthony's real name. When it came to details about leaving the country she didn't have much to offer.

"That's it?" Matt asked.

"Some of it is still being worked out, but we can transfer our assets out of the country and take them with us. We can go out the same way Maggie and Brad did. Matt, it's worked before. We already know someone that it's worked with."

"It sounds sketchy."

"Can you give me a better plan?"

"Yeah. Give me the tablet and we take it to the National Police together."

"You can't guarantee our safety."

"You can't guarantee that we can safely get out."

"No, of course not! But sitting around here isn't safe anymore. All of our friends are gone, Matt. We need to leave while we still can."

"Okay, okay." He held up his hands defensively. "Just let me think about it overnight. You're going to have to trust me on this. We are married after all. We're supposed to trust one another?"

"Yeah, Matt, but that trust goes both ways." Before he could respond she reached into the shower and shut the nozzle off. Jennifer didn't offer anything more to say on the subject. She opened the door and walked out. Jennifer had been so sure that her husband would be excited at the solution she came up with. Instead he wanted to turn around and take it back to the Party. *The Party!* With all the trouble she had with the National Police Jennifer was surprised that he wanted to seek refuge with the Party again.

Jennifer went downstairs and poured herself a glass of wine. She curled up on the sofa and activated her tablet. It gave that angry buzz and flashed red at her. She needed to reset the emergency lock. The tablet gave her some helpful nonsense phrases. She went with "galleon reactor" and repeated it to the tablet three times. It would make her say or type the phrase every day for a week to ensure that she memorized it. She didn't know if the Party had access to her tablet. She thought accessing the Valley Forge forum was safe and the rest of her tablet didn't matter as far as the prying eyes of the Party was concerned.

Matt came down a few minutes later. He went to the bar and poured himself a bourbon on the rocks. He plopped down on the opposite end of the sofa. Jennifer stayed focused on her tablet. He sipped his bourbon for a minute before finally turning the news on the OLED wall. She was done talking to him for the night. He needed to figure out what he wanted.

She logged into the Valley Forge forum and checked the news. The real news, not the propaganda that permeated on the net. Coalition forces had made gains in Florida. Their eastern spear had overtaken Jacksonville and the western one had Panama City under siege. In Texas the American counterattack for Austin was thwarted. Neither side had air superiority or control of the seas. Shipping remained relatively unmolested in the Gulf of Mexico. The Coalition had sent a lot of battle groups but had trouble countering the *Enterprise* carrier strike group parked in the middle.

Jennifer was engrossed in the news when a chat window popped up.

Diablo05: how did it go?

BaldPretty: I'm not sure.

Diablo05: not sure? how can you be not sure?

BaldPretty: He started acting stupid. Says this is our way back into the Freedom Party.

Diablo05: he wants to offer up VF as collateral?

BaldPretty: Something like that.

Diablo05: Would you leave without him?

Jennifer paused. Is that something she should consider? Could she leave America without her husband and strike out on her own? The task seemed daunting. All her life she had been surrounded by a support system, whether it was her parents as a kid or Matt and friends through college. The prospect of going through life alone frightened her, but the prospect of dying in Golden Gate Canyon was even worse.

BaldPretty: Yeah, I can leave without him if I need to. But let me give him a chance first.

Diablo05: if he says no he's a security risk. it changes things.

BaldPretty: Can you monitor him?

Diablo05: I already am :)

BaldPretty: Okay, I'll let you know.

She waited to see if he had any more to say but he logged out of the forum. She checked to see if her husband had spied her activity but he simply kept his eyes on the OLED wall. He sipped on his bourbon while the melting ice cubes clinked softly against the side of the glass.

Two glasses of wine was enough to make her sleepy. After announcing she was off to bed she snuggled under the thick down comforter. Despite their efficient house the temperature never seemed to get warm enough for her during the winter. She fell asleep almost immediately and didn't wake up when her husband joined her late in the night.

⋏

In the morning Jennifer woke up before him. With nothing better to do he could sleep in as long as he wanted. She pulled an onion bagel out of the fridge and spread some soy butter on it after she toasted it. Jennifer was back at her tablet again, taking sips of coffee along with her bagel. She heard her husband rise at ten o'clock and run the shower. When he came downstairs she asked, "You want some breakfast?"

"What do we have?"

"I had a bagel. There's some oatmeal if you want it. How about some leftover grapes?"

"You know what I miss? Scrambled eggs and bacon."

Jennifer smiled. "I think the last time I saw scrambled eggs was in that diner on Haslet Avenue."

"And bacon?"

"Not since the last time we went skiing."

"At least we have futter." Futter was the nickname of the faux butter product that had replaced real butter and margarine. It was supposed to be healthy and cholesterol free, but it had embarrassing side effects for a few people.

"Fresh out of futter," Jennifer said. She didn't care too much for it.

Matt made no move to make himself breakfast or pour a cup of coffee. He simply stared at her with anxiety in his eyes. Jennifer had seen this before. He had made a decision and would go over his options one last time. Finally he said, "Let's do it."

She arched an eyebrow. "Let's talk about it another time."

He walked around the counter and held her close. A light peck on the lips and he whispered in her ear. "Let's leave. But you and your friend have to include me on the planning."

She turned toward his ear. "Okay, I love you," she whispered.

"I love you, too."

"So, neither one of us have jobs. It's the middle of the work week. What should we do today?"

"Let's go to Breckinridge. Stay a couple of days. Get in some skiing. You're right, we have nothing else to do without jobs."

Jennifer beamed at him. "Can we get in?"

"I think we still have access. They haven't taken it away from me yet."

"Okay. Let's go."

She changed into some jeans and a tan sweater. He changed into the same, except opting for a long sleeve gray thermal shirt. She packed a bag for each of them while he rummaged around the garage for their ski equipment.

When they first got married both of them had been avid skiers. It was hard not to ski with so many good locations close by. Not long after marriage their jobs and lives with the Party had bogged them down so they went less. Jennifer went online and booked a room for them at the lodge. While their personal lives were still a wreck their membership status with the Party afforded them the luxury of a priority booking.

Matt came back into the kitchen as she finished booking the room. "Do you think we can still fit in our bibs?"

"How long has it been? Two years?"

"I think three."

"We are both pretty active."

"Not as much as we once were."

"Well, even if our bibs are too tight we can always buy more at one of the shops while we're there."

"That's true. Are you ready?"

"Let's go."

Matt wrangled both of their bags into the back of the Patriot. Jennifer smiled as she climbed into the passenger seat and waited. She hadn't felt this good in a while. They were doing something together without something from work or the Party demanding their attention. Maybe this would bring Matt back to her and out of the arms of the Party. He abruptly disturbed her thoughts as he opened the driver's side door and climbed in. She shivered as she was assailed by a gust of frigid air that followed him.

They worked their way out of Denver to the roads that would take them into the mountains. As the road wound through the canyons and passes, Jennifer spied little hamlets nestled into openings along the way. She had seen these before. It amounted to maybe a half dozen streets and a couple dozen buildings, most of which were houses. Coming from the city she had often wondered how people could live up here. To her it seemed like such a desolate existence yet they were still better off than her since they were far from the center of the Party.

Despite the fact that the Patriot was toasty warm a shiver ran through her. Climbing up the roads to the ski resort reminded her of the ride that had taken her to Golden Gate Canyon Protective Custody Center. This road with the rocks and ridges rising high on either side were identical. She dismissed the thought almost immediately. Jennifer didn't want to the let that thought ruin a good memory that she and Matt were creating right now.

The signs along the road warned that the way may be impassible due to winter weather but she didn't worry. Winter had barely started and the Party did a good job of keeping the passes clear to one of their beloved winter retreats. They reached the small town of Breckinridge before two o'clock and wound their way through the town to find the lodge. She smiled to herself. Jennifer loved that this town itself remained isolated from the Party and the world at large.

When they reached the lodge the valet took their car and the bellman had a cart that could carry their luggage and equipment. Jennifer stepped out of the Patriot and watched the skiers slalom their way down the mountain. Despite being mid-week the weather was perfect and the slopes were good.

The bellman followed them into the lodge with their luggage, as it bustled with activity. Jennifer tensed with apprehension. She recognized many faces from Party events and even a few that knew her. She wondered how much any of them knew about Matt and her. She reflexively tried to rub her head but her hand came into contact with wool knit cap on top. The anxiety hitched in her chest slowly started to subside. Everyone here seemed to be content to enjoy their own experience at the ski lodge.

Matt was able to get them checked in successfully. The bellman dutifully followed them to their cozy and large suite with the luggage. Jennifer had been to the lodge before and it was an extravagant expense, but she didn't want to question it with Matt. Jennifer reckoned that his generosity was related more to their predicament than any need for extravagance. Maybe he needed to blow off some steam and process what had happened to him? Regardless she found this escape to be more pleasurable than the dreary existence that they came from.

After they had settled into the room Matt asked, "What do you want to do?"

"Well," Jennifer said. "It's a sunny day and the slopes are perfect. There's still a good couple of hours of daylight. We should ski!"

Jennifer and Matt unpacked and put things away quickly. They changed into their ski bibs and took their skis and poles to the lobby. Jennifer felt a small sense of victory that her old ski clothes still fit. From there it was a straight shout out of the lodge and to the slopes. As they walked together to the lift Jennifer reflected on the familiarity, despite having been absent for several years.

"Which trail do you want to do?" Matt asked.

"Let's do the Spruce."

Matt's eyebrows shot up. "You want to start with the hard stuff right away?"

She grinned. "Neither one of us are going to live forever."

They worked their way to the crowded lift. Despite the long line people queued through pretty quickly. They took their spots on the lift as well and Jennifer felt the anxiety rise and hammer through her chest. The ski run always had this effect on her. It simultaneously frightened and made her feel alive.

They climbed ever higher above the snow. "Are you ready?" Matt asked. He had the same gleam of anxiety and excitement in his eye.

Her knotted stomach filled with butterflies told her no. Instead of answering she simply nodded. The lift came to the top and she worked her way on the skis toward the descent. If Matt had one last thing to say, she didn't hear him. Jennifer didn't want a moment's hesitation. She simply wanted to go down. With the descent looming before her she launched off the slope.

Jennifer immediately felt exhilarated at the descent and simultaneously alarmed of losing control. She needed to remember the forgotten skill of navigating the way down. The cold air bit her face where her skin was exposed to the elements. Despite the cold she could feel sweat trickle down her back. It was an odd feeling, given everything that had happened to her recently. The air whooshed by her and the skis hissed as they slashed through the snow.

Halfway down the slope Jennifer experienced a moment she thought she would lose control. It felt as if the skis wanted to go an opposite direction toward the darkened tree line. If she veered that way she was bound to knock herself out on one of them. She didn't want to go that way, so she adjusted her hips, bent her knees deeper and increased her speed to the waiting lodge below. Her knees wobbled and protested but she willed herself to keep them straight. Finally she came to the bottom of the run where the slope became shallow and she could slow her descent. She angled the skis and came to a halt. Jennifer turned around to see if Matt had followed.

A full minute passed before he appeared on the shallow of the slope. He spotted her and angled toward where she waited. When he came to a halt he said, "You came down that slope like a maniac!"

She winked at him. "Might as well make the most of it while we're here. Ready to go again?"

His eyes arched in surprise again. She was challenging him but she didn't care. At this moment, on this slope, she wanted them to feel alive. He had that same mix of anxiety and excitement while he worked out a decision. Finally he grinned and said, "Let's go."

They did the run again and then a third time. By the time the last run ended the sun was setting on the horizon and the slopes were clearing out. Jennifer's muscles felt warm and slightly achy. Since they had not done this in years she would be sore by midnight. She didn't care. It had been so long since she felt this alive.

They took off their skis and carried their gear into the lodge. Although the lodge was only three stories in height the elevator taking them to the top floor was extremely slow. It was also tight as other skiers piled in.

When they got to their room they stripped off their boots and bibs. With the sunny day she had worked up a sweat and their clothes were soaked through. Jennifer still didn't care. "Showers and dinner?" she asked.

"Yeah, sounds great. You go first."

Jennifer peeled off her sweat soaked clothes and laid them across chairs and the sofa in their room so they could dry out. She even took off her underwear and laid them out as well. As she pulled out her toiletry bag from her luggage she caught her husband staring at her. She blushed.

"You're as beautiful as the day I married you," he said. "I love you."

She grinned at him. "You're just saying that because I'm sweaty and naked."

"Maybe. Hurry up and shower already. Are you as famished as I am?"

"More!" She gave her hips an extra wiggle as she strode to the bathroom.

He jumped in the shower after she did. She lounged around their suite in the lodge's complimentary bathrobe. While Matt showered she powered up her tablet to see if Anthony had provided any updates. He had sent her a private message.

Working out the details of the plan. Should be pretty easy. Will update when I have more. Looking for a departure date of 12/27. Enjoy the skiing.

That was little over a week away. Jennifer typed a quick response saying that Matt wanted to be involved and that they should meet soon. She also wondered how he knew she was skiing but she quickly dismissed it. If the Party watched her then he watched them. He had to be monitoring their surveillance reports, which meant the surveillance had followed them to Breckinridge.

They had dinner in the main open area of the lodge. In the center stood a bar in a rough semicircle along the back with the kitchen entrance and exit doors flanking either side. Two pretty bartenders, a blonde and a brunette, worked behind the bar with huge layers of shelves lit from the bottom and stocked with bottles of liquor behind them. If the rest of the country suffered from any shortages it certainly wasn't apparent here. Atop of the bar shelves stood a large stuffed moose whose glassy eyes spied on the guests from above. As with most other ski lodges Jennifer had visited, this one had the same rustic appeal of walls made of wooden logs as well as chairs fashioned out of a shop somewhere in Amish country. The only thing missing was the fireplace but the lodge was cozily warm without it.

Since the restaurant was full Jennifer feared there would be a wait but the hostess showed them to a table near one of the windows that had a view of the slopes. She glanced out the window. Despite the dusk with only a hint of purple sky on the horizon, a few die-hard skiers slalomed down the lit slopes.

Jennifer rubbed her hand over her scalp, self-conscious that everyone in the lodge would recognize that she had been released from a detention center, but no one seemed to pay any attention to her. She relaxed a little. Her experience at the grocery store only a few weeks ago remained a fresh memory. Her bruises had long faded and her hair had grown out long enough to be called fashionably short. She still had the raw red scar from the car accident but she could tell the truth about that one.

A waitress approached their table and offered to take their drink orders. Jennifer opted for a cab and a glass of ice water. Her husband did the same.

"Still thirsty from this afternoon?" she asked.

"Yeah. Those slopes take a lot out of you."

He eagerly gulped down the water as she did, before starting on the wine. For good measure they both ordered additional glasses of water.

Jennifer read the menu. "There's steak on the menu!"

"You're kidding," Matt said.

"The filet is two hundred dollars."

"Are you worried about the money?"

"No. Are you?"

"We're here to have a good time. Let's make the most of it."

The menu featured many cuts of steak on the menu as well as seafood, chicken and hamburgers. Jennifer couldn't remember the last time she had seen steak on a menu. When the waitress returned Jennifer opted for the petite filet with grilled shrimp while her husband went with the porterhouse.

They drank their wine and water while waiting for their meals. Jennifer couldn't remember the last time they had a prolonged moment of intimacy such as this. For the first time in several years her husband was really into her. The moment was only interrupted when the server arrived with their meals.

Jennifer savored the first bite of her filet. Saliva rushed into her mouth and she tasted the char from the grill and the salty blood of medium rare. Neither of them spoke while they methodically worked through their meal. After the steak, dessert was offered. Jennifer chose the chocolate cheesecake while her husband went with the peach cobbler and vanilla ice cream. They both took turns taking bites from each other's plates.

After the meal Jennifer ordered another glass of wine and leaned back with satisfaction. "I haven't tasted anything that good in years."

"Weird, isn't it?"

"What's weird?"

"I remember you telling me about that lady you met at Golden Gate."

"Miriam?"

"Yeah, her. She's a cattle farmer, right?"

"She called herself a rancher."

"Well, we are always hearing how everyone needs to eat healthy and meats are bad for you. But here we are eating steak. We're not exporting all of it."

He was right. Here they were at a ski lodge enjoying luxury that they could only afford because they were members of the Party. Hamburgers weren't served anywhere anymore, much less steak. Occasionally you could find a restaurant that served chicken. She hadn't seen a Mexican restaurant in years. Jennifer wondered idly if such a thing as vegetarian Mexican fare existed.

"Does it make you wonder if the Party is being completely honest with you?" she asked. She looked around but didn't see anyone paying attention to them.

He shrugged. "Maybe."

The waitress interrupted their conversation to pour more wine for them, which they happily accepted. She sipped on the Cabernet and didn't want to spoil the moment or mood.

Matt leaned forward. "So about your friend..."

"Can we talk about it when we get back to Denver? I just want to forget about everything that is going on and enjoy the next couple of days."

He smiled. "Sure. Let's have fun. We can save the conversation for home."

"Do you remember the first time you took me skiing?"

Matt laughed. "Yeah, when we were in college. We'd been going out for three months?"

"Two."

"And I thought I could impress you by teaching you how to ski."

"And who taught who that day?"

"You did!"

Early in their relationship Matt had bragged about being such an avid skier. He kept had saying he would teach her. She had played coy with him and let him brag. He didn't know that she had already skied with her family for years. Even as he had placed his hands on her hips and told her how to turn she had kept the game up. For their first run he had picked one of the easier trails and she had surprised him with the speed she launched herself down the slope. He never caught her. When he reached the bottom of the slope she was waiting for him. He was less than a minute behind but she had laughed when he asked if she'd done it before.

Jennifer was pleased that they talked about the old times. Older memories were more fun to reminisce about than recent ones. They could talk about serious things in their bathroom at home. They finished their glass of wine and had another.

The restaurant had cleared out but the bar area remained busy when they left at nine. They went past the elevator and found the stairwell leading to their wing of the lodge. The stairs were quicker and easier than the elevator when they weren't encumbered with gear. Matt grabbed her by the shoulders and twisted her around after they reached the second floor landing. Jennifer was shocked by the abruptness of the move and surprised when he kissed her earnestly. She felt herself go into the moment and kissed him back. He pushed her back gently until her back was against the wall, then kissed her deeply some more. Minutes passed as they embraced on the stair landing, their moment interrupted as the first floor stairwell door crashed open as people entered laughing.

Matt pulled away but looked deeply into her eyes. He grinned and said, "Let's go back to the room." Without waiting for the answer he grabbed her by the hand and led her up to the third floor before the party crashers below could catch up to them. Matt barely had time to scan his dent on the door before they both crashed into the room. Their frenetic pace continued as Jennifer wrapped her arms around him and kept kissing him. He kissed her back and guided her through the suite to the king sized bed. Jennifer fell back against the bed with Matt on top of her. He pushed up her cream colored sweater and grabbed her breasts through the lacy bra. Matt mashed his face on the left breast then the right, gently biting the nipple through the fabric. She pushed him away for a moment, only to finish taking off her sweater and unhooking her bra. After those were out of the way he went back to sucking her nipples and massaging her breasts. She untucked the shirt he wore out of his pants and pulled it off him, then reached for his belt buckle. It stubbornly refused to unbuckle so he stopped what he was doing to help her. With the belt unbuckled she unbuttoned his pants. While she was undressing him, he undressed her. From his vantage point undoing her jeans was easier for him than it was for her. They frantically kicked off their pants, maneuvering around each other without losing their speed or urgency. With their clothing off he climbed atop her again and eased his erection forward. It found her hole and slid easily into her.

Now that he had found it, he started thrusting in a rhythm. She moved her hips along with his to stay with the motion. Jennifer leaned her head back and closed her eyes. She could feel the warmth permeating through her body as she was building to climax. As Matt began to thrust faster the pangs of disappointment arose. He was about to come quickly while she was nowhere near her conclusion. He shuddered while on top of her, then slowed down the stride at a pace that was long and deep. Her vagina ached to let go with the climax, but with his change of pace the warm feelings started to subside. He still kissed her passionately while slowly thrusting. Normally he would finish and turn over but the long deep kisses kept her warm. Almost imperceptibly she felt his stride quicken. Soon they joined together in the rhythm again, him moving with her. This time around she climaxed first. The orgasm racked her body while Matt continued his thrusting. She couldn't keep pace any more but he seemed not to notice. She rode her orgasm out then was pleasantly surprised when she came a second time. After her second orgasm Matt continued thrusting vigorously. Finally, he shuddered and let a moan escape as he climaxed for a second time.

Panting, he rolled off her this time and lay on his back. "Wow," he said.

Jennifer laughed. "We haven't gotten that crazy in a while."

Matt laughed with her. "We're going to be so sore tomorrow."

She leaned over and kissed him on the cheek. "It's okay. It was worth it."

"Are you up for doing it again?"

Jennifer laughed. Her thighs and glutes were singing to her with aches. "Not tonight. I think we truly wore ourselves out today. And tonight."

He smiled. "Yeah, you're probably right. I love you."

"I love you, too."

Jennifer rolled over and laid her head on his chest. She felt and listened to the beat of his heart. Soon she was fast asleep.

⋏

She woke in the middle of the night freezing cold with the lights of the room still on. Thankfully their curtains had been drawn during their sexual escapades. Jennifer used the bathroom quickly and gulped down two glasses of water to stave off any hangover that might rudely wake her in the morning. She put her panties back on and dug through her luggage until she found a T-shirt. After turning off the lights she climbed into bed under the covers.

Jennifer woke up before Matt did. Their suite featured a coffee maker that she turned on while she showered. When Jennifer finished showering she found Matt already awake.

"Should we order room service?" she asked. "Or eat downstairs?"

"Let's eat in the lodge and get some more skiing in."

The ski lodge featured a large breakfast buffet. Jennifer couldn't remember the last time she had seen so much food. Even when they were here years ago the fare had been more modest. Today the buffet featured pans heaped with sausages, bacon, pancakes and hash browns. One table overflowed with donuts, Danishes and other pastries. A chef stood at a station and made omelets and eggs benedict to order.

"I see bacon," Matt said. "Let's eat."

They had to wait fifteen minutes for a table to open up before they could hit the buffet. Jennifer had the chef make her a western omelet. She piled bacon from the buffet next to her omelet and grabbed a second plate. She couldn't help but feel uneasy with the excess. As she cut her steaming omelet with the knife, she regarded the other diners around the room. Many of the faces here were the same she had seen the night before. Everyone enjoyed the excesses that the Party had to offer them. She took another bite of her omelet, followed with a bite of crispy delicious bacon. Being here at the ski lodge took her away from her problems back in Denver. She realized that even though these were considered "good Party people", they had escaped their own problems with their visit to the ski lodge. The battlefronts in Texas and Florida were not going well. Did they subconsciously know that? She didn't want to dwell on it for too long. Jennifer was as guilty of escaping her problems as everyone else in the room.

Jennifer and Matt spent the rest of the day skiing. Her muscles were achy and sore but after going down one of the trails she started to loosen up. The sun filled the sky and made the slopes reflect brilliantly white. She found herself taking off her jacket and stuffing into a locker when they took a break for a late lunch.

They skied until dusk and found themselves famished for another big dinner. After dinner they made passionate love again in their room.

The pattern repeated on Friday, the last day of their trip - a huge breakfast, a day of skiing, dinner and lovemaking. During dinner that evening Jennifer mused that she hadn't felt the need to be glued to her tablet. She remained fully aware that they needed to escape but for now she enjoyed this time together with her husband. It was almost the same as when they had first started dating,

CHAPTER 12

When they checked out on Saturday the skies had turned grey. A lot of skiers reveled at the prospect of fresh powder but Matt wanted to get back down to Denver before the big snowstorm hit. He said Denver would be covered by the evening. With the help of the bellman they loaded up the Patriot.

Jennifer checked her tablet as soon as they were on their way. A message from Anthony said they needed to meet on Monday at the food court in the mall near their house. She guessed that the plan would be revealed then. Now that they left the ski lodge she went back into her intense escape mode. She didn't tell Matt. He would start peppering her with questions that she couldn't answer because the car was bugged.

The snow started to fall when Matt pulled the Patriot into the garage. Buoyed by the trip they returned from kept him in a generous mood. He told her to go inside while he took care of the equipment. Jennifer wrestled the luggage upstairs and started unpacking. While she unpacked the luggage she spied him heading for the bathroom. She dropped the jeans she had pulled from the suitcase and followed him.

Startled, Matt said, "I think I can handle this myself." He had unbuttoned his pants.

"He wants to meet."

"Oh. When?"

"Monday at twelve-thirty. He wants us to meet in the food court at the mall."

"The mall? Won't we be surrounded by people?"

"I think that's the point. More people, more noise and less conspicuous. He says we need to buy our lunches first then join him."

"Okay. Monday then."

With that Jennifer left him to his personal business.

⚓

One criticism that Jennifer could never level against the Party was that of their efficiency in regards to utilities and infrastructure. The Party apparatus along with the Denver Department of Transportation had kept the roads clear despite the winter storm that raged for a couple of days. By Monday morning all roads were traversable right down to the streets in their neighborhood. She remembered talking about it with Maggie and her dad at a dinner party one time. David made the remark about "keeping the trains running on time". It hadn't made sense and she'd asked him to clarify. He had muttered something about the efficiency of dictatorships.

Matt had to pull out the old gas powered snow blower to clear the driveway. It took him awhile to get it working and Jennifer was afraid they might miss their meeting with Anthony, but Matt got the driveway cleared in little time.

The mall was only fifteen minutes away from their house catered to the local wealthy neighborhoods as well as the middle class. Since a lot of the wealthy visited this mall, there were more cars in the parking lot then Jennifer was accustomed to seeing elsewhere. Still, the mall was built in a time when nearly everyone had a car. The vast parking lot remained largely empty. Matt parked the Patriot near the south entrance that was closest to the food court. Buses routinely pulled up and dropped passengers off near the same entrance.

"This place is busy," Matt said.

"Two days before Christmas, a lot of shopping to get done."

They hurried through the frigid air to be greeted by a blast of heat as soon as they entered the mall. The massive food court was up one level past the AMC Theater. Jennifer started looking for Anthony as soon as she entered the food court. She spotted him at a table near the center of the court.

He wore blue jeans and a black T-shirt with a black leather jacket. In other areas around town a black man would be conspicuous but there were enough brown and black faces here that he blended in.

"Come on," Jennifer said. "Let's get something to eat."

A few minutes later they joined him with trays of McSalads. "You're black," Matt said.

"He has been for years," Jennifer said. "Matt, just sit down before you draw attention."

Matt furrowed his eyebrows crossly at her for a moment. She was afraid that he might cause a scene, but he bit his lip and sat down only after Jennifer took a seat.

Jennifer felt an introduction was in order. "Anthony, this is my husband Matt. Matt, this is Anthony."

"Please to meet you," Anthony said.

"Are you sure you know what you're doing?" Matt hissed.

"Yes. I'm quite experienced at this." Despite Matt's fluster Anthony kept calm.

"Matt, let's hear him out first before judging," Jennifer said. She turned to Anthony. "Is it safe to talk here?"

He nodded. "Yes, too many people and too much activity. They didn't know we were meeting here so they couldn't prepare. You have two tails here who are watching you. I know who they are but I can't pick them out in the crowd without being obvious. There's too much noise for a parabolic mic to pick up our conversation as long as we keep our voices down." He maintained eye contact with Matt who only glared back at him.

Jennifer wanted to keep this conversation focused. "So what's the plan then?"

"First, you plan another ski trip this weekend."

"You told him about our trip," Matt said.

"I didn't tell him about our trip. He figured out everything from the surveillance."

"It's true," Anthony said. "You had a group of three agents that were quickly dispatched to Breckinridge. They had enough time to wire the room with audio and video. The mics worked fine but fortunately the video was black and white and grainy."

Jennifer felt herself blush. The National Police had witnessed their sex acts in that suite.

"You watched us?" Matt asked.

"No. I watched them, the agents. I don't believe in watching people having sex."

Jennifer wanted to get back on track. "So we're going skiing again this weekend."

"You're going to look like you're skiing this weekend. We're really going to get you out of here, but the ski trip will buy us some time. You're going to have about an hour, maybe an hour and a half, before they figure out what's going on."

"So where are we going then?"

"You're going to the Union Pacific rail yard just off Fox Street. Don't go through the main entrance, use the Fox Street entrance. Pull past the administration building and go into the container yard. That's where we'll make the switch."

"Switch?" Matt asked.

"Yes, we'll leave your Patriot behind. It's crawling with bugs and the GPS will beam the location to the National Police. If there's time the Patriot can be sold and cannibalized for parts. The proceeds will be added to your assets. I have a guy that can do this and he charges a big fee, but it's better than getting impounded by the police and letting it rot in a lot."

"About the assets?" Jennifer asked.

"Yeah, a pre-programmed executable will take care of that. Your assets will be moving at the same time the National Police think you're going back to Breckinridge. The timing is tricky on this. Too soon and they'll know what you're up. Too late and the assets are frozen then seized."

"Do you need our account codes?"

"I already have them. Remember, what the Party knows about you I know about you. A sniffer is assigned to you. Sniffers are good at what they do."

"What's a sniffer?" Matt asked.

"It describes a couple of things. One is a program that examines data looking for something specific, most of the time it searches for login and passwords. But a sniffer is slang for a cyber-agent that is assigned to monitor people like you two. Everyone has a digital identity. Wherever you go your dent gets scanned, a hundred times a day. A sniffer can learn every detail of your life and create a profile of you based on your digital identity alone."

"And our dents?"

"We will fix that when the time comes. I don't want to get into the details of that yet."

"Okay," Jennifer said. "We get to the rail yard then what? Are we leaving by rail?"

"No, but it might throw off the agents watching you. I think it'll buy you some time. At the rail yard you'll leave your vehicle behind. I'll direct you to where you need to go. And I'll be the one waiting to get you out."

"You'll take us to New Orleans."

"Not right away. I'll take you to a safe house where you'll lie low for a few days. Anytime someone 'disappears' from the Party they spend about three days looking for them, then they widen their search. After three days we'll head down to New Orleans to another safe house. It'll give us a couple of days in case there are issues with the ship I arranged."

"What are the risks?"

Anthony sighed. "Normally low. I've done this consistently for the last five years, but you and your husband have particularly drawn the wrath of the Party. They're watching you closely. This Inspector Jennings doesn't want to let things go."

"Chief Inspector," Jennifer said, and felt embarrassed at the correction.

"Is this dangerous?" Matt asked.

"Like I said, there's risk. There are always going to be risks. But I've done this before and I know what I'm doing."

"How do we know you won't rip us off?"

"Matt!" Jennifer hissed.

Anthony furrowed his brow. "You want references? There are not exactly references in this line of business. I already got your friends out of here. They don't seem to be complaining."

"Look, I didn't mean anything by it." Jennifer couldn't tell if he was genuinely apologetic or embarrassed.

Anthony waved off the apology. "I understand. You're stressed. There are a lot of things happening to you all at once. Any more questions?"

Matt remained quiet. Jennifer said, "Thank you for helping us."

"I'll contact you through the forum with additional information. In a few days you'll be out of here." Without saying anything further he stood up with his tray of empty paper plates and left the table. Jennifer followed him with her eyes as he discarded his tray. She wanted to see if anyone particular in the crowd watched him leave. With all of the activity in the food court it was hard to spot if anyone in particular paid attention to him.

"Jesus, are you checking him out?" Matt said.

Jennifer felt herself flush with anger. "I'm looking for the surveillance agents!"

"Oh." He kept quiet after that.

⚓

Jennifer booked the trip to Breckinridge as soon as they got home. She booked it the same way as before. Hopefully the agents watching them wouldn't think anything was going on. When she checked her tablet that night she had a private message waiting for her. Anthony sent her an app to install on her tablet, a navigation app that operated on the same private network that the Valley Forge forum used. It would tell them precisely where to go on the day they left.

Everything seemed to be in order with the exception of Matt. He fretted over every little detail of "the plan". Several times a day he would pull Jennifer into the bathroom for a "few more questions". The only doubts she harbored were the risks already associated with it. She was afraid that Chief Inspector Jennings would somehow find out. That was her biggest fear. Her husband split his worries equally between the plan and his doubts about Anthony.

Christmas Day was uneventful in the Hanson household. If District Leader Baker held another formal party the Hansons weren't invited. Matt checked with some of the work contacts he kept in touch with. They told him there were no social gatherings for Christmas. Jennifer was privately relieved that they weren't invited anywhere. She didn't want Matt to be tempted back into that life. The Hansons stayed home and made dinner for themselves. The recent events since Thanksgiving had dimmed their mood for the holidays. There were no decorations much less a tree with presents underneath.

On the day after Christmas the sky turned slate gray with snow flurries swirling throughout the neighborhood. Jennifer was up well before Matt, watching the snowfall as she sipped on a hot cup of coffee. Matt still slept but it wouldn't be long before he woke up. She didn't want to deal with his anxiety right now. He would have plenty to spare throughout the day. Jennifer wanted this moment to herself before they made their escape. She had finished her coffee when she heard the shower kick on upstairs.

Jennifer rinsed the cup out and set it down on the counter. Matt turned the shower off a few minutes later. She slipped into the steamy bathroom while he toweled himself dry.

"He wants us at the rail yard by ten," she said.

"Okay. We know where that is already."

"Yes, but we're going to follow the route on the navigation app I downloaded. Anthony is guiding us in. Remember, only small talk in the car. It's bugged."

"Right. Bugged. Got it."

She grinned. "Did you save me any hot water?"

He grinned back at her. "Yeah, maybe."

"Well, get dressed and start packing that equipment. After I shower I'll pack our bags."

After Jennifer showered she pulled out the suitcases for her and Matt. She figured they needed enough clothes for four or five days. They could buy new clothes when they reached Cuba. She smiled as she tried to picture Matt in a tropical shirt. Jennifer found a small photo album tucked in a closet. There were few pictures in there, mostly older ones before the age of digital uploads. The album got tucked into her suitcase as well. The suitcases were big and heavy so she had to wrangle them down the stairs one at a time. Jennifer took them out to the Patriot so that Matt could load them.

After the last suitcase was in Matt asked, "You ready?"

Jennifer had butterflies in her stomach. She simply nodded. Jennifer climbed into the Patriot and pulled out her tablet. She tapped the navigation icon and it booted up with the title flashing at the top, "SECURED VIRTUAL INSTANCE". The app had a text box that would let her chat with Anthony. She typed in, *on our way.*

Anthony replied back, *follow the route.* A vibrant green line pointed the way on the freeway with a last minute deviation to the rail yard. Jennifer reasoned that this getaway should be simple. For all intents and purposes they were heading back to the mountains and the only suspicion that should be aroused would be the moment they went off the freeway.

Jennifer mused while staring at the snow swirling on the road before them. Aside from being cold the weather wasn't a worry. The snow appeared more threatening than it actually was. There wasn't any expectation that the snow would stick to the roads.

An incoming message chimed on the tablet; *you are being followed. This was to be expected. Don't panic.*

"I'm excited to get back up to Breckinridge," Jennifer said. "Fresh powder." She wanted whoever tailed them to hear nothing but innocuous chatter. She also didn't want Matt to panic and obsess about a risk out of their control.

"Yeah, me too, babe," he said.

When they were a couple of miles from the exit to the rail yard Jennifer said, "You're going to hate me."

"What?"

"I need to pee."

"Didn't I tell you to use the bathroom before we left?"

"I didn't need to go then! Can you find a convenience store?"

"Okay, okay, next exit."

They had already planned this conversation beforehand. Jennifer hoped that it might buy them a few more minutes before the surveillance team caught on. Matt took the Patriot down the exit ramp. He turned to her for instructions. "Left."

The surveillance team could still track the SUV through GPS. They had only minutes to get to the rail yard and she followed Anthony's direction on the navigation app. "Keep going straight. Take this next right. Then through here."

They came in through an unmanned gate near the administrative offices of the rail yard. The green navigation line on the tablet showed that they had veered past the offices into the yard itself. She pointed to an access road on the right. "Go that way."

The extremely detailed navigation guided them as they wound their way through the maze of freight containers. Jennifer kept calling out lefts and rights. Finally they turned down an alley to find a big rig with a ramp leading into the darkened recesses of a trailer. Anthony and another man stood on either side of the opened doors. Matt hesitated. "Go up," she said.

Holding his pad in his hand Anthony waved them forward. Matt eased the Patriot up the tracks leading into the trailer. The SUV bumped its way up as he pulled forward. Once the back wheels had cleared he cut the engine.

"I guess we go?" Matt asked.

Jennifer didn't answer. Anthony was already up in the trailer with them and pounding the back glass with the palm of his hand. He waved at them urgently to come to him. She opened the door only to slam it against the side of the trailer. It was a tight squeeze but she was able to get out. She saw Matt experiencing the same struggle on his side. Jennifer worked her way between the Patriot and trailer side toward the back.

"We have maybe five minutes," Anthony said. "Leave your iGlasses behind. Matt, leave your tablet here. We don't need it." He pointed to Jennifer. "Give me yours right now. Make sure it's unlocked. And get your luggage."

After she handed the tablet to him he keyed some commands into her tablet, then his own. Then he inspected both tablets for a few seconds before facing them glass to glass. He hopped out of the trailer and set the tablets down together. Anthony pulled a roll of silvery duct tape then taped the tablets together. Jennifer turned and helped Matt struggle with the luggage.

"You brought all that?" Anthony asked.

"Yeah," Matt said. "Clothes for travel."

"Okay, but you have to carry it. We have four minutes but it's a short walk."

Jennifer realized how stupid it was to pack the huge heavy suitcases. The other man with Anthony was a Hispanic truck driver. He was already sliding the ramps under the back of the trailer. Jennifer simply tossed her suitcase off the back of the trailer and let it bounce off the pavement. She hopped off the trailer just as the truck driver slid in the second ramp.

"Three minutes," Anthony announced. The truck driver closed the trailer doors. As the truck driver climbed into the cab Anthony slapped the trailer indicating to the driver that he was free to go.

"Let's go," he said to them.

"What about our car?" Matt asked.

"Questions later. Right now we're running out of time."

He turned and walked between two containers toward the next row without waiting. Jennifer slid the handle out of the suitcase and followed while her rolling suitcase bounced across the pavement. The wind howled between the containers and the biting snow stung at their faces. Anthony went past one row of containers and into another row where a Ford cargo van waited with Fed Ex labeled on the side. It faced the southerly direction where the tractor-trailer had headed off north. He opened the back doors. "Come on. Get in."

Jennifer heaved her heavy suitcase into the van while Matt followed suit. Anthony slammed the doors shut behind them then got into the front. From where Jennifer and Matt sat in the back of the van they had access to Anthony.

"We made it," Matt said.

"We're not out of danger yet," Anthony said. "They're closing in now. We need to get out before they close the yard." He started the van up and it glided whisper quiet through the container yard. Anthony weaved his way through the containers using the heads up navigation on the OLED windshield. They drove through the south gate a couple of minutes later. Anthony took a left and paralleled the southern fence of the rail yard. "We need to get across the river and then we're free."

The seconds dragged as the electric cargo van rolled slowly silent down the street. On this side of the rail yard there was only one street leading away. Jennifer realized that if any police showed up right now they would be trapped between the bridge and the rail yard.

Anthony crossed the bridge and took a right heading south away from the rail yard. They were barely away from the rail yard when three black Suburbans passed them on the opposite side with their red and blue lights flashing. Jennifer's muscles loosened up as the immediate danger seemed to pass.

They headed south for thirty minutes before turning east for another thirty. None of them had anything to say during the ride. Anthony seemed content to drive while Matt simply stared past him through the windshield. Finally, Anthony eased the cargo van into an industrial warehouse district with only a few cars and trucks parked about. The corrugated steel siding on the warehouses had rust creeping up the sides. Anthony drove the van around to the loading dock behind one of the warehouses. He cut the engine to the van and said, "Your new home for the next few days."

"I thought we were leaving the country," Matt said.

"You will in a few days. We have to take care of a few things. First, we need to let the police do their best to find you. Their protocol is to do an intense search for the first seventy-two hours. After that the search is diminished locally. Their computers tell them that the best time to catch you is in the first three days. After that they assume you have escaped but they widen their net. They don't have the resources to catch every way in and out of the city. With the way the war is going they are running thin everywhere these days. We still need to take care of your dents."

Reflexively, Jennifer and Matt rubbed the palms of their right hands. The embedded RF chip was their identity everywhere they went. The dents would need to be replaced somehow. Most of the current espionage thrillers on the net usually featured an enemy spy who lurked about the urban landscape with a counterfeit dent. The thriller ended with the spy ferreted out and the fresh scar on his hand revealed as proof. Jennifer didn't relish the thought of having her hand cut open.

Anthony opened the van door. "Let's get you settled inside."

She and Matt wrestled with their large suitcases. Jennifer had to heave her suitcase up the steps of the loading dock. Anthony waited patiently with a bemused smile and didn't offer to help. He lifted the steel roll gate that lead into the inky black warehouse interior, while Jennifer and Matt followed him. She was apprehensive in the darkness but Anthony switched on a circuit breaker and round lights high above them began to glow. Anthony rolled the gate door shut.

The warehouse was starkly empty and remained dark even as the CFL lamps warmed up high above them. At the back of the warehouse was a staircase that led into what might be offices. Anthony headed straight for them with the footfalls from his boots echoing through the empty warehouse. Jennifer and Matt followed with their wheeled suitcases as they crossed the concrete floor noisily.

When they reached the staircase Jennifer regretted having packed a heavy suitcase. She let Matt take his up the staircase first then followed, heaving the thing up every step of the way. Anthony waited atop the stairs with the same bemused smile.

The insides of the offices were vastly different from the warehouse and could almost be described as cozy. Fluorescents lit up overhead to reveal an enclosed apartment with wood paneling and an avocado green carpet. A leather sofa lined up against the wall flanked by a couple of easy chairs. An old fashioned flat panel TV and a computer sitting on the desk on the far side of the room were equally archaic.

"This is the safe house we use for folks like you," Anthony said. "It's warmer than the rest of the warehouse. There's a thermostat on the wall if it gets too hot or too cold, bedrooms in the back, bathrooms as well. Don't worry, we keep it cleaned and maintained. TV works but the eye has been disabled so you don't have to worry about the National Police watching you. It's wired into the Valley Forge network so you can watch any programs you want to, same thing with the dumb terminal over there. Your Valley Forge login will work but you won't have access to the net at large. The kitchen is stocked, mostly canned foods and dry goods. Any questions?"

"Yeah, what happens with our car?" Matt asked.

Anthony pulled out a tablet from the inside his jacket. "Jorge was able to get out with your vehicle. We'll strip is down and sell it for parts. After costs and a modest fee we'll add the money to your account."

"Our assets?"

"The minute you went off the turnpike towards the rail yard I executed a command to transfer your assets. The transfer was completed through a couple of proxies and your money sits safely with the National Bank of Cuba."

"And my tablet?" Jennifer asked.

"I'm doing a memory wipe on it right now. With your access to Valley Forge we couldn't risk it falling into the wrong hands. I'll take it home with me and do some additional work. I'll bring it back tomorrow with a second one for Matt. The refurbished tablets will be tied to your new identities, as well as access codes for your accounts."

"Yeah, how are you going to change our dents?" Matt asked. "Surgery?"

Anthony grinned. "We'll save those questions for tomorrow. Get settled in. Matt, check out some of the archived entertainment from the old days. I'll see you later."

They quickly said their goodbyes and Anthony left them in the apartment. Jennifer's eyes welled with tears as she was overwhelmed with what they had done. She had always thought about their escape in a detached way. "I guess we should get settled in," she said.

They both wheeled their luggage to the back bedroom. The bedroom was plain but cozy. A thick green comforter on the queen-sized bed matched the carpet. They had finer furniture at home but this would do for the next few days. She set her suitcase down without bothering to unpack. There would be plenty of time for that later. On her way back to the main living room she checked out the bathroom. It was small and appeared to be clean with simple decor - a narrow shower stall enclosed in frosted glass, a plain white porcelain toilet and matching sink. Again, homesickness filled her with anxiety, but she couldn't turn back now. If they gave themselves up they would be incarcerated if not summarily executed.

Matt followed her into the living room. "What do we do now?"

"Keep ourselves entertained. You should check out the TV. If what Anthony says is true, there is access to banned programming."

Matt picked up an old fashioned remote and clicked the power button. The TV came to life but offered only a menu with options to choose from. He navigated to the TV shows category and browsed the menu. "Hey, I remember this show from when I was a kid. I haven't seen it in years."

"Watch that one then."

He confirmed his selection for "The Big Bang Theory" and the show started immediately.

Jennifer was more interested in checking the forums on the computer. She turned it on. When the screen didn't immediately light up it took her a minute to remember that the monitor needed to be turned on too. After the computer booted up it asked her for her Valley Forge credentials. She typed in her login and gained immediate access. It was the same forum she was used to seeing on her tablet but, just as Anthony had told her, there was no way to go out into the network. She reckoned that they needed to keep this location secret and couldn't risk the National Police snooping out this location through some sort of net surveillance.

Jennifer navigated her way to the local news forum. She wanted to see if she and Matt had made the news. Already a blurb had been posted thirty minutes earlier - "Local Party Official and Wife Wanted for Questioning". They had attached pictures to the news story but they had used an older picture of Jennifer with hair that they had lifted off of the elementary school's website where she had worked. Details were scarce since the story was still fresh. She checked the other forums that she read habitually. Jennifer got lost in the uncensored news of the outside world.

She was abruptly startled when Matt barked out laughter. "I forgot how hilarious this show was," he said.

Jennifer smiled and left the computer to join Matt on the sofa. It would be good to get lost in this comedy for a while.

CHAPTER 13

They spent the evening watching more episodes of the comedy Matt had accessed. Despite the archaic feel to the show it was still funny. There were a lot of cultural references that went right over their heads. They enjoyed the show until well into the evening hours.

With nothing better to do Jennifer and Matt decided to go to bed. She checked the news forum one more time but there was nothing new for her to read. The National Police had continued their search for a "prominent Party official wanted for questioning".

Jennifer worried that anxiety would keep her awake through the night, but she went to sleep quickly. Despite being smaller than their bed at home it was unexpectedly comfortable. The only thing she had to contend with was Matt waking her with his tossing and turning.

She woke up before him and showered. The kitchen had some bagels that she ate cold. After chewing through her bagel and washing it down with water she decided to check out the rest of the warehouse. Jennifer tested the door to see if it was locked. It turned easily and she stepped out to the metal staircase. When Anthony had left yesterday he had kept the lights on. Jennifer guessed that he anticipated they would wander about.

Jennifer walked down the stairs. The warehouse remained starkly empty with an open concrete floor. The only thing that broke up the open view were the steel beams that served as pillars. She shivered. While the apartment above was cozy and warm the interior of the warehouse was freezing. She turned around and saw a recessed door under the apartment. She tried the door handle but it was locked. Jennifer walked around the interior periphery of the warehouse but her wanderings yielded nothing interesting. Bored, she climbed the stairs back up to the apartment.

When she opened the door she found Matt eating a bowl of Cheerios. "I couldn't sleep last night," he said.

"Really?"

"Yeah. Are you sure we did the right thing?"

She mused on that for a moment. "Yes, we did the right thing. I'd already been detained by the Party once. Tortured even. They were bound to do it again sooner or later if not outright kill us. We did the right thing."

At noon the garage door to the loading dock rattled open. Jennifer leapt off the couch and rushed out of the apartment to see who had entered. Anthony strode into the warehouse with a large black bag he carried on a shoulder strap. He grinned and waved as he climbed the metal staircase. She stepped back to let him into the apartment.

"How are you all doing?" Anthony asked.

"Good," Jennifer said. "Any trouble outside?"

"Everything is going as expected. The National Police are searching for you. They're using the Denver Police and the Colorado State Police to find you. We're going to throw them off your scent in a couple of days."

"How are you going to do that?" Matt asked.

"By giving them something to chase. Your dents are going to leave a trail of breadcrumbs for them to follow. Ready to get started?"

Jennifer wasn't ready but she had anticipated this. He would dig the dents out of the palms of their hands and implant counterfeit dents. "Is the surgery safe here?"

"Surgery? You think I am going to cut out your dents?"

"That's how they do it in the movies."

Anthony snorted. "That's how most people do it. But I have planned something better than that." He opened up his black bag and started pulling out equipment. She recognized her tablet and he had a second one for Matt as well. Anthony pulled out an old fashioned laptop with several other gadgets and cabling that she didn't recognize. Anthony started piecing it all together. She and Matt waited patiently as all the gadgets and tablets were wired into the laptop.

When he was ready he told Jennifer to place her hand on one of the gadgets. She heard the gadget give off the familiar chime as it registered her dent.

"Is that connected to the network?" Matt asked.

"No." Anthony started to explain as he tapped into the keyboard. "A lot of people try to use counterfeit dents or dents stolen from people. Or, if you want to be ghoulish, dents from dead people. Sometimes they work for a day or two but the National Police figure out what's going on and catch up to them. Me and a couple of other guys figured out a way around it. The problem with changing the dent is that it always has to touch the database. So we just changed the database. Your dents are going to be tied to new identities. You can scan your dent anywhere without any problem."

"Doesn't the National Police have safeguards against that?"

"We figured a way around it. We can assign new RFIDs onto the chips that match what is in the database. As long as the dent scanner is happy and the database is happy, it doesn't raise any red flags. The only thing that we can't change is the listed serial number for the dent but the system doesn't check for that."

"What about facial recognition?" Jennifer asked. "Wouldn't everyone be looking for our faces to pop up on surveillance?" There were surveillance cameras everywhere. The facial recognition software that the National Police used was designed to recognize someone instantly.

"There's a chance of that," Anthony said. "So we'll stay out of sight as often as possible. Most of the cameras are tied to a third party institution, such as a bank or a restaurant. There's no direct link from the National Police to them. It'll take them a few days to put it together - if ever."

"And the trail of breadcrumbs?"

"Tomorrow the names of Matthew and Jennifer Hanson are going to pop up in Wyoming. It'll lead the police to focus their search there. In a couple of days we take off for New Orleans. Matt, your turn." Anthony gestured toward the dent scanner.

Matt placed his hand on the scanner and waited for the chime. "How are we getting to New Orleans?"

"A black Chevy Suburban. We're going to look like one of them. Our route is going to take us through Oklahoma City then through Shreveport. I want to avoid as much of Texas as possible. With the war going on right now that would be an added complication."

"What happens after we reach New Orleans?"

"An outbound freighter that has its first port of call in Havana. We've been working with this captain for a while now."

"So we'll be in Havana in about a week and a half," Jennifer said.

"About that long, yes. Starting a new life there or somewhere else. There's a large expat community in Cuba. And Australia. Smaller communities in Europe and Mexico if you ever wanted to go."

"A new life…" Things were happening quickly now. They would soon be on their way.

"Finished," Anthony said. He started to disconnect all his equipment. "So sit tight here for another couple of days and we'll leave on Monday. Any other questions?"

"Do you always personally accompany people?" Matt asked.

"Always. This is a scary process for someone in your position. You've never done anything like this before and you have concerns. I'm there to help you. I'm sharing the same risks that you are. Here, take these." He handed them a pair of tablets. Jennifer recognized the one she had surrendered to him yesterday. "Your new identities are on them and tied to your dents. Memorize your new details. If we're detained by the National Police, we want to be able to talk our way out of it."

After Anthony left curiosity got the best her. She logged into the tablet to see what her new identity was. Her new name was Mary Elizabeth Portnoy, wife to Jarrod Portnoy. There were some additional details to the false history. She wasn't too thrilled with the name but in the long run it didn't matter.

"I'm Jarrod," Matt said. "I sound like I'm from Indiana or something."

"Both of us," she agreed.

After spending some time studying her new persona she found the familiar π icon to Valley Forge Forum. She still had access and the forum remembered her preferred settings from before. It was like she had never left. Matt turned on the TV and found some classic banned programming to watch.

⬥

Since Anthony didn't return on Saturday that left them alone to entertain themselves again in the apartment. Both Matt and Jennifer started to go stir crazy. None of the electronic entertainment at their disposal could satiate their need to escape the warehouse into the open air. Matt was sullen and began to bicker in every conversation. Jennifer fared a little better. She started walking the interior perimeter of the warehouse. Despite the freezing cold the walks helped clear her head and she needed that time away from her husband.

On Sunday morning Jennifer and Matt were packed and ready. Anthony showed up at exactly nine o'clock in the morning. The loading bay door rattled up and spilled sunshine all through the warehouse interior. Jennifer raised her hand and shielded her eyes from the sun.

"Ready to go?" Anthony asked.

"Yeah, we've been ready," Matt said gruffly.

Anthony had backed a black Chevy Suburban into the loading dock. The back doors were open. White lettering was stenciled on each side of the vehicle that read "Lafayette Security Contractors". The vehicle had Louisiana plates. "Load up," Anthony instructed. Jennifer again regretted the decision of the heavy suitcase again. She did her best to shove it into the back of the SUV.

Anthony handed them black baseball caps that read Lafayette Security Contractors in bright white letters. He handed them each a pair of aviator sunglasses and well as some black jackets with the same lettering. "Wear these from now on. It will help hide you from the security cameras. If anyone asks us what we are doing we tell them we are independent contractors returning from assisting a National Police search for a couple of fugitives. Anyone digs deeper and the story won't hold up, but it'll get us by most people who ask."

"So we were helping the National Police search for ourselves?" Jennifer asked.

Anthony grinned. "Ironic, isn't it? Remember that as security contractors you have an air of self-importance about you. Be cocky and confident and people will believe the role that you're in. You wear your hats, jackets and sunglasses outside all the time."

Matt put everything on and grinned like a kid playing dress up.

"Somebody ride shotgun and somebody get in the back."

"Shotgun," Jennifer called out. Without waiting for argument she climbed into the passenger side.

The SUV was already warm inside from Anthony's ride to the warehouse. Anthony took his jacket off, Jennifer and Matt followed his lead. It would be a long drive so they might as well get comfortable. Anthony pulled away from the loading dock and started working his way out of the collection of warehouses.

"How long is it going to take to get there?" Matt asked.

"About three days. The maximum range these can go without a recharge is six hundred miles. We have a couple of safe houses we can stop at along the way."

The familiar environs of Denver gave way to ranch land in eastern Colorado. The scenery was not as exciting as when they skied in the mountains. Anthony explained that they would head to Kansas first, then Oklahoma City and skirt around Dallas through Shreveport before finally ending up in New Orleans. Matt had stretched out on his back in the back seat and fell asleep after they left Denver. Neither Anthony nor Jennifer had the inclination to listen to patriotic war music on the broadcast radio. Instead, Anthony had old R&B softly streaming through the Suburban's stereo system.

After miles of the soft music Jennifer asked, "Why do you do it?"

"I just believe in the old ways, that's all," Anthony said. She turned her head and waited patiently for more of an explanation. He caught her staring and blushed. "The system we had before the revolution wasn't perfect. It was a two party system with both sides holding extreme positions. It seemed like one side was for something just because the other was against it. They got to the point where they could never agree on anything. Can you believe there was a debate on vaccinations? Then things got worse. The economy never recovered from those crashes and things got too expensive. The people didn't care at first but when they couldn't afford to go to the movies or out to eat anymore, that was when we had the revolution."

"That doesn't sound like it was better in the old days."

"It wasn't a perfect system but until it got hard on people it was working. People had freedoms. They could say whatever they wanted. They could travel anywhere. They could own a gun. They had more freedoms to do whatever they wanted than we do now. Then we had the revolution."

The Second American Revolution was now taught in all the schools. The curriculum these days presented a tale of downtrodden heroes known as The Five rising up against the elitist politicians and the one-percenters. Jennifer had been a child when the revolution occurred and it wasn't as bad in Denver as it had been on the East Coast and West Coast. She did remember a few scary nights with mobs marching down the streets.

"Didn't it get better after the revolution?"

"We were united under the leadership of Hank Gregor and the Freedom Party, one party to rule over us all. Things did get better for a while. There was no more income disparity. Everyone was able to afford the stuff they wanted. Food and housing became affordable for everybody again. Then things gradually changed. It started with freedom of speech. Any criticism of the Freedom Party was considered seditious so no one was allowed to criticize the Party any more. Then it came to guns. Without anyone to speak up all guns were seized. There were a lot of firefights in the South and Texas, where gun ownership was a way of life. Then it was religion. Every religion was deemed offensive in some way so that none were allowed to exist."

"They still exist though, right?" Even today there were police reports of breaking up churches across the country.

"They still exist, in secret, in smaller areas of the country. The biggest hot spot is Utah where they're always cracking down on Mormons. These little towns that we're going through today have a church hidden in a basement somewhere. For some odd reason the Catholic Church is still allowed to exist. Nobody has figured out why yet. Probably because of all their money. For the most part people were content without free speech, guns or religion. More and more freedoms were taken away. TV programs changed. Books were burned. News was censored. Then food was changed. Every decision in our lives started being made for us. Now look at us, twenty years later."

"Progress?"

Anthony barked out a sharp laugh. "Yeah, progress."

"Did you know there are still huge cattle ranches up north?" She went on to tell about her encounter with Miriam at Golden Gate.

"Yeah, I knew about that. We still reel in lobsters in New England. There are giant chicken farms in Arkansas. Pig farms in Georgia. Some of it gets sold to the Party elite. Everything else is sold to China or some other high bidder. It started off as a benevolent dictatorship. Nobody had to worry because the Party made all the decisions for you. Even if you were unambitious and didn't want a job you got a stipend of food and cash from the Party. But they became more and more intrusive. The National Police was formed. They superseded the authority of FBI, CIA, NSA and any other law enforcement agency. Did you know the National Police have their own private army? Then the genetic testing started a few years ago. Only Type A parents can produce Type A kids. Now we have an elite group of people at the top dictating everything down to the rest of us. Just a different group of one-percenters to deal with."

Jennifer stared silently out the window. The memory of her own recent pregnancy was still raw.

"I'm sorry," Anthony said. "I forgot what you just went through."

"It's okay," she said. "I know you didn't mean anything by it. Can I ask you something else?"

"Sure, go ahead."

"How do people, um, like you, fare in this country?"

Anthony snorted. "You mean black people?"

This time it was Jennifer's turn to be embarrassed. "I didn't mean anything by it."

Anthony smiled, "I know. We fare the same as other folks. The Freedom Party is predominantly white but there are some black folks and Mexicans too. One of the founding members of the Freedom Party is an African-American." He was referring to Leo Jefferson. "There are not as many black people as the white people, but some. We all seem to be treated equally dismal as everyone else who is not favored by the Party. The biggest disparity is in the armed forces."

"What is the disparity?"

"In the enlisted ranks it is mostly black and brown. A lot of folks figured out they can join the army and send money back home to their folks. People in the army get treated better, higher reward with higher risk. I did my stint in the army."

"You did? Were you deployed anywhere?"

"No. I was too smart to serve in a front line unit. When I was a kid I tinkered with old computers. After computers it was tinkering with networks siphoning off free internet wherever I could. After I joined the army they figured out my aptitude and put me into cyber warfare. I remember the look on my drill sergeant's face when he stuck me in front of a computer for the first time. He thought I would freeze up on the first test. I hacked their test server in under a minute. After that they treated me as special. I knew they were using me but I was using them too. As a kid playing with computers you're limited in what you can do. In the army I was thrown into the biggest sandbox in the world with the best toys. I learned from them. I got promoted a couple of times during a four-year stint, but when they asked me to re-up I was out. Then I started hacking for myself."

"What do you do when you hack for yourself?"

Anthony laughed. "Make money! It's all just zeros and ones out there. Maybe in the old days pirates plundered ships or dug up treasure chests. There's so much money floating in cyberspace, people would be shocked at how easy it is to find. Grab a few thousand dollars here and there and you're comfortable. Grab a million and you're rich."

"Nobody catches you doing it?"

"Not until it's too late, and by that time I'm long gone. The money has switched hands through several proxies. The trail grows cold quickly. I've got buried treasure all over cyberspace. It's how I built your account using your assets."

"So you got into the people smuggling business to get rich?"

"I'm already rich. More money than I will ever need; dollars, euros, pounds, pesos, rubles, yen and bhat. No, I don't do this for the money. The more I hacked, the more I learned about the Party. The detention centers, the abusers, the people in charge holding us down. Too many foreign wars that didn't serve a purpose. It gnawed at my conscious and made me want to do something different. Now I help people."

"For a fee," Matt chimed in from the back seat. Jennifer wondered how long he had listened to their conversation. She felt a pang of guilt at having gotten caught excluding her husband from the dialog. Jennifer didn't know why but she wanted to keep this conversation to her and Anthony.

Anthony made eye contact through the rear view mirror. "There are a lot of assets I moved in place to get you out of here. The Party was already watching you closely. This is more challenging than my normal run."

Matt didn't comment any further. He stared at the passing countryside through the passenger window of the SUV.

☥

Early in the afternoon Anthony pulled off of Interstate 70 into the Loves truck stop. A half dozen rigs and trailers sat in the expansive parking lot designed for ten times as many. There were plenty of cars in the parking lot. Jennifer reckoned people in these remote rural communities gathered in places like this.

"Remember, hats and sunglasses on," Anthony said. "When we walk in here we act like we own the place. People are more likely to mind their own business."

Jennifer donned the cap, jacket and sunglasses as Anthony instructed. Stepping out of the SUV was a shock to her system. Despite the sunny day the weather remained frigid. Jennifer suppressed a shiver as she and Matt followed Anthony into the diner.

The mood changed as soon as they stepped into the diner attached to the truck stop. Most of the locals were dressed in jeans or overalls. The three of them stood out with their black attire. While Jennifer felt like a bug under a microscope Anthony strode through confidently towards a booth in the back corner. She followed him with Matt trailing behind her.

As soon as he sat down he handed out the laminated plastic menus to Jennifer and Matt. Anthony frowned while browsing the menu as a waitress approached. She had a yellow uniform that appeared as if it came straight out of the 1950s, except the once sunny yellow had faded to pastel after many washes. Jennifer noted that the waitress kept the frayed areas hemmed up with fresh stitching.

"How you doing, Grant?" the waitress asked.

Anthony grinned. "Just fine, Brandy, and yourself?"

"I'm doing good. Are you on your way to Denver or back to Louisiana?"

"Back to Lafayette. We finished some work in Denver."

"Y'all decide on what you want?"

Anthony reached into his breast pocket and pulled out a wallet. He took a couple of twenty-dollar bills out and laid them on the table. "Say, Brandy, is there something that isn't salad and tofu. You know how it is in Denver."

She quickly scooped the two twenties into the pocket of her apron. "We just got a mess of catfish. Serving them up with some fries, hushpuppies and some homemade tartar sauce. Thirty dollars a plate."

"You all okay with that?" Anthony asked.

Jennifer wasn't sure if she had ever had catfish in her life but she turned to Matt and he nodded.

"That'll do just fine," Anthony said. "And if you could be so kind we would like three sweet teas as well." He peeled out seven more twenty-dollar bills and laid them on the table where they quickly disappeared.

Jennifer wanted to ask him more but the warning in his eyes told her that this wasn't the time. A few minutes later the Brandy came out with their plates of catfish on the serving tray. None of the diners took notice as she set out the plates of contraband food in front of them.

The crispy fried catfish was delicious. Jennifer slathered a generous helping of the tartar sauce onto the catfish itself then dipped her fries and hush puppies as well. She couldn't remember the last time she'd had sweet tea. Jennifer had so many questions she wanted to ask but she and Matt we too busy shoveling food in their mouths. Anthony took his time as he smiled bemusedly as they indulged themselves.

After they'd finished they strolled back out to the Suburban, completely satiated. As soon as they climbed inside Matt beat Jennifer to the questions. "How did you know they would have catfish?" he asked.

"And I haven't seen that much cash in years," Jennifer added.

Anthony pulled the SUV out of the parking lot and turned eastbound on the interstate. "Out in the country they haven't changed as much. Cash is king out here but everyone has checking, savings and credit card accounts tied to their dents. They traffic in contraband. Nobody has gone meatless out in the countryside. They barter for different things or sell their excess. A trucker probably came through here with a haul of catfish."

"Will we see more places like that?"

"I've been doing this for a couple of years now. I try not to go to the same restaurant too many times but I'm a familiar face on this route. Everyone thinks I do consulting work throughout America. But, yeah, we'll hit a few more spots between here and New Orleans. Wait till you see that town. There's no way in hell they'll ever go meatless. I'll take you out the night before you leave."

CHAPTER 14

They were nearing Wichita when evening set in. The HUD on the windshield blinked the battery warning back at them in violent red. Anthony headed west on the 235 Loop then took the 21st Street exit. Finally he guided the SUV into one of the neighborhoods. The street was quiet but amply lit with halogen streetlamps. Older ranch style houses with brick or aluminum siding lined the streets. Anthony pulled into the driveway of one of the brick sided homes. He waited for the garage door to open a minute later. Boxes, a bicycle and other assorted items hung from the walls, but there was ample room to squeeze the Suburban in. Jennifer spied a petite African American woman standing in the doorway that led from the garage to the house interior. Jennifer doubted the woman reached the height of five feet. The pretty woman had an abundance of curves despite her short stature. She waited with a wide smile as they piled out of the SUV.

"Hey Lisa," Anthony said.

"Hey yourself," the woman replied. "You want to introduce me to your friends?"

Jennifer stretched her arms after the confines of the SUV. "I'm Jennifer. This is my husband Matt."

"Pleased to meet you. Y'all can bring your stuff in. I kept some dinner warm for you."

"That sounds nice," Anthony said. He pulled the vehicle plug from the wall and stuck it into the socket of the SUV.

Jennifer and Matt wrestled with their oversized luggage. Despite the awkwardness of the luggage she felt like she was becoming quite adept at handling it. She felt a pang of envy when Anthony led the way easily carrying his gym bag over his shoulder. The kitchen attached to the garage featured dated decor, sometime in the late 20th century if not older; it was warm, inviting and filled with the savory scent of home cooking.

"I'm afraid it's not much for dinner," Lisa said. "I didn't get a chance to go to the store today. It's pinto beans and cornbread, with a little ham hock. I have a homemade apple pie and some ice cream for dessert."

Anthony waited expectantly for her and Matt.

"That sounds wonderful," Jennifer said. "I can't wait to eat. Let me get this put away."

"I'll show you where you'll be sleeping," Lisa said.

The decor in the rest of the house proved to be as dated, but the house was warm and clean. The bedspreads in the guest bedroom were antiquely hand stitched. After unpacking a few items she and Matt joined Anthony and Lisa in the dining area attached to the kitchen. The steaming pot of beans sat in the center of the table, alongside a serving dish of cornbread cut into squares. A small bottle of Tabasco Sauce as well as a small bowl of futter garnished their meal.

"Let's eat," Anthony said.

They each took a turn ladling out beans into a bowl. When Anthony and Lisa added hot sauce to their beans Jennifer decided to add a few dashes to her bowl. Matt remained entirely perplexed. He dipped the spoon experimentally into his own bowl of beans and into his mouth. Jennifer could see that he had that vertical worry crease in the center of his brow.

"So y'all are from Denver?" Lisa asked.

Jennifer smiled. "Yes. On our way south. Are you from here?"

"No, originally from Saint Louis, moved out this way a few years back. Things are quieter out here."

"Why did you move here? It seems like Saint Louis would be more active."

Lisa gave her a tired smile. "Just needed to get away."

Jennifer flushed with embarrassment. "I'm so sorry. I didn't mean to pry."

"It's okay. We all have our reasons why we do things." Left unspoken was Jennifer and Matt's own reason for being in Wichita.

"Lisa operates this safe house," Anthony said.

"How many safe houses are there?" Matt asked.

"I don't know the extent of the network. Operational security. I only need to know which safe house I'm going to. Since I drive to New Orleans often, this place is a frequent stop. I think there are at least two dozen safe houses."

"Probably more," Lisa interjected. "I think closer to forty. The network is pretty big."

"Have you two known each other long?" Jennifer asked.

Anthony glanced at Lisa before answering. "Just for a couple of years, since I started doing this."

"You're the highest profile couple that Anthony has ever transported," Lisa said.

"What makes us different?" Matt asked. He pushed his half eaten bowl of beans away from him.

"You, sir. You're the highest ranking Party member that I've seen ever come through here. Sometimes we get a rich couple who want to take their money elsewhere. We get lots of people who are individually targeted by the Party." Lisa nodded toward Jennifer. Jennifer rubbed her head then caught herself. The stigma from her stay at Golden Gate Canyon betrayed her again.

"But you, sir," Lisa continued, "you don't seem like you needed to run away from the Party."

"Operational security?" Matt said. "It sounds like everyone in your network knows we're coming."

Anthony shrugged. "You're pretty high profile. Normally people don't pay attention to who the passengers are. Your case is a little different, I guess."

"I was the assistant to the deputy director," Matt said with a hint of pride. "More of an operator, really. I worked behind the scenes and connected people together."

"Do you want to leave America?" Lisa asked.

"I'm here because my wife wanted me to be here. She convinced me that we needed to go."

"So you did this out of love?"

"Of course." Jennifer could hear the doubt in his voice. Her heart sank as she realized he would never be entirely convinced about this endeavor.

"The beans and cornbread are delicious," Jennifer said. She felt the sudden urge to change the subject. "Not sure if I ever had them with hot sauce before."

"Oh, it's nothing," Lisa said. "Just a little ham hock and beans. The cornbread is from a mix."

"Anthony, what time will we head out tomorrow?" Matt asked.

He washed down a mouthful of cornbread with some water. "We should call it an early night and get on the road by six. It's not too far to Oklahoma City. From there we'll take back roads to Shreveport."

"Six AM it is then," Jennifer said.

After dinner Jennifer helped Lisa with the dishes. She was dismayed to see that the dishwasher was absent. In all the years of growing up in Denver she never saw a house without one. They did the dishes while the men hovered over an archaic paper map on the kitchen table. Matt asked Anthony a lot of questions about the route. Jennifer appreciated Anthony's patience with her husband. While this was Matt's only time doing this route, Anthony appeared to be well practiced.

It wasn't long before they all turned in early. Jennifer changed out of the jeans and bra, opting for T-shirt and underwear. She crawled into the little, full size bed while she waited for Matt. He chose to go with underwear only. Despite the chilly Kansas weather the house was cozy and warm.

"How about that dinner?" Matt asked.

"It was good."

"Are you kidding? That's how poor people eat."

"Matt, that's how a lot of people eat. Lower your voice! I don't want our host to hear you bad mouthing her food."

Matt rolled his eyes. "Please! We're paying them good money. We should get better food."

Their conversation was interrupted by voices in the next room. She and Matt glanced at each another guiltily. They could hear the voices next door but couldn't make out what they were saying.

"See? Keep it down."

"Okay, okay. But you didn't think the food was awful?"

Jennifer sighed. "No, it wasn't awful. It was actually pretty good and filling. It contained meat. Not a lot but it was there. I know it's not like the food that we're used to eating in Denver but we've gotten access to better food lately. Did you like the lunch we had today?"

"Yeah, the catfish and fries were delicious. I hadn't had that in a while."

"So keep an open mind about all of this. We're on the run from the National Police. We're going to experience new things. It'll be stressful. Just try to accept it."

This time Matt sighed. "Okay. I get it. We're in trouble and on the run."

Jennifer smiled. "Let's get some sleep. It's an early day tomorrow."

Matt turned out the light and climbed into bed. Light from the streetlamps filtered through the gauzy curtains. Jennifer was dozing off when a noise startled her. She reflexively kicked her feet under the covers and strained to listen. A rhythmic bumping came from the adjacent room. Soon soft moans accompanied the bumping.

"Oh my God," Matt whispered. "Do you hear that?"

"Yes." Her reply came out as a hiss.

Matt chuckled. "Do they know we can hear them?"

"I doubt it. If they did they wouldn't be making that much racket."

Matt slid his hand around her waist and cupped her breast. "So do you want to...?"

She jerked away from him. "No. Let's just go to sleep."

"Alright, alright," Matt said resignedly. "It's not a big deal."

Jennifer pulled the pillow over her head to muffle the noise. It helped mask the noise of the moans but she could still hear the bumping. She tried to focus on something else but the sounds of passion from the next room were intrusive. Jennifer didn't know why she was bothered by it. Lisa was a pretty woman and Anthony probably came through here often. Soon the bumping stopped and she fell asleep. If it started again during the night she never knew.

⚓

Jennifer had set the alarm on her tablet for five o'clock. That would give her plenty of time for a quick shower and a bite to eat. When the alarm went off she jumped out of bed and headed for the bathroom. The shower was hot but brief, enough to wake her up and motivate her to take the day head on. She changed quickly into jeans and a black long sleeve T-shirt. Matt was getting out of bed when she finished packing her suitcase. Since there was nothing to do but wait on the men, she headed to the kitchen.

Lisa sat there in a floral bathrobe drinking a cup of coffee. "Help yourself to a cup," she said.

Jennifer poured a cup and sat down. She winced as she took a sip.

"It's not real coffee," Lisa said. "But it is full of caffeine and will wake you up."

Jennifer smiled. "It's fine. Should be enough to wake me up for the ride."

"You want to be awake for that long drive? I would rather sleep through them. Ten minutes on the road and I'm out like a light."

"I never could sleep on the road. I get winks here and there, then finally just get frustrated and wake up. Hell, if Anthony would let me I would rather be the one behind the wheel"

Lisa snickered. "Honey, he ain't never going to let that happen, and he probably naps behind the wheel himself." With auto drive you could tell the car where you wanted to go. It always unsettled Jennifer to cede that much control to the car's AI but everyone else seemed okay with it.

Jennifer sighed. "I know." With nothing more than silence between them, Jennifer sipped on the hot coffee again. "So you and Anthony?"

"Do we have something going on? No, not really. We see each other every few weeks when he's making a run. That is, if his route comes through here. But given the nature of our business we don't have what the shrinks call a 'long term relationship'. When he does stop, I do enjoy his company though." Lisa smiled as she took another sip.

Jennifer sipped her coffee in lieu of response. She was relieved when Matt burst into the room several seconds later. "Anything for breakfast?" he asked.

"Some oatmeal on the stove," Lisa said. "Help yourself."

Some bowls and spoons were already set out next to the pot. Matt helped himself to a heaping bowl then scooped some futter and sweetener on top. Jennifer fixed herself a bowl. Anthony stormed into the kitchen with his gym bag. "Are you all about ready?"

"Yeah as soon as we finish breakfast," Matt said.

Lisa stood up from the table. "Let me fix you a bowl."

They didn't say much as the three of them eagerly scooped the sweetened oatmeal into their mouths. Lisa quietly sipped her coffee.

When Anthony pushed the bowl away, the spoon rattled inside and rang like a bell. "Okay, we gotta go."

Anthony tossed the gym bag in the back of the Suburban casually, while Jennifer and Matt struggled with their awkward suitcases again. They loaded up in the SUV and the garage door lifted open as they climbed in. Lisa waited quietly from the kitchen doorway as they piled in. Anthony started the SUV and selected the reverse button, when he stopped and put it back into park.

"Give me a minute to say goodbye," Anthony said as he opened the door. Anthony embraced Lisa carefully, whispered in her ear then kissed her deeply. He whispered in her ear once more and let her go to return to the vehicle.

"Sorry about that," he said as he buckled his seat belt. He reversed the SUV out of the garage.

"It's the least you could do," Matt said with a grin.

"I'm sorry?"

"After last night. That was quite a racket."

Jennifer felt embarrassed. "Matt!"

For the first time since she had met Anthony he was flustered. "I'm sorry," he said again. "I didn't mean for you all to hear any of that."

"No, I'm sorry. My husband is an ass."

Matt laughed. "What? I'm happy for the guy. He got lucky last night. I'm glad someone did."

"Let's just go."

Anthony put the SUV into drive and they headed off. There was no more talk of Anthony's sexual escapades with their host. Jennifer watched passively out the window as they worked their way out of Wichita and south to Oklahoma City.

⚔

They arrived in Oklahoma City before ten in the morning. Anthony worked his way east toward another interstate. After two hours heading east he turned off to another road called the Indian Nation Turnpike.

They had lunch in another truck stop. Unlike the day before, where they drew stares but were generally left alone, the people in Oklahoma barely masked their hostility. Anthony carefully explained to them that they should follow his lead. Even though the truck stop featured a full restaurant, none of them trusted the cooks and wait staff to not spit in their food. Instead they went to the self-serve pita bar and made wraps with hummus and roasted vegetables. They ate quickly and exited the truck stop under the watchful glare of the patrons.

After they left Anthony explained, "They don't much like outsiders here. Particularly people with my skin color."

Once on the Indian Nation Turnpike the scenery was pretty with lots of greenery, but starkly empty of any buildings outside of the occasional farmhouse that dotted the landscape. They soon grew tired of small talk amongst themselves. Jennifer and Matt buried themselves into whatever entertainment they could find on their tablets, while Anthony listened to the radio play the same patriotic war music they were already accustomed to.

They were north of McClesy when they spotted the roadblock. Jennifer had let the tranquil countryside lull her into a semi-doze, but she jerked upright to regard the roadblock closely. Two black and white police cruisers flanked a narrow opening between them. Another black panel van waited to the side. Flares and traffic cones marked the way between the two cruisers. One police officer stood twenty yards back and held an assault rifle. Another officer worked the line of cars with a tablet in hand. Behind the cruiser, next to van off the side were four other officers milling about. Despite the sunshine it remained bitterly cold and the officers' breath fogged the air.

"Matt, wake up," Anthony said.

"Huh?" Matt was groggy but instantly awakened as Anthony pulled in behind the line of six cars ahead of them. "What do we do?"

"Stay calm. This is nothing unusual. They throw up roadblocks all the time. Act natural and don't speak unless spoken to. They will want to scan your dents. Let them. Those dents have solid data behind them."

The Oklahoma Highway Patrol let a car through. They were now the sixth car back. "What are they looking for?" Jennifer asked.

"Could be anything," Anthony said. "Drugs. Subversives. Escapees." The next car went through the line and Anthony inched the Suburban forward. "There's even the off chance that they don't know what they're looking for. A lot of times they get orders to just scan the dents and feed the data back to see if it raises a red flag with the National Police."

"I've got a bad feeling about this," Matt said.

"Stay calm. This guy is going to wave us through this roadblock. Given the color of my skin I probably have more to be worried about in this state than you do." They were next in line.

The vehicle in front of them, a red Chevy electric compact, passed through. Anthony rolled the window down. "Afternoon, officer," he said.

The officer was bundled up in a heavy brown jacket. He wore his patrolman cap with his ears red from the cold. The officer scanned Anthony with eyes hidden behind mirrored aviator glasses. "Afternoon," the patrolman said. "Where you headed?"

"Back to Lafayette, Louisiana."

"Didn't want to drive through Dallas?" Dallas and then through Shreveport was the obvious shorter route.

"Too close to the front lines. Went through there just before Christmas and I got stuck half a day waiting for a military convoy to pass. Seemed easier to go this way."

The officer grunted an acknowledgement. "Where you coming from?"

"Denver. We did some contracting work up there for the National Police."

"What kind of work?"

"Crowd control."

The officer grunted noncommittally. "Okay, let me scan your dent." Anthony extended his right hand towards the window. The officer waved his electronic wand over Anthony's hand, waited for the chime of a successful read then checked the tablet. "Okay, you're good. Young lady, you're next. Just reach over your friend here so that I don't have to come around the other side."

Jennifer unbuckled the seat beat and leaned toward the driver side window. Since the dent was embedded in her right hand she had to lean across the console between them and over Anthony. She felt flushed with embarrassment as she realized that she could feel Anthony's breath on her left cheek. The officer waved the wand and checked the tablet after the chime.

"Okay, you're good," the officer said. He walked to the door behind the driver and rapped a knuckle on the glass. "Sir?"

Matt rolled down the window and quietly extended his hand. He had to do the same awkward reach over the left side of his body. Matt kept his gaze averted while the officer waved the wand over his hand.

"Are you okay, Mr. Portnoy?"

"Huh?" Matt replied. He withdrew his hand from the dent scanner after he heard the chime.

"You seem nervous."

"Me? No, I am okay." His voice took a high pitch.

"Can you extend your hand again, sir?"

"Is there a problem officer?"

Just do it, Matt, Jennifer thought. *And maintain direct eye contact. Look confident.*

"Sir, please extend your hand."

Matt reached across and extended his hand again. This time he maintained direct eye contact while the officer checked the scanner against Matt's face. For the second time he received a positive chime from the scanner.

"Okay, you're good too. Y'all can move along."

"Thank you," Anthony said. He rolled up his window and put the SUV into drive. Fifty yards past the roadblock Anthony said, "See? No problem."

"Are you sure?" Matt asked.

"Yeah. Everything in our dents backs up what I told him. They can even check the vehicle's dent and it will show that I tried to run this through Dallas last month."

"Did you go through Dallas last month?" Jennifer asked.

"No. But the record will show that I did."

"Will there be any more roadblocks?" Matt asked.

"Probably when we get deeper into Louisiana. That's a lawless state anyway, so roadblocks are pretty common. The key is to stay confident. You have to believe in your own story. You are Jarrod Portnoy, security contractor. In some circles that elevates you higher than these yokels in the country. Now onto Shreveport."

"How long till we get there?" Jennifer asked.

"It'll be a little after dark."

⋏

The remainder of the day's drive was uneventful. The weather remained sunny but cold. Jennifer thought that leaving the mountains for a southern climate would be warmer. Anthony explained that even though winter occurred down here, it would likely warm up and was certainly less harsh than Denver. When they reached Texarkana they took I-49 south to Shreveport.

It was well past dark and the battery cell flashed red again, indicating less than twenty percent life. As they turned on Riverside Drive the streetlights were active but the monolithic casinos stood dark and looming.

"None of them are open?" Matt asked.

"No," Anthony said. "This place has been hit hard. It started in the twenties when Texas legalized casinos. The casinos here and along the Oklahoma border died off. It didn't help with the continuous economic crises and the increasing expense of everything else. This part of the country has always been the hardest hit and the Party doesn't favor the Cajuns with any good grace. People couldn't afford to gamble anymore. Gambling still exists but mostly in small pockets."

They were the only vehicle in the street as they rolled past the darkened buildings. Jennifer tried to make out the dead structures and the signs, but with so little streetlight she couldn't read the names. Anthony turned the Suburban off Riverside into one of the lanes leading up to a casino. This time she could read the name - Gold Rush Casino and Resort.

"Where are we going?" she asked.

"You'll see."

He pulled past the main entrance and took a service road that led to the back of the casino, where they approached a large garage bay. Anthony put the SUV into park then got out and stepped toward the panel next to the door, where he keyed an entry code on the touch pad. The leftmost garage door rattled to life. When Anthony returned he pulled the SUV into the dark garage.

"Let me close the door and get some lights on before you get out," Anthony said.

They waited patiently as he made his way to the door to lower it. As the door closed Anthony flipped a switch on the wall. A bank of fluorescent lights hanging from the ceiling flickered to life.

Without waiting any further for an approval, Jennifer opened the door and stepped out. The garage was cluttered with antique limousines, gaming tables and slot machines that were gray with accumulated dust. Anthony pulled a power cord from the wall and plugged it into the Suburban.

Matt stepped out of the SUV. "We're staying here?" he asked incredulously.

Anthony grinned. "This is our safe house for the evening. A little different from last night. Tomorrow night we'll be in New Orleans."

"How did you manage to do this?" Jennifer asked.

"Grab your stuff. We're going to do some walking. I'll tell you on the way."

Jennifer and Matt wrestled once again with their oversized suitcases. They wheeled their suitcases up the ramp toward Anthony. He waited patiently for them by a service tunnel that led to the interior of the dead casino. He turned off the garage lights and flipped a switch for the tunnel. "I need to make sure there's as little light as possible escaping from the windows here. Can't have any people snooping around. We came up with the idea of using this place as a safe house a couple of years back. Nobody hangs out in this part of town and the previous owners kept this place buttoned up tight. Compared to the other casinos there's little issue with vagrants and vandals."

The service tunnel took a right turn and led to a fire door. Anthony opened the door after flipping the lights in the tunnel off and another set back on. He opened the second door and led them to the floor of the casino.

Anthony pulled out his tablet and entered a command. The casino came to life. Slot machines and other electronic games went through their boot sequences. The casino felt haunted as the lights flashed continuously and the dust motes swirled in the air. As the machines finished booting they started to ring and chime, begging to be played.

"This is incredible," Jennifer said.

"Does the electric company know about this?" Matt asked.

"The place has always been powered," Anthony said. "I did a little hacking with the records on the back end, so that the electric company doesn't know how much power this place draws."

"Do the games work?"

"No. These machines were invented long before dents. They take cash only and they don't dispense anything in return, but they're fun to look at."

They followed Anthony through the casino. Most of the screens were brightly lit but some of them were dark. They likely malfunctioned because of age and lack of maintenance. The bleeps and warbles from the machines entertained Jennifer. Past the slot machines were the long dead gaming tables. She was disappointed to find them covered with plastic. They passed through the casino exit and into the hotel lobby.

The casino abruptly died as Anthony switched the machines off. If there were lights for the lobby Anthony decided not to turn them on. Instead he produced a flashlight from his gym bag. The lobby windows were completely blocked so that not even streetlight or moonlight could filter through. Their footfalls echoed on the marble floors in the long empty lobby. Anthony made his way to the resort elevators, where he produced an old-fashioned brass key. The key managed to open the elevator with a soft chime and greeted them with soft music.

"Come on in," Anthony said. "It's big enough to carry your heavy bags." Once inside he pushed the button for the penthouse.

"Any worries about the elevator?" Matt asked. "I mean it has to be pretty old, right?"

"Never had an issue with it."

When the elevator arrived to the top floor the three of them stepped into darkness. The doors of the elevator remained open long enough so that Anthony could switch on the lights. Jennifer found herself in a short marble-tiled hallway, warmly lit by hanging chandeliers adorned in cobwebs. Large oak doors stood at the end of the hall. "Welcome to the penthouse suite," Anthony said.

He opened the doors and flipped on another light switch. Lavishly furnished, the suite featured tan leather couches in the living room. A small bar with three bar stools was off to the right. An old fashioned flat screen TV hung off the wall behind the fully stocked bar. On the left side of the room stood a white grand piano. There were glass doors at the back of the suite that led to a balcony. The suite was amply filled with windows, but they were all covered with blackout paper to hide the light. Despite the dated decor Jennifer noted that it was clean and free of dust.

"Wow," Jennifer said. "This place is huge."

"I like it," Matt said as he started to wander. "How do you take care of it?"

"We have a schedule," Anthony said. "About six guys take care of the place. Since we all take turns using the penthouse, we take turns keeping it clean. Sorry, no room service though. There are a couple of hot plates and a microwave. We have canned food and rations. I can get us take out if we get tired of the food here. There is even a small laundry room with a washer and dryer if we need it."

"I'm sure it'll be just fine," Jennifer said. "Any heat?"

Anthony turned up the thermostat next to the door. "It'll take a while to warm up, but we have heat."

They had hot running water as well, even though it took several minutes for the shower to warm up. Jennifer took a shower while the men sipped bourbon on the rocks at the bar. She dressed lightly, blue gym shorts and a black T-shirt. When she stepped out of the bedroom and into the living she blushed when both men gave her appreciative glances. "So, about dinner?"

"Some stuff behind the bar over here," Anthony said. "Help yourself."

"Every man and woman for his or herself tonight?" Matt asked.

Jennifer made her way behind the bar. There was a small larder of canned foods and dry goods, along with a few spices. She studied it for almost a minute and said, "I can make something for all of us out of this. Relax and go watch net programming or something. I'll let you know when dinner is ready."

She could use the small bag of white rice along with a can of beef tips in gravy. The beef tips would taste awful but fortunately they had a small bottle of Tabasco Sauce that was brown with age but should still add flavor. She also had a can of asparagus spears that she could sauté in a little olive oil that was fortunately still fresh. Soon the penthouse filled with the smell of simmering beef and asparagus. Jennifer set the table and announced that dinner was ready. She added a bottle of red wine she found from the bar.

"Let's eat," Jennifer announced. Both men stood up from the couch and came over to the small dinette table near the bar. They left the TV on to some football game.

"Smells wonderful," Anthony said as he sat down.

Jennifer poured glasses of wine for the three of them, as Matt served himself first then Anthony followed. Anthony ladled the beef and gravy on top of a bed of rice. He shoveled a bite into mouth. "Mmmmm. I didn't think you would be able to make this stuff tastes good."

"It's delicious, honey," Matt added.

Jennifer was impressed with her own effort to make a meal out of canned goods. They ate silently for a few minutes. "So what's the plan for tomorrow?"

"We can sleep in," Anthony said. "The drive to New Orleans isn't far at this point. There might be some checkpoints out here in swamp country. The Cajuns don't cotton to the city folk, so I don't think it'll be much of an issue. We should get past them. Even if we get up at ten tomorrow we'll make New Orleans by six."

"Another safe house?" Matt asked.

"Yeah, for a couple of days at least. The departure time depends mostly on the ship's schedule. I've worked with the captain before; it's nothing unusual." Anthony raised his glass in a toast. "So drink up and enjoy your evening." They toasted over the dinette table.

After dinner the men returned to the couch to watch the second half of the playoff game. Jennifer carefully bagged up the leftovers into a garbage bag and cleaned the dishes. She wanted to leave the safe house the same way they had found it. Somebody else would need to escape. Jennifer wanted whoever that was to have the same liberating experience. When the dishes were done she didn't feel like watching the football game with the men. She retired to the bedroom with her tablet. Once comfortably in bed she logged into Valley Forge website and caught up on the news she had missed during the day.

Apparently there was a push from the Coalition forces towards Dallas and a new column struck towards Houston. Despite her interest in the subject the wine and food made her drowsy. She placed the tablet on the nightstand and fell asleep with the lights on.

Chapter 15

Jennifer woke up and realized somebody was talking. A sliver of light shined through the crack of the door into her dark suite room. Slightly disoriented it took her several seconds to remember that she was in an abandoned casino in Shreveport, Louisiana. Were Matt and Anthony arguing? No, Matt remained sound asleep and lightly snoring next to her. She checked the time on the tablet - 2:14. She recognized Anthony's voice emanating from the suite.

After being startled awake she was curious about the conversation. Jennifer got out of bed, feeling the slight chill from escaping the warm covers. She peeked into the suite until she caught Anthony's eye. He talked through his headset but waved her in. Jennifer listened in on his half of the conversation. Her mother had always said nothing good ever happened after midnight.

"I understand," Anthony said. "All of them? Okay, what resources have not been compromised? How about the network? Who hasn't reported in? Okay, some of them might still be underground? Yes, I'll let the passengers know. Goodbye." He took the earpiece out. "We have a problem."

"What's wrong?"

"Most of the network is gone. It's been compromised. That chief inspector is a tenacious son of a bitch."

"Gone? What do you mean 'gone'?"

"Earlier in the evening the National Police raided locations around the country. Safe houses in Colorado, Oklahoma, Kansas, Missouri, Iowa and Montana have been compromised. The safe house in New Orleans is gone."

"What about this one?"

"This one is on the periphery of the network and is unmanaged. Only the transporters know about this safe house and we don't think we've been compromised."

"What about Lisa?"

Anthony lowered his eyes. "Gone. I don't know if she's dead or if they took her. She never knew anything specific about other safe houses so she can't compromise us."

"She might still be alive. Lisa might have gotten away."

"Maybe."

"But she does know you."

Anthony sighed. "Yeah, she knows me. At the moment I'm compromised as well."

"Can we still make it to New Orleans?"

"No. Every police agency in Louisiana is on high alert, especially in New Orleans. The National Police will have Homeland Security watching the airport and the port. It's too hot to get into and out of right now."

"This is all our fault, isn't it?" She felt hot tears well up in her eyes.

"Hey, hey, hey. None of that," Anthony stepped toward her and cupped her chin. "This is the fault of the National Police. They've been trying to roll up our network for years now. That's why we compartmentalized everything." He squeezed her shoulder sympathetically.

"You said it yourself. We're too high profile. They were looking for people exactly like us."

"They were looking for your friends when we came through here last month. The National Police caught a lucky break, that's all. It might take a little longer, but we're going to come up with a new plan."

"What are we going to do?"

"I don't know yet. I'll need to figure out some things."

⅄

Jennifer changed into jeans and a sweater. Awake and alert, she had nothing else to do but read the forum. Valley Forge was abuzz with the news of the raids. She wondered if the forum was compromised but Anthony said that it was hosted on a cloud server based in the Caribbean. He seemed reasonably sure the network remained secure but Jennifer sensed hesitation. Anthony stayed busy with his headset and tablet. He spent his morning dialing out to contacts, but most of the people he typically worked with seemed to have disappeared off the grid.

Jennifer was surprised when her husband broke her concentration. "What's going on?" Matt asked. Jennifer and Anthony stopped when his sudden arrival surprised them.

"I can tell by the look of you two something happened," Matt said.

"We can't go to New Orleans," Jennifer said.

"Why not?"

She glanced at Anthony who gave her a slight nod. Anthony dialed a number and walked to the other side of the suite. Jennifer went on to explain for several minutes that the New Orleans safe house was compromised and the port security was tightened.

After she finished Matt asked, "So do we have a new plan."

Jennifer shook her head. "No, not yet. That's what Anthony is working on right now."

Anthony disconnected his call and came back to the living room area. "She bring you up to speed?"

"Yeah," Matt said sharply. "I want to know what the fuck you're going to do about it."

"Calm down," Jennifer said.

"Right now I'm gathering information," Anthony said. "I need to know what they know and it'll take a little time and resources for me to do that."

"Well, can't you do your hacking thing?" Matt asked.

"Not at the moment. They're not just looking for you. They're looking for me too. Now all of us need to leave. I need to pause and come up with a workable plan."

"How long is that going to take?"

Despite Matt's hysteria Anthony stayed calm. "It'll take as long as it takes. The sooner the better, but it might not be today or even tomorrow. Now I'm going out. I need you two to sit tight here. Can I count on you for that?"

"Yes," Jennifer said. Her husband remained silent.

Anthony put on his security windbreaker hesitantly and left the penthouse.

When the elevator doors dinged shut Matt said, "This guy is going to get us killed."

"We don't know that!"

"We can turn ourselves in right now. Get leniency. Maybe even get our lives back."

"Matt, you don't know what it's like in there. This isn't a summer camp you're talking about. You're talking about concentration camps where people die."

"Oh, come on, it's nothing like that."

"Maggie's dad died in one of these places."

"He was old." His voice trailed off and he turned away. "He might not have died because of that place."

"Have you ever seen the inside of a detention center?"

"No."

"It's not a pleasant retirement home and I suspect the centers on the East Coast and West Coast are far worse. And Matt, listen carefully to what I say next - I will die before I go back inside to one of those places."

⚔

Anthony returned as dusk fell. He entered the suite with bags of Chinese take-out and some groceries. "There's a little mom and pop shop that can do some awesome fried rice. Meatless, unless you count tofu as meat."

"Did you find anything out?" Jennifer asked.

"Let's talk while we eat."

Jennifer quickly set out some dishes and silverware while Matt grabbed beers for everybody. Plates were piled high with fried rice and vegetable egg rolls. Anthony tore open a couple of packets of soy sauce and dumped it on the rice, then stirred in a packet of sriracha for good measure.

Anthony shoveled a forkful of rice into his mouth then bit off a chunk of eggroll. He quickly washed it down with some beer before speaking again. "So I'm pretty sure we're not in any danger at the moment. They figured out the cold trail I sent them on to Montana quickly enough. Their data forensics team started back tracking from there. They know the data breach was through a back door in their network, but they don't know where that back door is. They'll start combing through logins to figure out how I did it. It won't take them long to figure out that I changed the data tied to the serial numbers in your dents. Your dents are compromised. We're stuck here for a while until I can figure out a way out of that.

"I got rid of the Suburban. They had enough information on that vehicle and it was tied to me as well. There's a local guy here named Max. He's, what you might call, quasi-legal. He has little love for the Freedom Party and even less for the National Police. We lucked out that we're here in Louisiana. This state is not Party-friendly. Max is helpful to a point. He might not be entirely trustworthy but it's the best we got for right now. Anyway, the Suburban is gone, replaced by one of the 400 Series Volts.

"Louisiana is infested with the National Police right now. The effort is led by your Chief Inspector Jennings. The Cajuns will frustrate the National Police out of spite but we're on lock down at the moment. Our dents are compromised so we can't get very far anyway. If we stay low and quiet the National Police will assume we escaped Louisiana and widen their search again.

"The Port of New Orleans is closed to us. It's too hot of an entry/exit point for us to use. I wouldn't be surprised if the ship you were supposed to be on isn't seized. I'll work with the folks at Valley Forge to come up with a different exit plan. Bottom line – we're here for at least a week or more."

"So is there any good news?" Jennifer asked.

"There is! Valley Forge is secure for right now. We can still access and communicate through there. Contingency plans were set up for this scenario a long time ago. The entire site is rotating through several private clouds that are offshore. It's a pain in the ass and there'll be frequent downtimes, but the site is designed to stay one step ahead. Not sure how long that'll last. If the full weight of America's Cyber Command comes crashing down with all their processing cycles, we won't last for long. We don't think they can afford to take that away from the war effort.

"I developed contingency plans for this situation. They'll find my back door soon enough, but there's another account that I can activate. I can't tie it to my dent yet because they already figured out how I did that. I've a little bit more freedom of movement. But while your faces are everywhere, I am just another black face in a crowd of black faces. As long as I'm careful and keep my head down I should be able to move around without drawing too much attention."

"So we wait," Matt said. He didn't hide the disappointment from his voice.

"We wait, at least a week, to get out of here. You two are locked down here at the resort. I'll get out and work on a different exit plan for us."

After they finished dinner Jennifer cleaned the dishes. Matt simply watched television without comment. The Freedom Network played one of the new war movies that had just come out. Anthony was at the dining table working his tablet while talking through his headset again. Jennifer was concerned that her husband was sullen about the news. She didn't like that he went straight the Freedom Network right after dinner. When she finished washing the dishes she didn't join him, opting for the bedroom instead.

Jennifer was still wide awake and reading her tablet in bed when Matt joined her. "Are you sure about this?" he asked.

It was an open question but this was one of her husband's familiar quirks. He had returned to doubting this endeavor. "Yes. I'm absolutely sure about this. I need to escape."

"We can still turn ourselves in -"

"No! We can't! A national manhunt is underway to apprehend us as well as tear down the Valley Forge network. This is probably bigger than you and me now."

"Are you sure he knows what he's doing?"

"Yes. He's been doing this a lot longer than either of us has. He strikes me as a smart man with a lot of experience."

"Experience doing what?"

"He's an experienced veteran who has helped people escape for longer than two years. Why do you ask? Do you think that because he didn't come from money you're automatically smarter than him? If there is anything that I have learned in the last five months it's that money and party status is not the full measure of a person."

He looked wounded. Jennifer wasn't sure if she had gone too far or not far enough. Matt slid back to the safe and comfortable for him. "Well... whatever," he said. He stormed out of the room.

Jennifer got up from bed to follow him. She stopped at the doorway and looked out on the suite. Matt had the TV back on but poured bourbon into a glass at the bar. He caught her eye then ignored her, as he plopped down in front of the couch. Jennifer looked across the suite at Anthony. His eyes questioned her and she shook her head slightly. Reluctantly, she retired to the bedroom for the evening.

During the day Anthony would leave the resort to work on their "exit plan". This left Jennifer and Matt in the suite alone. Matt went through an entire bottle of bourbon in the first two days, then started working on the second one. He remained sullen during the day and questioned Anthony when he returned in the late afternoon or evening. Jennifer could tell that Anthony was being patient with her husband.

On the third morning she caught Anthony before he left. Her husband was sleeping off a hangover from the night before. "Can you leave me the keys today?" She referred to the keys for the penthouse and the rest of the resort.

"Sure," Anthony said. "But there isn't a whole lot you can do. There's no money and the machines don't operate without cash."

"No, it's not anything like that. I need to get out of this room and get some space."

"Are you up for a little walk?"

"Sure, I would love some fresh air."

"Well, you can't go outside but there's a little place where it's kind of like outside. Let's go." He took out the key ring from his pocket. "This one operates the elevator. It won't go to the penthouse unless you insert it. The others open and close doors. I would be careful about using them. This place is wired for alarms. Here, let me do this..."

He brought up a program on his tablet and toggled a few commands. "Okay, I disarmed the alarm that leads from resort to the garden atrium. I think you might like it there."

Anthony led her out of the suite towards the elevator, careful to give Jennifer instructions along the way. When they reached the lobby she was lost and didn't which way to go. "It's okay," Anthony said. "Just remember the way there and back. We're going this way." They passed the long silent lobby desk and walked toward the back of the resort.

Where the rest of the casino was dark the corridor was illuminated from sunlight from the clear glass twenty feet above them. The once maroon and gold carpet was now grey with over a decade of dust. Jennifer had never been in a casino resort before and was surprised at the size of the place. The walk to the garden atrium took her longer than she expected.

They found the atrium after several minutes of walking. The door was glass but covered with so much dust that she couldn't see in. Anthony pointed to the green colored key then unlocked the door. Jennifer didn't realize how enormous the garden atrium would be. It had to be the size of a football field. The first thing that struck her was the chill. She checked the ceiling and saw that many of the glass panels on the roof had shattered exposing the garden to the elements. At least it wasn't freezing. Most of the plant life had withered but the trees were still alive, albeit devoid of leaves. A tan marble walkway circled the atrium and led to an empty stone fountain in the center.

"Thank you for this," Jennifer said.

"It's the closest thing we have to a paradise here at the Gold Rush. Sometimes I need to get away from the passengers and just hide here."

"Have you ever brought a passenger here?"

"No," he said softly. "You're the first."

She reached out and grabbed his hand then held it. Her eyes locked on his for a moment then he averted his gaze. "I can't thank you enough for doing this for us."

Anthony gently pulled his hand away and kept his eyes down. "Is he going to be okay?"

Jennifer frowned. "I think so. The stress of all this seems to be getting to him. I told him that I need to leave and he's going along with that." She almost added "for now" but checked herself at the last second.

"Keep an eye on him. Tell me if anything changes."

Jennifer smiled. "I will."

"I'll leave the green key and the penthouse key with you. Lock up when you leave. I have to go now." As he handed her the keys her fingers brushed his for a moment. This time is was Jennifer who averted her gaze. "Stay as long as you like. The garden is pretty peaceful. I'll be back this evening."

Jennifer noted that this garden was still. Even though the structure was exposed to the air and sunlight came through the broken roof, the place was quiet. This area of the city had been abandoned when the casinos closed and was isolated from the activity of the city. She caught herself smiling. This was an excellent suggestion. The isolated garden atrium gave her time to relax away from her brooding husband. She sat on a cold marble bench and let the worries evaporate from her mind. Soon small signs of life began to emanate around the garden. It wasn't entirely empty. She spied a mouse running across the marble walkway, then shortly after a rabbit peered at her from under a dead bush. Jennifer had left her tablet behind. She had no idea how long she stayed in the garden. Without any way to tell time she quickly lost track. Only when the numbing sensation on her butt grew too uncomfortable did she decide to go back to the suite.

Jennifer worked her way back to the suite without getting lost. When she returned she found Matt awake and back to watching the Freedom Network.

He had a small stack of toast and a tiny jar of orange marmalade sitting on the coffee table. He didn't use a plate and crumbs were everywhere. He was at least drinking coffee instead of bourbon. He glared at her. "Were you with him?"

"No, he's out. I went for a walk. Why are you asking like that?"

"I've seen the way you look at him. And the way he looks at you."

"Matt, you're my husband. I'm here with you. I don't have any idea what's going on in your head but you and I are in this together. This guy is getting us out of here. When we escape we are probably never going to see him again. At most, and I mean the very most, I can call Anthony a friend. I don't know what has gotten into you but you need to let this... attitude... go."

He said nothing and took a bite of his toast with marmalade. A pea-sized chunk of toast fell onto his chest. He ignored it as he glared at her.

"What happened to the man who was chief of staff for the Deputy District Leader of the Freedom Party in Colorado?" she asked softly.

"He became a fugitive."

"Matt, we need to change. We need to adapt to a new situation. I need you to be strong. I need you to take care of me. Can you do that? Can you at least try?"

His eyes softened and then he nodded. "Yeah, I can do that. It's been so overwhelming these last few weeks."

She walked around to the back of the couch and hugged him from behind. She got a whiff of his soured scent as she kissed him on one stubbly cheek. "Come on," she said lightly. "You need a shower and shave."

Jennifer led her husband to the bathroom. She helped him pull off the stained sweatshirt and jeans and got the shower running. The bathroom steamed up quickly. She gently pushed him toward the bathroom but he held her hand and gave a soft tug. He wanted her to follow him. His eyes were hungry for her, his carnal eagerness to take her brazenly challenging. Jennifer quickly disrobed and hopped around awkwardly as boots, jeans and sweater all came off at once. Had she watched herself from afar she would have laughed at the spectacle she was making, but Matt was far too serious for frivolity. He lowered his gaze at her while his stiffening member continued to rise.

"Go," she said. "Give me a few seconds to untangle myself."

He turned and entered the bathroom while she finished taking off her underwear. Several seconds later she climbed into the shower with him. He turned toward her and reached to draw her in but she put a hand against his chest. "Take it easy, tiger. Let's clean you up a little first."

She squirted a dollop of shampoo in her hand and lathered his hair. As Jennifer shampooed her husband she massaged and scratched his scalp. She remembered he liked that sort of thing. The shampoo was rinsed out and she started with the body wash and a washrag. She lathered him up from head to toe, paying special attention to clean his erection. He softly moaned and she stroked him with soapy washrag.

After the body residue was cleaned off he couldn't contain himself anymore. He pulled her against him and kissed her deeply. His sourness filled her mouth; bile from vomit or acid reflux along with the lingering hints of smoky bourbon and sweet citrus of marmalade. She kissed him back, fighting off her instinct to retch instantly. He was her husband, after all, and she needed to do this for him. Fortunately the kissing didn't last long. He pushed her up against the shower wall and lifted her. After some fumbling, he inserted himself inside. She clung tight to him while he thrusted into her.

Jennifer was struck with an odd thought as her husband continued with sex- *this is another stress fuck*. She moved with him and made the appropriate moans but her mind was elsewhere and she wanted him to finish. Jennifer was concerned that Anthony would come home early and catch them. She felt like she would be disappointed if he found out she and her husband had sex. And she wondered if she still loved her husband.

Matt finished quickly. This was something she was already used to; he had many habits and quirks in regards to sex. She suppressed a sigh as he withdrew from her. The man who had been so caring and attentive at the ski lodge was gone.

"That was fantastic, babe," Matt said with a grin.

Jennifer smiled back at him but he turned to rinse himself off. It was done. There was nothing more for her to do. She had appeased her man for now.

After the refreshing shower Matt dressed into a clean set of clothes. He reminded her of the man that she had married all those years ago. He even managed to stay away from the bourbon.

Anthony arrived at the suite shortly before sunset. Matt headed for the bar as soon as he saw Anthony. Jennifer picked up on the trigger for Matt's behavior. Did he see Anthony as some sort of rival?

"Anything new to tell us?" she asked.

"New Orleans is still closed. Putting together a new plan escape through Texas," Anthony said.

"Houston?" Matt asked.

"No, too obvious. Any ports leading to the Gulf of Mexico are going to be watched. We will use a coyote to get us through Texas and into Mexico."

"What's a coyote?" Jennifer asked.

"A human smuggler," Anthony said. "Coyotes have been getting people over the borders for years."

"Isn't Texas a battlefield?" Matt asked. The American and Coalition forces were waging war just south of Waco, Texas.

"It is a concern and a fair amount of risk is involved. Even with the war the coyotes are still operating."

Matt splashed some more bourbon into his glass. "Sure, what's the worst that can happen? Is everyone getting across successfully?"

"No. Sometimes they are strafed by gunships on the American side. Sometimes the Mexicans mistake the coyotes for American troops. Which is why I'm going to be careful in finding the right person to get us across the border."

"Can we get across another way?" Jennifer asked.

"Not that I can see. We can try for Canada but that's a lot of territory to cross. And Canada is almost as bad as America. I don't like those risks. I think with all the chaos in Texas we can pass through unnoticed."

"Well, you're the expert."

"Yeah, expert," Matt said. "Hey, expert, you think you can rustle up some more bourbon?" He held up his glass and gave it a shake to clink the ice cubes together.

"What's on the bar is all we have," Anthony said.

"What? You're a talented guy. You're planning our grand escape. What's a little bottle of bourbon?"

Anthony looked at Jennifer. His eyes asked her if she was losing control of Matt. After a pause he said, "I'll see what I can do."

CHAPTER 16

Each day Anthony went out early in the morning. He continued to meet Max and make arrangements for their escape. Anthony would leave around eight o'clock and return shortly after dusk. Sometimes he returned with groceries or take out. He did get another bottle of bourbon for Matt.

In the mornings before Anthony set out for the day he would share breakfast with Jennifer while Matt slept off a bender from the night before. During the breakfast they would chat.

On the morning of the sixth day at the resort Anthony said, "I am concerned about your husband's behavior."

"I am too," Jennifer said. "I think he's just stressed about the situation."

"The situation isn't that stressful. We both have to keep a close eye on him. Make sure he doesn't compromise us."

"You mean if he reached out to his old Party contacts? He hasn't done that."

"The firewall would have caught any attempts to reach the outside. It's happened before."

"It has?"

"Yeah, a lot of people get cold feet. Especially the ones from the middle class like yourselves. They think they want to leave but when I start to transport them they become uncomfortable. No more luxurious houses or OLED walls. Out here they get to see how the common folk live and they want back in the comfort of the suburban home they left behind."

"Have you ever had an unsuccessful transport?"

"No, they've all gone through. Once they drop off the grid the National Police starts to search for them. Once you're picked up by the National Police you're dropped into a black hole and never return. I convince them of that. They still doubt, even after I get them on the boat. Right up to the point when they make landfall to Mexico or Cuba."

"And then?"

"Then they can't believe it. All the stories are true. They're in a free country where they can do what they want. Most stay where they land. Some head to Europe, South America or Australia. I see a few of them on the forum boards every now and then."

"When do you think we can make it out of here?"

"A couple of days, maybe. The plan for Texas is in place but the National Police are still searching Shreveport. There's a strong presence on the streets."

"Okay. Good. I think a big part of Matt's problem is that he's cooped up here."

"Keep an eye on him."

⅄

Jennifer awoke to harsh light and Anthony screaming. She bolted upright in bed and was disoriented for a moment. Why did Anthony scream at her?

"GET UP!" Anthony shouted.

"What's going on?" Jennifer asked.

"No time. We've been breached and we need to move now. Get him up and get dressed. We might have five minutes." He exited the bedroom.

Jennifer shoved her husband. "Matt! Wake up! We gotta go!"

"What?" Matt slurred.

"They're here! The National Police!"

His eyelids jerked open and he exhaled bourbon fumes in her face. "What? The police?"

Jennifer jumped out of bed and threw on her jeans. "Get dressed! We gotta go!"

Matt rolled out of bed onto the floor. After several seconds he stood up and started fumbling around. Jennifer stepped out of the bedroom to see what Anthony was doing. He stood in front of the TV with his tablet synced to it. The TV was laid out in a 2 X 2 grid of surveillance cameras. They were grainy and green but she recognized the casino in one of the boxes. Several dark shapes slinked their way through. "Is that them?" she asked.

"Yeah, their SWAT team."

"How long do we have?"

"They tripped the outside perimeter alarm five minutes ago. They breached inside just now through the front. We need to move as soon as you two are ready."

Matt stumbled out of the bedroom. "What's going on?"

"The National Police found us," Anthony said.

"Oh, God."

"No need to panic. We just need to get out of here."

"We're at the top of a hotel!"

"I said calm down! I always have a plan, even for this contingency. Now are you two ready to go? Grab whatever you can carry. Leave those suitcases behind."

Jennifer dashed into the room and stuffed her tablet in her purse. She glanced around. All that remained was clothes, luggage and toiletries. Those things can be replaced. She grabbed her coat and left the windbreaker emblazoned with the security logo behind. Matt just clumsily grabbed his coat.

When they entered the main living area of the suite they spotted Anthony standing on a chair in front of the door. The gym bag lay open next to the chair legs. He was attaching something to the wall above the doorframe.

"What are you doing?" Jennifer asked.

"Explosive device with a proximity sensor. It will arm itself thirty seconds after we leave."

"I thought you were supposed to put them by their feet," Matt said.

"That's where everybody expects them. Ready?" He didn't wait for an answer. He jumped off the chair and kicked it away, then opened the door. "Go! Go! Go!"

Jennifer rushed through with Matt right behind her. Anthony shut the door behind them and was now brandishing a pistol in his hand. "Follow me," he said.

The gym bag was slung over his back as he stepped down the hallway. Jennifer was surprised when he veered off away from the elevator. "Where are we going?" she asked.

Anthony turned quickly and shushed her, then turned back on his path. He led them to a side door that had a "stairs" icon. He pushed the door open and flicked on a small flashlight. The gun remained pointed ahead of him and he rested his gun hand over the other that carried the flashlight, as he worked his way slowly down the stairs. Jennifer could hear some activity on the lower levels; the movement of men and sharply barked orders. Anthony went down the staircase to the next floor carefully. He opened the door to a dark hallway while Jennifer and Matt followed closely behind.

Anthony led the way down the corridor, careful to keep the flashlight pointed ahead. They approached other corridors that branched off. Anthony took a right then a left corridor. He led them to a set of large black double doors. The pistol was hastily shoved into the pocket of his jacket while Anthony fumbled with his keys. After several seconds he found the key he was looking for and inserted it into the door lock.

The doors opened up to the maintenance station for the resort's maid services. An operational service elevator waited for them in the back of the station. Another key was needed to activate the elevator and open the doors. When the doors chimed open Anthony hustled both of them into the elevator. The elevator was strictly utilitarian and harshly lit with bright fluorescents in the high ceiling. Anthony stabbed the "2" button with his finger.

"How are we getting out?" Jennifer asked.

"Through the lower level housekeeping services. We'll go out through the laundry then out through the fire exit," Anthony said.

"What about the car?"

"They've breached the back entrance. We can't get out that way. We're going on foot."

"Oh, that's great," Matt said. "On foot. They won't shoot us at all, will they?"

"Everything is under control. I told you already that I have a contingency plan for this. Do you think I would put us at the top of a building if I didn't have a way out?"

He didn't wait for an answer as the elevator had reached housekeeping services. Anthony had his gun drawn as the doors opened. Light from the elevator spilled into the services area. Anthony turned toward Jennifer and Matt and mimed for them to stay quiet as they stepped out.

The area was bigger than Jennifer had anticipated. Giant industrial washers sat silently against the wall. She could only catch glimpses of them from the small amount of light reflected from their dusty window doors. The room was jumbled with dead equipment in the room and many crevices led away to different paths. Sheets hung from lines that crisscrossed from the high ceiling. Anthony led them through a winding path of equipment patiently.

He stopped and motioned them off to the left side on a maintenance path, between two large dryers. Matt was hustled in first while Jennifer followed with Anthony behind her. He shut off his flashlight and they waited in the dark. Jennifer was aware of her own breathing and heartbeat. She was sure that her panicked breathing echoed throughout the empty room and she could hear the blood pulse through her ears.

At first she couldn't see anything. Then she caught a glimpse of light through the narrow crevice where they were hiding. Footsteps whispered throughout the room, along with the jingle of equipment. Two men passed their hiding spot. They wore helmets with lights mounted on their heads and carried assault rifles. They walked past casually, as if they were assigned a duty instead of tracking anybody. After the SWAT officers had passed and the light had receded Anthony turned on his flashlight and led them out.

Another couple of minutes of walking passed with Anthony leading them through twists and turns. If they got separated now Jennifer wouldn't know how to find her husband or Anthony. They were surprised to turn a corner and found two helmet lights pointed at them less than ten feet away.

"Hey," a voiced shouted out.

A moment later Anthony fired, two shots to the one on the right then another two to the one on the left. Both men were knocked backward to the ground. Anthony followed up with a shot each in their heads. "Body armor," he explained.

"You just killed those guys," Matt's eyes were wide and his face was sweaty.

"Keep your voice down. They would have taken us," Anthony said.

Jennifer was shocked at the sudden violence. She stood completely dumbfounded. Jennifer's only experience with this kind of violence was from a war vid. Behind them shouts echoed from a distance. She turned to see the helmet lights dancing towards them. The two police officers that had passed them previously were now running toward them.

"Get behind me," Anthony said.

He stepped forward and grabbed one of the assault rifles from the slain policemen. Anthony dropped to one knee and sighted the rifle on the advancing men. When they were ten yards out he fired on them, short three round bursts in either man's direction. The men separated and broke for cover in opposite directions. Anthony fumbled with the corpse at his feet, found an object, and then tossed it toward the policemen. "Get down," he told Jennifer and Matt.

Jennifer huddled against the wall, waiting for something. A sharp explosion surprised her and then she experienced disorientation followed by a brief wave of nausea. She was confused for a minute while her head swam, then came to her senses as Anthony pulled her up and held her by the jaw. "You okay?" he asked. She could hear the words but they were muffled she nodded. "We don't have much time. Two minutes at most. Let's go."

He turned to find Matt picking up one of the assault rifles. "Put it down," Anthony said.

"Why?" Matt said. "We can use it."

"It won't work. The gun is bluetoothed to its owner. You get five feet away it will stop working or, worse, explode in your hands. Now let's move."

Matt dropped the assault rifle with disgust, as if he had just picked up a live rattlesnake. "You are going to get all of us killed," he muttered.

Anthony ignored the jibe. Again he shepherded Jennifer and Matt through the housekeeping facilities. He finally got them to a fire exit and motioned for them to stop. "This is the way out. We're on the north side of the resort complex, mostly maintenance buildings here. We're looking for one in the back. It has a maintenance tunnel that leads to the garage of a sister property to the east. It's abandoned as well. Keep your eyes open and follow any orders I give you. Got it?"

Jennifer nodded.

"I asked if you understood." He was looking past her at her husband.

She turned. "Matt?"

"Yeah, yeah," Matt said, "I hear you." His voice trailed off.

Anthony opened the door softly then peered out. After waiting for several seconds he stepped out and held the door open for Jennifer and Matt to follow. When they were through he closed the door softly. The night was clear and the half-moon above gave them enough ambient light to navigate. A helicopter was aloft using a searchlight around the resort complex. A muffled explosion sounded out above them, followed by tinkling of glass some distance away.

"They found your surprise," Jennifer said. The helicopter turned and focused on the penthouse explosion on top of the resort.

"Yeah," Anthony said. "They'll be confused for a couple of minutes but it won't take them long." They walked along the broken asphalt just outside of the resort. Anthony kept them close to the wall for cover. After he reached the edge of a building he peered around the corner. "Okay, it is clear. Jennifer, you follow. Matt, you follow her. We get across this alley quickly and keep moving." The alley was maybe fifteen yards wide. Anthony dashed quickly to the other side while Jennifer and Matt followed.

The helicopter now circled the resort again. Anthony was careful to keep them close to the shadows and the wall. They reached the corner of the building they were using for cover. A wide employee parking lot stood between them and the maintenance building. Anthony peered around the corner quickly. "Shit! They're right around the corner."

"Who are 'they'?" Jennifer asked.

"Two Joltvees. At least a half dozen men. A lot of lights and activity. Maybe seventy yards away from our location. I think they're using it as a staging area. If we keep to this end of the parking lot and stay in the shadows, we can probably get by them."

"Are you sure?"

"Nothing is certain, but I think we can make it. Same plan as before. Follow me, with you behind me and Matt behind you. Go where I go and stick to the shadows. If we get any trouble, you run to that building over there. Understood?"

"Yeah, got it."

Matt was silent.

"Matt, do you understand?" Anthony asked.

"Yeah, I understand," Matt said. Jennifer thought he sounded distant as if he was distracted by a passing thought.

"Let's go."

Anthony kept toward the end of the parking lot, carefully watching the activity to his left. He didn't quite run but casually trotted with gun in hand. The seconds passed by slowly. Even though Jennifer was in shape she never felt so slow in her life. Her footfalls on the asphalt were agonizingly loud as the squat maintenance building loomed closer. She would make it in another fifteen seconds. Anthony made to the building and turned to wave her in. She reached the building and took cover.

"Where's Matt?" Anthony asked.

"Hey!" A shout sounded out from across the parking lot. Matt stood halfway between the buildings with his hands in the air. "Heyyyyyyyyy!"

Jennifer started forward but Anthony held her back. "We can't expose ourselves."

"Heyyyyyyyyy," Matt shouted. "I surrender!"

The lights from the vehicles turned and trained their intense beams him. "I surrender," Matt shouted again. He began to run towards the policemen. "I surrender! I surrender! I surrender!" It became his chanted mantra.

Across the parking lot the men came around and trained their guns on Matt as he advanced. Jennifer heard their boot heels smack the pavement and their equipment jingle as they took their defensive stance. They shouted at Matt to get down on the ground. The pitch in the helicopter engine changed as it canted their way. Matt continued to close the distance while shouting his surrender.

"Get down, you idiot," Anthony muttered. He held her tight. She was aware that hot tears streamed down her face.

One of the policemen opened fired followed by two more. Matt dropped to the ground as bullets tore through him. One of the policemen shouted out a cease-fire which was quickly taken up by two more. Jennifer covered her mouth and stifled her own cry.

"We've got to help him," she said.

"We can't," Anthony said. "There's nothing we can do. We have to go."

"What's going on here?" A voice shouted above the other policemen.

"Wait," Jennifer said. "I want to see who that is."

A tall figure wearing a long overcoat strode through the throng of policemen standing over her husband's body. She recognized the owner of that voice. He had tortured her several times only a month ago. "That's one of them," Chief Inspector Jennings said. "There should be another one, possibly two of them. Fan out and search from here."

The searchlights of the helicopter began to move up the parking lot. They were behind the maintenance building, but their cover wouldn't last long. "We need to go," Anthony said.

Jennifer wiped the tears on her face with the heel of her hand. The adrenaline coursed through her now. "Yeah," she said and turned to follow Anthony. He grabbed her hand and led her along the wall of the maintenance building. A few seconds later they were at a steel door. He chanced turning on the flashlight to find the right key on his key ring. The helicopter swung around and the searchlight started crawling around the area. Anthony found the key just as the helicopter trained the searchlight on them. He opened the door and hustled Jennifer inside.

Once inside the flashlight was back on and he swung his gym bag around and searched it. He pulled out a grenade, pulled the pin, and places the grenade carefully against between the door handle and door. "Follow me," he said.

The maintenance building was small with tiny windows at the top where little moonlight filtered through. On the backside of the building was a staircase leading down. This door was unlocked and he hustled her through again. Before continuing he stopped and pulled out his tablet. The tablet came to life right away and Anthony started tapping.

Something blinked at Jennifer's feet. Timers were planted on either side of the doorway and they counted down. More explosives would go off in five minutes.

"Run," Anthony said.

Jennifer stood still and watched the blinking timers. *My husband is dead!*

Anthony grabbed her by the shoulders and shook her. "We have to run!"

Jennifer shook her head clear then nodded once. He maintained direct eye contact with her. "Okay, let's go," she said.

He started down the maintenance tunnel, the gym bag bouncing against his back. Behind them was a loud bang. That had to be the policemen getting through the door. They would hesitate now for fear of other traps.

Their run down the maintenance hallway lasted forever. All she could see in front of her were the bobbing flashlight and glimpses of the multi colored pipes running along the ceiling. She wondered why the maintenance building hadn't exploded yet when she was rocked off her feet. Jennifer was confused for a moment. The flashlight rolled across the floor. Anthony was on his back on the ground just ahead of her. The flashlight beams caught dust drifting off the ceiling. "Are you okay?" Jennifer asked. Her voice was muffled in her own ears.

"Yeah," he said. "We can walk now. They won't get through that any time soon."

"Won't they figure out where this tunnel goes?"

"They will. We're almost there. It'll take them about an hour, maybe an hour and a half, to figure out where we went off to. This tunnel branches off to the north and then two separate directions later on."

"Do we have a car?"

"No. I'll arrange something. I'll make the call right now." He put the headset in his ear and tapped an icon on the tablet. "Max? I need an extraction. There are two of us. Yeah, no longer a third. I understand that there are no refunds. We need extraction from the garage of the Fortuna Resort. Yeah, I know we have a lot of activity here. What? $30,000? Agreed. What else? Damn, okay, I'll call you back."

"What happened?"

"This is going to be dicey. He'll get us out but we have to meet his people. Too many cops patrolling the area right now."

"Where are we going to meet his people?"

"The backside of the Fortuna property. A lot of streets that intersect there. If that helicopter doesn't spot us Max can send his people to do the pick-up."

She followed Anthony as he walked through the tunnel at a brisk pace. He was right. It didn't take long for them to find steps leading to the other side. The door at the top didn't need a key, only a deadbolt that needed to be twisted. Anthony stepped out first, with his gun drawn. The garage was pitch black save for his flashlight piercing the darkness. "Careful," he said. "A lot of debris on the floor. Stay behind me."

Jennifer stayed close to him until she stumbled into some cans. They crashed on the floor making her jump. "Sorry," she muttered.

"Just be careful. If I remember it right there's a door over here."

Despite the darkness the garage felt cavernous with the clattering cans echoing throughout. They shuffled through the darkness for a couple of minutes before reaching the door. Anthony twisted the doorknob and peered out. After waiting several seconds he motioned for Jennifer to follow him.

They were at the backside of the second resort where a series of loading docks faced a wide alley. A large building stood on the other side of the alley.

Anthony called Max on his headset again. "Max, we're out. What next? Okay? Say again? Red diamond on the rear right fender? Okay, got it."

"What's up?" Jennifer asked.

"We go north. Quickly, to Delhi Street. There's a coroner's van waiting for us."

"A coroner's van?"

"It's our ticket out of here." A helicopter flew overhead high above them. Instinctively they both ducked even though they were hard to spot between the buildings.

Anthony led them north away from the Fortuna toward the freeway. They stayed off the freeway for several minutes while they walked east. Finally they found a drainage pipe large enough to walk through if they stooped. The water flowed through slowly at a height of six inches. Jennifer was glad that she had worn boots for the escape journey. On the other side of the drainage pipe was a street with some commercial buildings, relics of stores from the previous century that were now boarded up. Anthony led them to the other side of the street to lose the pursuing police in the alleys between buildings. Twice police cars howled by with sirens screaming. One car was a Shreveport PD cruiser while the other was the solid black National Police SUV. Each time they approached Anthony would pull Jennifer into the shadows until they passed.

They reached Delhi Street and headed west with little cover of darkness as the street was well lit with halogen lamps. They walked for a few minutes until they found a black van sitting silently on the side of the street. The taillights shined brightly. Jennifer and Anthony approached from behind on the right side of the street. As they reached the van Jennifer spotted the red diamond just behind the wheel well.

Anthony tapped the glass with his knuckle on the passenger side. The window slid down to reveal a thick ruddy face with salt and pepper mustache and beady black eyes. "You must be the passengers," he said in thick Cajun patois. "Let's get you in back."

Jennifer and Anthony stepped back to let the man out of the van. He was tall and heavy. Jennifer estimated that he was on the plus side of three hundred pounds. He likely ate a lot of rice and bread instead of the McSalads. The man wore a black windbreaker that had Caddo Parish Coroner's Office stenciled in yellow above the left breast.

Despite the man's size he moved rather lithely, as an athlete would. He quickly strode across the sidewalk and opened the back doors of the van. In the back were two bodies in the black bags. "Okay," the man said, "You are going to have to get in these bags."

"With the bodies?" Jennifer asked.

"No, no. We got separate bag for you. They are clean and new. I promise."

"Is this necessary?" Anthony asked.

"Yeah, it is," the man said. "You've caused quite a ruckus. Roadblocks are going up all over the city. We have to get through them and they are going to check. Get in. Time's a'wastin'."

Jennifer and Anthony climbed into the cramped van. Between the two of them and the two bodies it was hard to move around. She was finally able to slide into the bag which Anthony helped zip up for her. Then she waited while as Anthony climbed into the other body bag. The smell of rubber was overpowering but she was glad it wasn't the smell of decay.

"Can you help me here?" Anthony asked.

"Yeah sure, buddy," the big man said. "I'll take it from here."

She heard Anthony getting zipped up into the bag. Then she felt a weight on top of her. It wasn't directly on top but off to the side allowing her to breath. She realized that one of the bagged bodies had been stacked on top of her. She could hear the man climb into the passenger seat of the van and feel the van list to the right under his weight. "Hey, Rene, let's go."

Despite the fact that Anthony was only a couple of feet away and two other men were in the front, Jennifer felt alone in the black pit of the body bag. She was scared now. Did she fool herself into thinking it would be as simple as a cross-country trip then a boat cruise? Things went wrong as they always did. So far it seemed like Anthony had planned for anything that could go wrong, but now they were in body bags under corpses with two sketchy men driving them to only God knew where. Would these men turn them in? Was the reward high enough now for these defiant Cajuns, as Anthony defined them, that it outweighed the risk?

The coroner's van came to a stop. "You'll want to stay real still and real quiet for the next few minutes," the big man shouted to them.

Jennifer felt the van edge forward then stop every other minute. Finally a new voice spoke up. "Open it up. You know we got to check the back." Jennifer assumed the new voice was one of the police manning the roadblock.

She heard the big man step out of the van then the back doors open. "What do you got here?"

"Dead hookers dumped in a landfill," the big man said.

"Four of them?"

"You know that's an issue here, right?"

"Yeah, I heard."

"Check and see for yourself." Jennifer was amazed at how calm and bored the big man sounded.

The weight of the van shifted as the officer stepped in. She heard him unzip the bag above her. "Good God!" The police officer gagged.

"Hey, she's one of the pretty ones," the one named Rene shouted from the driver's seat. "The other ones are even more messed up. Check for yourself." He gave an evil laugh.

The bag was zipped up quickly. "No. No need to. Let 'em through."

The big man climbed back into the van and they moved through the checkpoint. Jennifer could feel her heart slowing down. The inside of the bag had gotten hot and cloying.

"You folks take it easy back there," the big man said. "We should be at the house in about thirty minutes."

The thirty minutes passed agonizingly slow. Finally the van came to a stop. Rene and the big man stepped out then around to the back. The two other body bags were tossed aside and they were unzipped out. Jennifer gasped and sucked in the freezing air. The cold winter never felt as good as it had in that moment.

"Feels so good to get out," Jennifer said, then gasped some more. Anthony climbed out of his own black bag. He was covered in sweat as well. Rene and the big man stepped back to allow them out. Rene, short with the wispy pencil-thin mustache, offered his hand to help Jennifer out. She smiled appreciatively but her gut reaction told her that Rene was a creep. Another man stood behind them, flanked by two bodyguards carrying pistols. The third man was tall but older. She pegged him on this side of sixty. He was bald with a white goatee. His eyes were whitish blue and she could feel him staring right through her. She realized right away that these were bad people.

The man smiled widely at her. "I'm Max, pleased to meet you." He offered his hand.

She took his hot, strong hand and could feel his frenetic energy pulsing through him. "I'm Jennifer."

They stood on the circular driveway of an old plantation house. A half dozen cars lined the driveway, flanked by cypress trees with Spanish moss hanging from the limbs. The house itself had a broad facade but was rife with years of neglect. The windows had black shutters that starkly contrasted against the peeling faded white paint of the house. The porch was lit and red lights burned in the windows.

Max released his grip from her and turned to Anthony. "How are you doing, Anthony?" he asked.

Anthony shook his hand. "Thanks for the pick-up. We appreciate you helping us out."

"No problem. We're glad to help the cause, provided that we're properly compensated for our trouble."

"If I could have my bag I can complete the transaction right now."

"Leon, get the man his bag,"

The big man walked to the front of the van and returned with Anthony's gym bag. Anthony fumbled through it and found his tablet. He punched in a few keystrokes. "Done. Thirty-thousand wired to your account in Cuba."

Max checked own tablet and waited. When he received the chime several seconds later he nodded and put the tablet away. "Leon, could you put them up in the big room on the third floor. It should be big enough for the two of you. You can sit tight for a couple of days before we get you off to Dallas."

"Follow me," Leon said. Jennifer and Anthony followed the big man up the wide steps of the porch. He led them inside the foyer of the plantation house, then veered left to a locked door. Leon fished out a key ring from the inside pocket of this jacket then unlocked it. The windowless room was small with old wooden shelving and drawers lined along the walls. "First things first. If you got weapons you got to surrender them here. Don't worry, I'll give you a claim ticket and you will get them back when you leave."

"Is this necessary?" Anthony asked.

"House rules."

Anthony sighed and placed his gym bag on the table in the center of the room. He fished out two pistols, several clips of ammo, a grenade and some plastic explosive.

Leon chuckled. "You expecting a war?"

"It helps to be prepared."

Leon carefully cataloged Anthony's arsenal on a ticket. "How about you, Miss?"

"I got nothing. Just my tablet," Jennifer said.

"No clothes or nothing."

"No."

Leon grunted. "All right. We'll see if one of the girls can scrounge up some clothes for you."

He led them out of the room and locked it up. Jennifer and Anthony followed him past the living room. She looked in the room while passing and saw two women sitting on a couch. The blonde woman was wearing a black bustier and panties while the Latina was in a teal baby doll teddy. Both women made eye contact for a moment with a mix of anticipation and apprehension in their eyes. They also appeared to be emaciated to the point where their ribs showed and they were covered with sores, scabs and bruises.

"Come on," Anthony said. He had started up the steps then stopped. "We should get to our room."

Jennifer realized that she had stopped and stared. "Sorry," she said, then followed them up the stairs.

The top of the stairs led to a long hallway lit with light fixtures on the walls. The peeling wallpaper was a garish green and gold. The bedroom doors were heavy oak. Someone had crudely painted numbers on them in white paint. As Jennifer and Anthony followed Leon down the hallway the exaggerated sounds of passion emanated from behind one of the closed doors. From another door they passed came screams of terror and the sound of a beating. Jennifer was disturbed by all of this. Anthony gave her a reassuring smile.

At the end of the hall Leon opened the door. The room was spacious but the walls were covered with that same peeling green and gold wallpaper. An enormous bed stood against the wall, covered with a bright red satin comforter and equally red pillows. "Welcome to the VIP suite," Leon said. "Don't worry. This is the cleanest room in the house. It has an attached bathroom separate for you to use. It's for special clients and transient guests such as yourselves. It'll be morning soon. We'll have breakfast in the kitchen at nine, if you want to join."

"Is this a brothel?" Jennifer asked.

Leon smiled tiredly. "Yeah, it is. Where did you think the dead hookers came from? Have a good night." He closed the door behind him on his way out.

"This is bad, isn't it?" Jennifer asked.

"I knew that Max was in this business but, yeah, this is pretty bad. Stay with me at all times. Don't leave yourself alone with anyone here. Not even the women. Understood?"

"How long do we stay here?"

"Just a day or two. The plan in Texas is in place. We just need to get out of Shreveport and to Dallas. And I still need to come up with a way to get around our dents."

"Should we get some sleep?"

"If you can. After tonight I'm too awake to sleep. Take the bed. I will take the floor."

She regarded the bed dubiously. "Is it clean?"

Anthony shrugged. "Maybe the sheets are. That comforter isn't." He sat down in an easy chair next to a small table near the sole window of the room. Anthony pulled out his tablet and starting tapping away.

Jennifer took off the filthy boots. The bottoms of her jeans were filthy with mud as well. She stared at them for several seconds. Anthony looked up from his tablet. "I have a pair of gym shorts you can change into," he said.

He had the luxury of being able to bring his scant luggage. Anthony reached into his gym bag, dug around for a bit and then came up the shorts. He tossed them to her from across the room.

She took them into the bathroom and flipped on the light. The shower was a garden tub with a glass door. Jennifer was relieved that the bathroom appeared to be clean. She unbuttoned her jeans and shrugged them off. Without any real place to put them she slid open the door to the tub and laid the jeans over the edge. Jennifer put on the gray gym shorts, cinched the drawstring as tight as she could and sat down on the lidded toilet.

It was the first time she had slowed down during the night. What had transpired only a few hours ago now crushed her. Her husband was dead. Dropped down in the middle of a parking lot under a hail of bullets. She was essentially alone now. Jennifer had to go forward with this escape without her husband and with a man she had just met last month.

The tears spilling from her eyes caught her by surprise. She wasn't ready for the tears and now that it had started her chest heaved with despair. Jennifer did the best she could to stifle her sobs. For some unknown reason she didn't want Anthony to hear her crying. She was afraid that he might judge her as weak as her husband was.

With Matt that was what it had amounted to. He couldn't leave that old life behind. The status, the privilege, the wealth - all of it earned or granted by the Party in some way. She had pushed him into this even though he wasn't ready and never would have been. Jennifer realized that Matt had kept thinking they could turn all this around. He didn't have the same experience that she did. He had never realized that their lives of privilege had ended and he had so desperately wanted to hold on to it. So rather than try to change he had ran to the Party looking for acceptance. And now he was dead.

So what next? She had no choice but to go forward. She, along with Anthony now, had to stick with the plan and escape America. But that was too far ahead. Right now all she wanted to do was sit on the toilet in this brothel and cry.

Jennifer was unsure how long she sat in that bathroom. Maybe ten minutes, maybe as much as thirty. She wiped her eyes with the heel of her hand, then splashed some cold water on her face. When she left the bathroom Anthony looked expectantly at her. She realized he had heard her and he wanted to help but didn't want to push himself. Instead, he said, "Try to get some sleep."

She pulled the covers back on the king-sized bed then climbed in. Jennifer didn't think she would fall asleep but she did.

CHAPTER 17

The bedroom had a perfect east-facing window that allowed sunlight to stream in. After the bright light woke Jennifer up she immediately checked her tablet. The time was almost ten o'clock. Jennifer searched for Anthony and found him curled up awkwardly with one of the pillows on the settee near the window. She got up and nudged him.

Anthony eyes flew open. "What?"

"I'm awake," she said. "Take the bed."

"Okay," he mumbled. He got up, walked to the bed and collapsed on it.

Jennifer took a shower but had nothing to change into except the same gym shorts and sweater she had already worn. She played with the tablet and checked the news. The lead story was about terrorists holding out at one of the abandoned casinos in Shreveport. The news report proudly boasted that one of them had been killed in a shootout. The National Police had six killed and eight wounded. Jennifer felt some sense of satisfaction in that.

She didn't want to stay cooped up in the room all day but she didn't want to wake Anthony either. Besides that she was starving. After mulling it over for a couple of minutes she decided to venture down to the kitchen to see if there was something she could eat. Jennifer was well aware that she was in dangerous situation, but she hoped she could dash in and out without notice.

She cracked open the door and ventured out into the quiet hallway. Jennifer figured that maybe business wouldn't be conducted until noon at the earliest. She worked her way down the staircase and started searching for the kitchen. She found it in the back of the house, occupied by a lone woman wearing a purple tank top and gold shorts, washing dishes by hand at the sink. She caught Jennifer entering into the kitchen. "Oh, hey hon," she said. "Are you new?"

Jennifer wasn't sure how to respond. "We came in early this morning and are staying in the VIP bedroom."

"Oh, y'all are the visitors. Sorry, we get a lot of new girls here all the time. My name's Rachel." She quickly wiped her hands on a dishtowel and extended her right hand.

"Nice to meet you," Jennifer said as she introduced herself.

"You want something to eat?"

"I'd be grateful."

"We got some biscuits left over from breakfast. I can warm some of them up for you. We got some jelly and futter you can put on them."

"That sounds great."

Jennifer sat down at the little kitchenette table in the corner of the room. Rachel pulled a half dozen cold biscuits from the breadbox, put them on a pizza pan and then in the oven.

"Well ain't you a pretty sight in them shorts." The voice startled Jennifer as she turned to the see a short thin man standing in the doorway. It was Rene, the driver from the coroner's van. She thought he might have been talking to Rachel but she realized he stared lecherously at her. He wore torn blue jeans, a stained white sleeveless undershirt and a LSU ball cap. "We should probably put you to work here."

"Rene, you leave her alone," Rachel said.

"Shut your fucking mouth!" His voice boomed across the kitchen causing Jennifer and Rachel to flinch. Rachel took a step back. Rene quickly reclaimed his composure. "My apologies, ladies. I'm just saying that a little gratitude would be nice. We pulled your fucking asses out of the fire last night."

"Gratitude?" Jennifer said. "I believe your boss was compensated this morning. Very well compensated."

"Maybe so. But he didn't compensate me. So I'm looking for something a little more for me." Rene moved across the room. Jennifer stood up from the chair and took a step back. That only seemed to encourage Rene to close distance. He rushed toward her until he was almost nose-to-nose. "So how about it, you fucking society bitch? Are you going to do something for me?"

"Is there a problem here?" Jennifer looked past Rene to see Anthony standing in the doorway of the kitchen. He stepped into the room.

Rene took a step back. "Hey, man, there's no problem here. The lady and I were just talking."

Jennifer took the opportunity to step around Rene and get behind Anthony. She spotted Leon coming down the hallway. "Behind you," she said quietly.

Leon stepped past Anthony and approached Rene. "What the fuck are you doing?"

"What?" Rene said. "I'm not doing nothing."

"We can hear you all over the fucking house. It's bad enough that the customers abuse the girls. We don't need you doing abusing them too. These are our honored guests who paid good money to be here. We're going to treat them as guests. Do you hear me?"

When Rene didn't answer, Leon slapped him across the face. The big man was quick and powerful. Leon casually swept Rene aside like a kid knocking over blocks. "You can't do that to me," Rene cried. "Uncle Max won't stand for it."

"Well, your Uncle Max left me in charge. That means I'm in charge of you too, you fucking idiot. I'll ask this question one more time. Do you understand me?"

"Yeah, Leon. Yeah, I get it."

"Good." Leon turned to Jennifer and Anthony. "You two okay?"

"Yeah," Anthony said.

Leon turned to Rachel. "Could you help the young lady with some clothes? She left in a hurry last night."

"Yeah, sure," she said. "I'll take care of her, Leon."

Leon turned to Jennifer. "Go with her. It'll be all right."

Jennifer looked at Anthony. He nodded and she followed Rachel out of the kitchen. She heard Leon say, "Let's talk," to Anthony as she left.

Rachel led Jennifer up the stairs. Several scantily clad women peered out from the doorways. They were curious about the ruckus Rene had caused downstairs. "Is it true that you were high society?" Rachel asked.

"I was."

"What happened?"

"I got in trouble with the National Police."

"You couldn't talk or buy your way out of it?"

"Once they focus in on you they won't let go."

Rachel sighed. "Ain't that the truth? I thought you Party types were exempt from rules."

"Not this time."

Rachel opened an unnumbered door. Inside the room stood racks of clothing. "Pick out some things. These clothes are old and the owners won't miss them. I'll run them through the wash for you."

"Are the owners dead?"

Rachel winced. "We don't ask questions." Then she sighed again. "Occasionally we get clients who are rough. Sometimes a girl will just OD. Rene gets rough with us when he thinks he can get away with it. Max is the boss so he can do whatever he wants. Leon's okay. He's a sweetheart really."

Jennifer pulled sweaters off the racks and compared them. "Do you ever think about getting out?"

"Sometimes, but where would I go and what would I do? Shreveport's dead. There are no jobs here. At least with this job I'm getting fed."

Jennifer tried on a couple pairs of jeans. They were the right length but a little loose in the waist. They would have to do.

"How long are you staying?" Rachel asked.

"A couple of days? Anthony's making arrangements to get us across the border."

"Is he your man?"

"No. He's helping us. I mean me, now. My husband was killed by the National Police last night."

"Oh my God! I'm so sorry."

Jennifer pushed the thought out of her mind. The last thing she wanted to do was cry in front of this stranger. She presented the clothing. "What do you think?"

"They look fabulous. I'll wash them for you. In the meantime stay in your room. Clients will start coming by soon and you don't want to be seen. Soldiers from the front on leave and we get a few from the National Police too. Wouldn't want you to get caught."

Rachel took the clothes from Jennifer. They left the room heading for opposite directions. She went back to the VIP room at the end of the hallway. Her stomach protested again. She never got the biscuits she was promised.

Anthony returned to the room a few minutes later. He had a platter of biscuits with marmalade, jelly, jam, honey, futter and molasses. He set the tray down on the table and offered a plate to Jennifer. She took it wordlessly and snatched a biscuit as well. The biscuit was split open quickly and lathered with soft futter. "What did he want to talk to you about?"

"Give me the lay of the land. What goes on here? Why we need to stay out of sight. They get a lot of people in here from military, the National Police and the Party."

"Rachel told me the same thing."

Anthony poured the molasses on his plate then mixed in some soft futter with a fork. He stirred the mixture until it was an amber color then broke off a piece of biscuit to dip into it. "Leon says we're on schedule to leave in two days. They have their fingers into shipping. Trucks are running to the front and he says Max can get us into one of them. They should get us into Dallas without being held up at checkpoints."

"What about our dents?"

"I think I got a plan for that?"

A knock sounded at the door. Anthony opened it and let Leon in. "I got the stuff that you wanted," Leon said. He dumped the contents of the grocery bag he carried in onto the bed. "You got a dent scanner, a bag of dents, a first aid kit, scalpel, tweezers, rubbing alcohol and suture tape. You know this is not going to work, right?"

"I just need it to work a couple of times," Anthony said.

"You said using other people's dents were a bad idea," Jennifer said.

"Normally, yes, but I'm out of ideas at the moment. And I have something more long term in mind."

Leon shrugged. "I hear you're a genius when it comes to this shit."

"Where did the bag of dents come from?" Jennifer asked.

"Do you really want to know?" Leon asked. "Let's just say that when an unidentified body is discovered at the landfill this is the reason why." He picked up the clear plastic Ziploc bag of dents and jingled them.

Jennifer shuddered. There had to be at least forty or fifty dents in that bag. She had never actually seen one. They were smaller than a quarter-inch and silvery-grey. Each dent represented a dead body, probably that of a prostitute.

Leon sensed Jennifer's uneasiness. He tossed the bag of dents on the bed. "I'll leave you two at it. Stay inside here for the rest of the day. Dinner will be brought up a little past six."

As soon as Leon left Anthony went straight to the collection of materials. He grabbed the bag of dents and the scanner and took them to the table. Still munching on the biscuits with molasses he dumped the bag of dents onto a white napkin then started separating them out.

"So do you want to tell me this plan?" Jennifer asked.

Anthony answered while working. "So the first part of the plan is to find some dents to replace our own. The healing wounds are going to be a giveaway but hopefully we don't get stopped or we pass somehow. The hard part is going to be finding a woman's name that sounds like a man's name. If I pick a dent with the name like 'Michelle' they're going to know something is up."

"And the second part of this plan?"

"A modification of my original plan. Tie our identities with the records I already set up in other countries; Cuba, Mexico, the European Union and a half dozen other places." He picked up a dent and scanned it. "Alexis Chumway?"

"Alexis is pretty."

"You are now Alexis. Now to find a name for me."

This took longer for him. One by one dents were scanned then carefully placed back into the Ziploc bag. Finally, Anthony said, "I think this one will work. Cameron Boudreaux."

"A girl?"

"Yes, but the name is masculine enough to pass a casual inspection. I didn't expect any men's names among these."

"They go through women here quickly."

Anthony sighed. "I don't like it any more than you do, but this was the nearest safe harbor I could find. And we'll be out of here soon enough."

Jennifer wasn't happy either but she couldn't argue. She was considered a criminal herself and, by Party standards, even worse than the people here. She left him at his work and powered on her tablet.

Anthony spent an hour working on his tablet. He established the dents into the American database as well as the other countries they might possibly enter. Anthony explained that the protocols for the foreign databases worked differently but were not entirely unbreakable. He couldn't pull the same trick with the serial numbers on the dents that he did before on the US side, but he was sure that he could do it on the foreign databases. That way when they went to the other side their dents tied back to their original identities, or, at least, a bare template of a built identity. He couldn't transfer their original identities across from America to Mexico. The Mexican firewalls were weak but the American ones were vigilantly monitored for data coming in as well as going out. If given time he could probably find an exploit on the website. Create a back door like they did on the Kongo Gumi wiki page. But there wasn't that much time and he had to limit his interaction with them anyway. After working with the dents and his tablet he announced, "It's time."

"Time for what?" Jennifer asked.

"A little surgery."

"Okay, I'm ready."

"Well, I need you to help me with mine first. I have to do my surgery one handed with your help. Come over here."

She hopped off the bed and sat down opposite him at the table. Enough sunlight shined through that they could see their work. Anthony laid out the scalpel, rubbing alcohol, the dent on a piece of paper labeled "Cameron" and a roll of suture tape. He cleaned a pair of tweezers with the rubbing alcohol then picked up the dent and dropped it into a small bottle with rubbing alcohol. He shook the bottle.

"Does the alcohol hurt the dent?" Jennifer asked.

"No, it'll be just fine."

When he was done shaking the bottle he fished the dent out with the tweezers and placed it back onto the paper. Then he rubbed the palm of this right hand, trying to feel for the dent. She did the same thing many times herself. Finally, he cleaned the scalpel with alcohol then the palm of his hand. "Now comes the hard part," he said.

Using his left hand he cut a small incision in the palm of his right hand, right above where the dent should be. Immediately he grabbed the tweezers and fished the dent out of his palm. The little blood that oozed out was cleaned with some gauze. After the area was clean enough he picked up the other dent with the tweezers and put it into the wound. "Can you cut me off a piece of that tape? About two inches." His brow was beaded with sweat.

Jennifer cut the tape as he instructed. She placed it on top of the wound for him and let him press down on tape to finish the seal.

"See?" he said. "That was easy. Now your turn."

Jennifer rolled up the sleeve of her sweater and extended her right arm. Anthony considered it for a moment then suggested that they switch seats so that her arm could rest on the table. After a minute of making the new arrangements Anthony started to work on her hand. He did the same procedure as before where he rubbed the center of her palm to find the dent in her hand and found it quickly enough. She realized that he never used anesthetic on himself nor did he offer any for her. Jennifer held her arm still as he sliced into her palm with the scalpel. A painful sting blossomed with fire as he cut in. She kept her hand steady and remarkably refrained from screaming. Anthony sensed her discomfort and worked quickly as he extracted her original dent and inserted the replacement.

After the suture tape was applied he announced, "All done. How are you doing?"

"Not bad, considering."

"Be careful with the hand for a couple days. By that time it should start heal up nicely. Let's test them." He took the dent scanner and passed his hand in front of it and nodded after receiving the agreeable chime. He then tested the dent in her hand.

"What are you going to do about those?" she asked. She nodded to the bloody dents sitting on the white paper.

"Flush them down the toilet."

"Really?"

"Yeah, dents are pretty sturdy. They will survive the journey through the pipes. Maybe the National Police will pick up their signal along the way." He folded the paper around the dents so they wouldn't spill on the floor, then carried them to the bathroom. Several seconds later he flushed them down the toilet.

⚔

They stayed in their room for dinner, a watery gumbo with some meat only identified as "like chicken". They also had some cornbread from a prepackaged mix along with some futter. And, as was custom in Louisiana, Tabasco Sauce accompanied the dish. Dinner was brought to them by a blonde woman in a pink see-through nightie. She didn't care that her breasts could be easily seen or that she sported a black eye. Jennifer felt fortunate that they were in an isolated room at the end of the hallway. The evening in the mansion became festive as the clients arrived to meet the ladies. Doors opened and closed all night long. Bells kept ringing constantly. Jennifer peeked out of the room once to see white old-fashioned egg-timers sitting in front of each door.

"Egg timers?" she asked Anthony.

"I guess they see clients by the hour. The clients need a cue to tell them time is up."

She offered Anthony the bed again but he declined. Jennifer started to feel guilty about the special treatment. The women of the brothel stayed busy late into the night. Jennifer fell asleep long before that.

The next morning they went down to the communal breakfast. Jennifer found a bizarre sight. Seven women were seated around the table, six of whom wore either lingerie or casual clothing. The last wore only a thong. Rachel and another woman in lingerie prepared breakfast, a large skillet of scrambled eggs with a second skillet filled with bacon. The other women eyed Anthony hungrily. Jennifer had seen this before but it was on the other side of the spectrum. Women who attended Party events did the same thing with the men in high power. Leon and Rene were also seated at the large table. Leon still sported the same lack of affect with his deadeye stare while Rene remained quietly sullen.

"Have a seat," Leon invited.

The prostitutes made a space where Jennifer and Anthony could sit next to each other. The girl in the thong maneuvered the seating so that she was on Anthony's right. "Glad you could join us," Rachel said from the stove.

"My name is Amy." The girl with the thong introduced herself. "Where are y'all from?"

"Amy, you know that's none of your business," Leon said. "These are our guests. They'll be leaving tomorrow."

"They're the ones on the TV that everybody is talking about," Rene said.

"You're speaking out of turn again." Leon glared at Rene until he cast his eyes down.

"You mean from the old Gold Rush casino shootout?" Amy asked. "I thought everybody died in that shootout? That's what they said on the TV."

Leon slammed his hand on the butcher-block table. "Enough! These people are leaving tomorrow. We don't need any questions about who they are, where they're from or where they're going. Are we clear?" Slamming his hand on the table had stunned them all to silence. The only sound that filled the room was the sizzle of bacon.

"It was nice to meet you," Amy said meekly.

"Likewise," Jennifer said. She introduced herself and Anthony. Amy smiled and the rest of the girls introduced themselves in turn. After the introductions Rachel brought breakfast to the table. The eggs were ladled out onto the plates while the platter of bacon went around.

"Where did the bacon come from?" Jennifer asked.

The girls turned to Leon. "What did I say about questions?" Jennifer could feel Anthony tensing beside her but then Leon gave a surprisingly warm smile. "I'm just teasing. We get a lot of things through barter around here."

"Barter? Here?"

Leon laughed. "You mean with the girls? No, but we operate a lot of different businesses. Any of the illegal foods we can get our hands on. Bacon is surprisingly cheap. Most of this homemade. Hell, I made my fair share of bacon when I was a kid."

"There are pig farms?"

Rene snickered. "Naw. Pig hunters."

Leon continued. "What my young friend is trying to say here is that while hunting is illegal there are still enough feral hogs that nobody cares if one or a hundred go missing. Nobody likes a feral hog in their soybean field anyway."

"You can turn a wild boar into bacon?" Jennifer asked.

"Not that much different from a pig. I grew up on a pig farm till the Freedom Party took it from my folks back in the late twenties. My daddy was sent to 'protective custody' when he tried to fight back. He died in protective custody. Broke my momma's heart. She drank herself to death a year later."

The breakfast table got quiet as Leon stared at the scrambled eggs on his plate. Jennifer was surprised to see that the women eyed Leon with some degree of affection for him. She wondered if there was more to the man who had taken them in.

As they continued to eat breakfast the table talk turned into a discussion of the previous night's activities. Jennifer was dismayed at the frank talk of sex. The women discussed who was the biggest, who was the smallest and who finished the quickest. Amy had the unfortunate experience of her last client being the drunkest. He had thrown up all over her and the bed in room six. She had showered and slept in the same bed with one of the other girls, saving the laundry as a chore for the morning.

When breakfast was over a couple of the girls cleared the table. Leon said, "You two come with me for a moment." They both got up from the table and followed Leon out of the kitchen. Rene followed them as well but was quickly stopped by Leon. "I got this," he said. "Why don't you keep an eye on the girls?"

Jennifer could tell that Rene was pissed off but he didn't say anything. He turned around and stormed away. Trouble brewed between the two of them.

Leon led them to an office with a large ornate desk and shelves full of old books. The bookshelves were covered with dust but the desk was clean. Leon waved them to the two overstuffed leather chairs in front of the desk, while he worked his way to the other side. He dropped into the executive office chair with an audible plop on the leather. "So you two are out of here tomorrow. I got a driver who comes through here hauling food for Stigman's. You should be out by tomorrow afternoon and in Dallas by evening. We're going to take you to the pickup location. The driver will drop you at a location just north of Dallas. From there you and he part ways and our business is concluded."

"We just hunker down in the truck?" Anthony asked.

"There's a false back to it, about three feet deep. It's lead lined so that most scans won't detect it. Cold though, so wear your winter coats." Leon grinned. "Maybe you two can snuggle."

"How will we get to the drop off?"

"I'll drive you tomorrow. Are we good?"

"Yeah, we're good."

"All right then. Stay in the room today. We'll set out tomorrow."

⋏

"It just seems like we hurry up and wait," Jennifer said.

They were sitting in the VIP room as the brothel was busy with clients. Amy had brought them tomato soup and grilled cheese sandwiches for lunch. The meals were eaten and the dirty dishes were sitting on trays, waiting for someone to collect them.

"Soldiers used to say the same thing," Anthony said. For a change he wasn't busy on his phone or tablet.

"What do you mean?"

"Soldiers spent most of their time waiting for battle. They would say the same thing. Hurry up and wait."

"Is that what we are? Soldiers?"

"In a way we are. We're fighting our way to freedom, getting through checkpoints and escaping the National Police."

Jennifer thought about Matt rushing towards the National Police two nights earlier. She turned and stared out the window. She was still frustrated that Matt chose to run back to the Party in a desperate attempt to cling to an old life that was no longer there.

"I'm sorry," Anthony said. "I wasn't trying to bring up what happened."

Jennifer smiled wanly. "It's okay. I think, deep down, he wasn't committed to this. I think he hoped that everything would go back to normal and that this was a huge misunderstanding. Do you think he would have made it in Cuba?"

Anthony paused before answering. "Probably not. Some people have a hard time dealing with change. Living in Cuba would have been a challenge for him."

That was a polite and safe answer. "I don't think he would have liked it. He was too attached to the Party. He wouldn't have found his place in Cuba." She mused on that for a moment. "Do you think I can find my place in Cuba?"

Anthony smiled back at her warmly. "You survived a stay in a detention center. I think you're strong enough to find your place anywhere."

"What are you going to do when you escape? Live a life of luxury?"

"I like living comfortably but I'll keep up the fight. I'll do what I can to link up with the Coalition Forces and give them intel. They'll probably be happy for my assistance."

"Maybe you can find yourself a senorita?"

"Maybe," he replied softly.

"I'm sorry. Were you and Lisa close?"

"We were a bit close, but it's hard to get close to anyone here these days. You never know when the Party is going to take your partner away from you."

Jennifer waited as he mused on that. Uncomfortable with the silence she asked, "Can you tell me how tomorrow is going to go?"

"I'm taking Leon at his word on the truck. They're getting paid pretty well for this. After we get dropped off we'll get picked up by another man. He's the coyote who is going to get us across the border. As I understand it all of the action is focused on Waco right now. This guy says he has a route well west of Waco that he has been successfully using since mid-December."

"Is it safe?"

"We're crossing a battlefield. So there are risks."

Risks. Two large armies clashing in Texas and Anthony simply called it "risks". Jennifer didn't share the same doubts her late husband did, but she was concerned. She had never seen battles outside of a movie or TV show.

"Don't worry," Anthony said. "We won't run straight into battle. This guy assures me that we're going around everything. Mexicans and Americans have been travelling across the border for years."

CHAPTER 18

It seemed that every room in the brothel hosted a client. Rachel hastily dropped off dinner. She came in, dropped off some gumbo and cornbread then explained that she had to get to back to business. Jennifer and Anthony wanted to be well rested for their trip the next day. They both packed their clothes, what few clothes Jennifer now had, into Anthony's gym bag. When it came time to sleep Anthony started setting up a blanket and pillow on the floor.

"We can share the bed," Jennifer said.

"No, we couldn't do that."

"We're sharing the bed or else I'm getting on the floor with you. Come on. You need your rest and you said it yourself, we have a big day tomorrow."

Anthony was dubious. "Are you sure?"

"Yes, I'm sure. It's a king sized bed. We can both take a side. It's not like we're going to fool around or anything."

"Okay. I guess it'll be all right."

Both had on gym shorts and a T-shirt. Jennifer didn't know why he made a big deal. She turned out the light while he climbed into bed. They had left the bathroom light on with the door cracked. Neither one of them were comfortable being completely in the dark while staying in the brothel. Anthony had propped up a chair against the door handle. With the light out she climbed in on the other side.

A good two feet of space remained between them. She turned and faced Anthony. Even with the little light from the bathroom she could make out his chest as he lay on his back. Surprised, she was aware that she watched him breathe. Her ears sought out the deep rhythm of his breath as his chest rose and fell. One of the girls cried out in passion down the hall. Jennifer was shocked at how loud the cry was. Was it for real or fake? Probably the latter. She was suddenly uncomfortable watching Anthony sleep. She turned to her side and faced away from him. Jennifer lay awake for a long time and was unaware of when slept succumbed her.

⋏

Jennifer and Anthony were eager for breakfast at nine o'clock. It was a surprise to them that the smell of breakfast didn't fill the plantation house. Anthony walked into the empty kitchen tentatively to find that all the stoves were off and the lights were out.

"What's going on?" Jennifer asked.

"Something's off," Anthony said.

"Good, y'all are awake," a voice said from behind them. They both turned around and found Rene wearing a jeans and a black hoodie.

"What's going on?" Anthony said.

"We told the girls to stay in for breakfast. Max has something that he wants to discuss. Y'all come to the office."

"Where's Leon?"

"Max sent him out to do an errand. Now walk on ahead."

Jennifer waited for Anthony to signal. He made eye contact briefly and shook his head slightly. Something had gone wrong. The office was the front room opposite the storage room, in the foyer of the plantation house. Rene trailed them closely like a shepherd.

Max sat comfortably in the office chair. On the desk blotter rested a gold plated .45 caliber semi-automatic pistol. He smiled but it lacked warmth as he waved to the chairs in front of him. "Sit," he said.

Jennifer sat first and Anthony followed a moment later. "I hope everything's okay," Anthony said.

Rene stepped around the desk and stood at Max's right. He reached behind him and pulled out a black semi-automatic pistol, then crossed his hands in front of himself as he held it.

"Well, that depends on you two," Max said. "I'm in a bit of a quandary with y'all. You see on one hand, well, a deal's a deal. You paid us good money to get you out of here and that's what we agreed to do."

"Paid handsomely," Anthony reminded him.

Max nodded as if to concede the point. "Be that as it may, Rene here seems to think that we would be better served turning you two in. There seems to be quite a bounty on your heads. What was it Rene?"

"Five hundred grand each," Rene said. "That's a million dollars."

"So your plan is to double-cross us and turn us into the National Police then?" Anthony asked.

"Let's not be hasty," Max said. "We can call this a renegotiation of terms."

"As you said I paid you handsomely. A renegotiation hardly seems fair at this point."

"You never told me what hot commodities you and this little lady are."

"Isn't this sort of thing against the ragin' Cajun independent spirit?"

Max cocked his head to the side to consider the point. "Normally, yeah, but a million dollars changes things."

"I don't have a million dollars."

Anthony had told Jennifer he had invented a bank account out of thin air. He could pay the sum but he held out.

"Well, what can you pay?" Max asked.

"I can transfer two hundred thousand now, then another three hundred thousand when we're in Dallas. That is a half million altogether."

"How about the entire half million now?"

Anthony smiled. "Call it 'insurance'. It's not the million that you would get for turning us in but on top of what I already paid it's a generous sum."

Max mused on that for a moment. "Okay. We have a deal. Make that transfer then."

"Let me get my tablet." Anthony started to get up.

"No, you two stay put. Rene can fetch it for you. Rene, go up there and get them their stuff."

"Sure thing, Uncle Max."

Rene hustled out of the room and stomped up the stairs. There was a pause and his voice boomed out. "I told y'all to stay in your fucking rooms."

Anthony said, "I trust there won't be any further issues with our deal."

Max grinned. "Nope. Not as soon as the money transfers." Jennifer didn't like the way Max grinned. If he double-crossed them once he would do it again.

"The first part of it anyway."

Rene stomped his way down the stairs and into the office with the gym bag. He slammed Anthony in ribs with it. "Here you go!"

The bag fell to the floor. Anthony leaned over the side of the chair to pick it up. He unzipped the bag and stuck his hand in it.

Max quickly picked up the handgun and pointed it at him. "You might want to be careful there."

"Max, you have my guns," Anthony said. "The only thing here I can threaten you with is my dirty underwear." He grinned at them.

Max guffawed and Rene echoed his uncle's laughter with his own. "I guess you're right," Max said.

Anthony fished the tablet out of the bag and turned it on. He tapped the screen a few times then said, "It's done. Check on your side to verify."

Max set the pistol down and pulled out his own tablet from the desk. "Yeah, you're right. Another two hundred thousand in my account."

"So we go to the rendezvous now then?"

"It's only 9:30. We don't need to be there until 1:00."

"So what do we do in the meantime? Play cards?"

"Wait in the living room. Rene will go with you and keep you company."

Rene brandished his pistol again. "Come on, fucktards! Let's go."

Anthony carefully placed the tablet back into the gym bag and picked it up by the strap handle. He nodded for Jennifer to exit the room first then he followed. Jennifer glanced behind her to see Rene pointing the pistol at the two of them. There was no way these guys were going to keep their side of the deal.

After exiting the room Anthony walked beside her. She watched him carefully to see if he had another move in mind, as Anthony clutched the gym bag to his chest. As they entered the living room he made eye contact and grunted, "Fall down." She dropped to the floor immediately knocking a lamp off an end table in the process.

"What the -" Rene said. He never finished his sentence. Anthony spun around and swung the gym bag against Rene's gun hand. The black semiautomatic pistol fell and slid across the floor in front of Jennifer. Both Anthony and Rene stared at one another for a moment, equally stunned that the move had worked. Then Anthony rushed him, wrapping his arms around Rene and shoving the thin man against the door jam.

Jennifer picked up the gun. She had never held a gun at in her life and wasn't sure what to do. Jennifer pointed the gun as Anthony and Rene wrestled on the floor but was afraid to pull the trigger. Anthony was on top of Rene pummeling his face with his fists.

Max appeared in the doorway with gun drawn. "What the fuck is going on?"

Jennifer swung the gun around and fired. She gave a surprise yelp at the noise and kick of the gun. A dusting of plaster puffed out of the wall from the right of Max's head, forcing him to duck out of the doorway.

Anthony's laborious beating of Rene wore him out as the punches slowed. Rene's eyes were closed and he wasn't struggling, but he at least appeared to be breathing. Anthony rolled off the top of him and gestured for the gun.

"What's going on in there?" Max shouted from the hallway.

Anthony hustled Jennifer to the back of the room. He kept one shaky hand holding the gun pointed at the doorway. He tried to move the couch one handed so that he could crouch behind it. Seeing what he was trying to do Jennifer pushed him back and started moving the heavy couch herself.

"What's going on in there?" Max repeated.

"How long until the Nats show up?" Anthony shouted.

"I don't know what you're talking about."

"This is a double-cross, Max. You're playing both sides for a profit. I know what you're doing."

"What are you talking about? We had a deal?"

"Yeah, we had a deal. Then you fucked us. So when are the National Police getting here?"

"You think I want them in my place of business?"

"So you have to bring us to them then?"

"Listen, why don't we just talk about it?" Max started to come through the doorway but Anthony fired, forcing Max out again. "You two are fucking pains in the ass," he shouted.

"Why don't you rush in and kill us?"

"I'm not trying to kill you. Will you just be reasonable?"

"Yeah, you're not going to rush in here for the same reason the National Police are not coming here. You need to deliver us to them alive. Am I right?"

"I wish I'd never met you two, but that payoff is going be so fucking sweet."

"Yeah, that's what I thought."

"So if you're so smart how are you going to get out of that room? There's only one way out of there. I mean, I would rather keep the two of you alive but I'm not going to risk my skin for it. Maybe I should just call the National Police and bring them here?"

There was only one way in and out of that room and that was through the door. The room had a window behind them and another to their left but they were barred. "Check the windows," Anthony said to Jennifer.

She went to the one on her left and opened the latch. A rush of cold air hit her in the face. She searched for a way out through the bars but they were bolted onto the window frame. She turned to Anthony and shook her head. Anthony waved her back. Just as she turned away she saw the coroner's van pull into the circular drive. Leon got out of the driver side wearing a long grey overcoat. Jennifer rushed back behind the couch. "Leon's here," she said. "Reinforcements?"

Anthony shrugged. Leon wasn't here for what had played out earlier. It was hard to say if he had gone along with this idea or not.

They heard the front door open and close then Leon asking Max, "What the fuck is going on?"

"Those two went crazy," Max said. "They beat up poor Rene."

Leon snorted. "What did Rene do this time?"

"Hey, Leon," Anthony shouted. "Are you in on this? Your boss wants to turn us into the National Police for a reward."

"What's he talking about, Max?"

"Don't listen to him," Max said. "He's off his rocker."

"Ask him about the reward," Anthony shouted. "There's a million dollar bounty on our heads. He extorted another two hundred grand from us."

"Boss, is this true?" Leon asked.

"I said don't listen to him," Max said.

Anthony pressed further. "Ask Max why he hasn't come in here with guns blazing? It's because he needs us alive. The reward is no good to him if we're dead. That's why he sent you away this morning. He didn't want you around for this double-cross. He knows how you feel about the National Police and the Party. Ask him to show you his tablet. Dare him to prove me wrong!"

"Leon, you work for me. You best remember that."

"Max, you working with those Party assholes," Leon said. "You know what they did to me and my family. Sure, we let them and the army and those Party fucks come in here and bang the girls. But we don't fuck each other to help them. We don't help them period." There was a cold edge to Leon's voice.

"Show him your tablet," Anthony shouted.

"Shut the fuck up in there," Max said. "I don't need to prove anything to anyone!"

"Are you turning them into the Party?" Leon asked. "Look me in the eye."

"Leon, this could be big for both of us. This is a big score."

The house was silent and still without a noise from upstairs or from Rene crumpled in a heap next to the doorway. The men outside the doorway had stopped speaking. Then a single shot rang out from the hallway. Jennifer ducked and looked at Anthony questioningly. Anthony only shrugged in return.

"Hey, Anthony," Leon said. "I'm coming in. Don't shoot."

Anthony stood up with the gun still pointed at the doorway. He waved for Jennifer to stay down behind the cover of the couch but she still peeked out from behind it anyway. Leon stood a step inside the doorway with his own gun drawn.

"What happened to Max?" Anthony asked.

"I shot him in the head."

"So what now?"

"Well, the way I see it is we already have a deal in place. We will get you to the pickup point so that you can make your way out of here. I would feel more comfortable if you lowered that weapon. You can keep it if you want. Consider it a sign of trust. But I get nervous about guns pointed at me. Agreed?"

"Yeah."

"On the count of three. One. Two. Three."

Anthony sighed as he lowered his gun.

"There. Isn't that better?" Leon asked.

With a trembling hand Anthony put the gun in the waistband in the small of his back. Jennifer breathed a sigh of relief and her muscles relaxed as the tension eased out of her body.

Leon stepped back into the hallway. "Rachel, come on out," he shouted. He waited for several seconds for the prostitute to appear. When she was at the bottom of the stairs he gave her further instructions. "I need four girls that you trust the most; two of them to take Max here and another two to take care of Rene. Get Rene up the stairs and into one of the empty rooms. Put a lock on it. I don't know what to do with him yet. After the other two girls move Max out of here I want someone to clean, clean and clean. They can take the rest of the day off afterwards. But we gotta move fast. We open in two hours."

"Do you want me to take Max to the shed?"

"Yeah. I'll cut his dent out first." Rachel bounded back up the stairs to gather the other four girls. "The lady might want to stay in this room for a minute. It's a bit of a mess out here and she shouldn't see it."

"I'm all right," Jennifer said.

"Just wait," Anthony said. "It's probably unpleasant." He turned back to Leon. "Are the National Police going to show up here?"

Leon pulled out a switchblade and flicked it open. "That's what I'm going to find out."

"Do you need help with his tablet?"

"No, Max gave us admin rights to his tablet. A lot of times he went on a bender and would be passed out for days. It made business bad when he did that. So he gave me and Rene access to it. That way we could still work. We just had to be close enough to his dent so the tablet would activate, which was shitty when Max was covered in his own puke and piss."

Leon stepped into the hallway with the switchblade. A few moments later he returned with the bloody dent pinched between his own bloody fingers. When Rachel returned with the four girls he asked her to get him some paper towels. After she returned with the paper towels he placed the dent carefully atop one of them, then used the rest to wipe the blood from his fingers. Then he retrieved the tablet from the office. During the whole time Jennifer and Anthony waited patiently. What if the National Police were coming? She didn't understand how Leon could be so calm.

After Leon returned he powered up the tablet and tapped on the screen. "Yeah, that's what I thought. There was no way he was going to let them in here. Too much risk. They might have arrested all of us and Max isn't that stupid. He was supposed to deliver you to them at noon today, at the local precinct in Shreveport. Kind of neutral ground I guess."

"What happens if we don't show up?" Jennifer asked.

"They'll come out here looking for you and Anthony."

"We need to go then."

"Yeah, I reckon so."

"Why are you doing this?" Jennifer asked softly. "I mean, Max was in it for the money."

Leon sighed. "Listen, I know I ain't no saint. I'm a pimp, a dealer and an enforcer. I was a lieutenant in this business but now, as of today, I'm the owner. We make good money already but we always had a rule, you know? Sell them dope, sell them pussy but don't help them hurt any of ours. You remember the story I told you about my mama's farm?"

Jennifer nodded.

Leon continued. "I hate the Party. I hate the National Police. I would hate the military but I know they're just doing their job. Hell, half of them got worse things to say about the Party than I do. Max crossed a line because he was greedy. He's been running things bad for a while and this little episode just forced my hand sooner than I thought it would."

Two of the girls had picked up Rene and were struggling to drag him up the stairs. The sheet lay over Max's body and was soaked in blood at the head. The coppery scent filled the air and made Jennifer's empty stomach do a slow roll. Leon stared at the body on the floor while lost in thought. Anthony stood closely behind Jennifer as if he feared Leon would change his mind and turn them both in. He cleared his throat. "Can we get our gear?"

Leon still stared at the corpse. "Yeah, yeah," he said absently. "It's probably a good idea to get you out of here. I still need to make a couple of calls."

He put his earpiece in and gave instructions to the tablet to dial out. While he did that he motioned for them to follow him to the storeroom near the front door of the plantation house. In the storeroom Leon pulled out Anthony's gear while simultaneously talking on the phone. He asked for a couple of guys to come in and run some odd jobs at the brothel. He also called a meeting for later but Jennifer hoped they would be in Dallas well before then.

"We got some other stuff here if you need it," Leon said. "Some other handguns." He rummaged through the bins and pulled out a couple of extra semi-automatic pistols and ammo.

With their stuff collected they waited in the living room for Anthony to give further instructions. There was still a possibility of a double-cross but it seemed less likely. Leon seemed to be genuinely pissed that Max had tried to double-cross them. Besides, Leon was in charge now, as he constantly worked Max's tablet.

A half hour later two additional men dressed in biker leathers came into the brothel. Leon conferred with them for a few minutes then approached with one of the men. "Don't worry," he said. "This is the guy who is going to take you to the drop off. You gotta go now and sit there and wait. Normally, I would like to time this so that we can drop you off and go but, well, circumstances changed today."

"By the way, I'm Steve," the man in the leathers said. "We go out in the van, wait a couple of hours till the big rig comes and then you're off to Dallas."

⊼

Leon's hatred of the Party and everything it stood for had superseded Max's greed. Jennifer and Anthony were fortunate for the way it had turned out. She mused on this as Steve drove them in a nondescript grey minivan to the rendezvous point. It could have taken a turn for the worse if Leon had been in on it.

For someone dressed like a fearsome outlaw biker Steve was quite amiable and talkative. He asked questions that Anthony was reluctant to answer but Steve took it in stride. "I get it. I've done a couple of these for Max before, escaping America and all that. I guess things got so hot for you two that you had to leave."

"Something like that," Anthony said.

"So how did you end in up in Louisiana?" Jennifer asked. She'd learned as a schoolteacher that the best way to distract children from inquisitive questions was to get them to talk about themselves. In her experience it applied to adults as well.

Steve was happy to comply. He told them all about how his family from Juarez had sneaked across the border in the late 80s. His mother was born in America and Steve had been born here as well. Steve kept talking as he pulled in at an abandoned warehouse just north of Shreveport. He was happy to tell his life story to anyone who would listen. Soon Anthony sensed how Jennifer kept Steve occupied and threw a couple of questions of his own.

Shortly before noon Steve pulled out a grocery bag with sandwiches. Thin slices of grilled tofu with melted Swiss cheese on toasted wheat. Jennifer was surprised that she liked the sandwiches.

Just before one o'clock a big rig belching smoke pulled into the parking lot of the warehouse. Behind it trailed a dirty white trailer without any markings on it. The rig stopped at the end of the parking lot. Steve flashed the high beams at the truck, which the truck returned with its own flashes before pulling forward.

"Do we get out now?" Anthony asked.

"He'll circle around us so that he can point that truck to the exit," Steve said. "Wait for him to come to a full stop."

The big rig pulled past them, did a one-eighty in the parking lot and pulled ahead of the van. The trucker hopped out of the cab and put on a fur-lined denim jacket. He walked towards the minivan, while scanning the scenery suspiciously.

"Okay, let's say howdy," Steve said. He hopped out of the minivan to greet the truck driver. Jennifer followed Anthony as he slung the gym bag over his shoulder.

"I'm Bobby," the truck driver introduced himself. "How do you do?" He shook hands as Anthony and Jennifer introduced themselves. Steve introduced himself as well, but Bobby regarded the biker dubiously.

"So we get in the back of the truck?" Anthony asked.

"Yeah, but you two are going to stay in a little compartment at the back of the trailer. Ready to go? I'm on a schedule."

The whole group walked to the loading doors of the trailer. Bobby took out a key and opened the padlock chain. The trailer opened to reveal boxes and crates on either side of the truck with a clear space through the middle. "Hop on up," Bobby said.

Steve hopped up into the trailer to help Jennifer climb up, then helped Anthony afterwards. He grinned and jumped back off the trailer. "I'll keep an eye out here while you get them settled in," he said.

"Follow me," Bobby said as he led them through the dark recesses of the trailer. "It's going to be snug for two people. It's a tight fit. You can stand but it's about a four-hour drive. I recommend you lay down on the floor or sit with your backs against the wall. This thing is lead-lined so X-rays won't pick you up. But if there's an inspection the Border Patrol will catch us. There are two checkpoints to get through before we make it to Dallas."

"Have you ever been caught doing this?" Jennifer asked.

Bobby smiled. "Little lady if I had I would be locked up right now. Or worse."

"Any issues with the ventilation?" Anthony asked.

"There's a small vent on the inside. You won't suffocate but keep your coats on it. It'll be a cold ride." Bobby flicked the hunting knife out of his belt holster and worked the blade into a groove at the back of the trailer. A slight twist of the wrist popped the panel with a hidden hinge. He reached in and turned on a light switch. "I learned a long time ago that having a light on helps. People who find themselves in the dark, they get all kinds of scary notions."

Jennifer peeked into the small compartment. It was tighter than she had anticipated. Three adults would be uncomfortable but two should manage just fine.

"If you folks need to use the bathroom do it now," Bobby said. "Otherwise your next chance is four hours from now."

"There's no bathroom here," Jennifer said.

"Maybe go on parking lot on the other side of the trailer?"

Jennifer considered it but shook her head. She imagined herself getting caught with her pants down.

"Okay, folks, let's get rolling. Time to button you up."

Jennifer squeezed into the small compartment with Anthony coming in right after her. Bobby put the hidden door back in place. There was no way either of them could sit without laying atop of each other. And they would have to sit since there were no handholds. "Let me turn around," Jennifer said. She tried to twist away from Anthony but there was no room to maneuver.

"Hold on," he said. "Maybe if I..."

The truck's engine roared to life. Jennifer hadn't heard the sound of a gas-powered engine since she wrecked her car. It startled her and she surprised Anthony with a yelp.

"Are you okay?" he asked.

"Yeah. It's just..."

Anthony smiled. "We're almost there. Just hold on a little longer."

With the truck bouncing all over the asphalt it was clear that they needed to find a way on the floor that worked for them. They tried sitting across from each other but found that it just tangled their legs. Finally they found a semi comfortable position by lying on the floor next to each other. Each had to lie on their sides and they lay facing each other. Jennifer was acutely aware that this was the closest she had been to Anthony.

"Are you comfortable?" she asked.

"We are lying in the floor of a tractor trailer. I'm about as comfortable as I expected to be."

"Do you have any doubts about our driver?"

"I doubt everything. I don't think he's going to turn us in though. Max got paid well for this. This guy was paid well too. These guys risk just as much as we do. If he turns us in to the Party they're going to question why he had this compartment in the first place. It's safer if he just delivers us where we need to go and he knows it."

"Are you leaving anything behind?"

"You mean like family?"

"Yeah."

"No, not really. I have some kin that I'm not close to. My dad died when I was young, an accident at the steel mill. Mama raised us, me and my brother, I mean. I was the one that got out and went into the army. My brother OD'ed when he was seventeen."

"I'm so sorry."

She waited as he struggled with his next words. "Yeah, Eddie was my older brother. He hated me tagging along with him when we were kids. Then I saw what he was doing to Mama. At the end he was stealing stuff to buy dope. This was before all the addicts were sent to the protective custody centers. One day he didn't come home. The police found him dead a couple of days later in an abandoned house. I think that's what broke Mama's heart."

Jennifer reached up and caressed his cheek. "I'm so sorry," she repeated. "Your mother?"

"She did the best she could but I think she died when Eddie did. On the inside, I mean. She caught cold in the winter and went into a tier five hospital with pneumonia. Died in her sleep. I was sixteen and became a ward of the state."

"No family took you in?"

"Nobody could afford to. Money was tight. The last thing anyone wanted was another mouth to feed. So I ended up in an orphanage."

"How long were you in there?"

"Only a year and a half. I was so scared but I knew better than to let them see it." Anthony laughed. "My brother always told me on the first day of school to go and find the biggest and meanest kid and beat him up. He said it was better to get it over with on the first day so you wouldn't have to worry about it for the rest of the year. So there I was, a scrawny sixteen-year-old kid in the activity room of an orphanage, getting sized up by the other kids and I see this group of boys across the room. All of them white boys and there's this big fat kid with beady eyes. You know the kind I'm talking about? His name was Chad. The first thing he said was, 'Looks like we got us a new nigger.' Then he and the other kids came right up to me with Chad grinning the whole way. I asked him, 'What did you say?' And I popped him as hard as I could and as fast as I could, before he could say it again. Chad dropped to the floor just like that."

"And they left you alone after that?"

Anthony laughed again. "No. They were shocked for a moment and the other four jumped me. But I threw a lot of punches. They kicked my ass but they left me alone after that. Did ten days in isolation but I was okay with that."

"No more trouble at the orphanage?"

"Not for me. Chad and his crew left me alone and I kept to myself. All the other kids were delinquents. There wasn't any future for them. So I studied and made good grades. I was never going to make it to Harvard or any other college, so the only way out I saw was the army. Computers came natural to me so they put me in cyber warfare school."

"Why did you leave the army?"

"I got a little taste of the world outside. Figured out everything we were doing around the world put us on the wrong side. Nobody liked us. It was bad before the Freedom Party but when the Party took over things it got much worse. And I learned that the Party lied to us. They rewrote everything that happened before 2019. Our country was founded on a different set of principles than the Party represents. That's why I always felt like we needed to take our country back."

"And you do this? This is your part about paying it back?"

"It might not be much but it's something. I'll still do what I can when we escape America."

"Maybe I can help you?"

Anthony smiled. "Maybe you can."

"I just hope that I'm strong enough after this. I feel as broken as I look." She caught herself rubbing the scar on her forehead. Five months ago she was the envy of every other Party wife. Now she had a crewcut with a two big scars on her head and a scattered collection of smaller ones on her face.

"You're not broken."

"Are you sure? My scars..."

"I think your scars are beautiful." Anthony smiled, reached up and rubbed the scar on her forehead. Then he caught himself. "I'm sorry."

Jennifer smiled. "No, it's okay."

They rode in silence, staring into each other's eyes for a few minutes until Jennifer felt the rig slow down then eventually come to a stop. "The checkpoint outside of Shreveport," Anthony whispered. "Shhhh."

The truck stopped and started continuously for several minutes. Eventually it came to a full stop. Jennifer could only assume that the driver presented his tablet while they authenticated his dent. She heard muffled voices outside of the trailer. Jennifer could also feel the warmth coming off

Anthony. A few minutes later the rig rolled through the checkpoint and was back on the interstate to Dallas.

Anthony smiled. "You can breathe again."

"Was I holding my breath?"

"Seemed like it."

"Come with me to Cuba." She startled herself after saying it aloud. "I mean, you can just as easily help the Coalition forces from there as you could from Mexico."

"I guess I could."

"I mean, the only people I know there are Maggie and Brad. But it's a good place to live, better than here." She was embarrassed at herself. Why did she stumble over words like a teenage girl with a crush?

"Better than here," he repeated back to her.

She never quite realized when the steady rhythm of the tires lulled her to sleep.

Chapter 19

Occasionally the truck would hit a rough patch on the interstate and jar her awake. She tried to keep her eyes open but was quickly lulled back into sleep again. When the rig slowed down and turned off the interstate Jennifer woke up sharply alert. "Are we there?" she asked.

"Probably just outside of Dallas," Anthony said.

"Did you get any sleep?"

"No."

"Do you think they'll be looking for us?"

Anthony mused on that for a moment. "Probably not. Dallas serves as a staging area for the war. They just want to make sure there's no one sending car bombs their way."

This checkpoint was noisier than the last. Whereas most of the vehicles on the roads used quiet electric motors there were a lot of old fashioned gas powered engines here. Gas powered engines meant military. Over the continuous din of the rumbling engines were shouts from the police and soldiers manning the checkpoint as well are the occasional warbling siren.

The rig stood still for a long time then the trailer doors opened up. Anthony put his finger to his lips and mimed for her to stay quiet.

Boots stomped along the floor. "What is all this?" a gruff voice asked.

"Food supplies from Atlanta," Bobby said. "Heading to the Stigman's DC in Frisco. It's all in the manifest and the TR-41 sheet."

"You telling me how to do my business?"

"No sir," Bobby said sheepishly.

The boot heels echoing hollowly on the pinewood floor of the trailer stomped methodically toward the secret compartment where Jennifer and Anthony hid. Jennifer held her breath. She was so afraid that the soldier could hear her breathing. The footsteps came right up to the compartment door and stopped. For nearly a full minute nothing happened. She was an anxious bundle of energy and it was all she could do to stay still. The soldier would take a couple of steps, pause, and then more steps.

"Open this box," the soldier commanded.

"Yes, sir," Bobby said. She heard the splintering of wood and the crash of boards.

"What is this? Contraband?"

"Looks like cans of beef stew. It's on the manifest. I promise."

"Well, I am keeping a few of these cans for myself."

"Yes, sir."

"Okay, you can go," the soldier said. Jennifer slowly exhaled, her heartbeat slowing down as she did so.

The rig was moving a minute later. "They won't hear us now," Anthony said.

"Are you sure?" she asked.

"Too much noise and activity."

Given that they were outside of Dallas Jennifer thought they were only minutes away from their destination. It turned out that they had to travel at least the better part of an hour before the rig stopped again. After stopping Bobby came aboard the back of a trailer to let them out of the compartment. They wiggled their way out and stretched when they stood. Anthony extended his hand to Bobby. "Thanks, again," he said.

"You're welcome," Bobby said in return. "I hope you two can make it to wherever you're going. Seeing things like this these days... well, I think I might not be too long behind you. We're in the parking lot of Stonebriar Mall. The mall has been closed for a couple of years now so the longer we sit here the bigger the chance that we'll draw attention... I think your ride's here."

Still stretching they worked their way to the trailer doors. Anthony slung the gym bag over his shoulder. Bobby hopped off first then extended his hand to help Jennifer.

She found herself in another abandoned parking lot where yellow dead weeds sprouted through the cracks of the concrete. Jennifer shielded her sensitive eyes from the stark winter sun. Bobby had parked some distance away from a white van that advertised pool cleaning. A man wearing blue jeans and a well-worn black leather jacket stood next to the driver's side door of the van. He checked his smartwatch impatiently.

"Good luck, folks," Bobby said. "I would see you off, but I'm already late getting to the DC as it is. They check everyone on their times these days." He closed up the trailer and climbed into the cab of his rig.

Jennifer and Anthony walked to the man waiting for them. As Bobby drove off Jennifer could see that the man waiting was Mexican, with long black hair and a thick droopy black mustache. "You're late," he said.

"We got here as fast as we could," Anthony said. "How late are we?"

"Twenty minutes. I was just about to drive off when I saw the truck pull in."

"We're glad you waited."

"Anthony?"

"Yes. You are Hector?"

"Yeah. Get in. We can talk along the way. This mall is dead but there's still a lot of traffic in this area."

Hector opened the back doors of the van. To Jennifer's surprise the van actually contained pool cleaning supplies. "Work your way around that," Hector said.

It took a couple of minutes to maneuver their way through the supplies packed in the back of the van. Once again they were in a confined cramped space. Still, it was better than the tiny compartment in the trailer.

"I got a place in West Plano," Hector said. "I can stash you two there along with everyone else."

"Everyone else?" Anthony asked.

"Yeah. There are more of you heading south. The rest are arriving tomorrow. We leave the day after that."

"Do we need to worry about checkpoints?"

"Here? No, too many roads and streets. The military and the National Police don't have the resources to watch them all. Oh, sure there are eyes in the sky, but they don't know what we're doing."

From where Jennifer sat she could see through the windshield. Few cars travelled the streets but there were plenty of military vehicles. Most were trucks painted in olive drab. She also saw plenty of Joltvees and helicopter gunships thundered overhead. They passed a hospital that had a wide swath of land surrounding it that was now filled with tents and barracks. Soldiers by the hundreds, wearing either green camouflage of the army or the black uniforms of the militarized National Police brigades, marched and drilled.

"Is it dangerous for us to be here?" Jennifer asked. With this much military activity she was almost certain that the army or someone else would round them up indiscriminately.

"Not if we stay out of their way," Hector said. "Sure, there are a lot of businesses closed. People bugged out and headed north. But there's a lot of money in Dallas. That means a lot of stupid *pendejos* who don't know any better than to get the hell out of here. So I get around with this van because these rich assholes still expect me to keep their pool cleaned while the world burns to the ground around them."

"So what do the rich people do here?"

"Oh, there are still places to go, just fewer places and fewer rich people."

Jennifer suppressed a sigh. What had been an initial escape plan out of New Orleans now stretched over a month. "And we're crossing a battlefield?" she asked. "Like bombs and bullets whizzing by?"

Hector laughed. "You watch too many movies. We just try to find a place where the American Army won't be and let the Coalition forces know that we're coming."

"You have contacts on the other side?"

"Yeah, we don't want them mistaking us for a scout force. As a bonus we give them as much info as we can about troop movements and stuff."

Hector took them into an area that was a mix of commercial and retail space. Storefronts lined the street but there were hundreds of apartments behind them. The shops were a mix of bars, restaurants and retails stores. Only a few stores were closed with lease signs in the dust-covered windows. Hector turned the van on one of the streets and headed for a parking garage. He slowly drove the van up a couple of levels, then parked where there were few cars. "Come with me," Hector said.

He exited the van and opened the doors in the back while Jennifer and Anthony extricated themselves from the pool supplies. Hector offered his hand to help Jennifer, which she accepted graciously. Anthony slung his gym bag over his shoulder as they followed Hector down a staircase. When they reached the street level he hustled them across the street to the apartments. "We have a few places here and there," Hector said. "They're spread out in the area, can't have too many people in the same location. This is going to be a big run so we're going to squeeze you in with another couple."

Hector led them to an apartment door where he quietly knocked. They waited close to a minute before someone behind the door asked meekly who it was.

"Hector," he said simply.

There was a twist of a couple of deadbolts before the door cracked open to reveal the pixie face of a petite blonde woman. "Oh, hey, Hector. Come on in." She had a thick Texas accent.

She let them into the spacious, if sparsely furnished, apartment. The furnishings in the living room were used and worn out. The brown leather sofa was patched with an abundance of silvery duct tape. A young man with a patchy black beard wearing blue jeans and a faded black Lynyrd Skynyrd T-shirt stood nervously near the patio door at the back of the apartment. "Who are these people?" the man asked.

"David, no need to be rude," the blonde woman said. "Please forgive my husband. This is David and I'm Kelly. We're pleased to meet you."

"We're going out tomorrow, right?" David asked Hector.

Hector sighed. "The day after tomorrow. Waiting on a few more people." He rubbed his forehead. "I miss the days when we were bringing in people instead of taking them out. These people are bunking here tonight and to-morrow. We head out on Thursday." He glared at David, daring him to argue about it. David cast his eyes to the floor and said nothing.

Hector turned to Jennifer and Anthony. "A couple of days."

"Okay," Anthony said.

⅄

Kelly and David didn't give out their last name and neither Jennifer nor Anthony pressed them on it. Sharing too much information gave risk to being compromised. Still, Jennifer felt the need to be social by nature and Kelly seemed to oblige. Jennifer found the cheerful pixie to be adorable. David, on the other hand, was the complete opposite of his wife. He remained sullen and suspicious. After Hector left he went and hid in the bedroom.

Kelly showed them around the rest of the apartment. It was clearly dated in terms of design and decor. The walls were splotchy from consistent dry-wall repairs over the years. The kitchen was antiquated as well. None of the appliances were connected through smart chips.

"Is there an OLED wall?" Anthony asked.

"No," Kelly replied. "Not even a flat panel. I hope you brought your own entertainment."

Finally, Kelly showed them the second bedroom. The furniture there matched the same in the living room - cheap and used. There was only one bed in the cramped little room. A set of lavender sheets awaited on top of the stained mattress.

"One bed again," Anthony said. "I can sleep on the couch."

"We can share again," Jennifer said.

"Are y'all not a couple?" Kelly asked.

"No, we're friends."

Kelly squinted at them for a moment then grinned. "Are you sure?"

Jennifer blushed. "We are, really," she said. She thought Anthony blushed as well.

"We'll, okay, then. Are y'all hungry?"

"Yeah, starved." The sandwiches in the van hadn't been filling.

$$\lambda$$

Dinner was nothing to be excited about. Everything was frozen or canned. The most exciting thing in the fridge was a package of burritos made with tofu and grilled vegetables. There was at least a jar of salsa to add flavor to it. Jennifer was delighted to find a bottle of wine. David stepped out the bedroom briefly to grab a plate then ducked back in. The three of them ate dinner around a small dinette table.

The wine seemed to loosen up Kelly. "David got into a spot of trouble," she explained. "His name came up in a sweep. The National Police were looking for resistance cells. David don't belong to any. But he knew a guy who knew a guy, so, you can imagine how that goes. Next thing you know we hear they are coming for us. David says he ain't never going into protective custody. So now we're heading to Mexico, maybe as far as Costa Rica. David said there are a lot of former Americans down there." Kelly finished her wine in a gulp and then poured herself another glass. "What about you two?"

Jennifer turned to Anthony for some guidance. His eyes warned her to proceed with caution.

"I'm sorry," Kelly said. "I don't mean to pry. It's just that David and me ain't seen anyone else besides Hector in a while. It's kind of fun to talk to somebody new again."

"I was in a protective custody center," Jennifer said. "I got out only after a few days, but it was enough. I think if I had stayed back in Colorado I would have been put back into the protective custody center for good."

"Were you there too?" Kelly asked Anthony.

"I was helping her," he said. "We had a different plan to escape. The National Police found out what that plan was so we had to change it."

"Are they chasing you?" Her eyes widened with alarm.

"Not any more. They thought they had us today but we got away."

"Are you sure?"

"The most they could figure out would be that we came to Texas. That's it. The chances of that happening are slim."

This time Jennifer finished her wine in a gulp and poured herself another glass. The conversation turned briefly to future plans. Kelly said that David was going to get a fishing boat but to Jennifer it sounded like a half-hearted plan. Jennifer admitted that she had no real plan other than to reunite with friends who left before her. Anthony reminded them both that his departure was sudden and unplanned. With dinner finished and another bottle of wine opened Jennifer helped Kelly clean what few dishes there were.

David made a brief appearance to refill his wine glass. "I wish this was beer," he said before disappearing in the bedroom once again.

The three of them shifted from the table to the ratty couch. With the added wine Kelly became a chatterbox. She was full of stories about rural farm life in East Texas. Jennifer figured that it had been a long time since Kelly had had another girl to talk to. She listened as attentively as she could, but as the clock neared nine o'clock she found herself nodding off to sleep.

"You okay, hon?" Kelly asked.

"Sorry," she said. "It was a long day and all this wine. I should be getting to bed."

Kelly patted her on the arm sympathetically. "You just go on to bed then. We can catch up tomorrow."

Jennifer picked herself off the couch and shambled into the bedroom. "I'll wait out here," Anthony said.

"I'm just going to change and you can come in," Jennifer said.

She quickly peeled off her pants and changed into an oversized T-shirt she had taken from the brothel. When she was done she opened the door and told Anthony to come in.

After Anthony entered the bedroom he glanced at her and then the bed. "I can sleep on the couch."

"Nonsense. The bed is big enough for two. You need rest more than I do. If it's that big of a deal I can sleep on the couch."

"No, no, it's okay. Just give me a minute."

She stepped back into the living room thinking Kelly would still be there but she had retired to the other bedroom. A couple of minutes later Anthony opened the door. He wore gym shorts and a grey sleeveless T-shirt. "Are you sure about this?"

"Yesh," she said, then became embarrassed at her drunken slur.

Anthony climbed into the far side of the bed, which was on the right. She climbed in the left, idly thinking that it was the same sides that she and Matt had always chosen. Her heart dropped for a moment. Had it only been a week since her husband was gunned down? She didn't want to think about those things right now, especially not after all the wine she had. When Anthony turned off the lamp she turned away on her side. If she was going to cry herself to sleep, she was going to keep as quiet as possible.

But none of that happened. Jennifer had endured hours for questioning and brutal torture. She felt like she was made of stronger stuff and would be damned if she was going to cry about it now. She fell asleep almost immediately. In the middle of the night the need to pee woke her up. Jennifer was surprised to find that she had turned back in the middle of the night and slept with her head on Anthony's shoulder and her arm across his chest. It alarmed her for a moment but she quickly got over it. A brief trip to the bathroom and she was back to sleep.

Jennifer woke up later in the morning than she thought she would. The sun was high in the sky and the bright light and warmth on her face kept her from falling back asleep. She turned to see if Anthony was beside her but he wasn't there. Her heart skipped a beat and, in a panic, she needed to find him. Jennifer sat up in bed, abruptly feeling the pain of her headache shoot through her head. As her hand reached the doorknob she heard his voice coming from the other side. She stepped out to find Anthony, Kelly and even David staring back at her from the dining room table.

"There she is," Anthony said. "Did you sleep well?"

"I have a headache," Jennifer said.

"Me too," Kelly said.

"Maybe not so much wine tonight," Anthony said.

"No, definitely not," Jennifer said.

"Want something to eat?" Kelly offered. "Got some oatmeal I can heat up. It's no bacon and eggs but it'll help with that headache."

"Yeah, that sounds good."

She sat down at the table opposite from David. Jennifer stared at him for a moment. He no longer seemed sullen like he was the day before. Uncomfortable and embarrassed David finally said, "Good morning."

"Good morning. How are you?"

"Fine. I'm sorry about yesterday. It's just that, well, we've all been through a lot lately. Anthony was just telling us everything you two went through to get this far. Ma'am, I'm sorry for your loss."

Did Anthony tell David the entire truth? It didn't matter. Where this man was sullen the night before he was now pleasant. Jennifer recognized that he was making an effort. "Thank you," she said.

During the day she made efforts to get to know David. It was mostly small talk and she found it tiring but she wanted things to stay smooth between the four of them. The last thing she wanted was a member of their group freaking out as Matt had.

Late in the afternoon Hector came to the apartment. "Waiting on another person," he said. "They should be in later tonight. Even if they are not here, we go tomorrow. We leave at noon and make our way west until we turn south. Most of the fighting is in Waco at the moment. We should be well west of it when we cross the battlefield. We got people waiting for us on the other side. Stay cool and everything will be all right."

After his announcement he waited for questions. Jennifer eyed her companions and but they didn't offer any. She was ready for this all to be finally over and for them to be safe on the other side. The other three stayed silent, as they seemed to share the same mix of anxiety and eagerness.

"Good," Hector said, then left.

Jennifer, despite still feeling tired from the hangover, managed to stay awake during the day. She even helped Kelly with dinner, which was several cans of different vegetables with tofu and spices added to it. They called it a soup and presented it for dinner. Kelly and David seemed to enjoy it but Jennifer had eaten better fare and could tell by Anthony's scowl that he was as enthusiastic about dinner as she was. A bottle of white zinfandel was opened. Jennifer only had one glass. She was never a fan and she didn't want a hangover the next day. Despite the shared wine everyone else seemed reluctant to indulge.

Just before nine o'clock they seemed to run out of things to talk about between the four of them. Kelly and David announced that the evening was late and retired to their bedroom. Anthony let Jennifer change first, before changing into his gym shorts and sleeveless T-shirt.

When they were ready they settled into the small bed. Anthony turned off the lamp on the nightstand, leaving them with only the ambient light from the halogen street bulbs filtering through the window.

Jennifer lay on her back and stared at the shadows playing across the ceiling. She sensed that Anthony was still awake beside her and could almost feel the energy coming off him. "Are you worried about tomorrow?" she asked.

"Yes," he said. "There are a million things that could go wrong. But these guys do this all the time."

"Do they ever get caught?"

"Occasionally a coyote will get caught. It doesn't end well for them."

"We're just so close." She sniffled and was surprised as the tears welled up in her eyes.

"Hey," Anthony said. "Hey, there. Whoa, now. Everything is going to be all right. I promised." He reached over and pulled her towards him, then wrapped her in an embrace. With her head on his chest she let the tears silently fall from her eyes and soak his T-shirt. The arm that embraced her was lightly stroking her back. After she had composed herself, she looked up at him. He smiled then drew her to him and kissed her on the forehead. She let him hold her there with the kiss planted on her forehead until he drew back. There they were, face to face, with only a couple of inches between them. Even in the dark she made eye contact with him and saw his reassuring smile.

After all the running for the past several weeks, the connection between them was stronger than ever. She leaned forward and kissed him on the lips. Was he shocked? She didn't know but she continued then sensed him acquiesce to it and returned with a kiss of his own. With each kiss returned she felt the passion build within her like a stoked fire. She turned and climbed atop of him, keeping him pinned against the bed, still kissing him earnestly. Jennifer felt him stiffen beneath her. She leaned back and started grinding against his pelvis. A plaintive moan escaped from Anthony. Jennifer pulled off the oversized T-shirt, leaving only the pink boy shorts underwear she had received from one of the girls working the brothel. Anthony reached up and caressed Jennifer's ample breasts. He tried to get up and take control but she pushed him back down on the bed. They experienced a quick awkward moment where they rushed through taking off the remainder of their clothes. She pulled his underwear off, the top of the waistband snapping his erection for a moment. Then Jennifer took off her own underwear, then climbed atop him again carefully guiding his erection inside her. Then she rode him, moving her hips up and down with his. With the sudden and frantic lust Anthony came quickly.

She expected that he would want to extricate himself from their tangled limbs but after a minute of slow thrusting Anthony maintained his erection and sped up. This time he insisted on sitting up and switching her around to where he was on top of her. His erection slipped out when they were switching positions but he deftly guided himself back in. This time the thrusts were more controlled and sensual. While he was fucking her he kissed her passionately on the mouth, then moved to her neck.

It seemed to last forever. Jennifer couldn't remember the last time that a man had demonstrated love to her in such a way. Not in years. She relished and savored every moment of it. Jennifer held back her own orgasm, carefully paying attention to his body and cues. She wanted to share the moment when they came together.

Anthony sped up, then arched his back. She let herself go with him when he shuddered and his skin became prickled with chill bumps. He moaned loudly, his groan of pleasure inciting one of her own.

This time he extricated himself from her body and lay on his back. He was panting heavily from the exertion. "I," he said, seemingly confused about what else to say after that. "Are you okay?"

"I'm wonderful," she said. She blushed with embarrassment at the dreamy quality of her own voice.

"I just want you to know that I'm not trying to take advantage of you."

She grinned in the dark. "I think I took advantage of you there."

"I," he began again, only to stop himself.

Jennifer turned toward him and kissed him passionately on the mouth. She was afraid he was going to ruin this with talk and she wouldn't let that happen. As she kissed him she reached down and stroked his slick member. A distant part of Jennifer's mind was idly curious if he could come a third time. She wasn't disappointed.

Jennifer was awake well before dawn. She lay there in the dark as Anthony spooned against her with his arm draped over her. She didn't want to sleep any longer and wanted to lie in bed even less. Jennifer carefully extricated herself from Anthony's grip. He snorted once then softly resumed snoring.

Today is the day. Nothing would stop her from escaping America. They would cross a battlefield, hopefully unnoticed. Jennifer gathered a few articles of clothes and her shower items. She stepped across the bedroom and headed to the bathroom completely naked, hoping she wouldn't run into either Kelly or David.

She ran a shower and stepped into it, luxuriating under the steamy heat. *Today is the day.* She silently repeated the phrase again. Many things could go wrong with today but she was strangely calm about it. She would get out of America or die trying.

Jennifer wasn't sure how she felt about Anthony. Conflicted was the word that came to mind. It was true that she and Anthony had grown closer over the last several weeks, well before Matt had been killed. Anthony was the man that Matt pretended to be. Her husband had only been dead a short while, but she admitted that her marriage had been dying over the last several months if not already dead. As she thought about it, while she washed herself, she had to admit that this escape would have never worked with Matt. His boyish petulance at everything that had happened was certain to derail their plan at some point. She still mourned for her husband but a cold calculated part of her mind whispered that it was better attempting this without him.

When she finished her shower and dressed, she was surprised to find Kelly awake and waiting to use the bathroom as well. "Couldn't sleep either?" Kelly asked.

"No, I guess I can't."

"Are you nervous?"

"Just anxious, I guess."

Jennifer had caught up with the news on her tablet while Kelly had showered. A column of Coalition tanks had spearheaded their way through Mexia overnight. They had punched through the front lines there and were heading unencumbered towards Corsicana until a wing of American drones had stopped them with anti-tank missiles. Now the fighting had focused at a set of crossroads that both sides were trying to hold. Jennifer hoped that the place where they were going to cross was well away from it.

After Kelly was ready and dressed she made a pot of oatmeal that they could all share. Kelly didn't seem to feel like talking and Jennifer was fine with that. They ate their oatmeal together wordlessly, while they waited for the men to awaken.

David woke up first and was as pensive as the first time they had met him. Jennifer had the sense that he was pensive overall but his anxiety was no longer directed towards Anthony or her. Anthony was the last to get up. He smiled at her sheepishly before heading to the bathroom. Jennifer didn't want there to be any bad blood between them so she chased after him.

She shocked him when she pushed her way through the door before he could close it. "Hey," he said.

Jennifer didn't give him the chance to speak any further. She pushed him back into the room and kissed him. He was startled at first, then gave into the kiss. After she felt the right amount of time had passed, she pushed him back. "I don't know what will happen today," she said. "But I don't have any regrets about last night. I need you to know that and I need to know that you're on my side."

She waited expectantly for an answer. Finally he said, "I'm on your side."

"Good. Now shower and get ready."

Anthony soon joined them in the living room, carrying his own bowl of warm oatmeal. He shoveled the oatmeal quickly in his mouth, then worked furiously on his tablet. Jennifer wondered why he seemed obsessed with his work. Everything was arranged at this point and there was little more he could do. After trying to puzzle it out she dismissed it as his own anxious reaction to the upcoming trip. She toyed with her own tablet but didn't pay attention to the content displayed.

At noon a booming fist pounded on the apartment door and startled a yelp out of Kelly. She laughed with embarrassment and said, "I'll get it."

Hector had arrived to collect them. "It's time," he said.

It only took them a minute to gather their things and they followed him out the door. Hector led them through the apartment complex and carefully eyed anyone that passed by or showed an interest in their little group. He led them back to the garage where little knots of people milled around three non-descript panel vans. "Okay, everybody, get in," he said.

Jennifer estimated that there were about twenty people altogether in the group. Kelly and David seemed to want to stay with Anthony and her, as they made their way to one of the vans. When she climbed into the van she saw bench seats lined against the walls. A single CFL bulb was wired into the ceiling and hung down loosely on a cord. At least they wouldn't make this journey in the dark. There was also a conspicuous bucket and curtain near the back corner. Jennifer had a pretty good idea what that was for. They moved towards the side of the van to allow the other two people to come in behind them. Once everyone was in and settled Hector climbed aboard.

"We're going to travel west then south. Our route is long and will take most of the day. We designed this route to avoid checkpoints. We might get there fast or it might take a while. After sunset we'll stop and eat. I can try to make a stop or two for restroom breaks but if we can't stop use that." He pointed to the bucket.

"Oh gosh!" Kelly said.

"Any questions?" The passengers remained silent. "Good. Now sit tight for a few hours." He tugged the cord and pulled the sliding door down.

Jennifer took a seat alongside Anthony against the wall on the right side. The engine rumbled to life, another gas burner. She was surprised since gasoline was so expensive. It didn't matter to her as long as they made their way south.

The bulb swung to and fro casting constantly dancing shadows all about the van. It wasn't long before Jennifer caught one of the other passengers staring at her. It was a Hispanic woman, short but athletic with short black hair. Jennifer was startled when she realized that she recognized the woman.

"Detective Hernadez," she said. An alarm rose through her.

"I wondered if you recognized me," she answered.

"What are you doing here?" Jennifer asked.

Detective Hernandez raised her hands defensively. "I'm not here to catch you. Don't worry about that."

"So are you running too?"

"Yeah, it was time to leave Denver." The detective paused contemplatively. "Did you know what happened in the wake of your departure?"

"No, I never heard anything else." Jennifer was well aware that everyone in the van paid close attention to this conversation.

"Oh that Chief Inspector Jennings has such a hard on for you. He turned Denver upside trying to find you and your husband. Everyone who ever met you was considered a suspect. I don't know how far his investigation went but he's bound and determined to find you any way he can."

Jennifer was horrified. "Was anyone hurt?"

Detective Hernandez shrugged. "I don't know. Maybe. Probably. After you and your husband disappeared it set the National Police in such a frenzy.

Every known associate was considered a suspect, even District Leader Baker. He stepped down, by the way."

"Stepped down? You mean resigned?"

"That's what they say officially, but no one has seen him since he left office."

"Why him?"

"Because your husband knew him so well. They figured that someone this close to your husband had to know something."

"He's probably in Golden Gate."

Detective Hernandez shook her head. "Probably some place bigger like Fargo."

Jennifer mused on that. Before all this happened she was barely aware of the protective custody centers. Golden Gate was already huge. She couldn't imagine some place bigger than that. "I'm so sorry this happened," she said.

Detective Hernandez waved it off. "It happened. I went over it in my head several times. If it hadn't happened to you it would have happened to someone else. That Chief Inspector Jennings is like a pit-bull. Once he has a bite he won't let go. I didn't like the way things were headed in Denver any more so I started working on a way out. Ironically, I'm here in the same truck with you. I think our fates are tied, wouldn't you say?"

"I guess." The thought of all those people rounded up and questioned. Did they include Doctor Gupta? What about Owen from the computer shop?

"Where's your husband?"

"He didn't make it. He was cut down by the National Police along the way."

"I'm sorry for your loss," she said simply.

With little to do in the back of the truck the passengers did their best to make small talk. The sixth passenger aboard was a stranger named Todd. He said he was from Louisville but little else. Jennifer found herself shifting uncomfortably on the wooden bench seat. The panel van kept hitting bumps as well, which didn't help the situation. She wished they could stretch out but there wasn't enough room on the benches and the floor wasn't inviting.

The drive seemed to last forever. She had no idea where they were going and the van kept turning left and right. Halfway through the ride it became apparent that everyone needed a bathroom break. They all fidgeted uncomfortably and eyed the bucket and curtain set up. Finally, Jennifer couldn't stand the urge to pee any longer. She got up, closed the curtain and used the bucket. When she was finished she found Anthony and the others staring at her.

"You can use it too, if you like," Jennifer said. That elicited a chuckle from the other passengers.

It was past six o'clock when they finally stopped. Hector opened the rolling door and cool air swept into the cargo area. Jennifer welcome the fresh air with a sigh, surprised at how cloying the back had become during the ride. "Everybody out," Hector said. "Stretch your legs. We got some grub for you. We are gonna be here for a few hours before crossing into Coalition territory."

Since Jennifer had been the first in the van she was the last out. Her knees protested the new position but she ignored them. Instead, she arched her back and stretched, feeling the muscles loosening up while her spine crackled. All three vans were parked in a large barn. There were stalls for horses or cows but they were empty. Despite the lack of livestock fresh hay covered the floor and Jennifer's nose subconsciously twitched in a psychosomatic allergic reaction.

Anthony touched her lightly on the elbow. "Let's get something to eat."

The "grub" was not much to speak of; white bread, sliced tofu and yellow mustard. It could at least tide her over for a while. Jennifer made herself a sandwich and took a bottle of water from an opened package. When she had her food ready she caught Anthony's eye and nodded at the bale of hay right next to the one that Detective Hernandez sat on. He followed her lead as she walked to it.

Jennifer took a bite of her sandwich and winced. Tofu and mustard didn't go together. Detective Hernandez chuckled at her. "Not like the dinners at the District Leader's mansion."

"It's food. I learned what all there is out there." She wasn't going to rise to the bait in any fight about the class warfare bullshit. "Do you know what you're going to do when you make it out on the other side?"

Anthony cleared his throat.

Jennifer turned to him. "What?"

Detective Hernandez chuckled again. "He's right. It's called 'operational security'. You don't tell me what you're doing and I don't tell you what I'm doing. It keeps us both safe. But it doesn't matter anymore. We're either going to make or we're not. I have no idea what to do next. I'm told I have some cousins in Mexico City, but I have no idea how to find them. All I know how to do is police work but will they let me work on the force?"

"You can come with us to Havana? I have friends there."

Anthony nudged her with his knee. Detective Hernandez caught the move. "I appreciate the offer. I might take you up on that. But, like I said, I'm kind of making this up as I go along."

The barn was chilly but not freezing cold. Winters in Texas were mild compared to the rest of the country. After the meal there was little to do but pace around the barn. Jennifer checked her tablet once but they were so remote that they couldn't get a signal. Hector sat stoically on a stool and patiently answered the occasional odd questions from the nervous escapees. Just before midnight he checked his smartwatch and announced, "It's time."

The other drivers got up and rushed to their vans. Everyone was anxious to get going. Jennifer felt the energy coursing through her. This was it. They were going to make it to their freedom. She was first in the van again, taking the bench across from where the fragrant toilet bucket had stood but was now absent. Anthony sat down next to her. "You ready?" he asked.

"Yeah, I am. I just want to be finished with this running and never have to look over my shoulder again."

He squeezed her knee reassuringly. "Just relax. We're almost there."

Although she couldn't see it she heard the vans pulling out of the barn one by one. Her van had been the deepest inside the barn so it was the last out. If she thought the roads were bumpy before they were worse now. They were immediately bounced off their benches during the rough ride. Jennifer understood why the toilet bucket had been removed. The thought of arriving in Mexico covered in piss and shit nauseated her.

They travelled that way for a while with everyone holding on to the bench seat and each other to keep from getting bounced to the floor of the van. Jennifer wondered if it would be like this the whole way. She didn't know if she would vomit from motion sickness or break a bone.

Anthony fell to the floor, tried to get up and then fell a second time. He grinned sheepishly while everyone aboard chuckled. He reached for Jennifer to help him up. She extended her hand to him.

That was when the world turned upside down.

Chapter 20

Screaming. It was the only sound that filled her head. A woman was screaming somewhere. Maybe it was inside her head? It was the only thing she could hear. She slipped in and out of consciousness while the screams echoed in her head. And she wished the woman would shut up. It was dark but she couldn't tell if her eyes were opened or closed. Jennifer kept thinking she was somewhere else. Like the dinner party. *It all came down to that damn dinner party. Why couldn't Maggie's dad just keep his mouth shut and not piss off that general?*

That scream pierced her skull again. This time she opened her eyes and realized that she was lying on the ceiling of the truck, but the only way that made sense was if the truck was upside down. A flickering light came through the open sliding door of the panel truck and casted dancing shadows. Absently her mind told her that there was a fire somewhere. There was a rhythmic thumping banging around in her head.

The scream pierced her skull again. Jennifer whipped her head around then regretted it as her vision swam and a bloom of pain intensified behind her eyes. Maybe she had hit her head when the truck turned upside down?

Kelly screamed to the right of Jennifer while she held her trembling leg. "Oh my God, what's wrong?" Jennifer asked.

"My leg," Kelly said. "It's bleeding. I think it is bad."

Jennifer leaned over her. The leg was covered in dark sticky goo. Jennifer realized that it was all Kelly's blood. "What can I do?"

"Can you get me out of here?"

"Maybe. Where's David?"

"Beside me," Kelly said softly. There was such sorrow in the response.

In the dark it was hard to see the other person next to Kelly. Jennifer had missed him in the dancing firelight. She leaned over Kelly to check him for signs of life. A six-inch piece of shrapnel poked out from David's right eye socket. The other eyed stared vacantly. "Is he?" She couldn't finish the question.

"Yes."

Kelly's man was dead and nothing Jennifer could say would change that. She shook her head clear, despite the brief pain that it brought, and focused at the task at hand. "We need to get you out of here. Where are Anthony and the detective?"

"That other guy just ran out. That detective lady had a hurt arm. Anthony got her out of here since she was screaming."

Anthony popped his head into the back of the truck. "Good, you're awake. How do you feel? I didn't know if you had a back injury or anything." He had a bleeding gash along the right side of his forehead above the hairline.

"Back feels fine. Head hurts though."

"Probably a concussion. That'll pass but we need to go right now. Can you help me with Kelly?"

"Yeah, but can you tell me what happened?"

"Missile. There's a gunship out there circling around. He knocked the truck over but he hasn't finished the job yet."

Jennifer recognized that the thumping she thought was in her head was the circling helicopter. "We don't have much time, do we?"

Anthony ignored the question and positioned himself above Kelly's upper body. "We need to carry her. Her upper body is going to be heavier so I'll take this. You grab the legs." He looked down at Kelly's agonized face. "This is going to hurt."

Kelly gritted her teeth. "Just do it."

Jennifer thought briefly about the most painless way to do this then realized it was futile. Anthony had hooked his hands into Kelly's armpits and was waiting for Jennifer to do her part. She grabbed both of Kelly's ankles and nodded. Without waiting for a count they both lifted. Jennifer felt herself swoon as Kelly's scream pierced her skull again. She gritted her own teeth and let Anthony lead them backward out of the back of the panel van. It was awkward for a moment, trying to maneuver their way out, but Jennifer just held Kelly's legs up while they worked through the twisted wreckage of the door.

After they were outside the cool air felt like a blessing. Anthony instructed her to lay Kelly gently on the grassy prairie. A fire raged near the destroyed truck. Jennifer got a better view of the damage from the outside. The entire cab of the truck had been obliterated. There was no way Hector and his driver could survive that carnage. Jennifer searched the dark horizon for the other trucks but didn't see them.

Detective Hernandez crawled forward on her knees with one hand pulling her along the ground and revealed herself from the dark. Jennifer noted that the lady had improvised a sling out of her windbreaker for her right arm. "How is she," Detective Hernadez asked.

"Bad," Jennifer said. "Losing a lot of blood."

"Let me see. I know first aid." Kelly had passed out from the pain and exertion. The leg was worse than Jennifer feared. With the light of the fire raging nearby she could see that Kelly's leg was black with blood and the color had drained from her face. Detective Hernandez checked the wound and frowned at Jennifer and Anthony with grim determination. "Find something like a towel or a piece of clothing to see if I can stop the bleeding."

Jennifer dashed back to the overturned truck. She searched around the cabin and spotted Anthony's gym bag. She grabbed it, knowing that it had guns in there as well. She slung it over her shoulder and climbed out of the ruined truck. Jennifer scrambled quickly to Kelly and tossed the bag on the ground. She unzipped it and started rummaging through then stopped as Detective Hernandez no longer put pressure on the wound. "What's wrong?" she asked.

"It's too late," Detective Rodriguez said. "She's gone."

The engine on the gunship above whined as it canted wildly to the left. The three of them turned their heads up at the noise. The gunship had been caught in the billowing black smoke of the growing prairie fire and circled around to the west side of the fire but it now hid them from the gunship's view.

"Why isn't it doing anything?" Jennifer asked. She coughed as the smoke blew into her face. The fire had shifted and was now threatening them.

"I think it's watching and waiting," Anthony said. "Keeping an eye on us while the ground troops arrive." As soon as Anthony finished his sentence headlights bounced along the prairie from the north. "We need to get out of here!"

"Which way?" Detective Hernandez asked.

Anthony pointed toward the ruined truck. "We go that way - south. The same place the truck was headed. Run!" He snatched the gym bag up and reached for Jennifer who still knelt on the ground. Detective Hernandez didn't wait at all. She was up and in the dark before Jennifer and Anthony could get moving. He reached into his gym bag and found a pistol, then checked to see if it was loaded and ready to shoot. Jennifer heard the engine of the vehicle coming towards them. No quiet electric motor in this one. With gun in hand Anthony said, "Let's go. Keep up with me. If you can't then get my attention."

He ran into the darkness with Jennifer following. At first a slow trot then, with a glance over his shoulder to make sure she was there, he sped up. She heard the circling gunship change direction and pursue after them. She wondered briefly how it could see them in the dark and realized that all these vehicles had some sort of night vision. She kept running anyway, even though the ground vehicle chasing them closed in. Jennifer's lungs were on fire and the muscles in her legs burned. She was only six feet away from Anthony when he dropped from view with a yelp. Jennifer stopped. "Are you okay?"

"Damn it! Careful, there's a gully here."

She walked toward the edge of the gully and peered down. It was black and she couldn't gauge how deep it went. The gunship stayed in position above them like a watchful hawk. "I can't see you," she said.

"I can see you. It's about a six-foot drop. Slide down the side of it and we can climb up the other side."

Jennifer sat down on her butt and dangled her legs over the edge, then slid down. She felt branches from scrub brushes scratch her hands and face on the way. When she reached the ground she felt around for Anthony.

"I'm here," he said from her right.

"Okay, up the other side."

"Okay," he said. He panted as he struggled to get up.

They were losing precious time but the gully was steep and reaching the bank on the other side was a high climb. With any luck the vehicle pursuing them would plunge into the gully and get stuck there. The gunship would still chase them but Jennifer would worry about that later. She climbed up the opposite site of the gully, her hands clawing into the dirt, with Anthony struggling behind her with his gym bag. After she reached the top she turned around and reached down. "Here!"

Anthony clasped her hand and clawed his way over her to the top. Momentarily they were a tangle of limbs until she could roll off him. "Come on," she said. "It'll take them awhile to figure out a way around this gully."

"Go."

"What?" The military vehicle was almost upon them.

"I said go!"

"What is this? Some last stand hero bullshit?"

"It's my ankle. I twisted it or broke it. I can't run but I can buy you some time."

"I'm not leaving you!"

"Go! There's no time!" The gunship still hovered about fifty feet above them. The vehicle bouncing along the prairie was about a half mile out. Two minutes at most.

"We find cover and make a stand here. No arguing. You can't make me leave."

She searched frantically for anything that they could take cover behind but could only find scant scrub brush and prairie grass. Jennifer carried the gym bag behind a bush on the edge of the gully while Anthony hobbled behind her. He dropped to the ground as soon as she did. She unzipped the bag and rummaged through it again, this time finding the cold steel of a semi-automatic pistol. Jennifer handed the pistol to Anthony, then fished for another pistol. She handed the second one to Anthony. "Can you make this thing work for me?"

Anthony dropped the clip out of the pistol, inspected it as much as he could in the light of the raging fired, then inserted the clip in and pulled the slide back. "Loaded and ready to go. Ever fired a pistol before?"

"Just once. The other day." She recalled the shot she took at Max in the brothel.

"This is a 9mm. Slight kick but you should handle it. Line this sight here between this other sight here." He pointed to the fore and aft sights on the slide. "The clip holds seventeen rounds. There are a couple more loaded clips in the bag, if you want to fish them out." Jennifer reached into the bag again and found one of the clips then stashed it into the pocket of her jacket. She tried finding the other but there was no time. Whoever was chasing them was almost on them. Anthony laid on the edge of the gully and poked the barrel of his gun through the scrub brush they used for cover. "So they're driving this way, right?" he said. "I hope they run right into that gully. And when they do we jump up and start firing on them."

It was the same idea that Jennifer had thought of. The gully was the perfect trap for the vehicle coming towards them. It would dive in nose first and force the occupants out of the vehicle to engage them on foot. With their perch above their pursuers they should have the advantage. Jennifer had no idea how many men were in the vehicle or what the gunship would do when the situation changed, but they were making this up as they went along any-way. "What about them?" she nodded toward the hovering gunship.

Anthony shared the same thoughts. "We worry about them later."

Jennifer poked her own pistol through the scrub brush and lined the sights up as Anthony instructed. She pointed it directly at the headlights. They were only yards away now. "I follow your lead?" she asked.

"Hold fire until I do."

The vehicle sounded like one of the Joltvees. It raced directly towards them on the opposite side of the gully. Despite the chill in the air she felt flush with heat as the sweat beaded in the small of her back. Jennifer waited with eager anticipation for the vehicle to take the plunge.

The driver of the vehicle hit the brakes with a squeal and stopped at the edge of the gully. The vehicle idled with the headlights pointed directly towards them. Jennifer's heart sank with disappointment. Whoever was driving the Joltvee had coordinated their efforts with the gunship above. The doors popped open and two men came out from each side.

"Hold fire," Anthony said.

The men were silhouettes against the raging prairie fire that was behind them. Three of them dropped to kneeling positions and aimed their assault rifles. There were eerie blue lights where their eyes should be, giving them a spectral appearance. Jennifer figured they were some sort of combat iGlasses. The last man stepped out with a pistol at his side and his trench coat billowing out behind him in the wind. "You're a hard woman to find, Missus Hanson," a voice called out over the noise of the gunship.

Jennifer felt her heart skip a beat and her breath catch in her chest. That voice would be etched in her memory until the day she died. "Jennings," she said quietly. He had doggedly pursued her to Texas.

"That's him?" Anthony said.

"Missus Hanson, why don't you and Mister Picollo come out here and we can all go home. I promise nothing bad is going to happen to you. In fact your husband is quite anxious to see you."

"Matt," Jennifer said.

"It's a trick," Anthony said

"Oh, I guess you didn't know," Jennings said. "Your husband survived. He's in a hospital right now, awake and asking for you."

The chief inspector was lying. There was no way Matt could survive that hail of gunfire. Still, the thought that her husband might be alive tugged at her heart.

"Missus Hanson, we know that you're right over there. The gunship above guided us in to where you and Mister Picollo are hiding. If I wanted you dead I could have killed you a dozen times already. I need you to come back with me to Denver. There are a lot of people who are anxious to talk to you and Mister Picollo."

"Are you ready?" Anthony asked quietly. "I think I have a shot on him."

"Are you sure?" Jennifer replied. "What if they kill us?"

"Do you want to go back with them? I would rather die here than do that."

The last thing Jennifer wanted was to be back in the clutches of Chief Inspector Jennings. "No, absolutely not. Take the shot. I'll aim for the guys on the other side."

"Missus Hanson," Jennings called out again in a melodic voice. "I really don't want to come in there and -"

Anthony fired his shot so quickly that it startled Jennifer. She had heard gunfire before but never this close. She quickly regained her composure and pointed her pistol in the direction of Jennings' men. Jennifer squeezed the trigger like Anthony had told her. The report from the gun startled her again and her ears rang. Had she hit the target or not? To her right Anthony still fired at the men crowding around the armored Joltvee. Jennifer kept doing the same, not sure what she aimed at much less if she hit anyone. She just kept pulling the trigger until the slide locked back and she couldn't shoot any more.

Anthony was already inserting another clip into his pistol. Jennifer pulled the clip out of her pocket but wasn't quite sure what to do. They had never covered reloading. She pushed the small button near the bottom of the pistol grip. The empty clip slid out and fell into the dirt.

Jennifer had inserted the second clip when Anthony shouted, "Get your head down!"

She saw muzzle flashes from across the gully. "Stupid," she said and put her face in the dirt as instructed. The rounds from the assault rifles zipped by her and snapped through the branches of the scrub brush. Jennifer was startled as her left bicep blossomed in hot pain. Instinctively she reached over with her right to find a bleeding wound. "I'm shot," Jennifer said incredulously.

"Cease fire!" Chief Inspector Jennings shouted from across the gully. "Cease fire, you fucking idiots!"

"I got hit too," Anthony said. "Above my right shoulder, I think my collar bone snapped. Is your wound serious?"

Jennifer wasn't a nurse. She was in pain but it seemed to be manageable. She tried to check her wound in the dark and gingerly touched it. "I don't know," she said. "Maybe it's okay."

"Missus Hanson," Chief Inspector Jennings called again. "Now you're starting to piss me off. You shot me! You didn't kill me though. This little wound here will be just fine. But you're really starting to piss me off! If you make me come get you it's only going to be worse for you and Mister Picollo."

Jennifer glanced to her right. Anthony took aim with the pistol but he grunted as he did so and his hand visibly shook. She picked up her own pistol from the ground but wasn't sure what to do with it. The slide was still locked back. "Anthony?"

He glanced and muttered, "The top button above the trigger. It snaps the slide in place and loads a round."

She found the thumb catch and pointed the pistol away from her as the slide snapped forward. The click startled her but felt satisfactory at the same time. Her left arm throbbed with dull pain so she held the pistol with her right hand and hoped she was strong enough to handle the kick.

"Missus Hanson, you are trying my patience -"

The hovering gunship to the west of them abruptly changed the pitch of its motor. She couldn't see it in the dark but the engine whined and it canted away from them. Something was happening and it was enough to distract Chief Inspector Jennings from his taunts.

The explosion made Jennifer jump. The only other thing she was aware of was the low swoosh just before the explosion above her, to see that the American gunship had exploded in a ball of fire. The engine gave a wheezing cough as it dove toward the ground just north of their position.

"What happened?" Jennifer asked.

A new gunship entered the area from the south. It circled the area slowly and was joined by a second gunship thirty seconds later. "Coalition," Anthony said.

The two gunships circled the area with their engines howling. One of the gunships pointed their nose at the Joltvee across the gully from them. Jennifer noted absently that this was the hated Coalition that she had always heard about in the newscasts. She felt grateful that they kept watch over them. The National Police troopers next to the Joltvee dropped to their kneeling stances again. This time they aimed their rifles at the gunship oriented towards them.

Anthony squeezed off a shot at the National Police and created instant confusion amongst the men across the gully. One of the men ducked while the other two open fired on the gunship closest to them. Jennifer wasn't a military tactician but it immediately struck her as stupid for the men on the ground to fire at the helicopter above. She heard Chief Inspector Jennings shout at the men among the din of gunfire, but she couldn't make out anything he said. He was easy to spot across the gully as he waved frantically for his men to cease-fire. Inexplicably he stopped shouting and dove into the gully.

Jennifer turned to see the Coalition gunship fire a missile. It tracked down toward the Joltvee. Jennifer was too close so she mashed her face into the dirt and hoped she wouldn't get killed in the coming explosion. Only a second later she felt herself lift from the ground and fall flat against the dirt again. Her ears rang and everything sounded muffled, as she felt disoriented and nauseous with pain again. She tried to shake her head to clear but it became much worse.

Jennifer didn't know how much time had passed while she was unconscious. She sat up and scanned the landscape around with alarm, worried that she might be surrounded by more National Police. Jennifer found Anthony to her right. He was sitting up now and held his head in his hands. The explosion had disoriented him as well. She looked across the gully at the ruin of the Joltvee but relaxed when she didn't see any of the National Police officers that were there before.

"Anthony," she said.

"What?" he asked.

"Are you all right?"

"I'm... I got hit by a round. Are you okay?"

Jennifer winced as she tried to flex her arms. She felt flushed as beads of sweat broke out on her face. "Just hurts. They make this look easy in the movies."

Jennifer couldn't tell the number of Coalition gunships circling above them. She thought there were two but there could have been a third one lurking about. It was just too much noise for her to focus. "Did the missile get them all?" She turned to the fiery wreckage of the Jeep across the gully.

"I don't know. Maybe?"

Jennifer couldn't see any bodies in the tall grass. The National Police that had been there previously had either been killed or incapacitated by the blast. "I think I saw Chief Inspector Jennings jump into the gully before the blast."

"He did?"

Jennifer was startled by a grunt emanating from below. A hand appeared and clawed the edge of the bank followed by another with a pistol in it. She felt around for the pistol she had lost. "Anthony," she shouted.

He had slumped over but now snapped to attention at the alertness of her voice. He whipped his head around wildly for a threat but spotted Jennings too late. Jennings climbed out of the gully with the gun pointed at Anthony. Jennifer frantically searched for the gun she had lost after the missile strike. It was too dark and the only thing she could grab were the handfuls of prairie grass. Anthony had his own gun in his hand but was bringing it up too slowly. Jennings fired a shot at Anthony and he slumped over.

"No!" Jennifer screamed.

Jennings straightened himself up. Jennifer hoped that maybe one of the Coalition gunships would fire at Jennings but they circled continuously. Chief Inspector Jennings placed his boot on Anthony's shoulder and kicked him to the ground. He turned to face Jennifer, the firelight gleaming in his eyes like dancing jewels. "Now where were we?" Chief Inspector Jennings said with a hint of amusement.

Jennifer felt her heart drop. It brought her back to the interrogation room at Golden Gate and the panic began to rise in her chest. She kicked against the ground, trying to get as much space between her and Jennings. Despite Jennings' injuries he was still quick and launched himself like a tiger on prey. He closed the distance between the two of them in scant seconds and kicked her in the midriff. Jennifer doubled over as the breath exploded out of her. She coughed as her head simultaneously swam with pain and nausea.

"Oh, I'm going to have so much fun with you," Jennings said.

Jennifer remained folded over in pain. Jennings placed a boot on her shoulder and kicked her to the ground the same way that he had with Anthony. She was flat on her back and coughing. She wanted to sit up or roll away but the pain overwhelmed her. Jennings quickly clambered atop her and straddled her belly. She tried to push him away with her uninjured arm but her effort was weak.

"Do you know how much trouble you've put me through?" Jennings asked. "They want me to bring you and him back but at this point it's all I can do to keep from killing you. I was actually surprised when you got out of Golden Gate. I really thought that I had you for good then your husband called in a lot of favors with Baker. And then you were out and I had to get you back in. You fucked things up by running. I never thought you would have had the balls to do that. Especially your husband! What a fucking pussy. I guess he got his in the end, didn't he? And now I got you. I don't give a fuck if you survive this night. All that matters is that I got you. Even if I kill you, I can explain that away to my superiors. Hell, they were worried about you and him getting away." Jennings leaned over her so close that they were face to face. She felt his erection pressing against her belly and was sickened by it. Jennings placed his cheek intimately against her hers, so close that she could feel his breath in her ear.

"I am going to keep beating you until you beg me to kill you," he whispered.

He sat up, taking the pressure of the erection off her belly, and smiled. Quick like a snake he grabbed her left bicep and inserted his thumb in the wound. Jennifer's head exploded in pain and she screamed. That only encouraged Jennings to insert his thumb deeper. The pain was so intense and she desperately wanted him to stop. She gave into the pain, let herself go while it succumbed her, hoping that this final torture from Jennings would end while she simultaneously hated herself for it. She had come so close. *So close!* The line of battle to Mexico was only miles away. It was so easy to let herself go to it.

Jennings eased his thumb from her wound. "Oh, no, this wouldn't be fun if you passed out," he said. "You don't get off that easy. Oh, no. No, no, no, no. I can't have you falling asleep on me." Pain exploded on her face. Her nose started gushing blood. She was ashamed that she had wished to pass out from the torture but was so tired that she wanted to simply fall asleep and die at the same time. Jennings would draw this out as much as possible.

He punched her again, this time above the eye. Then another punch punctuated with another one, leading to a staccato of punches, never heavy enough to knock her out but enough to keep her pain continuous. She struggled weakly and mentally reminded herself that this was a man who got pleasure from torture.

The punches seemed to go on forever but it could have been only been a minute. She just wanted the pain to go away and it did abruptly. In a daze she wondered what had happened and then she saw that Anthony had somehow pulled Jennings off her. Her vision was fuzzy and she was confused as to what she was seeing. Jennings appeared to be just as surprised as she was.

"You're still alive?" he asked. "Well, I'll take care of that."

Despite Jennings' surprise he quickly recovered and focused his efforts on Anthony. Jennings twisted and turned then stood up. "You're distracting me from the task at hand right now," he said. "That's okay. I don't imagine it'll take too long to take care of you." Jennings straddled Anthony and started pummeling him. "I'm going to beat you to death as hard and as fast as I can." Jennings ended each sentence with a punch. "I can't let someone like you distract me from Missus Jennings. She needs all my love and attention right now!"

Despite her pain Jennifer couldn't let Jennings beat Anthony to death. She turned over so that she could get on her hands and knees. Jennifer started crawling towards them. She had to save Anthony from this hateful man. As she crawled through the grass her hand fell upon something cold and hard. She gripped it and realized that it was her lost pistol. Jennifer picked the pistol off the ground, still locked and loaded from her last action with it. She took a few precious seconds and struggled to stand up. Jennifer absolutely needed to save Anthony.

She stood even though every nerve ending in her body was telling her not to stand. Jennifer took one tentative step towards Jennings, then another. The gun was in her right hand and shaking. She had to control it. For what she needed to do, she needed to be up close. Jennifer was only a few steps away from Jennings. The Chief Inspector kept hitting Anthony then paused out of some prescience. Jennifer aimed the pistol as he turned towards her. Awareness dawned in his eyes and he said, "Wait a minute."

Jennifer didn't want to give him that minute. She couldn't miss from this distance. She squeezed the trigger of the pistol just as Anthony had taught her and fired on Jennings. Blood exploded from his face. She shot him in the nose and his face was an instant ruin. Jennings' eyebrows arched and his mouth formed a shape of a surprised "O". He didn't cry out at all. He simply fell backward with his legs draped across Anthony's.

Jennifer dropped the pistol and rushed to Anthony. She tried picking him up by the shoulders. "Come on, let's go," she said.

Anthony cried out in pain. "No, I can't."

"Come on!" Hot tears ran down her face. "We're almost there!"

"No. I can't. I'm losing blood. Go without me."

"I'm not leaving you."

Anthony coughed and splattered blood all over his face. "Just go," he said weakly.

Jennifer was exasperated. They had come so and it was all going to end right here. *It wasn't fair!* She had already lost Matt and she couldn't afford to lose Anthony too. "Please," she said as her voice trembled. "Please try to go with me. Please." She was startled at how loud she was then noted that the Coalition gunships had moved away during the struggle.

"I can't. I'm so sorry. I can't go. Just hold me until I pass, then go without me."

Jennifer positioned herself so that she could cradle him against her lap. The tears stung her eyes and she was exhausted but she didn't want to give up on him. "Please, just try," she said. The words were futile despite her wishes.

Jennifer held him as he trembled. Anthony had the shoulder wound and another shot in his torso that was mortal. They were miles away from any help. Jennifer felt helpless about the situation. All she could do was hold Anthony and cry. She was ashamed that she couldn't do anything more than that.

Despite the chilly Texas air she felt warm as she held Anthony in her arms. She thought he had passed but then he coughed and came awake again. He was semi-conscious with his last words. "I love you, Jennifer," he said. He gave another weak cough then breathed no more.

In the pre-dawn hours on the Texas prairie she wailed solemnly. Jennifer was surprised at the depth of her own grief. All she knew to do was to hold him. Nothing else mattered any more. Someone would find her here, whether from the National Police or the Coalition. Or she would die here alongside this man. She realized that escaping America no longer mattered to her. Nothing seemed to matter at this point.

$$\blacktriangle$$

When the sun started to rise from her right her tears had been spent and Anthony had grown cold. From the behind her a voice sounded from the south. *"¡Alto! ¿Quién está ahí? Muéstrese."*

Jennifer turned to see the twenty men approaching her from south. They wore the tan camouflage uniforms of the Coalition with their guns raised as they approached. Jennifer was spent. She didn't care if they shot her or not. The closest soldier eyed her warily through his combat visor. He kept his assault rifle pointed towards her but his eyes were sympathetic.

Jennifer eyes welled with tears. She said, *"Por favor."* It was the only thing she could think of to say.

Epilogue: Thanksgiving 2043

Jennifer waited patiently for the woman sitting in the chair across from her to talk. The woman still had a bandage over her eye. According to her file she would keep the eye. That was a miracle by itself. She bore the scars from torture and battle. Her right arm was in a sling with bright red blood still seeping through the white bandages. Allison was a newly arrived refugee from America. It was Jennifer's job to counsel the woman for a smooth transition into Cuba. Allison hadn't been fully debriefed. She had only started talking a couple of days ago and Jennifer thought it was too early for a counseling session. The Cuban bureaucracy was only sympathetic to a point. They were still a bureaucracy after all. The influx of American refugees over the past year was starting to tax their system. A few fringe groups in Cuban society called for the refugees to be deported. Only a few though. Most Cubans were sympathetic and recalled a time in the previous century when Americans took in Cuban refugees.

Jennifer didn't let her mind wander too long. She still had a "client" in front of her, for lack of a better word. Jennifer was only six months into this role and it felt like the right one for her. Many of the American refugees were traumatized by their journey. Jennifer was plagued by her own nightmares about the last night she was in America. In some of those nightmares Chief Inspector Jennings killed her. In others he did far worse. She was sympathetic to Allison's trauma. Jennifer still had that itch to fill the silence with chatter but Doctor Cohen had taught her that the patient needed to do the talking and you just had to wait them out.

Doctor Cohen had been a godsend. She was a wizened old psychiatrist from Manhattan. She liked to say that she saw the whole thing with the Freedom Party coming before anyone else did. Doctor Cohen had emigrated from New York to Cuba long before the Coalition had been formed. The psychiatrist was somewhere in her seventies and still spry enough to live to a hundred, despite her distasteful habit of smoking Cuban cigars. The old lady said, "I heard about these things all my life and I'll be damned if they are better than everyone said they would be."

Doctor Cohen had been the first to counsel Jennifer when she had finally made it to Cuba after being picked up the Coalition forces. Cohen had been patient with her, letting Jennifer talk everything out and only prodding her with a few questions here and there. They had become fast friends and Jennifer had found her calling. Allison was now her sixth patient on her caseload. Doctor Cohen had advised her to let the patients tell their stories at their own pace.

"Did you ever experience hell?" Allison barked out sharply.

It nearly startled Jennifer into jumping but she needed this woman in front of her to be at ease. If they were both anxious the session would go bad quickly. "Do you mean did I have a bad experience in my own escape? Yes, I did."

"I heard you were a society type. What? Did they have the wrong brand of caviar on the boat?" Allison punctuated her question with a sneer.

Jennifer recognized the tactic. Whether Allison knew it consciously or subconsciously, she was trying to put Jennifer on the defensive. If Jennifer let Allison control the conversation and kept attacking her she would never get anywhere with the client. She had to share some of her own experience to connect with the woman.

"I watched a lot of people die. Some were good people. Some were bad. I killed a man by my own hand. I watched my husband die. I held another man I deeply cared for as he died in my arms. I crossed a battlefield to get here." Jennifer said all of this softly yet with conviction. Her intent wasn't to use her own experience to trump Allison's but rather let Allison see that they were connected by a shared experience.

"Did all that really happen?" Allison was twisting her hair around her index finger again. It was a nervous tic that Jennifer had picked up on.

"All of it did. You can check on it yourself." Jennifer rubbed the scar on her scalp through the short hair on her head then caught herself. It was her own nervous tic and she was trying to curb herself from it. It wasn't nearly short as it was when she was in the Golden Gate Canyon Detention Center, but she had kept it shorter than normal. Many of the ex-pats did the same thing, women with shorter hair while the men had their heads entirely shaved. When passing each other on the sidewalk they would knowingly nod to one another.

"Maybe I will," Allison challenged. Again with that sneer.

"If it's that important then by all means. We all went through something to get here. Some of us had a tougher time than others." She caught herself rubbing the puckered scar on her left bicep where a round had gone through the meat. Jennifer winced. Her own subconscious gave herself away again.

"A real battlefield?"

"With gunships and soldiers." The file on Allison said she had been found in one of the Central Florida swamps. She was severely dehydrated and disoriented, bloodied and alone. Allison had been transported to Miami then finally Cuba.

"I was raped," Allison said. "National Police. The militarized ones. There were three of them. They took turns with me in a barn." She hung her head.

It was the first real thing Allison had said to anyone since she had showed up the week before. Jennifer felt like prodding her to talk was still too soon but this was progress. "I'm sorry that happened to you," she said softly. It wasn't the first time she had heard of a refugee getting raped but it always made her heart ache to hear the stories. She felt fortunate that it had never happened to her but the nightmares she had about Chief Inspector Jennings sometimes took a wicked turn that way.

Jennifer didn't try to coax Allison to talk any more. This was a first session and there would be many more. Pushing too hard in the first session would push the client away. Doctor Cohen had taught her that. Allison had a few more things to say about her own escape but it was simply details about her journey, things that were glossed over with little depth. This was familiar territory to Jennifer as well.

The hour-long session was Jennifer's last for the day and it ended at three o'clock. Even though she loved her job this day was a little different than most. It was Thanksgiving Day and her lingering sense of national pride still held the day close to her heart, along with many other ex-patriots. After the session with Allison was over Jennifer scribbled the date and time of the next session on a business card and handed it to her. Writing down appointments was another thing Jennifer couldn't get used to.

Once Allison left the office Jennifer quickly shoved her notebook and tablet into her canvas backpack. She had picked up the backpack from one of the flea market stalls in Old Havana. It was the first thing she had bought here and she found herself strangely attached to it. There were better backpacks like the nylon ones from Europe or even a few illegal American imports, but she only wanted this one. During the summer Doctor Cohen had called her out on it. "You never go anywhere without it," she had said. Jennifer hadn't wanted to push the issue. Even though she had been a recent convert to therapy and counseling she still hadn't turned that same introspective eye to herself. Jennifer didn't care how Doctor Cohen would psychoanalyze it. She still loved her backpack.

Maybe she was trying to get away from her old self. She slung on her denim jacket then the backpack over her right shoulder. She had to admit that she was a completely different person from her old life. Before that fateful dinner party her only worries were the latest fashion designs. Now it was just jeans and a T-shirt most days.

She locked her office door behind her on the way out. Despite the recent modernization of Havana there were no electronic keypads that automatically recognized her dent. Fortunately, she had experience with keys and locks from her experience at the dead casino in Shreveport. Still, this was an older hospital though so it was all locks and keys here, and they were a novelty to her.

Her boot heels echoed through the hallway and down the stairs as she made her way to the exit. It was old-fashioned linoleum that was installed before the Old Cuban Revolution. An older heavy man with a white shirt and white mustache sat behind the desk near the building. "Early day for you, Miss Hanson?" he asked.

Jennifer grinned. "Special day, Ernesto."

"American Thanksgiving." Working in the hospital he was bound to learn of things uniquely American. "We're you lucky enough to get a turkey?"

Jennifer winked. "I was. My friends are cooking it right now. I'm headed over there."

"Enjoy your Thanksgiving, Miss Hanson."

Jennifer left the building and headed for the bike rack. Her Monark bike was only a year old and she took good care of it. She could have had a car, but the streets of Havana were already crowded with vehicles. Besides, for some reason, she felt like having a car would be wrapping herself back up in her old life. One night, during her first summer in Havana, she had caught herself looking at ads for classic BMW convertibles online before turning the tablet off.

The old gas powered cars were expensive and fetched classic car auction prices, but money wasn't an issue. Anthony had taken care of that for her. In early March of the previous year her tablet had chimed that she had received an email. It was the first time it had ever chimed for Alexis Chumway. She had opened it up to find an email from Cameron Devereaux. Jennifer had recognized the name immediately. It was the dent inserted in Anthony's palm when he died.

There was no way Anthony was alive. She had watched the Coalition forces bury him right there on the battlefield in an unmarked grave. She had asked the sergeant if the body could come back with her but the sergeant, with sympathetic eyes, had said that this was the best they could do. They were exploiting a weakness in the American flank and they had little time. She had got the impression that they were making a big concession as it was for even stopping at all. The sergeant had sent her back in a scout vehicle behind the Coalition lines.

There had been one line to the email instructing her to click the attachment. Since it was from Anthony she had intuitively trusted the link and been simultaneously afraid of what it might contain. The attachment had been an executable file. There was a quick install bar that had lasted less than five seconds, then another message had appeared. There was no video, just text. It read:

Jennifer, if you are reading this then the worst has happened and I hope you are still alive. I put this in as a failsafe in case I didn't make it. It was what I spent the last day doing in that apartment in Texas. I just want you to know that over the last couple of months I fell in love with you and care deeply about you. Even as I write this my heart aches knowing that if you're reading this then I didn't make it. I wish I could have. I will never know what future we could have had but I would have done anything for you. Since I'm not there I have done the next best thing and a little more. I have given you your name and life back. When you clicked the executable it tied your name and assets back to your dent. Jennifer Hanson lives and will always be in my heart forever.

Jennifer was still in the hospital when she received that email. She had only had her first session with Doctor Cohen two days earlier. After reading Anthony's email again she had curled up in a corner of the room with tablet in hand. Two more times she had read the tablet then it had chimed several times for Jennifer Hanson, new emails from International Bank of Havana as well as other European banks. They were all bank balances. Jennifer now had over three million euros to her name. She was independently wealthy, even by Cuban standards. She had simply sat in the corner and cried softly for the next couple of hours.

As she rode her bicycle home she reflected on this for maybe the hundredth time. Seeing the European and Japanese luxury cars always evoked this memory from her. Why did Anthony leave her all that money? It was more than she and Matt ever had. The only explanation that she could come up with was that he did it out of love. Still, she was frugal with the money and allowed herself only a few luxuries here and there.

Despite the influx of new automobiles over the last few years Havana was a bicycle culture. For every car that Jennifer saw on the streets there were three bikes. Her first biking experience in Havana had been harrowing. Jennifer had been intimidated by the aggressive Cubans, enough so that she had nearly cried and given up after her first experience. She didn't quit though, drawing strength from the last message that Anthony had left behind for her and bringing it up on her tablet when she needed it. Now she was a seasoned bike warrior. Any Cuban that tried to kick at her bike, assuming she was a helpless *jipata*, got a kick back. There was a guy next to her right now that was trying to elbow her into a line of cars at a stoplight. Jennifer glanced ahead and spotted the trashcan. She stole a glance at him and noted his scowling in return. The trashcan was more in his way than hers. With the right timing she kicked out and knocked him into it. She didn't turn back to see the result of her handiwork. A handful of other bike warriors, all familiar faces on this route, nodded to her respectfully. She had one or two of these run-ins a week and she won them more often than not.

Jennifer took a right turn on Chacon with the hope that the side street would be faster. It proved to be right. The street was lined with parked cars, foot traffic and other savvy bike warriors who knew about the shortcut. Jennifer had a small apartment overlooking the parks lining the canal that led to the Port of Havana. She had been smart enough to realize that she needed a support system as soon as she reached Cuba so she had found Maggie. It wasn't something she did right away. She needed to get herself right in the head first before having a conversation with her old friend. That was the time when the nightmares had plagued her nightly while the nursing staff administered tranquilizers to her.

After her first session with Doctor Cohen she had reached out to Maggie. The first thing Maggie did was admonish her for not reaching out sooner. They were different people before this, but given their different experiences in fleeing America Jennifer had felt further apart. What made it worse was that Maggie always talked about her escape as if it were a herculean task. Jennifer had glossed over her own escape. Maybe Maggie had picked up that there was more to Jennifer's escape than she was letting on. She had stopped bringing it up when they were together and changed the subject when it was brought up at social gatherings.

Jennifer had moved into the same apartment building that Maggie and her husband lived in. It was one of the new high-rise luxury apartments that glistened along Cuba Tacon. They were separated by ten floors. Jennifer's apartment was one of the smaller ones on the lower floors while Maggie had something spacious closer to the top. Ironically, Jennifer could better afford one of the top apartments while Maggie and her husband struggled. Still, Jennifer allowed herself this small luxury and she never let Maggie know the amount of money Anthony had left her. She figured the luxury was worth it if it allowed her to be close to her friend.

The approach from Chacon allowed Jennifer to access the backside of the building. Most of the residents came in this way or through the attached garage. Jennifer was used to walking in with her bike. There was a bike rack in the garage but theft was a huge problem, even in this part of the city. Another security guard greeted her. There were two here and Jennifer had made it a point to get acquainted with all of the apartment staff. Today Raul worked the desk. He was closer to her age and flirted with her somewhat modestly. A good job in a luxury apartment building wasn't worth getting in trouble over so he wasn't pushy with her, but Jennifer recognized that he was interested. And, against the rules, the guards let her take her bicycle up on the freight elevator.

"Good afternoon, Miss Hanson," he said as she passed.

She smiled, "Happy Thanksgiving, Raul."

His face lit up. "Thank you, Miss Hanson. Enjoy your holiday." The guard wasn't surprised about the holiday. More of the affluent expats lived in this area.

Jennifer took the freight elevator to her floor and dropped the bike off in her apartment. With the ever-present backpack slung over her shoulder she took the regular elevator to Maggie's place. She knocked twice when she reached the door.

Maggie's husband opened it. "There she is," he said. "Come on in."

Maggie came out of the kitchen licking the tips of her fingers. "Hey, dinner's almost ready. The turkey comes out of the oven in thirty minutes. The Garcias should be here any minute and Maria is coming too."

"Would you like a glass of wine?" Brad offered. "We have a nice Shiraz."

"Yeah, wine would be great." He poured out a generous glass of red wine for her. She took it and sipped slowly. Doctor Cohen had been concerned about alcohol abuse so Jennifer had cut back for several months. She thought the doctor might be overreacting.

"Tell me about your day," Maggie said.

Jennifer smiled. "In a minute, how's the baby doing?"

This time it was Maggie's turn to grin. "Why don't you go check on him?"

Jennifer took the glass of wine with her into the second bedroom. The baby was playing with large neon colored plastic toys in a big square quilted playpen. He looked up and laughed at her when she entered the room. She set the glass down on the dresser and he reached up for her from the playpen. Jennifer picked him up and hugged him.

"How are you today, baby?"

He just babbled at her. She walked over to the bed and sat on the edge with him in her lap. Every time she saw the baby she couldn't help but smile. His skin was light brown but nowhere near as dark as his father's and he had brown curly hair with hints of her blond. His eyes though... those eyes were big and bright blue. He definitely got that from her. That was her biggest surprise from last year. Of all the things she had experienced in her escape from America she never thought she would come to Cuba bearing a child. It was simultaneously a blessing and a heartache. Her heart ached because the father would never see his namesake grow up.

"And are you going to call me mama today?"

"Mama," Anthony said.

Jennifer gasped with exhilarated surprise. It was his first word.

THE END

ACKNOWLEDGMENTS

This has been my labor of love for the past two years and I hope you enjoyed it. Along the way I received tons of support and encouragement from my friends, family, colleagues and the writer's forum I belong to on Facebook. I would also like to thank my beta readers who gave me valuable feedback along the way. That brave group of people include Leslie Cohen, Valerie Lindemann, Rick Weber, Lisa Dewar and Shauna Decker. If you found mistakes in the book it is totally my fault and not theirs. Also would like to thank Cathy Helms for the cover design. If you are ever looking for any graphic design you can find her at www.avalongraphics.org. Follow me on Facebook here - www.facebook.com/authorkarnes/ and on Twitter @karnes68.

Made in the USA
Middletown, DE
09 June 2016